# THE
# PACT

# THE
# PACT

## SHARON BOLTON

First published in Great Britain in 2021 by Trapeze
This paperback edition published in 2021 by Trapeze
an imprint of The Orion Publishing Group Ltd
Carmelite House, 50 Victoria Embankment
London EC4Y 0DZ

An Hachette UK Company

1 3 5 7 9 10 8 6 4 2

A CIP catalogue record for this book is
available from the British Library.

ISBN (Paperback) 978 1 4091 9832 1
ISBN (eBook) 978 1 4091 9833 8

Typeset by Input Data Services Ltd, Somerset

Printed and bound in Great Britain by Clays Ltd, Elcograf S.p.A.

MIX
Paper from
responsible sources
FSC® C104740
FSC
www.fsc.org

www.orionbooks.co.uk

For Magdalen College School, Oxford, class of 2020:
It's been a dark year, but you are stars, and will shine all the
more brightly.

# Part One

# 1

When they thought of that summer, it was to remember the bitter taste of the river in their mouths and the spatter of lager froth on hot skin; to recall days that began after noon and ended as the night sky paled in the east.

They remembered long afternoons beneath the chestnut trees in University Parks and the particular shade of rose gold that the medieval spires turned in the evening sunlight. They remembered discovering the steampunk shop on Magdalen Bridge and dressing as glamorous vampires for the rest of the month, strutting the cobbles as dusk fell, to the amusement – and occasional alarm – of the foreign exchange students.

They remembered dust clouds at Reading and Truck Festivals turning nose-bogies black and the relentless mutterings of the drug dealers: 'Want any coke? Need any gear?' The answer was always yes, and they never needed to ask the price.

That summer was a time of neither hope nor promise but of certainty: they were the chosen ones, to whom the world belonged, and their lives, only just beginning, would be long and golden.

How very wrong they were.

Inevitably, that summer, they ended each day at Talitha's mock-Elizabethan monstrosity of a house a few miles out of Oxford.

Tal's dad was rarely around and her mum never bothered them – they weren't sure she was there much of the time – but the fridge was always full thanks to the housekeeper (who didn't live in), no one kept tabs on the bar in the pool house, and Domino's Pizza in nearby Thame delivered until midnight.

Mainly, they stayed outdoors, dozing away hangovers in the pool house or the circular, lead-roofed gazebo by the lake, waking as the sun came up before heading home to reassure parents of their continued existence. They slept the day away in their own beds and by four o'clock were ready to begin again. And so it had been all summer long, since the last A level exam, which had been Daniel's: Latin, on 4 June. (Went well, he thought, but you never really knew, did you?)

On the night before results came out, they gathered again at Tal's after an evening in the city. Xav sat on the edge of the pool, his feet in the water, as Amber flopped down at his side.

'I feel sick,' she muttered, letting her head fall onto his shoulder.

'Don't throw up in the pool,' Talitha warned. 'Mum had to get the filters cleaned last time. She'll make me pay if it happens again.'

Walking towards them across the terrace, weaving his way around huge terracotta pots and statues of mythical creatures, came Felix, holding a tray of drinks on the splayed fingers of his right hand. His hair, grown long since he'd finished school, glowed silver like the moon that hovered over his right shoulder. His easy, rolling walk gave him away as an athlete and on closer inspection, the over-developed right arm and shoulder, the huge thighs and slight twist in his torso might suggest an oarsman. The outdoor security lights activated as he passed them, giving the impression that Felix was creating his own light.

'I'm not pissed.' Amber sighed as Felix drew close. 'I mean I feel sick about tomorrow.'

'Today,' Daniel corrected from his sun-lounger. The smallest of the boys, and the least athletic, he'd never had the same success with girls as his two friends, and yet his face was perfect. Secretly, the others had asked each other if Dan might be gay. It would be totally cool, of course, as long as he didn't have a crush on either Xav or Felix, because then, you know, awkward.

'School doors open in six hours' – he looked at his watch – 'seventeen minutes and five seconds. Four. Three.'

'Do shut up,' Amber told him.

'Manhattans?' Felix offered the tray to Dan. 'Two shots bourbon, one shot sweet vermouth and a dash of orange bitters to jazz it up a bit.'

Felix had been the first to turn eighteen; the others, mindful of his love of chemistry, had bought him a cocktail kit, and he'd taken to cocktail-making with a passion.

Talitha shook her head at the offered tray of drinks; of the group, she always drank the least. Talking about it once, when she wasn't around, the others had wondered whether it might be out of a sense of responsibility – after all, they were nearly always at her house. 'Nah,' Felix had scoffed. 'She doesn't give a shit about any damage we might do – she just likes to feel she's in control.'

The terrace lights went out, leaving the garden in darkness apart from the glistening turquoise glow coming from the pool, and five pairs of eyes fell to watch the slender figure, pale as moonlight, glide over the tiles at the bottom. Megan's suit was a delicate pink, giving the impression that she was swimming naked.

'Is it just me or has she been weird lately?' Felix crouched at the pool edge to watch the sixth and strangest member of the group. There was something a little unearthly about the way she moved through the water with barely any visible propulsion.

5

'It's Megan, she's always weird,' Amber said.

'Yeah, but more than normal.'

'She's been quiet,' Daniel said.

'She's *always* quiet,' Amber insisted.

Megan floated to the surface. The mounds of her buttocks and her shoulder blades appeared a split second before she flipped and stood up. Water streamed down skin that had turned turquoise in the pool light. She looked a little like a mermaid, if mermaids had short, silver-blonde hair. A siren, maybe? Yes, Megan, with her quiet inscrutability, was more siren than mermaid.

'Six hours and fifteen minutes,' Daniel called to her.

'Keep the noise down,' Talitha complained. 'If we wake Mum, she'll make us go to bed.'

'Yeah, Dan, shut up.' Amber hurried to the pool steps. 'I know I failed theology.' She handed Megan a towel, holding it high so that her friend's body was shielded from view. It's possible she meant it kindly and that she hadn't positioned her own body so that Xav couldn't see Megan climb out.

Felix said, 'No one fails theology.'

'She means she got a B,' Xav said.

'Fair play, that would be a fail. In theology.'

Amber flicked her middle finger at Felix.

'We should go to bed.' Megan walked over to where she'd left her clothes on a sun-lounger and began pulling them on. 'It'll be tomorrow before we know it.'

'That's the last thing we should do.' Flopping down again at Xav's side, Amber nuzzled her face against his neck. 'I want to put it off as long as I can.'

'You two could have sex,' Felix said. 'That'll pass two or three minutes.'

Daniel sniggered. It's possible Megan smiled too, but she hid it well.

'If any of us don't get our grades, we might not be able to go to Tal's place on Saturday,' Daniel said.

'What?' Xav looked up over Amber's shoulder.

'If we don't get our grades, we have to go through clearing. We can't do that in Sicily.'

'We do have phones in Sicily.' Talitha sounded affronted.

'I'm only saying, I think we have to be here to – you know – hatch a plan B.'

Felix, who'd already drained his glass, stood up. 'We are not plan-B people,' he announced. 'We will all get our grades. And I know how we can pass the time. Dan, how pissed are you?'

Dan held out his right hand, palm flat, swaying it this way and that.

'Can you drive?' Felix asked.

'No.' Megan looked up from the sun-lounger.

'He's the only one of us who hasn't,' Felix said. 'Come on, Dan, you don't want to go down in history as the only chicken.'

Megan didn't back down. 'We said we'd quit.'

'Last chance.' Felix fished the cherry from his empty glass and swallowed it. 'We'll all have family things tomorrow and Friday. We fly out Saturday morning.'

'I'll do it when we get back.' Dan lay back on the sun-lounger, but his eyes stayed open and wary.

Felix shook his head. 'Won't be time. I'm going to the States, Tal's staying on Mafia Island till late September.'

'If you say "Mafia Island" in front of my granddad, you'll be floating face down in the pool the next morning,' Tal said.

Felix strolled up to her. 'Which would kind of prove my point.'

Tal was tall, but everyone was dwarfed by Felix. She took a step back to hold eye contact. 'And at your funeral, we'll build into your eulogy that you were a smartarsed shitbag.'

'Come on,' Felix took her hands and mimed pulling her towards the drive. 'Last chance for some real fun.'

'It's not a good idea,' Megan said. 'We were all sober.'

'Told you she'd gone weird,' Felix muttered, after a dark glance at Megan.

'I wasn't,' Amber said.

'You're never sober,' Felix told her. 'Come on, guys, it'll take an hour at most – Dan will officially be a grown-up.'

'I haven't passed my test,' Daniel objected.

'Oh, like that'll make a difference. "It's OK, Officer, I know I've broken every rule in the Highway Code, not to mention several laws, but look, here's my licence. Are we good now?"'

Amber got to her feet. 'I need to take my mind off things. You stay here, Megan. I'll come with you, Dan.'

'We all go or we all stay,' Felix said.

Xav stood up. 'I'm in.'

A sharp glance seemed to bounce between Talitha, Megan and Dan; Talitha shrugged, feigning disinterest. Then, looking troubled, Daniel stood up and Megan followed. Back then, when Felix and Xav agreed on something, it happened. That was just the way it was.

They had a secret, you see, that summer. On the rare occasions, in years to come, when they talked about it, they could never agree quite how it started or whose idea it had been. Maybe at the beginning, none of them really intended to go through with it; maybe it had simply been something fun to talk about. The coolest dare imaginable; simple and yet so freakishly, thrillingly dangerous. None of them could have said when the talk became reality, when they realised it was actually going to happen. All they knew was that one moment they were sitting around the pool at Talitha's house and the next they were speeding, at eighty miles an hour, the wrong way down the M40.

## 2

It was three o'clock in the morning the first time. Felix had been at the wheel – of course he had – and they'd seen no other cars. It had taken a little over two minutes, because Felix drove like a maniac down the centre lane. After the first minute had passed, when none of them spoke, when they'd all stared, wide-eyed and open-mouthed, into the darkness, the A40 had morphed into the M40. They'd sped another mile before Felix had braked hard, swinging the car round in a three-hundred-and-thirty degree turn to reach the exit slip road of junction seven. Two minutes of stupid, senseless risk and they were back on the right side of the law.

The car – Felix's mother's VW Golf cabriolet – had erupted with loud, jubilant noise. They'd laughed, screamed and hugged each other. None of them had ever felt more alive. They didn't sleep that night; they drank and talked till dawn and beyond. There wasn't a drug that could compare to it; they knew they'd never feel that way again as long as they lived. It had been a rite of passage; they'd bet against the odds and won. They were marked, special.

But even the purest high wears off, and it had only been a matter of time before Xav had wanted to do it too. Xav hadn't been quite so lucky as Felix. As he'd reached the M40, at a little over eighty miles an hour, Felix, who'd been in the passenger seat, had seen the taillights of a car on the opposite carriageway. It was a little way ahead of them, but they were gaining on it.

'Stop the car, turn round!' Amber had shrieked.

'No, slow down. They might think we're behind them, on a bend in the road,' Daniel said.

'Kill your lights. They won't see us.' Felix leaned across the driver's seat and switched off the headlights.

The night was dark, cloud cover and no moon; they were speeding into a black void. Amber screamed and Xav switched the lights back on.

'Fuck it,' he said, and floored the accelerator. The speedometer crept up to eighty-five miles an hour, ninety, ninety-two. Xav leaned forward over the wheel, as though willing the car to go faster. The rest of them froze, silent, turning as one to their left as they caught up with the car, a large red saloon, on the opposite carriageway.

For a second, the driver, the only occupant of the car, didn't see them, then instinct alerted him and he glanced their way. He looked away, checked his rear-view mirror, then looked back again. His face twisted with incredulity.

Felix raised his right hand and waved.

'Don't overtake,' Megan called from her uncomfortable position, squashed in the back. 'Stay level with him.'

'Why?' Xav was still hunched over the steering wheel.

'If you pull in front, he'll see our number.'

'There are lights ahead,' Talitha said. 'Something's coming at us.'

'Shit,' Xav steered to the right, onto what should have been the inside lane. The lights coming towards them on their own carriageway were high off the ground, widely spaced, powerful; the lights of a heavy-goods vehicle.

'You've got time,' Felix said, his voice hoarse with tension. 'The junction's coming up.'

Xav braked, the car on the opposite carriageway moved ahead, and the lights coming towards them grew bigger. A horn, low-pitched and angry, broke through the hum of their wheels on tarmac. The air in the car seemed to reverberate with it.

'Junction,' Felix snapped, as the sign, unreadable on its reverse side, became visible against the background of trees and hedge. Xav swung the car. They were going too fast, heading for the metal crash barrier. Amber screamed. Talitha wrapped her arms around her head. At the last second, Xav pulled the car back onto its course, and they were off the motorway.

A month went by, and nothing more was said about their two adventures, but then Felix and Talitha had an argument one night about why women should never be permitted in the armed forces. They simply didn't have the physical courage, Felix argued. To prove him wrong, as he'd almost certainly known she would, Talitha had insisted on repeating the motorway stunt. Once again, they'd piled into Felix's mum's car – the only one big enough to take all six of them. Felix had sat in the passenger seat; Megan, the smallest, had curled onto Daniel's lap. They had their designated places, by this time, with only the driver changing.

That time had been uneventful until Talitha had pulled off the motorway at junction seven and they'd seen a highway-patrol car in the layby of the A329. She'd panicked and stalled the car.

'Move,' Felix said. 'If you don't, he'll come over. Move.'

'What if he saw us?' Talitha's face was white with fear. 'What if he pulls us over?'

'If you don't move, he definitely will.'

Talitha had pulled out, away from the layby. Every head in the car turned to watch the police vehicle, but it had remained where it was. And that made three times they'd got away with it.

Amber had been drunk; it had been as simple as that. But even before she insisted on having her turn, it had become an unspoken agreement that the three-minute drive was something that, sooner or later, they were all going to do. They'd seen no other vehicles that night, which was probably just as well, because Amber almost certainly wouldn't have been able to react in time.

Megan, to their surprise, had proven to be the coolest of all at the wheel. In the early hours of a Sunday morning, she'd swung onto the A40 to see headlights almost upon her. Before any of the others had time to react, she'd swerved right onto the hard shoulder, screeched to a stop and killed her headlights.

'Duck, all of you,' she'd hissed as she'd dropped her own head onto the wheel.

No sooner had the other car flashed past than she'd restarted the engine and driven at eighty miles an hour along the inside lane to get them off the motorway.

'That's it,' she said, when they got back to Tal's house. 'We were bloody lucky just now. We're not risking it again.'

Shaken, they'd all agreed, and it hadn't been mentioned again. Until tonight.

And so now, after all, it was Daniel's turn.

Not long after three o'clock in the morning, the B-road heading north out of Talitha's village was empty. They drove with the top down, because Amber was still feeling queasy and the night air smelled of honeysuckle, which seemed to bode well, and muck-spreading, which didn't.

Daniel drove slowly and badly, his acceleration uneven, over-compensating on the steering. At the tiny hump bridge over the stream, he nearly hit the wall.

'Watch it.' Felix, as usual, was in the passenger seat.

'I'm not used to this car,' Daniel complained.

'OK,' Felix said, as they approached the junction with London Road. 'We all know the drill if we're stopped. We were heading back to Tal's house. Daniel wasn't sure of the way and got lost. We're all a bit pissed, and we weren't concentrating. "We're all terribly sorry and upset and we'll never do it again, Officer."'

'You don't have to do it, Dan,' Megan said. No one replied.

'Everyone got their seat belts on?' Xav asked.

'Hold tight, Meg,' said Talitha.

'No hesitation, straight into the middle lane,' Felix said, as Daniel turned right at the junction and drove onto the slip road that would take them down to the A40. 'You need some speed.'

Daniel edged the car up to thirty miles an hour; the bend in the road was sharp, veering south, then south-east. The correct route – the only legally permitted route – made an almost complete circle onto the A40 heading into Oxford. At its south-eastern tip, the carriageway split; one way entered the A40, the other allowed traffic to leave it.

Black and white chevrons, indicating that all vehicles should turn left, came into view, then came the no-entry signs that flanked the right-hand side of the carriageway. It couldn't have been clearer which way they were supposed to drive. Daniel gave a low-pitched moan.

'Hold your nerve.' Felix sat forward, as though craning to see around Daniel onto the carriageway they were about to enter.

'Oh God, I hate this bit.' Amber tucked her face into Xav's shoulder; Talitha sat forward, holding tight onto the back of Felix's headrest.

'And go,' Felix called at the crucial moment. The car swung right, past the no-entry signs, and onto the wrong carriageway of the A40. The dual carriageway ahead, two lanes, unlit, was clear.

'Oh, thank God, thank God,' Talitha muttered.

'You need some speed,' Felix warned. The car was moving at a little over thirty miles an hour. 'Two and a half miles, that's all. Less than three minutes if you get your foot down.'

Jaw clenched, eyes unblinking, Daniel pressed down on the accelerator and the speedometer moved up to forty miles an hour, fifty, fifty-five. The intermittent white line that divided the lanes flashed past.

'Nothing behind,' Megan called.

'We need to get a move on.' Felix was drumming his fingers on the dashboard.

'Not fast enough, Dan.' Xav's voice was strained with tension.

The gear box screamed as Daniel made a clumsy change into top gear.

'There's a fox. Watch out for the fox!' Amber grabbed hold of Daniel's shoulder.

'Fuck's sake, Amber,' Talitha snapped.

'I'm good, I'm good.' Daniel steered into the lane closest to the central reservation.

'Motorway coming up,' Xav said.

'I'm never doing this again,' Talitha moaned.

'Nearly there,' Felix said. 'Move into the middle lane when you can. The turn will be easier.'

Maybe the bend in the road took them all by surprise. One moment, all ahead was darkness, the next blinding lights were speeding towards them. Out of nowhere, another car had appeared.

Amber screamed.

'Hard shoulder!' Felix yelled.

All of them were thrown forward by the sudden loss of momentum as the acrid smell of brake fluid filled the car. Felix pushed the steering wheel out of Daniel's grip and the car swung hard to the right. It should have been enough.

But the other car matched their movements, as though a huge mirror had been dropped in front of them. They were feet away from it. Daniel had frozen, his eyes wide and staring.

Felix pulled the wheel back. The car rocked and seemed to scream at them. They could hear the squeal of brakes, the blasting of a horn. Light filled the car, illuminating their horrified faces. There was a split second of silence, then the other car was gone and they were stationary on the carriageway. The world had stopped spinning.

# 3

Tiny whimpering sounds filled the night and it took them a moment to realise they were coming from the car engine as its component parts protested at their treatment of it. A moth attracted by the headlights bounced against the windscreen and, in the heavy silence, they could hear its gentle, reproachful thudding. *What did you do?* It seemed to be saying to them. *What did you do?*

'Shit.' Felix dropped his head into his hands and spoke through his fingers. 'Get out of here, Dan. Now.'

'We didn't hit it,' Daniel said. 'That car. We missed it, didn't we? Someone tell me we missed it.'

'It's crashed,' Megan whispered, as though if she said it softly enough, it might not be true. 'It's hit a tree or something.'

None of the others moved.

'Dan, we have to get out of here.' Felix grabbed hold of Daniel's shoulder. 'Get out of the car. I'll drive.'

Daniel didn't resist Felix's shaking. He'd become limp, unresponsive.

Xav leaned towards the driver's seat. 'Dan, we can't stay here. Something else will be along.'

Gently, Talitha took Felix's hand away from Daniel. 'Dan, please,' she said. 'We'll all die if we stay here.'

Daniel turned on the ignition. Nothing happened.

'Again, do it again,' Felix yelled.

The second time, the engine started. Daniel swung the car onto the hard shoulder and stopped.

'What the hell are you doing?' Felix said. 'We have to get out of here.'

A smell of burned rubber flooded the car. The night was silent.

'We have to see if they're OK,' Amber said.

'Are you mental?' Felix snapped back. 'We'll go down for this. Dan, give me the keys.'

'Amber's right,' Xav said. 'We have to check.'

Dan glanced once into the rear-view mirror and clamped his eyes shut tight. On the other carriageway, a vehicle entered the motorway and sped away.

'I'm getting out.' Megan pushed herself up so that she could sit on the car's side panel. She swung her legs over.

Moving slowly, his eyes not quite focusing and his limbs unsteady, Xav opened his door. On the other side, Talitha did the same.

'I swear, if you lot get out, I'll leave you here,' Felix warned. 'Meg, get back in.'

'I'll go,' Xav volunteered. 'Don't let him leave me behind.' Still, he didn't move.

With a sudden rush of movement that took them all by surprise, Daniel climbed out through the driver's door and stood looking back down the carriageway. Seeing his chance, Felix jumped out and ran around the front of the car. Before he could reach the driver's seat, though, Xav reached forward and grabbed the keys from the ignition. Then, at last, he got out of the car. Amber slid across and followed him. On the other side, Talitha climbed out.

The six of them, diminished, stared back at the devastation they'd wreaked.

The other car, a white Vauxhall Astra, was thirty yards away.

Its rear wheels were still on the hard shoulder, but its front end had vanished into undergrowth. Its headlights illuminated a mass of vegetation and the trunk of a tree.

The tree seemed to accuse them, as though if they closed their eyes, they would hear it moan with pain. Then the silence was broken as screaming sounded from inside the wrecked car. Thin, high-pitched, terrified.

'I think that's a—' Amber stopped, unable to finish her sentence. Xav moved towards the Astra.

'Give me the keys,' Felix demanded. 'Xav, give me the fucking keys.'

Ignoring him, Xav took another step forward. Megan did too, as movement became apparent in the headlights of the crashed car; something hardly visible, nebulous, an upward drift. The screaming stopped, only to be replaced by the sound of hammering on glass.

Xav took out his mobile phone.

'What the hell are you doing?' Talitha demanded.

'We need help.'

She wrapped her hand around his, enclosing the phone. 'We can't call the emergency services.'

'Dan can turn the car round,' Xav told her. 'We'll say we were travelling the right way and there was an accident. We don't know how it happened.'

'Dan's over the limit,' Amber said. 'He'll go to prison.'

'Not necessarily.' Xav pulled away for Talitha. 'And only for a short time. It can't be helped. We can't get away with this.'

'Smoke,' Megan whispered. 'Smoke coming up from the bonnet. It's on fire.'

'OK, OK.' Felix strode ahead and turned to face them, his hands held up as though in surrender. 'This is the plan. We make sure they're OK, then we get back in the car. We drive to the nearest phone box and we call an ambulance from there. We won't give our names.'

'We can't leave them,' Megan said.

Felix reached out, his eyes darkening when Megan flinched away. 'They're probably fine.' He looked from one friend to the next. 'It's just a bump. They didn't hit us. Xav, you and me, we'll go and check now. OK?'

Without taking his eyes off the Astra, Xav nodded.

'Turn the ignition off,' Talitha said. 'You have to do that. It's the ignition that causes the sparks.'

'It'll be OK, guys. It'll be cool.' Felix put his hand on Xav's shoulder. 'Get back in the car and wait for us. Dan, get in the back. I'm driving us home.'

Daniel and the girls stayed where they were as Felix and Xav walked towards the car. They'd covered roughly half the distance when a bright bubble of flame appeared on the Astra's bonnet.

Talitha wailed. A second later, the Astra's petrol tank exploded.

# 4

The night was transformed, as though someone had turned on floodlights. A wall of heat hit them, and both Felix and Xav took an instinctive step back. For what felt like an age, no one moved and then the two boys, acting as one, turned and ran back to their own car. Xav threw Felix the car keys; Felix jumped into the driver's seat.

'What are you doing? We can't go?' Amber wailed.

Talitha grabbed Amber and threw her inside the car. She followed so quickly the two girls made a heap of flesh and limbs on the back seat. Daniel leapt in and then Megan as Felix pulled away. He drove a hundred yards along the hard shoulder before swinging onto the exit slip road.

The junction to the A329 was clear. Felix turned left and within minutes they were back on the village roads that led to Talitha's house. The world seemed oddly normal, as though nothing dreadful had happened.

The stone mansion was in darkness when they arrived, and that was one good thing at least. No need to start lying quite yet. They got out of the car, slowly, stiffly, as though their bodies had aged in the last hour; as though standing upright, walking forward, speaking normally, had become beyond them. Acting on instinct, moving like a small and damaged herd, they made for the pool house. At the last moment, Megan hung back, her attention caught, it seemed, by the glistening of the water, but when Felix took her hand and coaxed her inside, she didn't resist.

In darkness, they sat and waited, although it is likely that none of them could have said what they were waiting for.

Finally, Xav spoke. 'We won't get away with it. They'll find us.'

'I can't believe we left them.' Amber's make-up was streaked with tear stains. Tiny rivulets of water were running down her face and showed no sign of stopping.

'There was nothing we could do,' Felix said. 'Once the car went up, that was it.'

Amber stared back at him. 'We should have called the police.'

Felix kept his voice low, uncharacteristically gentle. 'They wouldn't have arrived in time. You saw how quickly it happened. We were right there and we couldn't do a thing.'

'The police will be there by now,' Talitha said. 'The next car along the road will have called them. There'll be a major incident now. Still nothing they can do. A car explodes, that's it.'

'We should go back and see,' Amber said.

'Are you mental?' Talitha snapped.

'We need to call the police.' Xav reached out and took Amber's hand. 'They'll find us, sooner or later. It'll be worse if we don't own up.'

'I'll go down for murder.' Dan was huddled in a corner of the room, sitting on the floor, his arms wrapped around his knees as though trying to hide himself away. 'It was me behind the wheel. You can't make decisions for me.'

'We're all to blame,' Amber said. 'We all agreed to do it.'

'That's not how the law will see it,' Daniel argued. 'The driver is responsible.'

'He's right,' Talitha said.

'I'll tell them,' Daniel said. 'I'll tell them you've all done it. I was unlucky, that's all.'

'You weren't unlucky, you twat,' Felix snapped. 'You were incompetent. If you'd driven onto the hard shoulder when I told you, we'd have missed them.'

Daniel wiped a hand across his nose. Even in the darkness, they could see the gleam on it. 'You grabbed the fucking wheel – you caused it!'

'Stop it,' Xav said. 'We stay calm. We work it out together.'

'We can't go to the police,' Daniel said.

'They'll find us,' Xav insisted. 'Someone died in that car tonight. I know no one wants to hear it, but we need to face facts. Someone died. I pray to God it was only one person, but—'

'There was a kid in that car,' Amber said.

There was a moment of horrified silence, and then Xav let go her hand. 'That's not helpful, Amber.'

'That screaming we heard, it wasn't an adult.'

'Amber, please don't.'

'Look, guys, we can't change what happened,' Talitha said. 'I wish to God we could, but we can't. We have to come up with a plan.'

'We say nothing,' Felix said. 'There were no witnesses. Or no witnesses left. Sorry to sound heartless, but we need to focus. No one but us knows what happened, and I am not waving goodbye to my whole future for nothing.'

'That car on the other side of the motorway,' Amber reminded them. 'The one that joined at junction seven. They would have seen us.'

'We don't know that.' Felix's voice was rising. 'The car hadn't exploded when it went past. We were all still in our car. There are no lights on that stretch of the motorway. They might have seen nothing. Or they might have thought they saw something but couldn't make out what. The chances of them having got our registration number are zero.'

'They must have seen something,' Daniel said. 'The police will know there were two cars involved.'

'We didn't hit it. There will be no marks on our car.'

'They'll find us,' Xav insisted. 'This isn't a prank any more. Someone was killed. The police will throw everything into the investigation. They won't rest until they know what happened.'

Amber started to cry audibly. Talitha stood up. 'I'm going to find my mum,' she said. 'I can't do this.'

Daniel scrambled up off the tiles and beat her to the door. 'Wait,' he said. 'Just a few more minutes. We can figure it out.' He looked from one face to the next and it seemed to the others that time had unwound in the last few hours, and Daniel had become the boy they vaguely remembered from years ago; small and shy, clumsy on the sports field, wary of showing his intelligence in class in case the bigger, cooler kids labelled him a nerd.

'Is anyone actually sober?' he went on, and his voice too seemed to have regressed to the time before it broke. 'If the driver was someone who'd passed their test and who hadn't been drinking, then all we need to do is say we were driving the right way and it was an accident. We might get away with a few points on some-one's licence. If we all stick together.'

'You want one of us to take the blame for you?' Felix moved a step closer to Daniel, his shoulders squaring up, fingers twitching, as though about to clench into fists.

'It was your fucking idea!' Daniel yelled. 'I didn't want to do it. No one wanted to do it but you and Xav. I'm not taking the blame for what you did.'

Felix stepped closer still, pointing a finger in Dan's face. 'You were behind the wheel, tosser. We can say we were innocent pas-sengers, who begged you not to do it.'

'You fucking shit.' Daniel launched himself at Felix. He was several stones lighter but, knocked off balance, Felix stumbled over a chair and both boys fell against the wall. Taken by surprise, Felix lay stunned as Dan rained several punches on the bigger boy's head and shoulders. Xav and Talitha rushed to pull them apart. It didn't take long. Neither boy really had the heart for a fight. Red-faced, sweating, they sank back down onto chairs.

'It's over for us, isn't it?' Felix's heightened colour drained as he spoke. 'Even if it's only Dan who gets prosecuted – sorry, Dan, but we might as well face facts – we're all accomplices. We all left the scene of an accident.'

In the silence that followed, more than one saw the bright bubble of fire again, felt the exploding heat against their faces.

Talitha said, 'Everyone will hate us.'

'No university will take us,' Amber said. 'It'll be in all the papers.'

'Why?' Xav looked around. 'It was a road traffic accident. They happen all the time. They don't all make the news.'

'Get real, Xav. We're the senior prefect team at All Souls,' Talitha said. 'Megan's head of school, for God's sake. We've all got Oxbridge places, or near enough. The rest of the world loves to bring people like us down. Don't kid yourselves – the newspapers will have a field day with this.'

'My dad could lose his seat,' Amber muttered. Her father was the MP for Buckingham.

'We've ruined everything.' Talitha, too, seemed on the verge of tears. None of them had ever seen her cry before.

Felix held up his hands as though to stop the others rushing him.

'Not necessarily,' he said. 'Only one of us needs to have been in the car tonight. He can say it was an accident, that he made a mistake. We had a plan, remember? Well, that's what we do.

We stick to it. A solitary driver made a mistake, and there was a terrible accident.'

'Don't fucking look at me,' Daniel said. 'I'm not letting you off scot-free.'

There was movement in the room, hardly noticeable, and yet somehow four of the others – Felix, Xav, Talitha and Amber – had formed a circle around Daniel. He stared from one face to another, like a trapped animal, desperate for a way to run.

From her seat by the door, Megan watched, her dark eyes wide and staring.

'Think about it, Dan.' Felix's voice was calm, his movements soothing. 'One of us has to pay for what happened tonight. There's no getting around that. But not all of us do. You're still young. Your record's clean. You're an exemplary pupil. You'll get a year or two, possibly. Maybe not. Maybe you'll get away with community service. Whatever happens, we'll make it up to you.'

Daniel stared at Felix with something like hatred in his eyes.

'What are you suggesting?' Talitha asked, and Daniel shot her an anguished look.

'This is what happened,' Felix said. 'We were all hanging out here and Daniel left. He was nervous about tomorrow and wanted to be on his own at home. He took my mum's car without asking, because he had no other way of getting back. He got confused, because he was tired, and a bit drunk, and not a very experienced driver, and he took a wrong turn. He panicked when the other car exploded and drove home.'

'I don't believe I'm hearing this,' Daniel began.

'Hush, Dan. Let him finish,' Megan said.

'First thing in the morning, he comes back here, and tells us what he's done.'

'Then I phone my dad, who can be here in less than an hour,'

Talitha said. 'He agrees to act for Dan – he will, Dan, I'm sure of it – and the two of them go to the police station.'

Tears were running down Daniel's face. 'No. I'm not doing it.'

'My dad might even get you off,' Talitha said. 'He's brilliant, everyone says so.'

'I'll go to prison. That's it. Life over. Why should I be the only one who pays? Why?'

'Isn't it better to have five friends who are doing well, who can look after you, make sure you get what you need when it's over, than five friends who are serving time in the next cell?' Felix said.

Daniel dropped his head into his hands. 'I won't. I won't do it.'

'We could draw lots,' Xav suggested.

Daniel looked up. 'What do you mean?'

'Felix's right,' Xav said. 'It's stupid for us all to take the blame. Why ruin six lives? Only one of us needs to do it. Question is, which one?'

No one spoke.

'We're all equally guilty,' Xav said. 'We've all done it. Any one of us could have been in the driving seat when someone got hurt. Got any straws, Tal?'

'You're not serious?' Felix said.

'Why not?' Daniel demanded. 'Not so keen on one of us carrying the can when it might be you?'

'You're a dickhead. You caused the crash, not me.'

'I'll do it,' said Megan.

It's possible the others had forgotten Megan was there, she'd been so quiet since they'd got back. On her foldaway chair by the door, she seemed unnaturally still, her arms wrapped around her body, her eyes on the floor.

'What do you mean?' Felix said.

She glanced up. 'I'll say I was driving.'

They all watched her take a deep breath. She closed her eyes, and for a second or more seemed almost to have turned to stone. Then her dark eyes opened but fixed on something that none of the others could see.

'I'll say I was alone,' she went on. 'That I got fed up hanging out with you guys, that I was nervous about tomorrow and that I wanted to go home.'

'That's not your way home.' Felix spoke slowly, almost suspiciously. 'And why would you take my mum's car?'

Another long pause. 'I was really, really fed up with you all,' she said at last. 'You were behaving like complete jerks.'

Her eyes held those of Felix.

'I got confused at the junction,' Megan said. 'Maybe I was upset, not really concentrating as I should have been, and when I saw the other car, there was nothing I could do.'

A few more seconds of silence.

'Why?' said Xav. 'Why would you do that?'

'Let her, if she wants to,' Daniel said.

'You and Felix are right,' Megan said. 'It's stupid for everyone's lives to be ruined. One of us can save the others. We've always said we're the best friends we're ever going to have. Now we show we mean it.'

'I can't believe you'd do that,' Xav said.

'One of us has to, and Dan simply isn't strong enough. No offence, Dan, but I think you just proved it.'

'What's the catch?' Felix said.

Megan got to her feet. 'The catch is that you will all owe me. You owe me your lives, because what I'm about to do will save them. Do you agree?'

'Yes,' Daniel said.

'Meg,' Amber began, 'I'm not sure—'

'What is it you want?' Felix said.

'Tal,' Megan said. 'You're our legal brain, go and get some paper and a pen.'

Tal half got up from her seat. 'But, what—'

'Just do it. Dan, go with her. There's a camera in her bedroom. She usually keeps it in the bedside cabinet. Make sure it's charged up and bring that too.'

With a nervous glance at each other, Talitha and Daniel left the pool house.

'What are you up to?' Felix asked.

'Keeping you out of prison,' Megan told him. 'You were happy enough for Dan to do it. What's your problem now?'

Felix opened his mouth.

'No, shut up,' Megan stopped him. 'I need to think.'

Seconds, then minutes ticked by. Amber buried her face in Xav's shoulder, Felix stared at Megan the way predators watch prey that they're hungry for but fearful of at the same time. Megan fixed her eyes on the water outside. Only once did she turn around, only for a second, to make eye contact with Xav.

The others returned, Daniel carrying the camera, Talitha with a clipboard, several sheets of paper and a pen. No one spoke. They were waiting for Megan.

'Write what I tell you,' she said to Talitha.

Talitha sat.

'Date it,' Megan told her. 'Today's date. Thursday the seventeenth of August, and put the time, three thirty-five in the morning.'

'Done.' Talitha's hand was visibly shaking.

'OK, now write this. "We, the undersigned, were travelling in the VW Golf, registration number V112 HCG, in the early hours of this morning. At approximately zero-three-ten hours, we drove onto the south-east-bound carriage of the A40. Shortly after the road became the motorway, we narrowly avoided colliding with a Vauxhall Astra, registration number S79 THO travelling in the opposite direction."'

'How did you get the number?' Amber asked.

'I've got an eidetic memory. Tal, keep going. "The Astra crashed, due to our actions, and a fire broke out. We were unable to help the passengers."'

Tal stopped writing and shook her hand, as though to relieve cramp.

'We should say that Dan was driving,' Felix said.

'Shut the fuck up,' Daniel snapped.

'This is about collective responsibility,' Megan said. 'Almost done, Tal. "We acted deliberately, knowing our actions were potentially dangerous. It was a dare, one which we'd done five times before, with each of us taking a turn at the wheel. We jointly and fully take responsibility for the accident."'

'I'm getting to the bottom of the page,' Talitha said.

'Is there space for six signatures?' Megan asked.

'Just about.'

'We all sign,' Megan said.

'Why are we doing this?' Felix said, when the paper was handed to him. 'What are you planning to do with it?'

'Keep it safe,' Megan told him. 'I'll only use it if I have to.'

'Why?' Felix's face had turned stony. 'What's the catch?'

'If I do this for you, you will all owe me. I'll take the blame, but you'll all owe me one favour, redeemable when I come out of prison. Or sooner. Whenever I ask, basically.'

Felix's eyes narrowed. 'What kind of favour?'

'Anything I ask.'

'I'm not agreeing to that,' Felix said.

Megan gave a tight smile. 'Then the deal's off.'

'What kind of favour?' Xav asked. 'What do you want? Money?'

Megan seemed to be thinking about it. 'Maybe,' she said.

'Here are my terms. You all agree to one favour each. Whatever I ask, whenever I ask it. If one of you reneges, he or she drops the rest of you in it.'

'In other words, you've got us by the balls,' Felix said.

'You like my side of the deal so much, you step into my shoes,' Megan said.

'We need to agree now what the favours are,' Talitha said. 'I mean, you could ask me to murder my mum.'

'I've always liked your mum.' Megan smiled. 'I might ask you to kill Felix.'

Felix's head snapped from one face to the next. 'What the fuck?'

'Kidding. If you're dead, how will I redeem your pledge?'

'Meg, this isn't you,' Xav said. 'Why are you doing this?'

'I'm not sure any of you really know me,' Megan said. 'You let me into your little group because I was head of school, but I was never one of you.'

'That's not true,' Amber said, but there was no conviction in her voice and she kept her eyes on the tiled floor.

'Whatever. Here's what happened tonight. We were hanging around, as usual, and I got a bit bored and tetchy with you all. I sneaked away, round about three o'clock, stealing Felix's mum's car. That's the last you saw of me.'

Felix scribbled his name on the paper and passed it to Daniel, who signed without a word. Amber signed next, then Xav.

'Tomorrow morning,' Megan went on, 'you go to school as planned. If anyone asks you where I am, you don't know. After an hour or so, ring my mum, go round to my house. Tal, when I send word, I need your dad to come and represent me.'

'Is that my favour?'

Megan's eyes flashed. 'No, it bloody isn't. And don't let him get out of it. Make him do it.'

The paper was handed back to Megan. She signed it herself, then passed it back to Talitha.

'Stand together, all of you,' she said. 'Tal, hold it up.'

The others did what they were told. Megan took several photographs, then she pulled the film from the camera and tucked it into her pocket. She held her hand out to Felix.

'Keys,' she said. He gave them to her.

'Good luck tomorrow,' she said. 'Have happy lives, all of you. Don't forget me.'

'Meg, wait . . .' Amber took a step towards her, but Felix caught hold of her by the shoulder.

'Xav, walk me to the car,' Megan said.

Xav gave a last, desperate look around the group, and then he and Megan left the pool house.

# 5

'. . .and is likely to remain so throughout this morning's rush hour. Finally, the northbound carriageway of the M40 between junction seven at Thame and junction eight at Oxford has reopened following the fatal car crash in the early hours of the morning. Police are appealing for witnesses after a mother and her two young children died in a collision. None of the victims have been named and it is not thought, at this stage, that any other vehicle was involved. Now back to David Prever in the studio.'

Xav switched off the car radio and felt as though his heart must surely be bleeding; nothing else could hurt this much. Beside him, Amber sobbed quietly.

It was eight forty-five in the morning. The sun was casting golden light on the ancient stones of the city, and the sky was a bright blue, dotted with cartoon clouds and vapour trails like paper cuts. Xav couldn't remember the world ever looking darker. His life had ended in the early hours of that morning, and now, zombie-like, he was stumbling through a pale semblance of it.

'I told you there was a child in the car,' Amber mumbled. 'I told you.'

*Two kids*, Xav thought. *Two kids died last night, thanks to us.*

The car park was getting busier by the second and the warm summer air seemed heavy with a tension that was entirely removed from the churning inside Xav, and altogether preferable.

Oh, to have nothing more to worry about than exam results. Accompanying parents didn't try to hide their anxiety, huddling together, white-faced, muttering to each other that yes, they'd been dreading it, and no, it didn't get any easier, and they wished the school would open the doors and get it over with.

What they didn't talk about, because they could never bring themselves to be quite so honest with each other, or even themselves, were the enormous sums of money they'd invested in their children's education, but they were all bitterly conscious that in a few minutes, they'd know whether or not their investment had paid off.

The school-leavers made a credible attempt to brazen it out with a bit of half-hearted banter, but like their mums and dads, their eyes kept flickering to the dining-room doors. From his seat behind the wheel, Xav could see people inside: catering staff, the usher, the woman who ran the office; even the master had been glimpsed in a fondant-pink suit, but the doors were locked and would remain so until the stroke of nine.

'I can't do this.'

Beside him, Amber was shaking. Her face still carried traces of last night's make-up, and her breath in the confined space was sour. He guessed his would be too.

'Amber, you have to hold it together. We get our results, then we go back to Tal's and talk it through.'

'I can't. *Two kids*. I can't, Xav.'

Not for the first time that morning, Xav wished he were alone. He could barely deal with the contents of his own head, and keeping Amber calm might prove beyond him. How could he not have known, twelve hours earlier, that his life was perfect?

'Here they are.' He felt a moment of relief as Talitha drove her Mini into the car park and reversed into one of the few remaining spaces. Felix was in the passenger seat, Daniel in the back.

SHARON BOLTON

All three looked like shit when they got out. Daniel leaned against the car door, as though he barely had the strength to stand upright, but Felix made straight for Xav and Amber.

'Did you have the radio on?' Xav asked when they were close enough.

Felix gave a curt nod. 'It makes no difference.' Like Xav, he kept his voice low. 'Two kids, twenty kids, we can't do anything about it now. The important thing is, they don't think any other vehicle was involved. Have either of you spoken to Megan?'

'She's not answering her phone.' Amber blew her nose. 'She said she wouldn't.'

Felix gave a nervous look around. 'Yeah, but it's different now. If they think that other driver lost control, they won't be looking for anyone else. Megan doesn't need to fess up. We have to find her.'

'I'll try her again.' Xav dialled Megan's number. 'Nothing,' he said, after a second.

'What time is it?' Daniel asked.

'Eight forty-five,' Talitha told him. 'We have to go inside in fifteen minutes.'

'I'll drive round to her house,' Felix said. 'There's still time to stop her going to the police. Xav, can I take your car?'

'I'll come—' Xav began.

'Xav, no.' Amber clung to his hand.

Biting back what he really wanted to say, Xav handed over his car keys. Felix jumped into the silver Peugeot 205 and accelerated out of the car park.

'It's too late,' Xav said, as they watched Felix drive away. 'She'll have gone to the police by now.'

He should have talked her out of it when he'd walked her to the car. Wait, he should have said, give it time, let's see what happens. But he'd been knocked sideways by what she'd said to him.

34

Two members of staff, sports teachers, with matching smiles of sympathy, made their way through the crowd. They'd seen it all many times before.

'Oh, for God's sake, come on.' Talitha glared at the dining-room doors as though she might will them open. 'Let's get it over with.'

'I don't care,' Xav said. 'I really don't care what I've got. If I've failed the lot, I couldn't care less.'

In a way, he almost hoped he had, as though exam failure might act as part payment for what he'd done the night before. He hadn't though; he always found exams easy.

Amber wrapped her arms around his waist, and Xav took a deep breath, because the urge to throw her off was close to overwhelming.

'Amber, you need to pull yourself together,' Talitha snapped. 'You can't go in in floods of tears.'

Grateful to Tal for voicing his own thoughts so that he didn't have to, and guilty at those same thoughts, Xav gave his girlfriend a hug. 'We'll say it's nerves,' he said. 'Then relief.'

'Or dismay, if she does fail theology,' Daniel said.

# 6

He was on time, he had to be. It was still early; she wouldn't have done anything yet. The accident was bad, he wouldn't try to pretend otherwise, and he'd have to keep a close eye on Amber and Dan over the coming weeks, possibly Xav too, but they'd get through it, just as long as Megan hadn't made the phone call yet.

As Felix turned the corner into Megan's terraced street and pulled over on a single yellow line, he realised he'd never actually been inside her house before. On the few occasions he'd dropped her off after a night out, he'd pulled up outside her front door to let her jump out. He'd never been invited in and neither, as far as he knew, had any of the others.

A few seconds after he'd set off towards her house on foot, he saw the police car.

Double-parked, blue lights flashing to warn other road users, it was directly outside Megan's place. That was it then; he was too late. Felix almost turned on his heels, but common sense kept him moving forward. A few yards closer and he could see a tow truck lifting a vehicle onto its cargo bed. A few more yards and he realised it was his mother's car that was about to be towed. *('One more parking ticket, Felix, and I'm taking you off the insurance – I mean it this time.')* Felix heard his mother's voice loud in his head and ignored it. A car being towed was the least of his problems right now.

Closer still and he could see the uniformed officer on the

pavement, watching the car being lifted. Felix took the last few steps that committed him.

'Excuse me,' he looked from the police officer to the man in the yellow vest who was directing the loading of the car. Heavy chains had been wrapped around the wheels and two crane-like lifts were preparing to raise it off the ground. 'That's my car. What's happening?'

The man in the yellow vest looked a question at the officer, who nodded at him to continue.

'Can you give me your name, sir?' the policeman asked. 'This car is registered to a Mrs Elizabeth O'Neill.'

The lifts bounced, the chains tightened.

'She's my mum. It's her car, really. She lets me drive it. I'm Felix O'Neill.'

'And did you park it here?'

Steady. He needed to be worried, but not too worried, not yet.

'No.' Felix fixed his eyes on the car that was now several inches off the ground. 'I lent it to my friend last night. I mean, I sort of lent it.' He glanced around towards Megan's front door. 'Is she in? I came to find her. She needs to be at school.'

'Would that be Megan Macdonald, of 14 Warren Road,' the officer said, after glancing at his notebook.

'That's right.' Felix looked again at Megan's front door, at the railings outside where two bikes were chained. 'What's going on? Has something happened?'

Ignoring the officer's grumbled objection, Felix strode up to Megan's house. As he pushed open the gate and banged hard on the door, he told himself that he was doing well, that he hadn't put a foot wrong so far, he just had to keep it up.

He glanced right to the narrow strip of land that passed for a front garden: gravel, a broken planter, some weeds breaking through.

A hand landed on his shoulder. The policeman had followed him.

'Steady on, son. There's no one in, I can tell you that for a fact. Now, when did you last see Miss Macdonald?'

'Last night. What's happened? Is she hurt?' Felix looked back up the road towards the tow truck. 'I need to tell my mum if the car's been damaged. Can I go and see what's happened to it?'

The police officer raised his hand, effectively blocking Felix's way back onto the street. 'What time last night did you lend Miss Macdonald your car?'

Felix pretended to think, then gave a vague shake of his head. 'I don't know.'

'Ten o'clock? Eleven o'clock?'

Down the street, his mother's car was swinging in the air as it was raised towards the truck's cargo bed. People had gathered to watch, mainly kids, but one or two adults on doorsteps. His mum would kill him. On top of everything else, she'd never let him drive her car again. Not that that mattered now – nothing mattered now – but it was odd all the same, how he kept having thoughts that belonged to . . . before.

'No, later than that,' he said. 'We were in the Lamb and Flag till last orders.'

The police officer seemed to make a decision. 'Mr O'Neill, I think it would be a good idea if you came with me to the station.'

Panic raced through Felix like a swig of strong spirit. 'Why? I mean, I can't. I have to be at school. It's results day. We should both be there, me and Megan.' He felt tears spring into his eyes and didn't try to blink them away.

The officer seemed to be thinking for a moment, and then he nodded and stepped back, out of Felix's way. 'All right,' he said. 'Go and get your results. We've got your details. We'll talk to you later.'

*

The master of the school – a tall, thin woman with spiky, grey hair – spread her arms wide.

'My crème de la crème,' she said. 'Well done, darlings.'

Knowing it was expected, Talitha, Amber, Xav and Daniel stepped forward and let the master enfold them in a group hug.

'So proud of you,' she said, a second later when she released them. 'Five As,' she said to Xav. 'Superb.' She put a hand on Amber's shoulder. 'And you too, straight As.'

'Even in theology,' Xav glanced at Amber, who didn't react. She'd retreated into herself, her eyes had lost focus and she hadn't spoken since the doors had opened thirty minutes ago. People were only going to buy the nerves excuse for so long. He had to get her out of there.

Around them, though, the gathering in the school dining room was turning into a party. Two hundred people or more were talking too loudly, full of excitement and relief. For the first twenty minutes or so, after the doors opened at nine o'clock, a nervous quiet had prevailed as the leavers lined up to get their envelopes, leaving the parents hovering at the opposite end of the hall. Gradually, as more and more envelopes had been opened, as leavers had shared results with each other, with parents, with teachers – who knew them already, but pretended afresh to be delighted – the noise levels had grown and the two groups had merged.

Every few seconds, a flash of light appeared, as the official photographer captured the tiny moments of triumph and relief.

The master's eyes flicked from one face to the other. 'No parents here?' she said. 'I hope you've told them.'

'We stayed at Tal's house,' Xav explained. 'We've all phoned results through. They're thrilled.'

'And rightly so.' The master's face fell. 'Where's Megan? Did she slip away? And Felix, too. I was going to have a photograph with the six of you, but in the circumstances, maybe . . . Is she all right, do you know?'

'We haven't seen Megan,' Talitha said quickly. 'She didn't come in with us. Felix went to look for her.'

'There he is.' Xav had spotted his car, with Felix at the wheel, pulling into the car park.

'Hmmm,' the master said. 'Excuse me, folks. I'd better just . . .'

She walked away without finishing her sentence, towards the desk at the front of the hall where a teacher – Mr Sparrow, Latin – sat with an almost empty box. She and Mr Sparrow spoke for a few seconds, then both glanced back at the group.

Without conferring, acting on instinct, the four of them moved a little further from the crowd of people.

Talitha said, 'Did you see her face when she mentioned Megan? She knows something.'

'It's too soon,' Xav said. 'She can't.'

'We should ring again,' said Daniel.

'No,' Talitha argued. 'Wait for Felix.'

Felix and the master reached them at the same time. Her face was troubled, his unreadable.

'When did you last see Megan?' the master asked. 'Have any of you heard from her this morning?'

'I've just come from her house.' Felix kept his eyes on the master's, not looking at any of the rest of them. 'No answer.'

He was going to be the best liar; Xav stored the knowledge away for future use.

'She was with us last night for a while,' Daniel added. 'Then she went home.'

The master gave a vague nod, seemed about to speak, but then walked away.

'Something's wrong,' said Talitha.

'Oh, you think,' Xav said.

'I mean something else. She's worried about Megan, but how can she be? Unless the police have been in touch already?'

'You don't think she's done anything stupid?' Daniel said. 'Megan, I mean?'

'What happened?' Xav said to Felix. 'Did you see her?'

Felix shook his head. 'Not here. Come on, let's go.'

They were almost at the door when Talitha remembered. 'Felix, your results.'

They waited as Felix walked to the desk and was given his envelope by Mr Sparrow. He opened it as he walked back to them, and his face didn't change. By this time, most people were leaving, the youngsters into the city to celebrate, the parents back home or to work.

'Four As,' Felix said, as he reached them.

'Well done, mate,' Xav tried to smile and failed.

'Not one of us got less than an A, not in any subject,' Daniel said. 'We're the "crème de la crème" all right.'

'Yay us,' said Talitha.

At that second, a flash blinded them. The official photographer had caught up with them and the moment was immortalised.

# 7

This was not how it was supposed to be. They should have been in town now, dancing their way down the high street, heading for the Eagle and Child, the Turf Tavern, or any of the town-centre pubs that would serve champagne to kids who might technically be old enough to drink alcohol but almost certainly couldn't be trusted to handle it well. Their phones should have been ringing constantly with congratulatory phone calls. This was their moment, the first day of the rest of their lives, their triumph.

They should not have had to slip out of the hall, avoiding eye contact and the well-meaning enquiries of friends' parents, mums and dads they'd known since they were tiny, and who it would have been nice to be hugged by, possibly for the last time; they should not have had to slink back to Talitha's house, avoiding even the housekeeper whose attempts to congratulate them – the daft cow had even made them a cake with a decorative firework – seemed like nothing more than a taunt.

'We all did great,' Talitha told her. 'This is lovely, thank you. Can we take it to the pool?'

They left her behind, bruised and bewildered, and retreated to their den to lick their wounds and plan their next move. If they had one.

\*

Felix finished his phone call. 'It hasn't been taken to the city pound,' he told the others. 'They told Mum that much. It's in police custody. They can't tell her when she can have it back. She's fricking livid.'

'They'll find nothing on the car.' Talitha pulled the firework off the cake, sniffed it and tossed it into the corner. 'Nothing that will tie us to what happened.'

'Our DNA will be in it,' Amber said.

'We go in it all the time. It will mean nothing.'

'We need to find out where Megan is,' Daniel said. 'Where she is and what she's said. Has anyone got her mum's number?'

'Xav, what did she say to you? When you walked her to the car last night?' asked Felix.

Since they'd arrived back, Xav had taken no part in the conversation. Uncharacteristically silent, he was sitting with his elbows on his knees, gazing at the laminated floor. 'Nothing,' he said. It was as though the effort of getting through results had worn him out; he had nothing left.

'She must have said something,' Felix insisted. 'Did she say where she was going?'

'Home.' He glanced up briefly. 'She said she was going home.'

'We should have followed her,' Felix told the rest. 'We need to know what she did with that letter we signed and the film. If the police are searching her house, they'll find them.'

'Megan's not stupid,' Talitha said. 'She won't have left them lying around.'

'Where then?' Felix's attention was still focused on Xav. 'Where would she hide them?'

'Fuck should I know?' Xav said.

'Why you?' Amber asked him. 'Why did she want you to walk her to the car? I'm her best friend?'

Talitha snorted. Amber turned on her, 'What? You think you are?'

Xav got to his feet. 'I don't know why me,' he said to Amber. 'Maybe because Dan's a drip, you couldn't stop crying, Tal's a bitch and it was all Felix's fault to begin with. Maybe I was the lesser of five complete shits.'

A silence fell, as though Xav had voiced a truth they'd all known but had been keeping hidden; that they'd been drawn together by nothing more than a smug acceptance of their shared privilege, that they were none of them particularly nice, certainly not good, people.

And yet they'd worked hard, been polite and respectful to those in authority, they'd supported charity and given their time to the school. They'd broken no laws before last night, because no one really counted under-age drinking, a few recreational drugs and the odd bit of driving over the drink-drive limit. They might not be angels, but they were decent enough and things like this didn't happen to people like them.

'I keep thinking I'm going to wake up,' Amber said.

'The police.' Daniel jumped to his feet and looked ready to run. 'The police are here.'

The windows of the pool house overlooked the drive and a police car was parked close to the front door of the house. Two uniformed officers had already left it and were walking around the pool towards them. A few minutes later, all five were on their way to Oxford City Police Station.

# 8

'Has something happened to Megan?'

The detective, a thin, fair-haired man in his early forties, wearing a pink shirt and glasses the same shade of lilac as his tie, blinked hard at Xav and said, 'Why do you ask that?'

Xav couldn't keep still. Since he'd been shown into the small, windowless interview room, he'd repositioned his chair a half-dozen times and felt an itch on every part of his body. It was as though the ants that haunted the grass around Talitha's pool had hitched a lift in the police car and were determined to take part in the interview.

He'd found a stray paper clip on the tabletop and had broken it into three pieces. The detective who was fond of fondant colours had already asked him to stop jingling the keys in his pocket. Xav was being annoying; worse, he was giving too much away. He knew it, and still he couldn't stop. Right now, the heel of his right shoe was tapping against the tiled floor and he couldn't remember ever doing that in his life before.

'She didn't turn up at school this morning.' He realised he was talking too fast and made a conscious effort to slow down. 'She wasn't at her house when Felix went to find her, and the car she borrowed last night was being towed away. It doesn't take a genius to work out something's happened.'

Xav's mum reached out a hand, laid it on her son's knee and

45

applied gentle pressure. He forced himself to stop the heel tapping. He was scared by how much he wanted to hold his mother's hand.

Being a couple of weeks short of eighteen – his birthday wasn't until the very end of August – Xav was the only member of the group who was technically still a child. It had meant he'd been allowed, expected even, to have a parent or guardian sit in the interview with him. He'd been offered a solicitor too. *'Let's see how it goes,'* his mum had said.

'He's upset,' she told the detective now. 'This has been a difficult morning for my son and his friends already, and to learn that something might have happened to Megan on top of that is very disturbing.'

Never had Xav been so grateful for his mother's calm demeanour, her quiet air of authority. Nothing seemed to faze her. She was beautiful too, even in her mid-forties, and her looks never failed to have an impact on those she came into contact with. People behaved differently around the very attractive; he'd seen it with his mum and, in the last couple of years, experienced it directly.

'Megan's a good friend of yours?' the detective asked Xav, after a polite nod and a hint of a smile at his mother.

'We're all fond of Megan,' his mother said, before Xav had chance to speak. 'And naturally we're worried.'

'Megan's here in the station, helping us with our enquiries.' The detective was watching Xav carefully. 'She isn't hurt, but we have reason to believe she was involved in a road traffic accident in the early hours of this morning.'

'Was anyone else hurt?' Xav's mother asked.

'Xavier, I'd like you to tell us about yesterday,' the detective said. 'Start from the time the six of you met up.'

OK, he could do this. Stick to the truth as far as possible, Talitha had warned them all after Megan had left them the night before. That way their stories would match. He started to talk, feeling his voice grow in confidence. The six of them had met in University Parks at four. The girls had brought food, the boys Pimm's and lemonade. They'd played Frisbee, talked, sat and chilled, with no idea that fate had planted an incendiary device over all their lives and the timer had started its countdown. Restless, with nerves about results kicking in, they'd walked to Port Meadow, but it had been cold by that time, too cold for bridge jumping, so they'd given up and made for the Lamb and Flag.

'How long were you in the pub?' the detective asked.

'He spoke to me shortly before eight,' Xav's mother said. 'I wanted to know if he was coming home for dinner. He said no, and I heard a lot of noise in the background. I asked him where he was. He said he and the others were in the Lamb.'

'Thank you.'

'Just trying to be helpful.'

'Go on, Xavier.'

Xav said, 'We were in the Lamb until it closed and then we went to Park End.'

'You mean the nightclub on Park End Street? How long were you there for?'

Xav gave a quick glance at his mother. She didn't know that he'd had a fake ID for months to get him into the city's nightclubs with the others. 'We didn't get in,' he said. 'Dan and me were wearing trainers, and they were having a clamp down on dress code. We went to Tal's house instead.'

The detective glanced down and read out Talitha's address. Xav confirmed it.

'How long did you stay there?'

And this was where he had to stick to the script. 'Amber, Tal, Felix, Dan and me stayed the night,' he said. 'We were at the pool, and then in the pool house when it got cold. I must have nodded off, because when I woke up, Megan was gone.'

The detective reacted: his eyebrows raised, and he leaned back in his chair, giving Xav an appraising look.

*Shit*, thought Xav. *I've got it wrong.*

# 9

'How much longer do you plan to keep us?'

Barnaby Slater QC, a tall, wiry man in his late fifties, sat upright in the chair beside his trembling daughter. He didn't look comfortable, but then he never did. Talitha liked to boast she could count on the fingers of one hand the number of times she'd seen him wearing something other than a suit. She wasn't entirely kidding.

'This is an exceptional day for my daughter,' he went on. 'She's achieved brilliant exam results and she should be celebrating with her family and friends.'

Even in a small space, Slater pitched his voice, as though towards the back of a crowded courtroom. Each time he spoke, and he hadn't exactly been reticent about chipping in, the detective constable leading the interview flinched.

'I'm sure we'll be done soon.' She was a young woman with untidy red hair, trying hard not to appear unsettled. 'Can you answer the question, please, Tabitha?'

'Tal-ee-tha,' Slater corrected her. 'Emphasis on the second syllable.'

'Are my friends still here?' Talitha asked. Being separated from the others had thrown her; she'd expected they'd be questioned together, that they could double-check with each other and confirm their stories, and she was struggling to remember what she was supposed to say. And *she*'d been the one who'd decided what they should say! Stick to the truth, until after midnight, and then be vague. *We all went to sleep. We don't remember Megan leaving.* That had been what they'd agreed, what she'd told them, hadn't it?

'I believe so,' the constable said. 'Let me ask you again. How did Megan seem last night?'

'Well, she was . . .' Talitha glanced at her father for a steer, but you could never tell what he was thinking. Eighteen years of getting to know him, and she still struggled to tell whether he was pleased or annoyed, proud of her or disappointed, anxious or totally relaxed. In the absence of concrete information, she usually assumed the negative; it seemed safer.

'She was OK, I guess,' she said. 'A bit quiet, but Megan's always quiet. And we were all nervous about this morning.'

'Why do you think she left so early if the plan was to spend the night at your house and go in together?'

'I don't know. I'm not sure I even saw her leave. I remember, I think, that Felix was wondering what had happened to his mum's car, and we assumed Megan had taken it.'

'Did she do that a lot? Take other people's cars without permission?'

'No. I mean, maybe.'

'Which?'

Talitha turned to her father. 'Dad?'

Talitha's father didn't move, but then he rarely did unless he had to. He never squirmed in his chair or scratched at his head. More than once, when they'd been together in the evening, Talitha had secretly timed him to see how long he could last without moving a muscle. Each time, she'd got bored before he'd moved.

'Answer the question, Tal,' he said without looking at her. 'Did Megan make a habit of stealing your cars?'

'It wasn't stealing – Felix didn't mind.'

At last, her father's head turned and he peered down at her. 'If she took your car without permission, I would consider that theft.'

No. It was bad enough that Megan was taking the blame for the accident, Talitha wasn't about to accuse her of theft as well. Except, did it really matter now? If Megan was going to be charged with causing death by careless driving, what did a bit of car theft matter?

'Well, Talitha?' the detective said. 'Has she taken Felix's car, or yours, or' – she glanced down at her notes, 'Xavier's without permission?'

'I don't know. I can't remember. Maybe ask Xav, he was with her.'

No, that was wrong. She shouldn't have said that, that was a part of the story she could never tell, that Xav had walked Megan to her car after she'd agreed to save them.

The detective hadn't missed it. She eased herself forward in her chair. 'Xav went with her last night when she left?'

'No, no, I didn't mean that. I meant they spent a lot of time together. Usually. So, he'd know about the cars thing.'

'Did they spend time together last night?'

'Maybe. Usually they did.'

'Were they dating?'

'No, Xav is going out with Amber. But I always had a feeling that Megan liked him too. She never said so, but you can tell, can't you? It was always him that she'd sit next to or look for when we were out together. And she talked about him a lot when he wasn't there, like she was looking for an excuse to bring his name up.'

She heard her father give a heavy sigh.

'Did Amber know this?' the detective asked.

This couldn't be harmful could it? The Xav–Amber–Megan thing? This was safe?

51

'I think she was wary of Megan. Megan's very smart. And attractive. I wouldn't be surprised if Xav liked her.'

Talitha's father cleared his throat. 'I'm not sure what this has to do with the matter in hand, Officer, and the morning is slipping away.'

Ignoring him, the detective said, 'Is it fair to say Megan was the odd one out in your group?'

Oh, that hit home. Not that the detective had asked, but that she'd spotted it so soon.

'I don't know what you mean,' Talitha said, although she did. 'We've known each other for years, but I suppose we only really became good friends in the upper sixth.'

'When you all became senior prefects?' the detective prompted.

Talitha risked another glance at her father. Again nothing back.

'That's right,' she said, on slightly firmer ground. 'We had to spend a lot of time together. We had the end-of-year ball to organise, and the visitors' rota, quite a lot of charity stuff, and car park duties for open days. We started meeting up before school most days and it went from there.'

'Yes. But Megan's background is quite different to yours? To the others? Wouldn't you say?'

Talitha looked at her father again. Nothing. Christ, what was the point of him being there?

'She was a scholarship girl,' the detective said. 'Her mother wouldn't have been able to afford the fees to All Souls' School, not without financial help.'

'We didn't care about that,' Talitha said quickly. 'She was one of us.'

Even as she said it, Talitha knew it was a lie, and somehow, it was a lie that hurt more than the others she'd told already, than the others she had yet to tell. It felt more of a betrayal of Megan.

'We raised our daughter to judge people on their merits.'

Barnaby Slater spoke at last and it wasn't lost on Talitha that he did so to speak for himself, rather than his child.

The constable gave him a long, appraising stare. 'Of course, you did,' she said, before turning to Talitha again. 'My point is, could Megan have felt that she never really belonged?'

'I don't know. I never thought of it like that.'

'Possibly not. But something you never thought about could have been a big deal for Megan.'

'What's your point, Officer?' Tal's father asked.

'Oh, I'm simply wondering what Megan might have been prepared to do for a group she was desperate to be accepted by.'

## 10

Amber had agreed to be interviewed without a solicitor – she'd wanted to get it over with – but five minutes in, she was on the point of changing her mind. Maybe an hour or so's delay would have helped, given her time to think and get her story straight. On the other hand, if she asked for a solicitor now, she'd look guilty, wouldn't she?

'Tell me about Megan,' Rachel asked.

Rachel was the name of the detective who'd been assigned to speak to her, although she didn't look much older than Amber herself. Her blonde hair, home-dyed – Amber could always tell – was swept up in an elaborate bun and she wore a lot of make-up. Maybe she was a trainee or something, and that had to be a good sign, that they hadn't put her with anyone more experienced. They were ticking the boxes; it would be over soon. They weren't even in the sort of interview room that Amber had seen on television, but instead were sitting in a quiet corner of the police cafeteria. Rachel had actually offered Amber coffee.

There was a recording device on the table in front of them, though. And an open laptop.

'What do you want to know?' Amber said.

Rachel smiled. 'Anything that comes to mind. How long have the two of you been friends?'

This didn't feel right. Why wasn't Rachel asking about last night?

'I suppose we only became good friends when we were all made senior prefects,' Amber said cautiously. 'But we've known each other since we started at All Souls'.'

'She was in your house: Faraday, isn't it? You'd have seen her for registration every morning and afternoon. How many pupils in a houseroom?'

Amber heard the faint sound of an alarm bell ringing in her head. So few people knew about the workings of independent schools, but this woman, who looked like she had a Saturday job on the cosmetics counter in Debenhams, had done her homework.

'Twelve,' Amber said.

'Six girls, is that right?'

'Four. There are more boys at All Souls'. It used to be single sex.'

'Four girls, and you and Megan were two of them. I'd have thought it would be natural that you'd become good friends.'

'I had other friends. Girls I'd known at primary school.'

'That would be Collingdale Preparatory School, with fees of nearly ten thousand pounds a year,' Rachel said.

'What's that got to do with anything?'

'Megan went to Chorley Wood, the state school up the road from her house. She was a scholarship girl at All Souls'. Is that why you didn't like her?'

This felt all wrong, like Megan had been complaining about the rest of them.

'No. And I did like her. She helped me with maths in the run-up to GCSE. I wasn't that good at it, and if I didn't pass, I wouldn't have been able to stay on in the sixth form. Megan spent hours with me, and she didn't have to. I got a B thanks to Megan.'

Amber wondered, briefly, whether she'd ever actually thanked Megan for all the time she'd spent with her in fifth form helping her get through her exams.

'Were you resentful when she was made head of school and not you? I know you were interviewed for the position.'

Yes, she'd never admitted it to a soul, but she bloody well had been.

'No,' Amber said. 'Head of school is a lot of responsibility. I was happy to be a senior prefect. And any of us could have been given the job, that's what the master said. Megan got lucky. I didn't blame her for that.'

'Was it a bit of virtue signalling on the part of the school, do you think? Make their head girl the scholarship pupil? The one from the single-parent family?'

Amber shrugged. 'Maybe. Probably.'

Rachel dropped her eyes and began typing; she typed fast. Several seconds went by.

'I mean, she was clever,' Amber said, 'there's no denying that, but her social intelligence isn't all it should be. She wasn't that popular in school.'

Rachel paused in her typing and looked up. 'Did the fact that she was keen on Xav cause any friction between you? He's your boyfriend, right?'

'Yes. And who says she was keen on him?'

Rachel made a puzzled face. 'Sorry, I thought it was generally understood that Megan and Xav got on well.'

'Not by me.'

The detective typed some more. 'Let's talk about Megan being clever,' she said, when she'd stopped again. 'She was offered a place at Cambridge, is that right?'

'That's right. St Catharine's College. To study natsci.'

'Natsci?'

Miss Smartarse didn't know everything then. 'Natural sciences,' Amber explained. 'It's one of the most oversubscribed courses in the UK, possibly the world. You have to be good to get on the natsci course.'

'But only if she got her grades. Three As, is that right?'

'Megan would have got her grades. Of all of us, she was the least worried. She'd have got five As, no question.'

'Like Xav?'

'Yeah. They both did all three sciences, maths and further maths. We call it the "Full Asian Five", or the "Flasian Five", because its mainly the Asian students who do all five. I'm not being racist, they're just cleverer than the rest of us. Apart from Xav and Megan.'

'You're a smart bunch, aren't you? Even if you didn't all do the Full Asian Five?'

'We did all right. We worked hard, we had good teachers. We were lucky.'

The detective looked directly at Amber. 'So, can you explain why Megan failed to get anywhere near her expected A level grades?'

It took a second for Amber to even process the question. 'What?' she said in the end.

Rachel glanced down at her laptop. 'She got four Cs and a B. The B was in Maths.'

This was a trick, although for the life of her, Amber couldn't see where it was heading. 'That's not possible,' she said.

Rachel gave the smug smile of someone who's won a small victory. 'We spoke to your head teacher earlier this morning. She was very worried about Megan, on the point of going round to her house when we contacted her. I think she suspected her of having done something silly because she couldn't face how spectacularly she'd let herself down.'

It was absurd, but of everything that had happened in the past few hours, hearing of Megan's failure seemed the biggest shock of all. It was as though the world had somehow tilted, and everything was the opposite of what it should be.

'You're lying to me,' Amber said. 'She'd have told us if she'd done badly. We've been with her all summer. She never once said she was worried about her results. Well, no more than any of us.'

Even as she spoke Amber remembered that Megan had been different that summer, quieter, even more reserved than usual. When asked if anything was wrong, she'd simply shrugged and said she was a bit sad at how completely everything was about to change, and that she would miss her friends.

'*Two of us are coming with you to Cambridge, you daft bat,*' Talitha had said once, and only Amber had noticed the gleam of tears in Megan's eyes.

The detective smiled. 'As you say, Miss Pike, you weren't really very good friends at all, were you?'

# 11

The detective, a portly man in his early fifties whose hair seemed to have fled his head only to reappear in the form of fungi-like sprouts from brow, nostrils and ears, slid a photograph across the desk towards Daniel.

'Mrs Sophie Robinson.' The detective spoke slowly, as though bored. Daniel had seen him yawn twice and was hoping it was a good sign. 'Thirty-six, married, two young children. A GP. Well liked, by all accounts. About to go back to work after maternity leave. This picture is a few months old. The baby, Maisie, would have been closer to nine months. Until the early hours of this morning, that is. Lily was four.'

Daniel really didn't want to see the picture. He didn't need to know that Sophie Robinson had dark hair and that her face looked as though it smiled a lot. He certainly didn't need to see that she clutched her daughters to her body as though the wind might pull them out of her arms.

He wanted to close his eyes, but the picture held him, firing up details of the Robinsons' lives like tiny, stinging missiles. It had been windy when it was taken, because Sophie's hair was blowing up around her head and a strand had caught in the corner of her mouth. He could see a solitary swing in the background of the family's garden and what looked like the edge of a rabbit hutch. They'd had an apple tree, which possibly wouldn't produce much fruit that year because the wind had blown away most of the blossom.

Just as well, really, because no one would be around this autumn to pick them.

Sophie, Mrs Robinson – oh God, he'd never be able to hear that song again – was wearing a polka-dot shirt with a stain on the right shoulder where the baby had dribbled, and she had a tiny scar above her left eyebrow. The older child was about four, with curly dark hair and shining eyes; the baby was plump and creased and scowling.

Sophie, Lily, Maisie. He wondered which of the three they'd heard screaming last night. Not the baby, surely; no baby could have screamed that loud.

'The little girl was alive when she arrived at the JR,' the detective continued, JR being common parlance for the John Radcliffe Hospital. 'Badly burned, but alive. She lived about an hour.'

Daniel opened his mouth to say he'd heard about the accident on the radio and remembered in time that the detective hadn't yet told him how the family had died. He should really be asking what the Robinson family had to do with him, shouldn't he, although maybe he'd already left it too late? And wasn't that something his solicitor should have asked? It had been a mistake to agree to the duty solicitor; he should have called his dad, who would have made sure he found his own. The others would have done exactly that, he was sure of it. Talitha would have her dad, and Felix would insist on waiting till his parents had found the best possible solicitor.

Better advised than he, any one of them could drop him in it, in spite of what they'd agreed last night, in spite of the promises they'd made to each other. And still, details from the Robinsons' lives were bouncing up to wound him afresh. There was a cat in one of the flowerbeds, a black cat with a white vest and white tips to its ears, lying in that contorted way that cats have, licking its fur, totally self-absorbed.

'We'll be releasing this photograph to the media in a short while,' the detective said, before Daniel had a chance to speak. 'We haven't named the victims yet. Mr Robinson, who is understandably devastated, wanted some time to contact all his family members. It seemed the least we could do.'

'What does this have to do with my client?' Daniel's solicitor asked, and it was about fucking time.

The detective stuck a finger in one hairy ear and scratched. 'Oh, did I not mention? They were killed in the early hours of this morning on the M40. Just shy of junction seven. By your friend, Megan Macdonald.'

Not by Megan, though, by him. Not that it had been his fault; Felix had grabbed the wheel, had wrenched it out of his hands. It had all been Felix's idea anyway; they'd practically forced him into going along. It should be Felix who'd confessed, not Megan.

'Mr Redman? Have you nothing to say to that?'

'No. I mean—' He had to get a hold of himself. 'What are you talking about? Megan wouldn't kill anyone.'

'She confessed. We have her signed statement.'

'I don't believe you,' he managed. 'I mean, how?'

So, she'd done it. Until that moment, Daniel hadn't really believed she would. He'd been convinced she'd change her mind at the last minute and tell the police what really happened. He'd even wondered if she'd never meant to take the blame at all, had simply wanted to be the only one to own up and get more lenient treatment. All night, while the other four had dozed, even slept from nervous exhaustion, Daniel had been going over scenario after possibility, weighing up probabilities and coming to the inescapable conclusion that he was fucked.

Even now, he was reticent, knowing that the police pulled all sorts of tricks in interviews. They could be trying to catch him out. Even his solicitor could be in on it because, let's face it, he'd been useless.

'She was driving the wrong way down the M40,' the detective explained. 'She joined at junction eight, where it becomes the A40 into Oxford, and went onto the wrong carriageway.'

'She wouldn't have done that.'

He was going to be fair to Megan; he wasn't going to throw her under a bus. 'She was a good driver,' he went on. 'Better than the others. She passed her test first time.'

'The others?' the detective echoed. 'You don't drive then?'

'No. At least, I'm learning, but I haven't taken my test yet.'

He had, though, he'd taken it twice, although the others only knew about one time. After his first failure, he'd kept his second date secret. He would never pass it now, he realised; he would never get behind the wheel of a car again.

He should admit to that, or they might wonder what else he'd lied about. Or he could just say he'd made a mistake, said 'taken' when what he really meant was 'passed.' His dad would be pissed off, he realised, about his decision not to drive. His dad still hadn't given up hope of his only son one day taking over what he called 'the estate', but which really was only a big farm.

God, it was so hard to keep his mind focused.

The detective was talking again. 'The A40 into Oxford would have been the most sensible route home for her,' he was saying. 'Straight down to the Headington roundabout, round the ring road and then into town via the Iffley Road.'

'Sounds right,' Daniel said.

'So, what do you think made her turn right onto the A40 instead of left? It's not as though it isn't obvious – there are chevrons, no-entry signs.'

Of course there were. If he closed his eyes, he could still see them.

Daniel shrugged. 'It was dark. And late. She'd have been tired.'

'With respect, my client can't be expected to know what motivated Miss Macdonald,' the solicitor said. 'By her own admission, she was alone in the car.'

The detective's eyes peered into Daniel's. He knew, Daniel realised. He knew everything; he'd been right, this was a trick, and—

'She'd been drinking.' He hadn't meant to say that – it just slipped out.

'Megan had?'

'We all had. We started at four o'clock, in the park. Then we went to the Lamb and Flag till last orders. Then Talitha's house and Felix started making cocktails. We were all hammered. Amber was throwing up at one point.'

The detective frowned. 'If you were all drunk, how did you get from the Lamb and Flag to Talitha's house?'

Daniel looked at his solicitor.

'Daniel? How?' the detective insisted. 'Did someone collect you? Did you get public transport? A taxi?'

'Felix and Xav both had cars,' Daniel said. 'They didn't drink much in the pub. When I said we were all hammered, I meant later, when we were at Tal's. By then, we didn't think we'd have to drive again.'

'But Megan did? Any idea why?'

'I was asleep. I didn't see her leave.'

'More than one of you claim to have been asleep when Megan left. If you were all asleep, I wonder what could have happened to make her, of all of you, feel the need to go home?'

Daniel's solicitor spoke up. 'My client has told you he was asleep. He can't possibly know.'

The detective ignored him. 'But you do know that she was drunk?' he said to Daniel.

'He can't necessarily know that either,' the solicitor said. 'He wasn't inside her head.'

'Apologies. Daniel, you said that she'd had a lot to drink.'

'Yes, she had,' Daniel said. 'That must have been what happened. She had too much to drink, got it into her head that she needed to go home, and then made a mistake at the junction because her judgement was impaired.'

He'd done it now, turned Megan into a drunk driver who'd killed a mother and two young kids. Being drunk was so much worse than making a mistake when you were tired. He'd really dropped her in it now. But it had been her idea; she'd wanted this.

The detective produced another photograph and turned it to face Daniel. It showed an Oxford street of terraced houses.

'Do you recognise that car?' the detective's fat finger pointed to a red Golf convertible.

'Yes, that's Felix's. At least, it's his mum's, but Felix drives it.'

'I'll tell you what puzzles me, Daniel,' the detective leaned back in his chair. 'We spoke to the owners of the other two cars in the picture – the ones to the front and back of the Golf – and they hadn't been moved since early the previous evening. That means that when Megan got home last night, having just caused a fatal accident, and drunk according to you, she nevertheless managed to park the car perfectly in what is a very tight spot.'

The detective stared at Daniel for several seconds before he spoke again.

'How do you think she managed that?'

# 12

'Megan took a blood test at nine o'clock this morning,' Felix and his solicitor were told by the detective who'd been assigned to them. He was a thin man wearing a pink shirt and a purple tie. 'It found no traces of alcohol in her bloodstream.'

Felix's solicitor, a woman of about his mother's age, gave a slight shake of her head; they'd already determined that that meant keep quiet. Felix had insisted on waiting until his parents found a solicitor trained in criminal law to attend his interview. So far, it seemed to have been a good shout; she'd won every single stand-off with the officer.

'Felix?' the detective prompted.

'That wasn't a question,' the solicitor said.

'I'll try again. Given what we know about how alcohol leaves the body, and given the six-hour interval between the fatal crash and the blood test, it seems unlikely that Megan was, to quote you and one or two of your friends, "well away", "hammered" and "out of it" when she drove your car home.'

'Again, that is a conclusion on your part, not a question,' the solicitor said.

'So, would you like to reconsider your view that she was drunk?' the detective asked.

Felix made a 'How should I know?' gesture. 'I wasn't keeping tabs,' he said. 'I made the drinks – I didn't pour them down anyone's throats. I assumed she was drunk because the rest of us were. She might not have been. I don't know.'

'I think my client has answered that question,' the solicitor said.

The detective glanced down at the notebook he was using as a question prompt. 'You say the news of her poor results came as a surprise?'

This time, Felix had no need to seek advice from his solicitor. 'Too right. I'd have put money on Megan doing the best of all of us.'

'So, what do you think went wrong?'

He genuinely had no idea. Megan's near-genius was something that he, like the others, had always taken for granted. 'Problems at home?' he said. 'Something she didn't tell us about. I'm speculating, to be honest.'

'Which isn't helpful to any of us,' his solicitor added.

Now that he thought about it, there had been something off about Megan that summer; she'd been on edge a lot of the time, quicker to snap, especially at him. And out of the whole group, she'd become the only one really prepared to stand up to him. He'd ignored it, refused to acknowledge that he might be being challenged for leadership.

'Would you say she was a good driver? Careful?' The detective had apparently decided to ignore the solicitor.

Felix shrugged.

'For the tape, please.'

'She was OK,' he said. 'Not great. Maybe a bit careless.'

No sooner were the words out of his mouth than he wondered if they were a mistake. Megan was actually a pretty good driver, and the others would probably say so.

'And yet you let her drive your mother's car?'

The solicitor said, 'It's already been established that Miss

Macdonald took Mr O'Neill's car without his permission in the early hours of this morning.'

'Where had you left your keys?'

'My what?'

'Your car keys,' the detective clarified. 'I assume your mother's Golf needs them in order to work. Most cars do.'

Felix looked at his solicitor; this time nothing came back.

'Felix?'

'I can't remember. I told you, I was drunk.'

'Most people keep their car keys in their pockets. Did you?'

'I guess so. Sounds about right. Except, no, I couldn't have done, because then Megan couldn't have got them without me knowing about it.'

'We had plenty of time to talk to Megan while we were waiting for your solicitor to arrive,' the detective said. 'And we asked her how she got hold of your keys. What do you think she said?'

'My client has no possible way of knowing what Miss Macdonald said in her interview.'

The detective's eyes sharpened as he looked back at the solicitor and, for the first time, seemed her equal. 'He would if the two of them were both telling the truth,' he said.

'I'm sorry,' Felix said. 'I can't remember what I did with my keys. I'm always leaving them lying around when I've had a few. She could have picked them up anywhere.'

A page, and then another, in the detective's notebook were turned. The solicitor sat stony-faced. Felix looked at the clock. It was nearly noon. He'd been here almost two hours.

'Where were you in the early hours of Wednesday the seventh of June?' the detective said at last.

For a moment Felix had absolutely no idea and had opened his mouth to say so, when the significance of the date hit home.

'I've no idea,' he said anyway.

So, this was how everything ended, in a dingy beige room with no windows and dust in the corners. And still, he had no real idea of how it could have gone so badly wrong. He should be in the Lamb right now. They'd had a table booked for six, their champagne-breakfast celebration.

Because Wednesday, 7 June was the night he'd driven his car down the M40 the wrong way; the night it had all started. Megan had betrayed them.

'Have a think about it.' The detective seemed oblivious to the turmoil in Felix's head. 'It's what, nine, ten weeks ago – early in the summer holidays, not that long.'

'I'd need a diary. I left it at home.'

Felix wondered if he might be about to cry.

'Specifically, what were you doing around two forty-five, three o'clock in the morning?'

Megan had stitched them up, after promising faithfully that she wouldn't.

'We can have your diary brought in,' the detective said. 'Maybe one of your parents can get it – we'd like to talk to them too. I'd also like to know where you were on the nights of Sunday the twenty-fifth of June . . .'

In the Golf, Xav at the wheel.

'Monday the seventeenth of July . . .'

Talitha's turn.

'Tuesday the twenty-fifth of July . . .'

Amber. Bet the bitch hadn't told them about her own stint in the driver's seat.

'And Sunday the thirtieth of July.'

'My client has already told you he can't recall without the help of a diary,' Felix's solicitor said. 'So, I can't really see the point of these questions.'

'I'm getting to the point.'

Felix had no idea how it had happened, but the mousey detective had changed, become bigger somehow, more in control of the room.

'And you can be sure we'll be asking the same questions of your friends,' he added. 'One of them might have a better memory than you, Mr O'Neill.'

One of them would drop them all in it, if they hadn't already. Amber, probably. But if Megan had already told them everything, it was all over anyway. He would kill her, Felix realised. If she'd thrown them to the wolves, he would find her, and he would kill her. It didn't matter how long it took.

'You see, in the early hours of Sunday the twenty-fifth of June, we had a call from a lorry driver who'd stopped at the Oxford service station on the M40, junction eight,' the detective explained. 'He'd been driving through the night from Antwerp and needed some fresh air. He went for a bit of a walk towards the edge of the grounds that surround the station.'

The detective stopped to let his words sink in.

'He saw headlights entering the A40 directly opposite where he was standing but travelling in the wrong direction,' he went on. 'Being from the continent, he's very conscious of how easy it can be, especially when a driver is over-fatigued. He thought it might be a fellow European, making a big mistake.'

It hadn't been a mistake. Xav had been at the wheel. He'd driven the wrong way down the slip road, pushing sixty miles an hour.

'We weren't unduly worried at the time,' the detective continued. 'There had been no reported accidents. We assumed, like our witness, that it had been a mistake, with no unfortunate consequences, luckily. But then we had another call, from a driver who'd seen a car driving the wrong way down the M40 in that area that very same night. The car had actually kept pace with him for a while, and he was sure there was more than one person in it.'

'What does this have to do with my client?' the solicitor asked.

The detective said, 'Were you in that car, Felix?'

'No.'

'Do you know who was in that car?'

'How could I?'

'Was it your mother's car?'

'It couldn't have been.'

The detective reached down into a briefcase on the floor, which Felix hadn't noticed before, and pulled out a photograph.

'Two reports made us take the incident a little more seriously,' he said. 'So, we approached the service station, and it turns out they have a CCTV camera that captures traffic on the opposite carriageway.'

Felix's solicitor leant forward to study the photograph. 'This is very indistinct,' she said. 'I can't even make out what model of car we're looking at.'

Felix could, but he had the advantage of knowing exactly what make of car it was; he'd been in it at the time. Objectively speaking, though, his solicitor was right. In the photograph, the car appeared nothing more than a blur against the dark background of the trees. There were no lights on that stretch of the A40, thank God, and the lights from the service station didn't come anywhere close.

Sunday, 25 June. There had been no moon, and they'd talked about how dark the night was. Amber, who'd always had a fanciful side, had mentioned its possibility for black deeds. Shortly afterwards, Xav had announced that he was going to do the dare; his words had made it a dare, one that would ultimately challenge them all. Until that moment, Felix's escapade a couple of weeks earlier had been a one-off.

'Do you have a registration number?' the solicitor asked.

They couldn't have, Felix realised. If they'd had the registration number of the car back in June, he'd have heard of it long before now. For a fleeting second, he found himself wishing they had. Xav would have been fined, they'd all have been in trouble, but it would have blown over and they'd never have risked it again.

'Not on that occasion,' the detective said. 'But we went back through the service station's CCTV footage. It took us a while, but we found images of the same car entering the A40, in the early hours of the morning, travelling in the wrong direction, on five separate occasions.'

All five. They'd been recorded on tape every time they'd done it. How could they not have thought of that possibility?

'Do you have a registration number?' the solicitor repeated.

They couldn't have. They'd have come for him long before now.

'I'm coming to that,' the detective said. 'So, you see, Felix, I'm not buying this story that last night was a one-off because Megan was overtired or drunk, because in the first place, she wasn't drunk, and in the second, she – or someone – had very obviously done it before.'

# 13

A telephone rang as Amber and Xav followed Megan's mother along the narrow hallway. Megan's mother turned quickly, her tear-stained face alarmed and hopeful at the same time.

'That could be Megan,' she said. 'I need to get it.' Standing to one side, she indicated the stairs. 'Go on up. Second door at the top.'

Amber felt Xav's fingers against her spine, pushing her on.

'Hello!' Megan's mum's voice was loud in the cramped space. 'Meg? Is that you?'

On the landing, they faced four worn white doors.

'Second one.' Xav wanted to get this over with; Amber didn't want to start.

She shouldn't be surprised at how small and – yes – how mean Megan's house was. She'd been outside it more than once, had seen the narrow front door, the dustbins in the street, the bikes chained to railings because there was no room for them in the houses. She should have expected the depressing interior but had simply never thought about it before. Megan's life, her life outside the gang, had never entered Amber's head.

Megan's room was small, barely space for Amber and Xav to move around past the single bed, the desk and chair and the coat stand, strewn with Megan's coats and jackets, which was serving as a wardrobe. Most of Megan's out-of-school clothes were from the city's charity shops and Amber had always assumed it was because Megan's style veered towards the edgy, the retro, the quirky. In Megan's bedroom, in an instant, Amber realised it had been driven by necessity. The whole room spoke of 'not enough'.

Not enough money for new clothes. Not enough space on the narrow bookshelf for Megan's collection of paperback classics. Not enough time or inclination to keep the windows cleaned or to repaper the walls.

Above the bed, the only ornamentation in the room beyond Megan's own possessions, was a cork noticeboard covered in photographs of the six of them: on the river, in Port Meadow, in front of ancient stone buildings. In the centre was the official portrait taken after they'd been appointed senior prefects. The six of them leaned, gleaming and fresh, just a tiny bit smug, over the rail of the first of the white bridges leading to School Field.

'Am, check the bed.' Xav was already making his way through the bookshelf, pulling out volumes and shaking them to loosen anything tucked inside. 'Get a move on.'

Amber dropped to the carpet – thin and a bit sticky – and felt beneath the bed for a large envelope, maybe a slim plastic bag. She slid her hands between the divan and mattress and shook first the duvet and then the pillow. The divan drawers were overflowing with Megan's school clothes.

Downstairs, the muffled sound of talking had stopped. Megan's mum was as slight as Megan herself, and would make little sound on the stairs.

'Am, for God's sake. Behind that board.'

On her feet again, Amber had lifted and replaced the cork board when the door opened. They were out of time.

'They've charged her.' Megan's mum grabbed at the doorframe as though the climb up the stairs had exhausted her. 'They've charged her with murder.'

'What?' Xav dropped the book he'd been holding as Amber felt something vice-like grip her chest. Murder? What was the woman talking about? Causing death by dangerous driving, Talitha had said, if they were unlucky; death by *careless* driving if things went Megan's way. The harsher charge carried a maximum fourteen-year sentence, but Megan would serve seven years at most, fewer probably, because of her age and it being a first offence.

'How can it be murder?' Amber's voice sounded like it belonged to someone else. 'She didn't mean to kill anyone – it was an accident.'

Out of the corner of her eye, she saw Xav lean back against the desk.

'There was a witness.' Megan's mum looked on the verge of collapse. An unhealthy sheen of sweat had broken out on her forehead. 'On that bridge, the one that goes over the motorway.'

'The A329,' Xav muttered.

'This witness said Megan drove straight at the other car. They said she meant to hit it.'

It was true, or sort of. They had driven into the path of the other car. Amber saw Xav's face, as white as her own must be, saw his hands shaking, the clenching of his jaw as he swallowed hard. Dan had frozen at the wheel, unable to move, and Felix had grabbed it, trying to steer them to the hard shoulder. The other driver, though, had done the same thing and they'd only avoided a head-on collision because Felix had quickly steered them back again. To anyone watching, it could have looked like a deliberate attempt to cause a crash.

'They said she's done it before,' Megan's mum went on. 'That she's been doing it all summer. They won't even let me see her.'

As though in a daze, Xav picked up the dropped book and put it back onto the shelf.

'She's eighteen,' Megan's mum said, as though announcing a

fact they couldn't possibly have known. 'That's an adult. I have no rights. I can't do anything to help her.'

'Does she have a solicitor?' Xav said. 'A good one, I mean. We can talk to Tal's dad. He'll know someone.'

'Why, Xav? Why would she do such a thing?' Megan's mum – for the life of her Amber couldn't remember her name – looked from Amber to Xav and then back again. 'Did something upset her? Did she fall out with you two?'

It had been a massive mistake coming here. It should have been Talitha and Felix; they would know what to say, what lies to tell. There were no words in Amber's head, and Xav seemed equally at a loss.

'There's been something wrong all summer,' Megan's mum went on. 'Something happened. I thought it was boy trouble.' Again, her eyes went from Amber to Xav and then back again. 'Did she say anything to you?'

'We can't understand it either,' Xav said at last, and he sounded like a robot. 'We didn't find the book, sorry to have bothered you.'

Megan's mum gasped, as though suddenly the room was short of oxygen. 'She was going to Cambridge,' she wailed. 'How could this have happened?'

## 14

Talitha had been at the window of the pool house for nearly half an hour, waiting, when finally, Xav and Amber came back. As she waved at Xav she saw, reflected in the window, Felix pouring himself another drink, although she'd already said it wasn't a good idea. Dan was worrying her even more than Felix. Since getting back from the police station, he'd closed in on himself, barely speaking, knocking balls around randomly with the pool cue, although she'd never known him show the slightest interest in the game before. He hadn't even told his parents what was going on.

'Any luck?' Talitha asked when Xav and Amber had joined them in the pool house.

Amber shook her head. 'We felt like complete heels.'

'We *are* complete heels.' Xav collapsed into a chair. 'Her mum's an absolute mess and she's got no one with her. There's something else, guys. She told us—'

'She let you look though?' Felix was still behind the bar and if he stayed there much longer, Talitha was going to drag him out; she didn't care what weight advantage he had over her. 'Did you get into her bedroom?'

A ball, the blue, rattled against the wood and Daniel watched it bounce back over the green felt. He hadn't even acknowledged Xav and Amber. Occasionally, his eyes drifted to the TV, playing silently in the corner.

'It's not in her bedroom,' Amber said. 'Listen, there's some—'

'Somewhere else in the house?' Talitha said.

'We could hardly search the whole house,' Xav snapped. 'Besides—'

'We can when her mum's at work,' Felix suggested. 'Drink, Xav?'

'No!' Talitha almost yelled. 'For God's sake, Felix, no one should be drinking.'

'Keep your hair on.' Sulkily, Felix put the bottle down. He didn't though, abandon his own drink, keeping his hand firmly wrapped around the glass, as though Tal might take it from him.

Daniel had flinched at Talitha's raised voice, as though still struggling with a hangover. 'She may have left it in the car,' he said.

'Shit, I didn't think of that.' Felix was getting nasty. 'I should have climbed inside while the tow truck had it swinging in the air.'

'If she's hidden it in the car, we can get it when the police release it,' Talitha said.

Felix downed his drink. 'She didn't go to the trouble of getting proof only to hand it right back to us. It's somewhere in the house and we have to look when her mum's out.'

'It's risky,' Talitha said as Xav and Amber shared a look she couldn't interpret.

'So is leaving it lying around,' Felix replied. 'I'll sleep a lot easier if we know Megan can't change her mind. Without that letter and the photograph, it's her word against ours.'

'Guys!' Xav raised his voice. 'You need to—'

'Shush,' Talitha darted to the TV and turned up the volume.

'*Oxford police have confirmed tonight that eighteen-year-old Megan Macdonald, a former head girl of the prestigious All Souls' School in Oxford, has been charged with three counts of murder.*'

Silence gripped the pool house as a photograph of Megan appeared. Taken shortly after becoming head of school, she crouched with the master's dog, Poppy, by the river in Christ Church Meadow. She looked serious and beautiful, and with her short silver-blonde hair, a little bit edgy; the scholarship girl from a single-parent family who hadn't only survived her six years at the most academic school in the country but had thrived there and come out on top.

'*Megan Macdonald will be remanded in custody until the trial, expected towards the end of the year,*' the newsreader read on, as the picture of Megan vanished. '*And now the weather—*'

Talitha switched the television off, amazed to see that her hands were trembling; she hadn't known hands really did that.

'Murder?' Felix said. 'How the hell can it be murder?'

'We need to keep our voices down,' Talitha said in hushed tones. 'Dad's in the house and sound carries with the windows open.' She glanced out at the terrace as she spoke, as though her dad might be lurking outside. 'He said earlier that the police are always asking themselves, "What are we not being told?" He was looking right at me when he said it.'

Daniel said, 'You think he suspects something?'

'He always suspects something,' Talitha said. 'It's his nature.'

'How can it be murder?' Felix said again. 'Dangerous driving, you said, Tal, at worst. Obviously, she didn't mean to kill anyone.'

Xav said, 'She didn't kill anyone. Daniel did.'

Daniel's hands tightened around the pool cue.

'Don't.' Amber put a hand on Xav's arm. 'There was a witness,' she added.

It took a second for Amber's words to sink in. 'What do you mean?' Talitha said, and then she, Dan and Felix listened, in growing horror, as Xav, with occasional input from Amber, explained what they'd learned from Megan's mum.

'A witness will have seen us.' Daniel looked ready to run. 'We all got out of the car. That's it, game over.'

'Not necessarily,' Xav said, hurriedly. 'Am and I were talking on the way back. If we'd been seen, they'd have arrested all of us by now.'

'But—' Daniel couldn't go on.

'I think you're right, Xav.' Talitha was struggling to stay calm. 'But a witness could make a big difference.'

At that moment, the door opened and Talitha's father stood in the doorway. None of them had noticed him crossing the terrace. 'Did you all see the news?' he asked.

As Talitha nodded, Xav said, 'We were wondering what you thought about the murder charge. We heard there was a witness on the bridge.'

'Apparently so.' Barnaby Slater didn't even look at Xav. 'A couple who missed the junction were performing an illegal U-turn on the A329 above the motorway. The passenger saw the near collision and then both cars stationary, one on the carriageway, the other having crashed.'

'Did they stop?' Xav asked. 'Did they try to help?'

'Apparently not. They thought the incident might be gang related, so they didn't risk it. They drove onto the next exit and alerted the emergency services.'

Talitha felt tension draining from her.

'Will Megan be convicted?' Felix asked.

'Too early to say.' Talitha's dad continued to address thin air rather than look at Talitha or any of her friends. 'The CCTV footage the police got from the service station will be significant. It proves Megan was lying when she said she'd driven that way once, by accident.'

'Suggests, not proves,' Talitha corrected her father. 'That's what you said earlier. The police can't prove the car on camera was Felix's mum's, and if they can't do that, they can't prove Megan was driving.'

Barnaby looked down his nose at his daughter. 'Nevertheless, there's a reasonable chance a jury will believe it was your mother's car, Felix, and that it was Megan behind the wheel each time,' he said. 'And if the jury believe she deliberately put lives at risk six times, they won't be at all sympathetic and they won't consider it an accident. The sentence could be harsh.'

'How harsh?' Amber asked.

Barnaby shrugged. 'Life. We're talking two young children. Mind you, a lot can happen between now and the court date. The police will be wanting to talk to all of you again. You can certainly forget about going to Sicily on Saturday.'

'Will they let us see her?' Xav asked.

'Almost certainly not,' Barnaby snapped. 'And if they do, you should assume your conversation will be witnessed or recorded. You all need to be very careful.' He looked round the pool house, from one pale face to the next, finally making eye contact. *He knows*, Talitha thought.

'It's probably not a good idea for you to spend too much time together in the coming weeks. And on that subject, Tal, your mother and I would like you to join us for dinner. Ready in five minutes. Drive safely on the way home, the rest of you.'

The door swung shut behind him.

Amber was the first to break the silence. 'We can't do this. Megan wasn't even driving the car.'

'It makes no difference,' Felix said. 'Sorry, but it doesn't. If we confess, it won't get her off. We'll go down with her.'

'Felix's right,' Daniel said.

'Well, you would say that,' Amber snapped. 'Three people died last night. I can't believe how selfish we're all being.'

'Amber, shut the fuck up. We have to focus,' Felix said. 'The fact they let us all go means nothing. They need time to compare our stories, look for inconsistencies. They'll want to talk to us again, and when they do, we can't afford any mistakes.'

He looked at Xav. 'Before you two got here, we were going through the dates when the car was seen on the road and talking about what we should say.'

'We think, keep it vague,' Talitha interjected. 'That's what I did today. Each time they threw a date at me, I said I couldn't remember, that I was probably with you lot, because we've been together most of the summer, but I couldn't say for certain.'

'I said the same,' Felix said. 'I told them I needed to check my diary.'

'We should stick to the truth as closely as possible,' Talitha said. 'We can say we were here on those nights, that we've had a chance to think back, look at diaries, ask parents, et cetera, and that we were definitely here. It's the truth, so we shouldn't try to pretend otherwise.'

Felix was nodding. 'We got here, sometime late evening, probably after the pubs closed, and then we hung out, swimming, playing pool, watching movies. We went to sleep at some point and didn't notice Megan slipping away.'

'I think that's right,' Talitha said. 'Be vague, don't make anything up, because someone else might contradict it.'

'You realise this all depends on Megan,' Xav said. 'It doesn't matter how well we play it, if she—'

'Do you think she'll keep quiet?' Dan asked. 'She must have so far, or we'd be under arrest too. But will she in future?'

'We can't know,' Talitha said.

'What do we say when they ask us why Megan did it?' Amber asked. 'Why she kept driving her car the wrong way down the motorway? I mean, it's totally not what Megan would do.'

'We say we don't know,' Felix said. 'Don't try to second guess, don't make shit up. Say you have no idea.'

'But she has been odd this summer,' Amber pressed on. 'I didn't really think about it until today, until we found out her results, but there's been something bothering her.'

'I noticed that too,' Xav said.

'Guys, it doesn't matter,' Felix said. 'The point is we don't know, so that's what we say.'

'What did your dad mean, we shouldn't spend too much time together?' Amber asked Talitha.

'He means we're guilty by association,' Xav said. 'Everyone knew we were best friends with Megan. Our reputations will be tainted too, and it will be worse the more we hang out together. He wants to break us up. We should expect our parents to do the same thing.'

'You and me?' Amber asked, her face creased up in dismay. 'Will we have to stop seeing each other?'

'They'll try,' Xav said. 'They'll be praying that none of the rest of us gets dragged into it, and if we escape charges, they'll want us to have nothing to do with this friendship group ever again.'

'They can't stop us meeting up, though, can they?' Amber said. 'We're all over eighteen, even you in a couple of weeks.'

'They're probably thinking they can do it for the rest of the holiday,' Xav said. 'Come October, we'll all be going our separate ways anyway.'

'We hope,' Felix muttered.

The door opened again and Barnaby appeared. He tapped his wristwatch. The group got to their feet.

'I'm just seeing them out,' Talitha announced.

'Dinner's on the table,' her father objected. 'A considerably nicer meal, in much better surroundings, than the one your erstwhile friend Megan will be enjoying tonight.' He looked around the group, taking in each one of them with his cold stare. 'I suggest you all dwell on that in the days to come.'

# 15

Four months later

Since he'd been a kid, when he'd first discovered and fallen in love with the periodic table, Felix had formed a habit of assigning chemical elements to people in his life. He never felt he really knew someone until he'd given them an element, sometimes a compound of two or more. Megan, though, he'd always struggled with, and the closest he could get was bismuth. Long and – wrongly – considered stable, bismuth did decay, but infinitely slowly; one could never see it, or measure it, but beneath the surface, something was definitely going on. And that was all Megan, reliable head of school, calm, even-handed, as good at contributing to a team as leading it, Megan seemed entirely unremarkable for much of the time, but with occasional flashes of the extraordinary. In the same way, bismuth appeared dull, a bit uninteresting, but crystalised into fragile, rainbow-coloured structures of an astonishing beauty. On balance, Felix thought, he'd got it right. Bismuth was Megan, or at least the Megan before all this happened to her.

Because in the last few seconds of her trial, from his seat at the back of the public gallery, Felix was forced to watch Megan lose her composure. As the judge completed sentencing, she seemed to curl in upon herself, as though an invisible fist had punched into her stomach. Her mouth opened, but any sound she made was drowned by the uproar in court; if the guilty verdict had been popular, the sentence was bringing the house down.

A life sentence, with a minimum tariff of twenty years.

At the front of the public gallery, Michael Robinson dropped his head into his hands. Sitting next to Felix, Amber did the same thing, and it was Dan, not Xav, who put a comforting arm on her shoulder. Amber and Xav were no longer a couple.

Then Megan's head lifted, slowly, and she might have aged ten years since the trial began. Her hair had grown, its silver spikes giving way to an inch of dark roots. Her face, always pale, had blanched, its flesh seemingly melted away and her eyes sunken inwards. Her skin was coarse, like cheap paper, and the skin of her lips had cracked and split. Megan Macdonald, the most despised young woman in England, might, at last, be absorbing the gravity of her situation.

Felix watched her eyes moving upwards, finding the gallery, possibly even seeking him out, and had he thought there was the remotest possibility of hiding, he might have shrunk in his seat. He had no chance of avoiding her, though; he was probably the biggest person in the room.

Sensing that something might be unfolding, heads began to follow Megan's gaze, looking perhaps for her mother, but no, Mrs Macdonald had been at the opposite side of the gallery since the trial began, and she'd collapsed now, onto the shoulder of someone sitting next to her.

Was Megan looking at Xav? Glancing to the side, Felix saw Xav's face tight with tension. Down in the courtroom, Megan's hands gripped the rail in front of her, as though she might even be on the verge of clambering over it. For a second, she held eye contact with Xav and her mouth opened.

And then the spell was broken by the court officers who took hold of Megan's arms and eased her out of the courtroom. Felix felt a split second of relief. The drama, now, would be outside the court. The TV cameras – plenty of them, the 'Daredevil Driver' case had caught imaginations worldwide – would be waiting in the street. There would be statements: from the police, from the victims' family; there might even be a glimpse of the windowless van that would take Megan out of this life and into another. Nobody wanted to miss this; people began to move.

Like stones embedded in the sand as waves wash away from them, Felix and the others watched the emptying courtroom. Around him, all sound dulled, as though the court had become a TV set on which someone had turned down the volume. He saw the judge's mouth move, and Talitha, perhaps, would have known what he was saying, maybe thanking and dismissing the jury; he watched the barristers pack away their papers and the detective in charge of the case, who turned out to be the blonde who'd interviewed Amber on the first day, checking her lipstick discreetly in a pocket compact.

People in the main body of the court were leaving with barely concealed impatience, and those in the gallery followed suit. The press, who'd been sitting at the back to be in poll position, had already gone, as fast as they decently could. Megan's mother was led away, weeping. She didn't speak to her daughter's friends. It was possible she hadn't even known they were there.

'We have to go.' Felix leaned across Amber to address the others. 'We'll be seen if we stay. Come on.'

Like sheep, exhausted but cooperative, they went with him, and all kept their eyes down as they slid out of the wooden benches. They'd managed to keep their profile low during the five days of the trial, but reporting restrictions would be lifted now, Tal had warned, and as far as the country's media were concerned, it would be open season. Journalists desperate for copy wouldn't be able to reach Megan in her prison cell, so they'd come for her friends.

With Felix at the front, which possibly wasn't wise, because with his height, build and colouring he'd always be the most recognisable, they followed the last of the court occupants out. On the street, TV cameras were trained on the lead detective, wrapped up warmly now in a pink coat, on the legal team at her side and especially on Michael Robinson, the victims' husband and father.

'These last few months have been the worst imaginable for Mr Robinson,' the detective was saying, as a reporter held a fluffy grey microphone towards her face. 'His entire family was wiped out by the thoughtless and cruel actions of an over-privileged young woman who thought she was above the law. Today's sentence will send a strong signal that no one is.'

'There they are!' A woman in a padded jacket was pointing directly at them. 'Megan's friends.'

The waiting, watching crowd seemed to act as one, and there was something pack-like in the way every head turned in their direction. Cold eyes locked onto targets and a man holding a camera on his shoulder moved towards them.

Felix grabbed Talitha's hand. 'Come on.'

Heedless of the Christmas traffic, he dragged Tal into the road, dodging around a bus, ignoring car horns. Xav, Amber and Dan followed, but further along the road lights had turned against them and the traffic was slowing. The chasing pack caught up on the opposite pavement where the sheer number of pedestrians made it difficult to move at speed. Faces turned towards them, because people love nothing more than a street brawl, as long as it involves someone else.

A camera was pointed into Talitha's face. 'Talitha, did you know about your friend's daredevil game?'

Felix pulled her aside, and they dodged around a bus queue, but the news teams had far more practice in pursuing reluctant interviewees than the gang had in evading them. The hunters kept pace with prey as they fought their way along the busy pavement.

'Do you think she was trying to commit suicide after her terrible exam results?'

The sharp bristles of a Christmas tree carried over someone's shoulder scratched against Felix's face.

'Amber, were you expecting such a harsh sentence?'

'Were you ever in the car with her, Dan?'

This was disastrous; he had to get them away. 'Meadow,' Felix called over his shoulder.

Christ Church Meadow, an area of open land in the city centre, and one the gang knew every corner of, was close by. In Christ Church Meadow, they could run, and the news teams with their heavy equipment would struggle to follow. The meadow, though, was locked at dusk, and at a little before four o'clock in the afternoon, the December sky was already turning the rich blue of twilight. Dusk was an indeterminate time and they might, or might not, be lucky.

Out of breath, they reached the entrance to see the groundsman standing by the gate as the last people left. Felix dragged Talitha through.

'Hey,' the groundsman called. 'I'm shutting up.' He stepped forward, perhaps to argue, although Felix and Tal were already some way along the darkening path, and in doing so, lost his chance to stop the other three. Xav pulled Amber through the half-open gate and Dan followed. Admitting defeat but only to a point, the groundsman pushed the gate closed and the journalists were shut out.

'Keep moving,' Felix said, as the others slowed to get their breath. Daniel, who looked on the verge of an asthma attack, had even produced a blue inhaler from his pocket and was sucking at it. 'That's a frigging big gate we'll have to climb if we get shut in here.'

He led them east along the Broad Walk, a wide gravel path that took them through the ornamental gardens at the side of Christ Church College.

'That's us on the evening news,' Xav said. 'Running for it as though we've everything to hide.'

'My dad will kill me,' Talitha said. 'I promised him I wouldn't go.'

'Where's he think you've been the last five days?' Felix asked.

'Library.'

'They might not have caught us on camera.' Dan still sounded out of breath. 'We might get lucky. My folks won't be thrilled either.'

'Where will they take her?' Amber asked, as they left the grandeur of Christ Church behind and the day darkened further. They were walking now between Christ Church Meadow and Merton Field.

The others waited for Talitha to reply. Studying law at Cambridge, with access to her father's expertise, she'd become the go-to on all legal matters.

'Tonight, she'll probably stay in Bullingdon where she's been for the trial,' Talitha said. 'Over the next few days they'll move her somewhere more permanent. Dad thinks Durham is the most likely. Women serving long sentences nearly always go there.'

'Handy for you, Dan,' Felix said, without a smile.

Daniel, who'd just completed his first term reading classics at Durham, didn't see the funny side either.

'Were you expecting her to get that long?' Amber asked Talitha.

'Not here,' Felix said, as Tal opened her mouth. 'We need to get somewhere we can't be overheard.'

Dan turned a full circle. 'The place is empty.'

He didn't care. 'I'm taking no chances,' Felix insisted.

'Grab a coffee somewhere?' said Xav, who wasn't as warmly dressed as the others. 'I'm freezing.'

'We can't,' Talitha objected. 'We've no idea who else will be in those places.'

'Come to Queen's.' Amber named her Oxford college, not far from where they'd emerge at the other edge of the meadow. 'I can sign you in. We can use the library. There'll be no one there at this time.'

They seemed to be waiting for Felix to agree, and he couldn't think of a better plan. 'Let's go,' he said and hurried them along even faster.

They reached the river and turned north. Merton Field was on their left, the botanic gardens on their right. The gate at this end, being less frequently used than the main gate, was still open, and they left the meadow. Hurrying along Rose Lane, they crossed the high street and turned right into Queen's College. Michaelmas term had ended, but the students still had access to the general areas. Amber signed them in at the porters' lodge and then they followed her through the main quad and up the spiral staircase to the seventeenth-century upper library. All of them, even Felix and Xav, were out of breath by this time.

Widely regarded as one of the most beautiful libraries in Oxford, the upper floor of Queen's library was a long, oak-floored hall with freestanding cases filled with rare and venerable books. The carved ceiling was painted shades of white and pearl grey. The huge arched windows were black by this time. The room looked empty, felt empty, but Felix strode its length, checking each alcove between the giant bookcases. Satisfied, he came back to where the others had gathered around a reading table.

'No one,' he said. 'We're good.' Even so, he kept his voice as low as the subdued reading lamps around them. They pulled out the red leather-backed chairs and sat, none of them removing their coats. The library wasn't cold, but there was a sense among them that they might have to flee again at any time. Talitha kept her arms wrapped around her upper body, as though trying to warm herself; Daniel, inhaler in hand, glanced round at the spiral staircase every few seconds.

For several long moments, no one seemed to have anything to say; no one could make eye contact with any of the others.

'I didn't think she'd go through with it,' Xav spoke at last, but addressed his words to the polished oak table. 'The last four days, especially today, I kept expecting to see her turn and point to us.'

'Me too,' Amber agreed.

'She didn't look at us once,' Xav went on. 'She must have known we were there but for four days, not a glance, until that last minute.'

'I really thought that was it,' Talitha said. 'I was sure she was going to say something then.'

Felix said, 'Fair play to the girl – she's got more balls than any of us.'

Silence fell again. Downstairs, a muffled thud sounded, as though a book had been dropped. Daniel, who'd been jumpy as a kitten since the accident, got up and walked silently to the staircase. He peered down for several seconds before shaking his head and walking back.

Daniel, in Felix's head, was a mixture of the soft, malleable copper – useful enough, but never going to set the world alight – and iodine, a dull substance that was displaced by just about every other element in its group. If there was a wimpy element, it was iodine. In his more generous moods, Felix admitted to himself that he wasn't being entirely fair on Daniel, but God, when was the guy going to grow a pair?

And what was with the inhalers? He'd never been asthmatic in school; he'd been a pretty decent cross-country runner.

'Twenty years. I had no idea she'd get that long,' Xav said. 'Can she appeal?'

Once again, everyone turned to Talitha.

Tal had been the easiest of the lot. Pure mercury – the fascinating, irresistible metallic that took liquid form in standard conditions. Mercury was relentless and ruthless; it was smart, slippery, toxic as snakes. Exactly like Tal.

'To be honest,' she said, 'I'm not entirely surprised. Dad said a couple of days ago he thought it wasn't going her way. The fact she'd done it before' – she held up a hand to stave off protests that might, but probably wouldn't, have been coming – 'I know, I know. But from the point of view of the court, it looked bad. The witness statement went against her. And the press coverage has been vicious. Public feeling isn't supposed to impact trials, but it does.'

'And the mental health assessment found her perfectly sane,' Felix added.

'"Curiously detached", that's what he said,' Amber said. 'That psychiatrist bloke, he said she was cold and distant, removed from what was going on around her and not properly grasping the significance of what she'd done.'

'He also said she might have psychopathic tendencies,' Daniel said. 'Did you ever think that about her? I can't say I ever did.'

'She was lying through her teeth to protect us, no wonder she sounded weird,' Xav snapped. 'And I don't know about any of you lot, but I'm not sure I can go through with this.'

Around the table, something shifted. More than one body tensed, and Felix heard the whispered intake of breath. Xav, with his brilliance and physical beauty, was gold, of course: rare, fascinating, with a hundred different uses, but ultimately rather soft and unreliable. People had lusted after gold since the dawn of time, but no one had ever built a house from it.

'What do you mean?' Talitha said. 'And keep your voice down.'

Xav ran his hands over his face. 'It's on my mind, every second of the day, from the moment I wake up.' He looked up. 'I barely sleep. I'm at risk of being thrown off the course. I can't focus on anything I'm being taught, and I've no interest in socialising or getting involved in any of the college stuff. I'm turning into a zombie. It's eating me away.'

Amber reached out towards him. Xav looked coldly at her hand and tucked both his own into his armpits.

'I know what you mean.' Amber's eyes had darkened at Xav's snub. 'Every morning, for a split second when I wake up, I think everything's all right, and then I remember, and it's like someone's dropped a massive weight on my chest.'

'I'm frightened of fire,' Daniel said. 'I can't be in a room with a real fire, even a small one. I can't stand the sound of the crackling and the spitting. It makes me want to scream.'

Felix gave a heavy and audible sigh. Across the table, he caught Talitha's eye. They'd expected this, not necessarily so soon.

'I walk round college at night after everyone's gone to bed,' Daniel went on. 'I'm checking for anything that could start a fire. People think I'm mental, hardly anyone talks to me any more, but I can't stop it. My tutor said I need to see a counsellor but what good would that do when he's going to want to get to the root of what's causing my problem and that's the one thing I can never tell him?'

Felix said, 'This is getting us nowhere.'

'I've requested a change of rooms to one on the ground floor,' Daniel didn't seem able to stop. 'I've got a rope under my bed for when the fire breaks out. I'm a mess.'

'We're all paying the price,' Talitha said. 'Not just Megan.'

'Well, I think she might swap with any one of us right now,' Xav said.

'You have to get a grip, mate,' Felix said to Dan. 'We all do, or we'll all end up exactly where Megan is now. They won't release her just because we confess. She'll still be serving twenty years and the only difference is we will be too.'

He met Talitha's eyes again and gave her a small nod. Taking it as permission to speak up, she said, 'If we're on the outside, we can help her. Felix and I have been talking that we can help her financially.'

'How do you mean?' Amber's head lifted. 'She can't spend money in prison.'

'In a few years, we'll be earning money,' Talitha explained. 'Quite a lot, if we all pull ourselves together. We can set up a trust fund and pay a percentage of our income into it every year. When Megan gets out, it can help get her started.'

'And that's doing something real to help her,' Felix argued. 'Throwing ourselves under the bus because we can't cope with the guilt won't achieve a thing.'

The mood was shifting, he could sense it. Daniel's eyes were gleaming, Amber was definitely listening.

'I like that idea,' Amber said. 'If we each set aside twenty per cent, it will give her an equal share, won't it?'

'Twenty per cent might be pushing it,' Felix said. 'Especially at first. But ten will be good. Ten per cent will add up.'

Even Xav seemed to be thinking about it.

'And we should tell her we're doing it,' Talitha said. 'So she knows we haven't abandoned her.'

'How? Are we going to write?' Amber asked.

'God no.' Talitha looked shocked. 'We never, ever, put anything about what happened in writing. Someone has to go and see her as soon as possible. It can't be me – Dad will hear about it.'

'I'll go,' Xav said. 'As soon as we know where she is. But we all need to visit, not just once, but regularly, as long as she's inside.'

Amber nodded quickly, followed a few seconds later by Dan. Once more holding eye contact with Talitha, Felix let his own head fall and rise. He had no plans to visit Megan, and he was pretty certain Tal would go nowhere near either, but for now, the weaker members of the group had to be kept on side.

'People don't serve their whole terms though, do they?' Dan asked. 'She won't actually be in prison for twenty years. It's not like she's a serial killer.'

'Dad thinks she'll serve at least ten years,' Talitha said. 'Possibly more. Michael Robinson's legal team will oppose any attempt at early release.'

'Ten years?' Xav said. 'I can't get my head round the next ten days.'

'There's something else we need to think about,' Felix said.

'What's that?'

'Megan could change her mind at any time. We really need to find that letter she made us all sign. And the film.'

'I agree,' Talitha said. 'But where do we look? We can't go round to her house again.'

'Well, we have to keep looking because even if she's as good as her word, there'll come a time when she gets out. And we owe her, remember, we all agreed. She could ask us for absolutely anything.'

# Part Two

## TWENTY YEARS LATER

# 16

The summer had barely begun when Megan came back into the world. At All Souls' School, Trinity term had been underway for exactly a week and the various sports teams had already made an impact on the league tables. On the other hand, building work on the new science block was behind schedule and a potential new donor had pulled out. The governors were scheduled to meet at six, and Daniel wasn't looking forward to giving them the bad news, especially as he suspected Megan's recent, much publicised, release from prison had been a factor in the wealthy businessman taking his cash elsewhere. He could only hope they wouldn't find out she'd been on the premises immediately before their arrival.

'She's in reception.'

He could offer them Pope's proverb, he supposed: 'to err is human; to forgive, divine', but had a feeling it might fall on deaf ears. Megan Macdonald was not an alumnus that All Souls' was ever going to view with pride. In fact, long before Daniel's appointment as master, every removable trace of her had been wiped from school records. And now she was back, in the flesh, less than an hour before the governors were due. He might have laughed, but sometime, over the years, he'd forgotten how.

Ellen, the school secretary, was standing in the doorway and, fair play, making a passable attempt at disapproval. Daniel had known Ellen for years, though; he could see the glee in her eyes.

'Who is?' he asked.

He'd said nothing to Ellen about Megan's visit, but she knew exactly who Ms M. Macdonald was; the *Oxford Mail* had covered her release – front page no less – as had BBC Oxford, and the school had been buzzing with rumours. Half the juniors had claimed to see her in School Field, gazing at them from across the river like the ghost of forgotten scandals.

'Your old friend,' the secretary said.

Daniel had never discussed his past with Ellen.

'Do the governors know she's here?' she went on.

'Thanks, Ellen.' He opened another document on his computer screen, an attempt to look busy that probably wouldn't fool her. 'I'll get her in a few minutes. See you tomorrow.'

'I don't mind fetching her.'

Daniel didn't look up. 'I'm not quite ready. And you'll miss your bus.'

Ellen left, but it was a safe bet she'd be exiting the building via reception to get a glimpse of the bogeywoman. Daniel gave her five minutes head start; then a few more for luck.

How was he feeling? Cornered, would be the only way he could describe it. Since Megan had made her appointment the previous week, after repeated attempts and refusing to be put off, he'd barely slept more than a couple of hours at a time, and when he did drop off, he was plagued by nightmares. In each of them, he was running through the Oxford of his teenage years, chased by a formless shadow that he knew to be Megan.

All Souls' might have been educating the gifted young of Oxford since the fifteenth century, but the original buildings had long since gone. The school that had appointed Daniel as master was an eclectic collection of structures arranged around an open space, known as The Yard, that the governors wouldn't allow him to turn into a car park. Heart thumping, he crossed into the main building via the covered bridge, scuttled through the art department and down the back stairs past the staff room to reception.

Megan, who knew the school almost as well as he did, had positioned herself so that she was facing the door. They saw each other at the same moment.

His first thought was that the youngsters who'd claimed to have seen her watching the school had been talking rot. The woman on the other side of the glass door looked nothing like the photograph that had appeared in the *Oxford Mail*, nothing like his memory of an eighteen-year-old girl. Her amazing silver hair had grown long and dark brown, dull as mud; her lovely face had turned skeletal and corpse pale. She'd always been thin, but her limbs had become angular and hung from her torso as though stuck to her body with pins. She was like a marionette, discarded after years of use. She looked ill, and to his shame he felt a surge of hope; this wreck of a human being couldn't possibly be a threat.

Meanwhile, he'd stopped moving, and they were looking at each other through the glass. He was trying to read her expression and wondering how soon after he pulled open the door would the accusations start. Why didn't you visit me? Why didn't you write? How come you've been nowhere near me in twenty years? Maybe she'd cut straight to the chase and tell him what she wanted, what he had to do for her now in return for everything she'd sacrificed. He'd been a fool to agree to meet her here, in front of witnesses, and yet she'd been so insistent.

'You all right, Dan?'

Daniel started. Without his noticing, one of the PE staff had followed him down and couldn't get past. Pulling himself together, he opened the door and stepped out into reception.

'Megan.' He held out his hand, praying she wouldn't expect a hug. She seemed to sway as she got to her feet, as though her legs weren't steady, and when she put up a hand to brush hair from her face, he saw an ugly scar on her right temple. A deep cut, not properly stitched up, had left reddened and puckered skin behind.

'Master.'

She smiled, and he couldn't tell whether she was congratulating or mocking him. Her hand felt cold and damp, and he let it go as soon as he decently could.

'Are you signed in? You've got a badge, I see.'

The receptionist gave Daniel a pointed stare, and he knew before the week was out that every member of the school community from the youngest junior to the usher would have heard of Megan's visit. The receptionist and Ellen between them had the board of governors, the parents' association, the various catering and cleaning supply companies and the staffroom covered.

'Right then, I'll lead the way. You OK with the stairs?'

It was a stupid thing to say, but she looked so frail, as though a strong wind would blow her over. He wasn't surprised that she fell behind before they reached the second floor. At the top, Daniel watched her struggle up the last few steps, breathing heavily, with a fine sheen of sweat on skin that, he saw now, had a yellow tinge.

'How long have you been—' he began.

'Out?' she offered.

He'd meant that. 'In Oxford,' he corrected.

'A couple of weeks. I've been ill, or I'd have come before.'

'Well, it's good to see you,' he said.

She recoiled and her eyes gleamed like steel. *This is it*, he told himself, *this is when it comes*. 'This way,' he told her, although, of course, she knew the way to the master's office. She walked behind him so quietly that halfway along the corridor he looked back to check she was still there, only to find her disturbingly close on his heels. Leaving her in the study, he made tea in Ellen's room. When he got back, Megan was at the window.

'I'd forgotten how lovely the view is,' she said.

'I never tire of it.'

It was, he realised, the first honest thing he'd said to her. The master's study looked out over Christ Church Meadow with the famous dreaming spires in the background. The sun was low in the sky and the buildings were turning their twilight shade of warm honey. There were evenings when Daniel sat for hours at his window, when the school had fallen quiet around him, and watched the sunset glow grow cold, the spires vanish into night, and the twinkling lights of the city appear like stars. Looking out at Oxford, alone at the end of the day, Daniel came closest to remembering a time when he'd been happy.

It didn't seem the moment to tell Megan that, and so he poured and tried to remember how she took her tea.

She said, 'Last time I was in this room, I was drinking champagne.'

And just like that, the memory was alive and shining in his head: the day of his last exam, a Thursday in June; the others had all finished before him but had come back into school at the master's invitation. She'd served them cake and champagne and thanked them for a sterling job as the senior prefect team. There'd been a professional photographer present, and the customary group shot had been taken for the yearbook.

He remembered admiring how confident Felix, Talitha and Xav were with the master, as though they knew all authority had slipped from her with their last exams; that they were her equals now and might one day outgrow her. She still made him nervous, Amber too, he could tell. Megan though? Now he came to think of it, there had been something wrong with Megan that day; she'd withdrawn into herself, barely speaking. He'd wondered if he'd done something to offend her.

'I don't have any chilled, I'm afraid,' he said, 'but I did stop at Sainsbury's for some chocolate digestives.'

It was a poor joke. Megan gave him a half-smile, took the tea, tasted it, and added three spoons of sugar.

'So, tell me everything,' she said, as she eased herself carefully into one of his armchairs. 'I would not have predicted you'd end up here.'

'Me neither.'

When Daniel had seen the master's job advertised, he'd thought he'd rather cut off his own arm than be back in that same environment every day. But as the days had gone on, he'd been unable to get it out of his head and, when the nightmares started, he'd wondered whether confronting his horror head on might help. On the last day that applications were open, he'd submitted his CV, almost as a dare to himself. When he'd been offered the job, he'd seen it as fate stepping in. He'd been right though; being back did help in some way he couldn't begin to explain.

'Well, the full story would take a long time and send you to sleep,' he said. 'But in my last year at Durham, I started coaching some of the first years and learned I had a bit of a gift for it. I did my year's teacher training and haven't looked back. I'm also not bad at raising money, which is probably how I landed the job here. Did you see the plans downstairs for the new sixth-form centre?'

'I did. Looks a big improvement on what we had.'

'It will be. And it'll cost us upward of ten million.'

She inclined her head in a small acknowledgement, and he wondered if she was toying with him. Sooner or later, she was going to say it. Twenty bloody years! Where the hell were you?

'Any family?' she asked.

He shook his head. 'Something else I learned at Durham was that I had an affinity with the religious life. I joined an order in my early twenties.'

He had to stop mentioning Durham. Megan, too, had been in

Durham for most of the last twenty years, a matter of miles from him in a high-security prison.

Megan's eyes, that he remembered being wide and such a dark brown as to be almost black, seemed smaller, bloodshot, even when she opened them wide in surprise. 'An order? What are you, a monk?'

He forced a smile. 'Yes, in a way. A lay monk. I live in a religious house off the Cowley Road with a dozen other brothers. We all work in the community, but we dedicate our personal lives to study and prayer.'

She blinked, twice, three times. 'Blimey. What do the others think about that?'

'The others?'

He knew exactly who she meant.

Megan's mouth lost its amused twist. 'Xav, Amber, Tal and Felix.' She spoke the names as though reading them from a card. 'You know, the others. Our friends. The gang.'

Daniel realised he was twisting a button on the cuff of his jacket, something he'd never done in his life before. 'Oh them,' he said. 'To be honest, I haven't seen much of them for years.'

Megan's stare hardened.

'Xav works in London, although I think he and his wife still live in Oxford. Felix travels overseas a lot, Talitha's law practice keeps her nose to the grindstone, and as for Amber, well, you must have seen her on TV. She and I don't move in the same circles any—' Daniel stopped talking. Something had happened; something indefinable in the room had shifted.

'Xav's married?' Megan said.

'They all are. Apart from me, of course. Xav was the last. The summer before last I think it was. In Wiltshire. Nice country wedding.'

As he spoke, Daniel had a sense of a fragile structure crumbling, as though he'd pulled a supporting card from a stack and they were in that split second before the whole lot tumbled. Something was happening, and he didn't have a clue what it was.

The teacup in Megan's hand tilted, as though she'd forgotten she was holding it. Pale brown liquid splashed into the saucer and then out, onto the carpet. She paid no attention to it at all and he thought, *She's not normal any more. Something essential inside has gone.*

'Megan?' he said.

With a start, she saw what had happened, and put the cup and saucer down. The carpet was marked, but she ignored it.

'You've all done so well,' she said.

'Well, our old friends did very well, of course,' he said. 'I'm just a humble schoolteacher.'

Her eyes flashed. 'Beats where I ended up.'

Daniel picked up his cup to break eye contact. It was coming. She was going to tell him what she wanted from him. A job? Money? Whatever it was, it would be a big ask, because she was going to punish him for neglecting her all these years, for not being the friend he'd promised to be. He almost wanted her to get on with it. At the very worst, he'd know where he stood. When he looked up though, her eyes had lost focus and were staring at something over his shoulder.

'Megan, what are your plans?' he said. 'Are you staying in Oxford?'

'Where else would I go?'

'So what – I mean – are you looking for a job? I'd offer to see if there's anything here, you know, in the kitchens, or maybe with the cleaning contractors, but – you know – DBS checks. I don't think it would work.'

What the hell was he doing? Megan Macdonald had once got

through to the international stage of the Physics Olympiad and he was telling her she wasn't good enough to clean the lavatories in her old school.

Megan didn't notice, or ignored, his lack of tact. 'Yes, I'll need a job,' she said. 'There are schemes to help with that, although they'll be fairly entry level. I'm also planning a course in September, when they all start up again.'

'Do you have somewhere to live?'

She pulled her face into an empty smile and gave him a hard stare. 'Actually, I was hoping you might have a spare room.'

Something clutched at his stomach. 'Megan, I live in a religious house. Only men are allowed.'

The smile stayed as cold and brittle as single-glazing in the north-east. 'I'm kidding. I have a bedsit on the Iffley Road,' she told him. 'Until the neighbours find out I'm there, of course. I've been told I may have to move a few times.'

She was miserable, wretched; she needed pity, not fear. And yet . . .

'Have you thought you might be better off outside Oxford?' he asked.

'Oxford is my home. My friends are here.'

Her eyes drifted from him again, as though she'd retreated into some internal private space. This time, he left her there. The hour he'd allocated to Megan was slipping away, and he could not let the governors arrive and find her here. After a minute or more, she leaned forward.

'Dan, did you come and see me?'

'I'm sorry?'

'You and the others. Did you come and see me in prison?'

He had no idea what to say. They hadn't, of course. Their parents had insisted they cut all ties with Megan Macdonald and while they were eighteen, officially adults, they were all still financially dependent. Their parents could still tell them what to do and know they'd obey. In all fairness, though, he doubted a single one of them had pushed back. Even Xav, despite his promises, hadn't been near her.

But why was she asking? She would know the answer already.

'I had a head injury,' she answered his unspoken question. 'When I'd been there about five years. Someone threw me down the stairs. I spent days in a coma.'

His eyes went to the scar on her forehead, barely visible now that her hair had fallen forward again. A head injury would explain a lot, her vagueness, her habit of drifting off. He said, 'I had no idea. I'm so sorry to hear that.'

Even as he spoke, a memory churned inside him. He remembered Tal, years ago, telling them all that Megan had had an accident in prison. Tal had played it down, implied that Megan had needed nothing more than a sticking plaster and some aspirin, and none of the others had even tried to learn more. They'd fallen into the habit of never talking, or even thinking, about Megan when they could help it. It had been easier that way.

Megan shrugged. 'It happens. But it means I can't remember very much at all about those early years.'

And at that, the feeling in his gut became a small twist of excitement. He hated it, even as he allowed it space to grow.

'For a long time,' Megan went on, 'I couldn't remember the trial, or being sentenced, or the first few years inside. After a while, memories started to come back, but they were vague and really confusing. I'm still not sure whether they're real or things I made up to fill the gap.'

'That must have been very disturbing.'

'I had no idea what I'd done. Think of that, Daniel. I'd gone from waiting for my A level results that last summer to being an inmate in one of the worst prisons in Britain, and I had no idea why.'

She was lying to him, she had to be. And yet he could see no hint of deceit in her eyes.

'But, I mean, someone told you, surely?'

There were tears shining in her eyes now. 'They told me I'd killed a mother and two young children,' she said. 'That I'd deliberately driven my car onto the wrong carriageway of the M40 and that I'd done it lots of times before. That I was convicted of murder and given a life sentence.'

He wanted to hate himself at that moment for how he was feeling; instead, he hated her for giving him hope that could be snatched away at any time. She could, still, be messing with him.

'But it sounded so unlike me, Dan. Did I do that? Did I really kill those people?'

Daniel honestly thought he would have given anything at that moment to tell her the truth and yet, to his shame, he didn't even try. The one thing he could say in his favour was that he couldn't look at her when he spoke next.

He said, 'You did, I'm afraid, Megan.'

When he looked up, the tears were rolling down her cheeks.

'I was hoping there'd been some mistake,' she said. 'I felt sure once I saw you again, you'd explain it all to me.'

'Meg,' he used the old diminutive without thinking. 'I can't explain it, I never could.'

And that, at least, was the truth; he would never be able to understand what mad, self-destructive force took hold of them that summer.

'So, tell me, please,' she said. 'Tell me what I did. I know you were with me that night, at least for the early part of the evening. Tell me how it happened.'

All this should be provoking some sort of emotional reaction in him. He should want to be sick, or to break down and admit the truth. Instead, Daniel could feel everything inside him freezing over. He wasn't sure he'd feel anything again.

'Megan, there's no point.'

Her voice rose. 'There's every point. I couldn't believe what they were telling me. It seemed impossible. I'll believe you.'

Her faith should have moved him; it didn't.

'We were at Tal's,' he said. 'We were drinking. I think you were in the pool for a lot of the time. We mostly fell asleep, in the pool house. When we woke up, you were gone.' He got to his feet, determined to end the charade the meeting had become. 'That's all I know, Megan, I'm sorry.'

She stared back at him, her eyes big and frightened, the scar on her forehead reddened and ugly. 'But why, Dan? Why would I do something so stupid, so reckless? Was that like me?'

'No.' He felt no shock at how hard his voice had become. 'It took us all by surprise. No one could believe it. Megan, I'm sorry, but I have a governors' meeting and I have to get ready. I have to see you out.'

She made no move to get up. 'Oh. I thought, maybe, we could have a drink, or something.'

'Not tonight, I'm afraid.'

Never. Never again would he be in this woman's company. He took a step closer to the door and outside, in the car park, recognised the car of one of the governors.

'Soon then,' she said. 'I've been trying to get in touch with the others but it's hard to get phone numbers. I've called Amber's office, but she hasn't got back to me, and I wasn't sure what Talitha's firm is called.'

'I imagine Amber's very busy. They all will be.' Daniel forced a smile. 'At least you got me. I'm a bit tied up for the next few weeks, but maybe in the summer we could have coffee or something? Is there a number I can get you on?'

He had no intention of meeting her; he just wanted her out of there.

'Can you give me any numbers?' she said. 'You must be in touch with them.'

He was at the door to his office now. 'Not really. Not any more. Different circles, Megan. I'm just a humble schoolteacher.'

At last, she got to her feet. 'You haven't answered my question,' she said.

'What question?'

'Did you come to see me before I had my accident? I know you didn't afterwards. I sent out so many visiting orders, but none of you came.'

He turned from her. 'We'd have been at university, starting jobs.'

'I was in Durham, Dan. Like you.'

He jumped when he felt her breath on the back of his neck. She'd moved very close, was touching his shoulder.

'It's OK,' she said. 'I was a monster, I understand that. You had to distance yourselves. Is that how you still feel?'

Yes, more than she knew. He said, 'No, of course not. But lives have moved on, Meg, you must understand that.' He pulled away, gently, but she held on.

'Will you tell them that I'd like to see them? Will you let them know I'm back?'

'Of course. But I'm hardly in touch with them myself. I'm not sure when I'll see any of them again.'

She nodded, slowly and sadly, and didn't speak again as he led her down the stairs. At the front door, she reached for the handle and seemed to lack the strength to pull it towards her. He reached round and opened it.

'You don't look well,' he said. 'Are you registered with a GP? I can help you with that.'

'I have kidney disease,' she told him. 'I caught a virus a few years ago. It affects my liver too, but the kidneys are the worst affected. Prisons are not healthy places.'

'I'm sorry.' He was running out of other things to say and a few yards away, the chairman of the governors was getting out of his car. 'Is it treatable?'

'No. It will deteriorate over the next few years. Faster if I drink heavily, which I probably will, because most ex-cons do. I really need a donor, but convicted killers are way, way down on the approved list of organ recipients.'

The room seemed to tilt. For a moment, Daniel thought he was falling. He even reached out and caught hold of the wall. There was absolutely nothing he could say to her.

She stood, on the threshold of his school, looking up at him and he knew, almost word for word, what she was going to say next.

'My one chance,' she began, 'and it's a slim one, is to find someone the same blood group as me.' She smiled then, and he caught a glimpse of the old Megan.

'Someone who owes me a favour.'

# 17

The governors' meeting ran over time and Daniel had to excuse himself. He left quickly, even rudely, cutting more than one conversation short. Outside, the evening was mild, plenty of light left in the sky, but he pulled his coat closed and raised the collar all the same as he left the school premises. He was halfway down the road when it occurred to him that he was hiding. He even stopped and looked around, in case Megan was lurking somewhere nearby.

A hundred yards further, he slipped into a narrow, cobbled cul-de-sac, darker than the evening he'd left behind. At its end, he pressed a four-digit key code to open a tall iron gate to let him into the grounds of Old School, the oldest of the school buildings, built when Victoria was on the throne. His footsteps crunched over the gravel as he made his way to the portcullis at the entrance to the choristers' tunnel.

One of the biggest excitements for new pupils at All Souls' – he could still remember his own glee all those years ago – was the discovery of the secret passage, a stone tunnel that ran beneath the main road. All pupils, up to but not including the sixth form, were expected to use it to cross the road.

At its opposite end, fifty yards away, Daniel could see a dark silhouette. Talitha had let herself into the tunnel with the key code he'd texted her and was walking quickly towards him, her heels rapping on the stone.

Years ago, Talitha had sacrificed her fabulous hair on the altar of looking serious in court. She couldn't do anything about the curls though, and it still spread out around her head like a glossy brown halo. In better light, Daniel would have been able to see the gold highlights that picked up the flecks in her brown eyes. Still thin, with that creamy southern European skin that didn't seem to age, he never saw her without thinking how striking she was. And yet, there was something about Talitha's looks that seemed to repel rather than attract. As teenagers, it had been the softly pretty Amber who'd gained all the male attention. And Megan, of course, but most boys had been in awe of Megan.

'How was it?'

The gate clanged shut as Daniel led Talitha away from the tunnel. All Souls', being a city-centre establishment, had little in the way of grounds, but did boast one piece of Oxford real estate that was completely its own – School Field, a large island, bound on all sides by the River Cherwell. It was possible that one or two people on the upper floors of the school or the nearby colleges might see Daniel and Talitha on the island, but they couldn't possibly overhear.

From the rose garden in front of Old School they followed a gravel path, via two ornate wooden structures known simply as The White Bridges. The land beyond was slipping into darkness.

He said, 'She doesn't remember.'

Speaking too quickly, probably too loudly, but desperate to get Tal's take on it all, he repeated what Megan had told him about her head injury and subsequent memory loss. He couldn't have been making much sense because more than once Talitha made him stop and repeat himself or clarify something. Eventually, even she seemed to accept that a miracle had happened.

'Wow,' she said softly. 'We didn't see that coming.'

By this time they were on the island, following an indented

path formed by generations of children trooping around the pitches to the pavilion. It was flat and firm enough for even Tal to cope with in her heels.

'She asked me to tell her what happened,' he said. 'What she did that night.'

'Well, I guess you were in as good a position as anyone to do that.'

There were times when Daniel could cope with the darkness of Talitha's humour, times when he even found it funny. This wasn't one of them.

'I told her it was true,' he said. 'That she really had killed those people. I heard the words coming out of my mouth and I didn't believe what I was doing, and I kept on doing it. I think I broke her.'

Tal squeezed his arm. 'She's been in prison for nearly twenty years. She was broken long before tonight.'

'I could have changed everything. I could have told her she didn't kill anyone.'

'No, *you* did. Is that what you should have told her?'

Daniel stopped walking. After a second, Talitha did too.

'I'm sorry, Dan, I shouldn't have said that. We were all responsible for what happened. But if Megan really doesn't remember that night, then it's over. Finally.'

Knowing exactly what Talitha meant, Dan still couldn't allow himself to feel it. Not yet. If anything, he felt worse than he had before. He'd been given a chance at redemption that evening and hadn't taken it. So many years, and he was still a coward at heart.

'We can help her,' Talitha said. 'At a distance, obviously. There's the fund, for one thing. I'm not sure how much—'

'A little over a million,' he told her. 'I asked Xav last night.'

The trust fund, born from guilt and desperation, had become a meaningful reality over the years. Felix had contacted them all in their first year in employment to nudge them into setting it up. Xav, already a rising star in investment banking, had managed the fund and it had grown well. Amber and Daniel, on more modest salaries, hadn't been major contributors, but they'd done their bit.

Talitha gave a soft whistle. 'Well, that's great,' she said. 'That's a huge deal for someone in Megan's position. She can buy a flat, maybe move abroad. That's what we should encourage her to do. Did you tell her about the money?'

'She asked me if we'd visited her before she had her accident,' Daniel said. 'I had to tell her no, that we'd abandoned her.'

'And she really has no memory of what happened that night? Did she actually say that? We need to be sure.'

'She begged me to tell her there'd been a mistake, that she wasn't the monster the world had labelled her.'

They'd reached the sports pavilion, a picturesque white-washed folly built in the 1930s. Climbing onto the veranda, they sat on damp wooden chairs.

'We knew this was coming,' Talitha said. 'We knew she wouldn't stay in prison for ever.'

'No, even you couldn't manage that.'

Talitha's breath whistled. Glancing sideways, he saw her face tense.

'It wasn't me,' she said, in a low voice. 'It was Dad.'

'Oh, come off it, your dad retired years ago.'

Daniel had never challenged her about this before, but the five of them had talked, in the beginning, about the possibility that their parents might suspect the truth. Not a single mum or dad had said anything, but there'd been a subtle shift in how they behaved around their children. Amber had explained it best; she'd said, 'It's like they love me a little less.'

What had really convinced them though, was the discovery that Talitha's father had actively taken steps to prolong Megan's incarceration. He'd instructed a team from one of his firm's subsidiaries to offer services to the family of Megan's victims. They'd argued at her trial for the maximum sentence, had opposed every attempt at appeal, every application for early parole. Had it not been for the interference of Talitha's father, Megan might have been released years ago.

Megan had no idea, of course, how terribly she'd been betrayed.

And now, Daniel wasn't buying Talitha's denial. She'd taken over her father's firm; she was its senior partner and nothing would be happening without her knowledge and agreement.

'And even Dad had nothing to do with her accident,' Talitha said. 'It was a prison brawl, nothing more.'

Daniel turned to look at Talitha.

'You told us it was something and nothing, a bang on the head, soon mended. It was more than that. I saw her scar. What else have you been keeping from us?'

Talitha's jaw clenched tight. 'I didn't know about her memory loss.'

'But you knew she'd been hurt?'

'There was an appeal shortly afterwards, for early release on compassionate grounds. It was rejected, thanks to Dad.'

'Nothing to do with you?' he repeated.

'No.'

Talitha wouldn't look at him. As kids, they'd joked about Talitha's Sicilian family and their possible connections to organised crime. They'd enjoyed the dark glamour of the idea, and Talitha had never denied it. They'd never actually taken it seriously though.

Arranging an accident in prison? It happened all the time, he knew that. But the thought that Talitha might have been behind Megan's head injury was something entirely new to grapple with. He didn't want to know, he realised.

'If she ever finds out . . .' He didn't finish his sentence. He didn't need to.

'No reason why she should.'

'She wants to meet up.'

Talitha's voice had hardened. 'I hope you told her it wasn't a good idea.'

'I said we weren't in touch any more, that I don't see any of you from one year to the next. I'm not so sure she'll give up easily though.'

Talitha stood up, brushed down her coat and moved towards the steps. 'See her one more time,' she said. 'You can tell her about the money, as long as the others agree. We'll give her the cash if she promises to leave Oxford and never come back. Maybe there's a way of paying an annuity, so the cash gets cut off if she starts making trouble. Xav will know. I'll call him tonight.'

At that very moment, Talitha's phone began to ring. She glanced at the screen and Daniel saw it too. *Unknown Caller*, via Facetime.

'I'm expecting this,' she said. 'I won't be a sec.'

She pressed the receive button and held the phone up so she could see the screen. Daniel could see it too, although he shifted sideways so that he wouldn't be seen himself. A face appeared in front of them. Megan.

'Tal,' she said. 'Good to see you. You cut your hair.'

'How did you get my number?' Tal asked.

'Dan gave it to me.'

He had to give Talitha credit; she didn't allow her eyes to so much as flicker in his direction.

'Are you actually on School Field?' he heard Megan say. 'I'm sure I recognise that pavilion.'

Tal frowned. 'I'm at my stepson's school,' she said. 'St Joseph's in Summertown. It does look a bit similar. I don't think I've set foot on School Field for years.'

Fair play to Tal, she was a great liar.

Megan said, 'Do you remember the madrigals on the river? That time Xav and Felix were punting and Xav lost his pole?'

Daniel remembered, even if Talitha didn't. A school tradition, towards the end of Trinity term, when the school choir sang madrigals from half a dozen punts. He and the girls had been watching from the bank. Xav had lost concentration, almost fallen in, and his pole had gone. They'd pissed themselves laughing.

'Long time ago,' Talitha said. 'What can I do for you, Megan?'

Megan didn't reply, and Daniel wasn't surprised. Even he was taken aback by the coldness of Talitha's tone.

'You can get the old gang together,' Megan said after a moment, and this time her tone matched Tal's. 'This weekend works for me.'

Tal's eyes flickered up to Daniel.

'Someone with you?' Megan asked.

'A groundsman. I thought he might want to speak to me. I'm going to have to go, Megan, I need to get my stepson and a couple of his friends home.'

'Shall we say Saturday? I can be at your lovely house by one. The forecast is good. We might even be able to eat outside.'

'I'm not sure . . .'

'No, you're probably right. It's still a bit chilly. Can I leave you to get in touch with the others? I'd ask Dan, but you know what he's like. Tell him you want to go to a brewery and he'd struggle to programme the satnav, never mind organise the piss-up.'

'Megan, I'll have to let you know,' Talitha said. 'The others, I mean, I hardly see them any more. It's quite short notice. And Amber – well, you don't just call up people like that and order them round for lunch. I think—'

Megan's voice cut through Talitha's protests. 'You know what, Tal, I don't call twenty years short notice at all. I'd say they've had more than enough time. One o'clock. I'll see you there. Say good night to Dan for me.'

The reflected light vanished from Tal's face. Megan had gone.

Tal glared at Daniel. 'You gave her my number?'

The fear was back; the Megan who'd returned to them was not someone he knew. 'Absolutely not,' he said. 'I don't know how she managed that.'

Talitha gave a scared look around, as though even now Megan might appear from behind the dark trees. 'She knew you were here – did you tell her we were meeting up?'

'She recognised School Field, Tal. It was obvious you were lying.'

A shudder. It unnerved him to see Talitha so rattled. 'She was – different.'

'I know, I heard. She wasn't like that with me at all. She was meek as a mouse.'

Talitha tucked her phone away. 'Well, it's not happening. Mark will have a fit if I bring her into the house. And there's no way the others are going to play ball.' She almost ran down the pavilion steps.

'You're going to have to deal with it, Dan,' she called back. 'Clear it with Xav and the others about the trust fund and then have one last meeting with her. Tell her about the money but make it clear she goes a long way away.'

Daniel had to admire the way Talitha thought every problem could be fixed with money and a firm hand.

'It's not going to be that simple,' he said as he caught up with her.

'Dan, she doesn't remember. We can't change what happened. She paid the price for what we did, and now we have a chance to pay her back. But we can't be friends again.'

Talitha strode on as though trying to leave him behind, and they reached the first of the white bridges. She stopped at the apex and looked down into the dark waters of the Cherwell. They'd spent so much time on this circle of water in the old days, punting, paddle-boating, picnicking.

Joining her, he said, 'We can't risk it.'

'What do you mean?'

'We can't assume she's telling the truth when she says she doesn't remember.'

Talitha's face fell slack. 'Why would she lie?'

He wasn't sure. He had his suspicions, but speculation wouldn't help. They needed to deal with facts, right now, not guesswork. Talitha of all people would appreciate that.

'She's ill,' he said. 'A virus she caught in prison has jeopardised her kidneys. She needs a transplant.'

Talitha gave a small and rather cruel laugh. 'She's got no chance.'

'She knows that. She needs a private donor; someone whose body is compatible.'

'And again, she's got—'

'GCSE biology, Tal. We all did it. Remember that time we all found out our blood groups?'

Talitha was sharp as knives. She got it. 'Oh Jesus,' she said.

'Megan and I have the same blood group,' he told her, because maybe he needed to hear it said. 'We even joked about it. If we ever needed a donor, we had each other.'

Even in the moonlight, Talitha had visibly gone pale. 'You think she remembers?'

'I'm sure she does. Those favours we all agreed to? I think she's about to call mine in.'

# 18

Daniel had been lying when he'd told Megan that he didn't see much of the old gang. There had been a time, shortly after graduation, when the five of them had tried to go their separate ways, but in his early twenties, Daniel's mental health problems had kicked off. He lost interest in socialising, had trouble sleeping, even more getting out of bed in the morning. He rattled with the combination of uppers and downers he took daily and was on the point of quitting his job. His therapist, a lay Franciscan and the reason he eventually joined the order, told him he had unresolved issues dating back to his school days (well, no shit, Sherlock) and that sharing his feelings with others would help.

Amber had been the most welcoming, the others more reticent, but not one had refused to meet up, and since that first reunion, they'd all, gradually, coalesced around Oxford again. Tal had never really left, of course, and Felix's company was a mere fifteen miles away, but both Xav and Amber, with every reason to base themselves in London, chose to move out and commute.

They never talked about Megan, or what they'd done, although Dan was sure that summer was always on their minds, floating beneath the surface like some toxic weed. It helped, on some level he could never fully understand, to be around people who were as guilty as he.

He wondered now if they'd been waiting for exactly this: for Megan's return.

And so they met the following night, in The Perch at Binsey because it was rarely busy in the early evening, to make sure everyone was up to date with events and to start to form a plan, if they could. Daniel arrived first, by bike, followed by Felix in his Aston Martin.

When, sometime in the lower sixth, Felix had admitted his fondness for assigning elements from the periodic table to people he knew, and not necessarily to a pleased response (copper wasn't too bad, but iodine – fuck's sake!), the others, especially the two chemists, had wanted to know which Felix had given to himself. Preening, Felix had told them caesium, a silvery-gold alkali metal that was super-reactive, exploding on contact with water and burning rapidly. Caesium, he explained, was too hot to handle.

'Nah,' Megan had snapped back. 'You're fluorine, Felix. You kick off left, right and centre but you can't do a thing by yourself. You latch onto other people and you don't let anyone see the real you.' Xav had laughed like a drain and for a few months after, the two of them had re-christened their friend *Fluorix*.

The driver window of the Aston Martin rolled down. 'I'll be five, mate,' Felix called over. 'Get me a pint. And a bottle of white for the girls.'

Talitha and Xav arrived together a few minutes after Felix. Amber pitched up last, in her own car, not the one issued by the government, and came into the pub wearing sunglasses and a hat over hair that was still a very distinctive strawberry blonde. She refused the wine Felix was on the point of pouring and asked for mineral water instead.

'I can't be stopped for drink-driving.' She checked her phone and switched it off.

'Could be the least of your worries,' Talitha muttered.

Amber had been one of the first parliamentarians to embrace social media, and had built up a massive following, even among people who'd never dream of voting for her party. In a 280-character tweet, Amber could display an insight and a wit that was rarely apparent in her conversation. The others had speculated, a bit meanly, that she might have an intern handle her social media accounts. Xav had stamped out the idea.

'She's actually very funny,' he'd said. 'She just doesn't play to the gallery.'

It seemed odd, for someone who made no secret of wanting to be prime minister, but the others had taken his word for it.

'Dan, how sure are you?' Talitha asked, when the two of them had filled the others in with their two conversations with Megan. 'That she's only *pretending* to have lost her memory, I mean?'

'Eighty per cent.' The last twenty-four hours, Daniel had thought about little else. 'I think she was testing me, seeing if I would come clean. I didn't. I failed. When she spoke to Tal less than a couple of hours later, she was different.'

'She was pissed off,' Talitha added.

Xav said, 'You'd have been on edge, not thinking properly. Maybe you saw things that weren't really there.'

'And the accident was real?' Felix asked Talitha. 'She definitely had a bad head injury?'

'I've seen the medical reports,' Talitha replied. 'You can't fake those. No mention of amnesia though.'

'It could be true,' Xav said. 'We could be worrying unnecessarily.'

No one spoke.

'If she really has lost her memory, we're home and dry,' Felix said. 'We don't even have to release the trust fund. I can certainly use that cash.'

'We still would, though, wouldn't we?' Amber said. 'We'd still give it to her. It's the least we can do.'

Xav lowered his voice. 'Did she actually ask you to donate an organ?'

'No,' Daniel said. 'But she used the word *favour*. And she looked me right in the eye when she did so.'

'It's a common enough word,' Xav said.

'She was toying with me.'

Amber looked up. 'She can't ask that, Dan. She can't.'

'She can ask anything she likes,' Felix said. 'She has us by the short and curlies.'

The music stopped at that moment. Over the silence, they could hear the barman pulling glasses from a dishwasher. They sat, without speaking, until the music began again.

'So, what do we do?' Amber asked.

'Easy,' Felix said. 'Dan gives her a kidney. No big deal – people do it all the time.'

Felix and Daniel made eye contact across the table; the challenge in his eyes said, 'Come on then, argue.'

'No, he doesn't,' Talitha said, and Daniel had never felt so grateful for his oldest friend's resolve. 'If she's prepared to take pieces of Dan's body, what the hell will she want from the rest of us?'

Xav shuddered. For a moment he looked about to get to his feet. 'I'm all ears for the alternative plan, Tal,' he said.

Tal pulled her huge leather bag onto the table and reached inside. 'These are known as burner phones.' She placed a mobile phone in front of each of them. 'They work on different numbers to our regular phones and, this is the important bit, the numbers aren't traceable.'

'Why is mine green?' Felix asked, as Daniel noticed they had all been given coloured cases. His was dark blue.

'I've programmed all our numbers into each of them, so I had to be able to tell them apart,' Talitha answered. 'You'll also be able to distinguish them more easily from your personal phones. There's quite a lot of credit on each, but not unlimited, so don't use them for anything other than calling each other about this particular issue.' She looked around the group. 'Is that clear?'

Felix's face was a frown line away from a sneer. 'Is this really necessary?'

Talitha said, 'Of the two of us, Felix, who knows most about criminal behaviour and how the police monitor it?'

Daniel was pleased to see Felix hold up both hands in submission. He always enjoyed Tal's small victories over their mouthy mate.

Amber slipped hers into her bag. 'It's a good idea,' she said. 'I can never be sure my phone conversations aren't monitored as a matter of routine.'

Talitha was on a roll.

'If Megan starts making accusations, we can expect any police investigation to include confiscating all our tech,' she said. 'A sudden flurry of text messages and calls between us will look suspicious. Even when we use the burner phones, we shouldn't say anything incriminating.'

Lips pursed, Felix put the green phone in his jacket pocket. After a moment, Dan and Xav followed.

'We also need to be very careful where and when we meet,' Talitha went on. 'A sudden pattern of meeting up more than usual will look suspicious.' She looked around the bar. 'We don't come here again for another couple of months at least. Each time we meet, it's somewhere different, where we're not known, and where anything accidentally overheard won't create suspicion. Are we clear on that?'

No one argued.

'And we keep conversations to a minimum,' Talitha said. 'I know its uppermost in all of our minds right now, but we only talk when we have something to say. The rest of the time, we carry on exactly as normal.'

'Anything else?' Felix wasn't quite able to keep the sarcasm from his voice.

'Yes,' Talitha said. 'We need to find the proof. That's the alternative plan, Xav. We find the proof and we destroy it.'

The proof, something none of them had spoken of for years, that they might even have been trying to forget existed. Twenty years ago, in Talitha's pool house, they'd looked disaster in the face and been thrown a lifeline. They'd leapt for it, eagerly, shamelessly, and had been swinging ever since, unable to reach solid ground. And now, they had to think about the proof that, with its razor-sharp edges, was more than capable of cutting the lifeline clean through.

'After twenty years?' Amber said.

'I agree,' Talitha said. 'We should have done it back then. We were idiots, and we were in shock, but we're not now. Megan hid that letter and the photographs somewhere, and we have to find them. Without them, if she starts throwing accusations around, it's her word against ours and who are people going to believe?'

No one argued. A junior minister, the senior partner in a law firm, a self-made millionaire industrialist, an investment banker and the head teacher of one of the best performing schools in England. Their word against that of an ex-con child killer.

'She won't need proof,' Amber said. 'If this gets out, even as an unsubstantiated accusation, I'm finished.'

'Without proof, we won't be charged,' Talitha insisted. 'None of us will face prison time. None of us will lose our families or our livelihoods.'

'If Megan doesn't have proof, she won't push it,' Felix said.

'Especially when we offer her the money to stay quiet. She's not stupid.'

'She's a very long way from stupid,' Xav said. 'She was smarter than any of us back then, and she won't be a pushover, even now.'

'So where is it?' Talitha said. 'There were limited places she could hide it that night. She went to the police first thing next morning.'

'We searched her bedroom, remember?' Daniel said. 'It wasn't there.'

'Someone should have gone with her that night,' Felix said. 'I mean, we should have followed her.'

Amber said, 'None of us were thinking straight.'

'Except Megan,' Xav said.

Something occurred to Talitha. She said to Xav, 'You took her to her car that night. Did you notice anything? She didn't – I don't know – show an unusual interest in one of those big terracotta pots on the terrace?'

Xav spoke slowly as though trying to remember. 'She had the letter in her hand when she got in the car. She put it on the passenger seat. The film must have been in her pocket. And Dan's right, they weren't in her bedroom. I think she must have stopped off somewhere on the way home.'

'We need a map,' Amber said, but Felix was way ahead of her. He'd already opened Google Maps on his iPhone.

'Wherever she put it, it may still be there.' Talitha moved her chair around the table so that she could see the map of Oxfordshire. 'She's hardly had a chance to retrieve it since she's been back. Especially if she's been ill.'

Felix made a scissor movement on the screen to widen the map. 'It's a needle in a haystack,' he said. 'It's eleven miles from your old house to where she was living back then, and that's assuming she went straight home.'

'Her old back garden,' Amber suggested. 'Her mum sold the house, but she could climb over the fence to get it back.'

'Needle in a frigging haystack,' Felix repeated.

'I'm not suggesting we start treasure hunting,' Talitha said. 'I'm going to have her followed.'

'You can do that?' Amber asked.

'We're one of the most successful divorce law firms in the northern home counties,' Talitha said. 'We have miscreant spouses followed all the time. I can put a tail on Megan before the night's out.'

'Expensive,' Felix said.

'I'll reclaim it from the fund when we're home and dry.'

'Does anyone feel guilty about this?' Amber asked. 'I mean, Megan saved us and we're planning to shaft her all over again.'

Daniel couldn't help it. 'Wait till she comes for your vital organs.'

Amber didn't back down. 'If hers are damaged, it was because of what she did for us.'

'Fine, then you go under the knife,' Daniel said. 'You give the kidney that you might want to hang on to in case your husband or one of your kids needs it one day. Oh, I forgot, your blood group isn't the same, so you're off the hook.'

'Megan had less to lose than we did,' Felix said. 'She'd screwed up her exams. She wasn't going to Cambridge, and she almost certainly knew that. If anyone was going to take the rap for what happened, she was the obvious one.'

'I'm not sure she sees it that way,' Daniel said. 'We were supposed to stand by her. Tal's dad was supposed to be her solicitor, not act for her victims. If she's pissed off now, heaven help us when she learns about that.'

As he finished, he watched Amber's eyes widen and saw Xav's puzzled frown. Felix, he noticed, remained unmoved. So, not all information about Megan had been equally shared over the years.

'Dan makes a good point,' Talitha said. 'Although not the one he was intending to make.'

'What?' Amber said.

'She's going to want something from each of us. If we can't find the proof, we need to be prepared.'

'So, we give her the money,' Amber said. 'It's a lot of cash.'

Tal shook her head. 'I'm not sure it's going to be enough. I think she'll want something big. Something that hurts. You all need to start thinking what she might want of you.'

'I already know,' Xav said.

All eyes turned to him.

'She told me that night,' he went on. 'That's why she wanted me to walk her to the car.'

Amber said, 'You told me she had nothing special to say, that she just wanted some company.'

'She had plenty to say,' Xav said. 'She told me exactly what my favour was and made me swear I'd say nothing to any of you. If I told you, the deal was off.'

'What?' Talitha said. 'What did she want? What did you have to do?'

'Stay single,' Xav replied.

Daniel could see from the faces around him that none of them were following. Neither was he.

'I had to stay single until she was released from prison,' Xav went on.

'Why?' Amber had gone pale.

Ignoring the others, Xav directed his next words at Amber. They hadn't been an item for years, but Daniel was reminded then of how close they'd once been. 'She told me she loved me,' he said, as Amber's eyes opened wider. 'That she had done for years, and would have said something before, but then I started going out with you. She said that had all changed, that I had to break up with you and stay single.'

He picked up his drink and downed it. They gave him the time he seemed to need.

'She said she was going to prison for the best years of her life and would lose her chance to meet someone and fall in love. She said she didn't want to come out in her late thirties and be a sad, old spinster. So, I had to wait, and when she was out, I had to marry her. That was my favour.'

'But, you and Ella . . .' Amber began. 'Xav, you married Ella two years ago. What the hell were you thinking?'

Felix leaned back in his chair and gave a bitter, hollow laugh. 'Man,' he said. 'You are so fucked.'

# 19

They agreed to show up at Talitha's house that Saturday for Megan's welcome-home lunch. They had no choice. Daniel could usually organise his weekends to suit himself, but the others would all have to reorganise schedules, placate annoyed spouses, deal with difficult kids and invent a dozen excuses afterwards. It didn't matter; they had no choice.

Talitha's home was an ultra-modern construction on a wide, tree-lined road north of the city centre. Most of the other houses dated back a hundred years or more, but somehow Talitha had got permission to knock down the Edwardian mansion and erect her own monument in concrete, coloured glass and granite. Her white Range Rover stood on the drive next to her husband's larger model in steel grey. A scattering of mud-encrusted rugby boots lay around the front step, and Daniel could hear young voices from an open upstairs window. Talitha had no children of her own, but her husband had three sons from his first marriage.

The disarray of youth was at odds with the pristine landscaping of the front garden and the gleaming front elevation of the house, but comforting at the same time. This too, it seemed to say, is a normal family home, and in normal family homes terrible things don't happen.

Daniel, wheeling his bike up the drive, told himself to hold on to that thought.

He was about to ring when he heard tyres on the gravel and turned to see a black electric BMW pulling up. He didn't recognise the car, but it turned out to belong to Sarah, Felix's wife – a tall, rather plain blonde with Pony Club manners. Daniel watched Felix reach into the back seat for their two-year-old son, Luke, as Xav climbed out of the other side.

No sign of Ella, Xav's wife.

Barely had the four of them reached Daniel when another vehicle pulled in, this one a massive black Volvo with Dexter, Amber's Afro-Caribbean husband at the wheel. With the ease of long practice, he executed a three-point turn so that the vehicle might be ready for a quick getaway, and then he too turned to help his children out of the car.

While none of her friends would have suggested for a moment that Amber married Dex to help her career, being part of a glamorous, mixed-race couple had done her no harm. Together with two of the prettiest little girls imaginable, Amber and her brood were poster children for the modern British family.

The two families turned to greet each other, the mothers to exclaim over the children, the three men to exchange handshakes, and Daniel had his customary moment of feeling left out. The world of the family was one from which he was permanently excluded. He rang the bell and Mark, Talitha's husband, answered immediately.

'Good game?' Daniel had no interest in rugby but had learned from experience that Mark could talk of little else. He could smell the outdoors on the other man; also the glass of red wine he held in one hand.

'Bloody excellent.' Already Mark was looking over Daniel's shoulder for the more interesting arrivals. 'Marlborough College. Wiped the floor with us last season, couldn't get a try past us this morning.'

From upstairs came an explosion of sound that managed to sound feral and electronic at the same time.

'How many have you got up there?' Daniel was used to the exuberance of Talitha's stepsons but they seemed to be taking it to another level that morning.

'Five,' Mark told him. 'One of Gus's friends did something to his knee and I sent him to A and E. We've got his brothers. Come on, you all know the way – you come here often enough.'

Daniel hung up his coat, turned to say hello properly to the others and braced himself for the usual ritual of hugging and cheek-kissing. A lifetime of celibacy had trained him to avoid physical contact, but he'd never managed to make the others understand that. The women seemed to feel they were doing him a favour with their tactile behaviour. When they finally let him be, he followed Mark through to the large kitchen at the back of the house.

Large, though, was an understatement; it was a huge space, stretching up two floors and constructed of floor-to-ceiling glass. Impossibly hot in summer, in Daniel's view, it was tolerable in late spring.

'Could have done without this,' Mark muttered. 'I'm on call, and Tal can't manage my three on her own let alone with a houseful of guests.' He glanced Daniel's way. 'No offence. I'm certain we saw you all the other week though. Too much of a good thing.'

Daniel was used to Mark. He meant well, and besides, he was inclined to agree.

'No Ella?' Daniel asked Xav as the others piled in behind.

Xav shook his head. 'I told her it was a work thing.'

Talitha, at the kitchen counter, turned to face them and her smile barely broke the rigid set of her jaw. Her hair was scraped up, out of the way, and the style didn't suit her. It left her face looking too large, too angular. She hadn't even bothered with make-up. Daniel was about to approach her when the women and children flowed past him to engage in more hugging. Freeing herself from Sarah, Tal came over to him.

'She's here already,' she whispered in his ear. 'Don't look round.' She moved swiftly away; Daniel saw her leaning to kiss Xav and knew she was saying the same thing to him.

*Don't look round? What the hell did that mean?* Turning to talk to Felix and Sarah, Daniel saw something in the periphery of his vision. Lifting his head, he found her.

The most notable feature of Talitha and Mark's grand design was a wide internal balcony running the entire width of the house. From the ground floor, Daniel could see the upstairs landing behind a half-wall of reinforced glass and, leading off it, five bedroom doors. Standing in its centre, looking down at them, was Megan. Daniel's first thought was that she looked so much better. Her hair had been freshly washed, held back from her face by a pair of red sunglasses. Knowing what he did now about her feelings for Xav, he realised she'd made an effort for his friend that she hadn't felt necessary for him.

'What you staring at?' Felix followed Daniel's gaze and then, one by one, the others noticed – Talitha was already there, of course – and they all looked up, like players on a stage, at their one-woman audience.

'Who's that, Mummy?' Amber's oldest asked.

'I'm Megan,' she replied. 'Hello, everyone.'

Megan's skin was still pale but had lost the horrible yellow tinge he'd seen when she'd come to the school. Better dressed, she looked fashionably slim, not anorexic and angular. She was even wearing make-up and Daniel had a moment to feel very grateful that he was not Xav.

'Don't hide away up there on your own,' Mark called. 'Come on down.'

Megan waited a second longer and then walked the length of the balcony before vanishing onto the staircase.

'Who's this?' Felix's wife, Sarah, asked.

'Old school friend,' Felix said.

Talitha sidled close to Daniel. 'She decided to show herself around,' she hissed in his ear. 'She's been acting like she owns the place.'

'Maybe that's your favour,' Daniel couldn't resist replying. 'Maybe she fancies your house.'

He almost felt guilty at the stricken look on Talitha's face.

'Does Mark know?' he asked. 'Who she is, I mean?'

She shook her head and shrugged. Exactly – what would she say? They'd all work it out eventually though: Mark, Sarah, Ella and Dex. He was lucky, in a way, that he had no one he'd need lie to. God didn't count. He already knew.

Megan's heels sounded on the pale stone floor and she reappeared. Determined to prolong the grand entrance as long as she could, she stared at them all from the doorway.

'"There is no friend like an old friend who has shared our morning days",' she said. '"No greeting like his welcome, no homage like his praise".'

'Who's that?' Felix asked, a little too loudly. 'Shakespeare?'

'Oliver Wendell Holmes Senior,' Megan replied. 'Hello, Felix, did you miss me?'

Daniel had a sense, then, of them all standing on a jetty, looking out over a freezing lake, knowing they needed to jump and putting it off for as long as they could. Felix went first, which should have surprised no one, and Megan vanished inside his hug. One arm around her waist, he steered her towards Sarah and little Luke. For the rest of them, it felt like a stay of execution, but Felix was never one to sacrifice himself for long.

'You remember your bestie.' He pulled Amber forward. 'We

call her the Right Honourable Lady now. And we all pretend we vote for her party; she gets mean if we don't. This is Dex, her long-suffering, and the two adorables, Gunmetal and Tungsten.'

'Pearl and Ruby!' the girls chorused. Felix had been doing this for years, but they never seemed to tire of it. He was being too jolly, trying too hard, but Daniel couldn't exactly blame him; none of them knew how they should behave.

Megan had run a finger fondly down the toddler's cheeks, but at the sight of the girls she seemed to melt. Dropping to her knees, she held out a hand to each of them. 'Well, you are too beautiful,' she said. 'How old are you?'

'Five,' Pearl told her. 'Ruby's three. Who are you?'

'I'm an old friend of your mummy's.' Megan stood up and reached out for Amber, who didn't move, and there followed an awkward embrace of arms and hair while their bodies, even their faces, remained inches apart.

'This is so sweet of you all.' There were tears in Megan's eyes as she smiled round at them. 'I'm so grateful.'

'And Xav, of course.' Felix seemed determined to act as ring-master. 'Step up, Xav, take your seat at the table.'

Daniel felt the group bracing itself as Megan and Xav's eyes met.

'Talking of which, I'm starving.' Mark's hands landed, one on Daniel's shoulder, the other on Xav's, effectively cutting off whatever greeting Megan had in mind for her one true love.

They sat around Talitha's huge glass table and tried to do justice to the lunch she'd organised. She'd had caterers in, of course – Tal had never cooked a meal in her life – and it was typically fabulous: salads gleaming with fruits and vegetables, a giant ham with a sweet, blackened crackling, a whole brie garlanded with figs and honeycomb, peppered fried chicken. Apart from the five teenage boys though, none of them could eat much.

Daniel had been worried the conversation would be stilted, that no one would know what to say, that they'd have not so much an elephant as a mammoth in the room. To his surprise, it was anything but, even though the five old friends took little part in it. Megan was the life and soul. She talked school rugby to Mark, horses to Sarah and the perils of being a parliamentary widower to Dexter, and you had to admire her, really, because every word that came out of her mouth had to be bullshit.

She said nothing to Xav, he noticed, possibly because Tal had tactfully seated him on the same side of the table, several places down – eye contact between the two of them was tricky. Xav, for his part, spoke hardly at all, checking his phone from time to time, once leaving the room to take a call that Daniel felt sure was from Ella, eating next to nothing.

'So, how do you know this bunch?' Mark asked Megan at one point. Daniel was sure he'd been told already that she was an old school friend, but Mark rarely absorbed information that didn't affect him directly.

'I was at All Souls',' Megan replied.

'Megan was head of school.' It was the first time Amber had spoken, other than whispers to her daughters, for the better part of an hour.

'I was a scholarship girl,' Megan said. 'It was a token appointment really, a chance for the posh private school to flash its progressive credentials. One pupil in a hundred was a peasant, so they made the peasants as prominent as they could.'

'That isn't true,' Xav said quickly.

Megan leaned forward across the table so that, turning her head, she could see Xav. They stared at each other for a second. Xav had taken off his wedding ring.

'No, you were the smartest of all of us,' Amber added quickly.

'So, where've you been all these years?' Mark, thankfully, seemed oblivious to the tensions around the table. 'Abroad? More ham anyone?' He picked up the carving knife and waved it in the air.

'I'll have some,' Felix held his plate out, even though he hadn't eaten most of what was on there already. His glass, on the other hand, was empty.

'Me too,' Daniel said in solidarity. 'Actually, give me a sec to finish this lot. Fabulous, Tal, as always.'

'What's Cooking in Summertown,' Tal said. 'Never let me down.'

'I've been in the north-east,' Megan told Mark. 'In Durham.'

'Lovely place.' Mark turned to Daniel. 'You were at uni there, weren't you?'

Daniel's mouth was full of unchewed ham; he could only nod.

'Amber's having a birthday party in a few weeks,' Dex said to Megan. 'You should come. I'll send you the details.'

Daniel could have laughed at the horror on the faces around him, and probably would have done if he hadn't been feeling the same way. Amber's parties were always fancy affairs: black tie, marquee on the lawn, the great and good of the local party showing off their titles and tiaras. Megan wouldn't be the first law breaker to attend by any stretch of the imagination, but there's a big difference, when you're close to government, between creative accounting and mowing down a young family in the dark.

For several seconds, they could only hear the electronic beeping from the kids' devices. Talitha poured wine into glasses that were already full, Amber wiped a non-existent mark from Ruby's mouth, Felix checked his phone and Daniel caught Mark and Dex exchanging puzzled glances.

'How kind,' Megan said. 'I'd love to.'

'Any luck replacing your accountant?' Xav asked Felix, and the table seemed to sigh with relief at a new topic. Felix's head of finance had left him in the lurch a couple of weeks ago. He shook his head. 'Plenty of applicants – none I'd consider up to the job.'

'You can contract it out, can't you?' Mark said. 'We use a local firm. I can give you their details.'

'I can, and I have been, but it costs a bloody arm and a leg.' Felix put his knife and fork down as though relieved at an excuse to stop trying to eat. 'And I'm already stretched with the new factory in Uganda. The trouble is, we're too close to London. All the decent ones commute in for double what I can justify paying.'

'In the meantime, Felix's doing it all himself,' Sarah chipped in. 'He's working every night till nearly midnight. Luke's started bursting into tears when he sees his own father.'

'I wouldn't go that far,' Felix grumbled.

'I would,' Sarah snapped, and there followed that awkward moment, when a couple have overshared in public.

'I'll do it,' Megan said.

And the awkward moment went into orbit.

'I have a degree in finance and accountancy.' She waited for one of the others to react. When they didn't, she picked up her wine glass and looked around at them over the rim. 'What?' she said. 'You thought I'd waste twenty years in prison?'

Sarah gasped. The boys at the end of the table, who'd been engrossed with mobile phones, fell quiet. Even five-year-old Pearl's eyes widened as she mouthed the word *prison* to herself.

'You were in prison?' one of the boys said.

'What for?' another asked.

Megan opened her mouth.

'No.' It was rare for Amber to raise her voice, but when she did, they were all reminded of why people were seriously talking about her as a future prime minister. 'This is not the place.'

Talitha got to her feet. 'Boys, you and your friends can have dessert in the games room.'

The five boys, reluctant to leave the drama, began to argue. 'I mean it,' Talitha warned. 'Take Pearl and Ruby and look after them.'

A brittle silence held while the kids helped themselves to dessert and left the room. Talitha checked the door was properly closed. Still no one spoke. Luke squawked and Sarah got up.

Megan said, 'You must remember how good I was at maths, Felix. Well, turns out I'm equally good at finance. And I can start on Monday.'

As Megan spoke, she lifted her sunglasses from the top of her head and shook her hair out, before folding them beside her plate. Her evident self-possession, though, seemed at odds with the sunglasses, the ends of which were chewed and discoloured.

'I mean Tuesday,' she said. 'Monday's May Day, of course. A bank holiday this year – should be madder than usual.'

'Tal, what's in this?' Sarah said, as she peered over a bowl of what looked like trifle. 'Can I give it to Luke?' She looked at her husband, though, not Talitha, and even Daniel could read the message in her eyes.

'Oh, Christ no – it's laced with brandy!' Tal stared towards the games-room door. 'I've just given the kids hard liquor.'

Amber gave a soft squeak and turned an alarmed face to Dex.

'So, we'll have a quiet afternoon,' Mark shrugged. 'Won't do 'em any harm.'

'Easy for you to say,' Amber snapped back. 'Your youngest probably weighs more than I do. Ruby's only three.' She got to her feet. 'Honestly, Tal.'

'They'll be fine.' Dex, whom Daniel had never seen ruffled, took hold of his wife's hand. 'Sit down.'

'What do you think, Felix?' Megan said.

'What about this tart thing then? Is this safe?' Sarah's voice had grown shrill.

'Oh, for God's sake, Sarah, it's not my responsibility to feed your child,' Talitha snapped.

Xav closed his eyes, as though he could make the whole scene go away.

'I'll take ten grand a year less than you're offering.' Megan addressed Felix as though theirs was the only conversation in the room. 'But only for the first six months. By that time, I'll have more than proved myself.'

Felix said, 'How do you know what I'm paying?'

'You were advertising on LinkedIn and the *FT*,' Megan replied. 'It's hardly a secret.'

*Surely one of the others will step in now*, thought Dan, *give Felix a hand?* It was a bit like watching a snake stalking a rat, though; they couldn't take their eyes off it.

'Meg, if you need money, I'm happy to help,' Felix said. 'I can get you back on your feet again.' He glanced around at the rest of them and the words *trust fund* seemed to dart around the group like a telepathic message. Xav nodded his head slowly, silently giving Felix permission.

'We should discuss this,' Sarah muttered.

'I don't want a loan, I want a job,' Megan said.

'Not a good idea,' Sarah repeated.

'It's quite specialist,' Felix said.

'Not really. Your annual turnover is fourteen million pounds, operating profit margin is seven per cent, and you've been growing ten per cent a year, which is all good. Problem is, you haven't thought through your strategy for financing the growth. As the business has grown, the finished goods stock has expanded, as has the credit offered to your customers. All this needs finance and, in short, you're running out of cash, which is why you're late paying suppliers and your credit rating is slipping. Don't you remember the old accountants' saying: "Turnover is vanity, profit is sanity and cash is reality"?'

'How do you know all this?' Felix looked stunned.

'You file your company accounts every year and your credit rating is listed on Dun and Bradstreet. You have a website, several social media accounts. It's not hard.'

'I want to know why you were in prison.' Dex grinned around the table, as though to give the impression he was joking. They all knew he wasn't. 'I may have to reconsider the invitation to my wife's party.'

Amber found her bag. 'Let's talk on the way back,' she said to her husband. 'Tal, thank you, but I think we need to get the girls home.'

'Actually, maybe I should be—' Daniel began.

'Twenty years ago, I stole Felix's mother's car and drove it the wrong way down the M40,' Megan said. 'I hit a car and killed the three passengers, two of whom were very young children.'

Sarah clutched her son a little tighter.

'Shit, that's who you are.' Mark gave his wife a 'What the fuck?' look.

'Was it an accident?' Dexter asked.

'No, Dex, because nobody gets the sentence I did for an accident, at least not unless someone powerful is trying to stitch them up.'

Megan didn't look at Talitha as she spoke, which was probably as well, because Talitha had turned the colour of a corpse.

'I did it for fun,' Megan went on. 'For a laugh, I did it a lot – there was CCTV footage to prove it. I was reckless and dangerous, and I was sent down for twenty years. At eighteen years old, imagine that.'

Xav got to his feet. 'I need some air,' he announced, before striding out of the room.

'Did you know?' Dex said to his wife. 'I mean, at the time. Did you know she was doing that?'

'Oh no,' Megan jumped in. 'None of my friends had any idea. They were out of their heads on drugs that summer – they had no idea about the dark little games I was playing.'

She got to her feet and leaned over Amber's shoulders. 'Probably not information you want in the public arena. Don't worry, I can be discreet.'

'Come at eight o'clock.' Felix spoke with his eyes closed. 'I'll have some time to show you the ropes before most people get in. We'll give it a try.'

# 20

A short while before dawn on May Day, thousands of the city's residents left their beds to listen to Magdalen College choir sing from its famous tower to welcome in the spring. As usual, Daniel was one of them; as usual, he wished he could be anywhere else in the world.

Daniel hated May Day. He hated the forced jollity and the sense of being in a crowd that had no beginning and no end; he hated the pools of vomit on the pavement and the girls in torn ball gowns fast asleep on street benches; he hated the blanket of litter left behind and the sheer bloody cost of policing it. Nevertheless, as master of one of the principal schools in Oxford, he had a standing invitation to the May Day breakfast at Magdalen College.

He took a call as he was approaching Magdalen Bridge. It was Tal. He could barely hear her above the noise in the background, which told him that she, too, was in the city centre. He was running late, didn't really have time to talk, and the crowd ahead had merged into an impenetrable mass.

'Where are you?' He squeezed his way towards a wild-haired, green-faced bloke throwing blossom into the air.

'By the covered market,' Tal replied. 'I've lost Mark and the kids. Bit of luck, I won't find them again.'

'How was it after I left?' he asked.

SHARON BOLTON

After Felix had agreed to give Megan a job, she'd seemed exhausted by her victory, and Daniel had called an Uber to get her back to her bedsit near Iffley Road.

'Amber and Dex left close behind you,' Talitha replied, 'acting as though I'd poisoned their kids, and the others went soon after, Sarah giving Felix some serious grief.'

The green-faced man had two stag-like antlers protruding from his head. He had his back to Daniel and there seemed no feasible way around him.

'Mark is livid,' Talitha was saying. 'The boys found coverage of the accident on the internet. He can't understand why I invited her to the house.'

'You didn't say anything, did you?' Daniel sidestepped onto someone's foot. His face came up against a mass of hawthorn blossoms; already they were on the turn and stank of piss.

Talitha said, 'What do you take me for?'

'Tal, we need a plan. We can't let her blackmail us like this.'

'What if she's not blackmailing us, though? What if she really can't remember? If we keep our nerve, it could all settle down again.'

It was impossible to move forward by this stage, the crowd having become a solid mass of flesh and bone. Daniel pushed his way sideways until he was right up against the steel barriers that kept people away from the bridge wall. On the other side was a narrow walkway, lined with security guards.

'We need to give her the money,' he said.

'Giving her the money could be what jogs her memory. Shit, they've found me. I'll call you later.'

Directly in front of Daniel, a young man with glazed eyes and an Eastern European accent was arguing with one of the security guards for permission to leap from the bridge.

'You have to let me,' he said. 'I am a professional.'

The guard shook his head.

In the old days, students, often still in the formal dress of the previous night's balls, marked May Day by leaping from Magdalen Bridge into the river below. More than one jumper had been seriously injured though, and for as long as Daniel could remember, jumping had been banned. That morning, the line of security staff resembled a presidential visit.

'I have done it before,' the young man tried.

Another headshake from the massive guard. Daniel pulled his invitation card from his inside pocket and held it out.

'Can you help me out?' he called to the guard. 'I have to be in the college in five minutes.'

The guard took his time, took in the smart suit, which didn't look like he'd been wearing it all night, and the gown, and then shrugged. 'You'll have to climb over,' he said.

Daniel stepped up onto the barrier, took the guard's offered arm and leapt for it. The guard caught him and Daniel managed to get himself, and his gown, over.

'Hey, how come he is allowed to jump? Who is he, anyway? Batman?'

'Thanks, mate,' Daniel said.

On the river side of the barrier, he could make his way quickly to the other side of Magdalen Bridge. He was within spitting distance of the college when he heard his name being called.

'Dan!'

He couldn't believe it. Megan was waiting by the entrance, formally dressed in a blue suit and heeled shoes. 'I was beginning to think you weren't coming,' she went on and for a moment, Daniel was completely lost. Had he invited her to meet him here?

'Good morning, Master.' The porter on duty moved the barrier aside to let Daniel through.

He hadn't, of course, but he had been talking to Xav about the

May Day celebrations on Saturday. She'd overheard them.

'Lovely day, sir. This lady with you?'

Daniel opened his mouth to say no, but Megan was steering him along the short, cobbled path and into the main quad.

'You don't mind, do you?' she whispered into his ear. 'I've always wanted a closer look.'

The quad was packed with people.

'What fun,' Megan said. 'Do we go up the tower? I expect the view is something else, especially today.'

'We wouldn't fit.' Daniel stopped short of the crowd. He'd already spotted several people he knew and did not want to be forced into introductions. 'Megan, what are you doing here?'

Her excited face fell, like that of a reprimanded child. 'I needed to talk to you,' she replied. 'Saturday was a bit awkward.'

'What did you expect?'

She opened her mouth to respond as the clock chimed the hour. Beyond the walls, the chatter of the crowd settled into a buzz of excitement and more than one shout rang out. In the quad, every head turned upwards and Daniel was glad to do the same. At 144 feet, Magdalen Tower was the tallest building in Oxford. On its platform, beyond the high balustrade, Daniel could see robed figures between the gaps in the stonework.

The clock chimed four, five and six times. There followed a split second when the city held its breath and then the choir began to sing the *'Hymnus Eucharisticus'*.

*'Te Deum Patrem colimus, Te laudibus prosequimur . . .'*

Amplified, soaring into the sky, the centuries-old hymn was magnificent, and Daniel could never hear its opening verse without tears springing into his eyes. Normally, he joined in quietly – it was a piece he loved – but he couldn't bring himself to do so in front of Megan.

'Can you understand it?' she whispered.

He had a doctorate in classics – of course he could understand it.

'We adore you, O Jesus, you, the only begotten Son,' he translated from the Latin for her as the choir reached the second verse.

The hymn came to an end. A deafening cheer rang out from the high street and Daniel saw a helium balloon, blue as the sky, float up over the tower. Airplanes had started to fly, and vapour trails cut across the blue like mathematical drawings. Up on the tower, the rector of the college began to read the opening verse of Genesis, about how God made the world and, especially, the light.

'And the earth was without form, and void, and darkness was upon the face of the deep.'

A shudder grabbed a hold of Dan's whole body; even Megan noticed and looked at him in surprise.

'Let us pray,' the rector announced, and, in the quad, every head lowered for a prayer about the waking of the spring and the return of the light, and Daniel realised at last why he hated May Morning. It was a celebration of the end of winter; a ceremony to mark the return of all that was good and light and strong in the world. But for those who lived their lives in darkness, there would be no return to the light. Daniel had spent twenty years looking for redemption and each springtime saw it slipping from his reach. And the woman beside him, if not the cause of that, was its living symbol.

He didn't hear much more after that. The choir sang three madrigals, and he didn't doubt they were as lovely as always. He watched several more blue balloons sail towards the heavens and they seemed to Daniel to be prayers, climbing ever upwards in search of a kindly ear. His prayers would never fly, he realised that morning; they were destined forever to be earthbound.

In paying the price that should have been his, Megan had stolen his redemption.

They watched the choir return to earth and applauded their journey across the quad. They were no longer angels, just kids and young men with good voices, and they wanted their breakfast.

'Can we go up?' Megan asked, meaning the tower.

There was no reason why not, now that the choir had come down, and the queue into breakfast would take some time, so Daniel led the way and they climbed the narrow spiral staircase.

'It was beautiful,' Megan said, when they reached the parapet. 'That bit about the birth of an early morning, welcoming the light after a long darkness. It felt like it was spoken just for me.'

Most people turned north-west when they climbed Magdalen Tower at dawn, to see the turrets, pinnacles and spires in the early sun, but Megan went to the southern edge. Daniel joined her and they looked down at the people on the high street. Like a block of ice melting at the edges, the crowd was starting to drift away. It would take time, though; there could be twenty thousand people in the city centre and most wouldn't be hurrying. They'd be heading into the nearby pubs, maybe to watch the morris dancing at St Giles. The carnival atmosphere would last for the next few hours at least.

Megan turned east, squinting into the sun. He opened his mouth to tell her he had her sunglasses, which she'd left behind at Tal's on Saturday.

'I don't have anyone else,' Megan said, without looking up.

Dan waited.

'You and the others, you're all I have,' she said. 'One doesn't make friends in prison, one forms alliances, and allies. Even those who are outside now, are no use to me any more. I won't live the life of an ex-con, Dan.'

*No, you want to steal our lives.* It was a thought in his head, nothing more; he wouldn't have dreamed of uttering it.

'What about your family?' he said instead.

She glanced around at him. 'Mum died, didn't you hear?'

He hadn't. But then he'd made no attempt to keep in touch with Megan's mother.

He shook his head. 'I'm sorry, I didn't know.'

'I think I wrote to you at the time. To one of you at least, but by then I was resigned to none of you writing back. Did you even read them, Dan?'

'Meg,' he sighed. 'It was a long time ago.'

'I'm not going to quietly slip away, you know,' she said. 'You and the others, you need to accept that. One way or another, I'm coming back into your lives.'

'You don't know what—' he stopped. He'd been about to say, you don't know what you're asking, except maybe she did. Maybe she knew exactly what she was asking; and had yet to ask of them.

'Do you really remember nothing about that summer?' he asked.

Megan looked him directly in the eyes and he thought, *This is it, she's going to come clean now*. Instead, she shook her head in the gesture that was becoming familiar, like she was trying to dislodge something that was stuck inside it.

'I'll tell you what it's like,' she said, and her face was screwed up in concentration. 'I want you to picture something, close your eyes.'

Dan did what he was told; he couldn't see any choice.

'A child's bicycle goes rolling into a pond,' Megan said. 'There's no one riding it – don't worry. It breaks the surface, sending frantic ripples racing to the edges, and then it topples, landing flat among some reeds.'

There was something about Megan's voice that was almost calming. Daniel felt as though she was telling him a story, one she'd rehearsed many times.

'There it remains,' she went on. 'Winter comes and the pond

freezes over. The bike is captured in ice. One of the handlebars, the spokes of most of the front wheel and part of the seat remain above the surface, the rest is below. We can see but not touch it. It's inaccessible. You can open your eyes now, Dan.'

He did. She'd moved a little closer to him. He wanted to take a step away but was right up against the stone wall of the parapet.

'That's what my memory's like of that summer,' she said. 'Parts of it I can recall clear as day, but the rest? I know it's there, I can almost see it beneath the surface, I just can't get to it. That's how it is for the murder. I know I killed Sophie Robinson and her children. It's all in my head, I just can't find it.'

She spun around and stepped away, back to the edge but further from Daniel; he thought, *She's not lying, she really doesn't remember. We're safe.*

Leaning out again, Megan looked down. 'What's with the green costumes?' she asked. 'They're a bit scary.'

'People have been dressing up in green for hundreds of years,' Daniel told her. 'It represents nature, rebirth, the springtime.'

From the quad below came a whiff of bacon. He was on the point of suggesting they go down for breakfast.

'Paganism,' she said. 'On such a Christian morning.'

'You'll find churches all over Europe sporting images of the green man,' Daniel said. 'The lines between Christianity and paganism are notoriously and endlessly blurred. Look, do you want to go—'

He was stepping towards the ladder.

'I'm going to try hypnosis,' she said.

Daniel stopped moving. 'I'm sorry?'

'I'm going to be hypnotised. See if I can't find some of those memories I've locked away.'

His appetite was gone.

'Are you sure?' he managed. 'I mean, what would you gain?

You know it happened, you paid the price. You can move on now, surely? Put it behind you. We'll help you. Actually, there's been something I've been meaning to—'

'But that's the point, I can't put it behind me until I understand,' she said. 'I need to know what made me do such a stupid thing. When I had my whole life ahead of me, and such great friends. We were going to conquer the world, weren't we? Why would I throw that away?'

She was so very convincing.

'I can't move on,' she said. 'Not until I can remember exactly what happened that summer.'

She could be telling the truth. On the other hand, maybe she remembered everything and was torturing him. He had no way of knowing for sure.

And then a thought came out of nowhere, so unlike him that Dan could have believed it had been implanted by aliens. Megan was standing by one of the pinnacles. Only her head and shoulders would be visible from below, if anyone were still looking up, and most people wouldn't be.

He'd thought of a way of bringing everything to a close, of ensuring that they were completely safe, now and always. All he had to do was run at Megan, grab hold of her by her ankles, lift and tip. She'd plummet 144 feet to the hard stone below.

And that would be that.

# 21

Felix's office was on the upper floor of the industrial unit, facing north over a car park and feeder road, a mile outside Thame town centre. He watched a bus pull up at the stop a hundred yards away but couldn't see who'd got off. There were too many trees in the way.

He forced himself away from the window and poured his second cup of coffee. He drank it white, with full-fat milk and two sugars. When he was alone, he added a dessertspoon of Irish whiskey from a bottle he kept at the back of the locked cupboard in his desk. He didn't keep a dessertspoon and in his more honest moments, acknowledged that the dessertspoon had morphed over the years into a tablespoon, possibly a serving spoon and, by the time the morning was out, would probably be the measure of a fucking soup ladle.

He drank, feeling the familiar warmth spreading from his heart outwards, calming his nerves, smoothing out the trembling. After an hour, it would be back, of course. It would help if he could eat, soak up some of the alcohol, but his appetite, poor for years, had dwindled to non-existence since the news of Megan's release.

And now here she was, walking towards the front door of his factory, wearing a green belted raincoat and carrying a bag over her left shoulder. She stumbled as she stepped off the kerb, almost over-balancing, and it lightened his heart to see her vulnerable.

He swallowed down his coffee and grabbed a couple of mints from a packet he always kept on his desk, before running down the stairs. It was too early for anyone to be at the front desk, and he had to unlock the door to let her in.

'You made it?' he said.

'As you see.'

'Get the bus all right? Not too crowded?'

She gave him a look that was half amused, half pitying, but still he continued to make stupid small talk as he showed her to the desk she would use in the general office on the upper floor, not too far from his own room, and then took her on a tour around the building.

'This is Megan,' he said to the warehouse staff who always arrived first. 'She'll be with us for a while, sorting out the accounts. Time someone did, I know.'

He was conscious of odd looks as he left the warehouse behind, but maybe with Megan beside him he was more perceptive than usual; maybe the odd looks had been there for some time. From the warehouse, they walked through the stock rooms and here, among the products, rather than the people, he felt a little easier. Chemicals didn't judge. There had to be five hundred or more unique compounds on the shelves in front of him, and he understood the precise formula of each. The compounds spoke to him; he understood them in a way he never would people.

'We're sourcing materials from extreme environments for our male grooming range,' he said, as Megan lingered by the shelves. 'I'm stoked about this. Listen, for a plant to survive in some of the toughest conditions on earth, it has to develop its own natural protective compounds. We harvest them and turn them into active ingredients in the products. The idea of thriving in harsh environments is an absolute gift when it comes to marketing to the male psyche.'

He leaned over and took a small plastic bottle from the shelf behind Megan, turning it so she could see the name and formula on the label. 'Black crowberry juice from Lapland,' he told her.

Megan made an impressed face. 'What does it do? Apart from appealing to the male psyche?'

'Improves microcirculation and increases skin firmness,' he told her. 'Our clients – L'Oréal, Unilever, Proctor and Gamble – they buy this from us, with advice on how it can be assimilated, and use it in their own products.'

He put the bottle back on the shelf. 'This is perlite.' He took up another bottle. 'Natural volcanic glass.'

'Exfoliant?' Megan asked.

For a split second, Felix was reminded that he'd once liked Megan, rather a lot in fact; she was the only person he'd ever met whose passion for chemistry came close to his own. 'Exactly,' he said.

She fell behind as he led the way out. 'That's a lot of sodium hydroxide,' she said, looking at a stack of drums in one corner of the room.

Felix made a face. 'Cock up,' he admitted. 'They should have gone to the new factory in Uganda. It's where our soap range is being made. I need to get them returned.'

The folk in the lab, PhDs all, gave him curious looks as he steered Megan around the fume cupboard, the row of homogenisers and the centrifuge, but he'd already started to suspect that *they* had started to suspect that his drinking might be teetering on the edge of out of control. His voice was too loud, and he was laughing too much. The only person in the company to seem unperturbed was Megan, who walked beside him as composed as a visiting royal.

'Cosmetics?' she said, when they were back at her desk and he'd made her coffee. He didn't think he'd ever made a member of staff coffee before. He'd poured them drinks, of course, at Christmas, but coffee? No.

'Personal care products,' he corrected. 'Cosmetics are what women, usually, put on their faces. We work on the entire range of personal care – deodorants, moisturisers, hair-removing creams, self-tanning products – but it's really all about the chemistry.'

She smiled, and he would have given anything to know what she was thinking. He remembered that the two of them had often worked together in the school labs. Not when Xav was around, of course.

'OK, right. All outstanding invoices are in this tray. I've put the accounting system password on your desk.'

She said, 'I always knew you'd do well, Felix.'

'Thanks. But, you know, we all did. I mean, who would have thought Amber—'

She interrupted him. 'But you're the one with the big bucks.'

The Scotch was definitely wearing off. He'd need another shot before the hour was up. 'Oh, I wouldn't say that. The factory in Uganda's been a big stretch. Xav's doing OK. He doesn't talk about his bonuses, but we're pretty sure he doesn't have a mortgage on that place he and Ella have bought on St John Street.'

Megan's eyes fell and he felt sure she was mentally storing away Xav's address. He'd been stupid to give it away, but she'd have found it sooner or later, one way or another. In his pocket, his phone buzzed. The green-cased burner phone that Talitha had given him. He glanced at the screen. Daniel.

'Do you have everything you need?' he asked Megan. 'Take your time, I'm not expecting immediate results. Get a feel for the place. Pay day isn't for another two weeks, so don't worry about the salary run today.'

'What's his wife like?' Megan intended her voice to sound

casual, he could tell; it didn't quite come off. 'I bet she's super glam, like Sarah.'

She was flattering him, and his wife. Sarah was attractive enough, in an ageing Boden-catalogue model kind of way, but a long way from 'super glamourous'. A long way from Ella.

His green phone buzzed again. Xav, this time.

'You'll have to judge for yourself,' he said, and was conscious of the spite creeping into his mind, if not his voice. 'I'm sure you'll meet her before long.'

'When did he and Amber split up?' Megan asked.

For a second Felix was tempted to accept the call from Xav and hand him over; let Xav explain himself to the woman scorned. 'Not long after we all went to uni,' he said instead.

'Who dumped who?'

He put his phone away. 'He broke it off with her in the first term. She was gutted. She went up to Cambridge a couple of times to try and sort it out. I know because she stayed with Talitha at Downing and she filled me in. It was no use though, Xav had moved on.'

'He was seeing other girls?' Megan's eyes had fallen, as though she didn't trust herself to look directly at him any more.

Felix caught hold of his next thought and held onto it. Xav had been shagging his way around Cambridge, according to Tal, but saying that to Megan didn't feel entirely wise right now.

'I couldn't say. We lost touch for a while.'

In his office next door, the desk phone began to ring. Felix excused himself and left her to it. In his own room, he poured himself another drink. This time, he didn't bother with the coffee.

## 22

Talitha, better than the others, knew the benefit of self-possession and keeping her own counsel. In the days that followed the disastrous lunch party, she picked up the phone several times to ring one of the others, but each time put the phone down before the call went through. When Daniel called her towards the end of the week, it was almost a relief and she readily agreed to meet up.

'As there's been nothing in the papers,' she said, when the two of them stepped through the giant stone arch and into the walled garden. 'I'm assuming you didn't do it?'

One of the oldest scientific gardens in the world, the Oxford Botanical Garden stood on the high street, almost directly opposite Magdalen College. Were Talitha and Daniel to turn at that point, they would have caught a glimpse of the tower through the rim of specimen trees. Instead, they made their way towards the wilder sections on the perimeter where they would encounter fewer people. It was a cloudy day, cold and damp, but there were always visitors in the gardens.

'Course I didn't bloody do it,' Daniel said as their footsteps crunched past fallen ranks of tulips. 'There was a moment though, Tal, when I thought she was going to jump of her own accord and, God help me, I'm not sure I'd have run to stop her.'

A sudden gust of wind threw pink blossom into their faces

as the sky darkened. Talitha turned up the rim of her coat and thought she could feel rain in the air.

'Here's what I don't get,' she said. 'You say she was threatening you—'

'Warning me – us – not to underestimate her.'

'Whatever. In which case, why play games? Why not simply come out and say what's on her mind, tell us what she wants and call in the favours? Why is she keeping us guessing?'

They edged their way around a tour of grey-haired women. 'The land you're standing on was once a Jewish cemetery,' their guide was saying. 'Four hundred years after the Jews were expelled from the city, thousands of cartloads of muck and dung were needed to raise the land high enough above the Cherwell to make it suitable for planting. No wonder things grow so well here.'

'She's talking about hypnosis,' Daniel said when they were out of earshot. 'Will it work, do you think?'

'If she's only pretending not to remember, it's definitely going to work,' Talitha replied. 'I just don't understand why she's going through the charade.'

'Because the balance of power has shifted. She has nothing to lose, we have everything. She's enjoying herself.'

The rain had started and the elderly visitors were heading towards the main glasshouse close to the garden's entrance. Talitha and Daniel made instead for the smaller greenhouses by the river. Inside, the air was close, the glass opaque with condensation, and their steps were punctuated by a constant, almost musical dripping.

In the waterlily room, tendrils curled like the waiting tongues of predatory insects, and the hanging flowers seemed more like chemical explosions than blooms. The central tank was a patchwork-quilt of leaves the size of saucers, of dinner plates, of manhole covers. They reached a wooden bench, dedicated to the memory of someone in whom they had no interest but took advantage of the generosity of his friends all the same, and sat.

'It doesn't sound like Megan,' Talitha said. 'She wasn't underhand or manipulative.'

'We knew her years ago,' Daniel replied. 'Before she spent twenty years in prison. And I'm not sure we even knew her back then. Did she tell anyone she'd screwed up her exams?'

She hadn't. Looking back, Talitha thought, there had been signs, a subtle withdrawing from the group, as though Megan had known that her place as a member wouldn't hold out against the revelation that was coming. At the time, though, they'd all been so completely self-absorbed. None of them had given it much thought.

'We need the proof,' Daniel went on, and Talitha could hear him trying not to sound accusatory, or impatient, because this was a task that had been entrusted to her.

'By the end of the day, we should have it,' Talitha told him.

'What's happening?'

'I wasn't going to say anything, because I didn't want to get anyone's hopes up, but I'm going round to Megan's bedsit after this.' She looked at her watch. 'In forty minutes.'

'How will you get in?'

'Someone I know will open the doors,' Talitha replied. 'He'll be dressed as a workman, with ID convincing enough for most people. Once he's inside, he'll call me and we'll search the place together.'

Daniel looked around, as though afraid they might be overheard, and lowered his voice. 'What if you're seen?'

'Megan's at work. Felix has promised to call me if she leaves, but there's no reason why she would. If anyone else sees me, I can be a supervisor or something. We're talking about a bedsit in student land, Dan. No one will care.'

Daniel scratched at his head, not for the first time. Talitha had already noticed a fine sprinkling of dandruff on his jacket shoulders. 'We should have done it before,' he said. 'She's had time to hide it somewhere else.'

'Well, excuse me, but one doesn't look on Yell.com for private detectives who have a relaxed approach to breaking the law. These people take time to find.'

'Can he be trusted?'

'No, which is why I'm going too.'

'Be careful, Tal.'

'Want to take my place?'

She laughed at the expression on his face. 'Relax. I have another job for you. For whatever reason, you're the one she's focusing on right now.'

'Maybe I'm the only one she can get hold of.'

'Whatever the reason, she talks to you, feels comfortable with you.'

'So, what am I supposed to do?'

'Find out as much as you can. Start with twenty years ago. Something happened back then, something that threw her off course, made her fail her exams. If we find out what it was, we might begin to understand what drove her back then. What's driving her now.'

# 23

Parking a car in central Oxford is close to impossible, and Talitha had long since given up trying. A bike, especially a modest, low-powered one, was so much easier. After saying goodbye to Daniel, she retrieved her bike from Rose Lane and steered back up the high street, passing him before the bridge; from The Plain roundabout she turned into Iffley Road. A mile or so up, she turned left again and pulled up six doors down from the house where Megan had a room. Ten minutes early. Checking no one was in earshot, she made a phone call.

'Hey,' Felix said after only two rings. 'What's up?'

Talitha asked, 'Is she still with you?'

'She is. You about to go in?'

'Few minutes. I need you to call if she leaves the building.'

'No worries.'

'How's she been?'

'Surprisingly good. Sorted out the backlog in two days. Rearranged several of the systems and everyone agrees it will make a big difference in the long term. People like her.'

Unsure whether Megan's unexpected success rankled or not, Talitha asked, 'Anyone know who she is yet?'

'Not yet. I'm trying to keep Sarah away. She's bloody livid about the whole idea and I've more or less told her I've changed my mind, that I'm planning to sack Megan.'

'You lied to your wife?'

Felix sighed down the phone, 'Tal, I think we're all going to be doing a lot worse before this is over.'

It was a fair point; she was about to indulge in a spot of breaking and entering.

Further down the street, a white van pulled up at the side of the road. In the driver's seat, Talitha could see a man in his forties looking down at a clipboard.

'I think we're in business,' she said. 'Don't let her leave.'

She hung up and waited. The man approaching her was wearing the dark blue jacket with turquoise sleeves that was the latest uniform of a British Gas engineer. There was no BG insignia on the jacket, though, partly because they were tricky to get hold of, and partly because impersonating a utility official to gain access to a property was a criminal offence. This way, the two of them would only be breaking the law once they were inside Megan's room.

They did not introduce themselves.

'We good?' he said, when they were close enough to talk.

Nodding, she held open the gate that would lead them to the front door of the three-storey terraced house. A double row of doorbells indicated that at least eight people lived in the building. Her companion took something from his pocket and slid it into the gap between door and frame. Five seconds later, they were inside. It always paid to wait for a professional.

'Flat seven,' she said, although she had told him this already.

'Top floor.' He led the way up, leaning a little to the right to compensate for the tool kit he was carrying. The blue carpet on the stairs was dusty, worn in places. There were scuff marks on the walls and the lampshade they passed on the first landing was full of a dark substance that she saw, with a shudder, was a heap of dead insects. They heard the sound of a TV from one room, the shouting of a woman from another, the yell of a baby from a third.

There were only two doors on the top floor, where the ceilings sloped at acute angles and the old carpet had finally given up the ghost. The bare boards of the landing floor had been painted, but not recently.

'New lock,' Talitha's companion remarked.

'Can you open it?' She kept her voice low, fearful of listening ears behind the other door. The new lock was a good sign. If Megan had seen fit to install a new lock, it could only be because she had something to hide.

Without replying, he dropped to his knees and opened his toolkit. Talitha tiptoed across to the door of number eight and leaned towards it, stopping when she could feel the wood against her hair. She held her breath for several seconds but could hear nothing from inside.

The man in the blue-and-turquoise jacket picked up one tool and then the next. He blocked her view of the lock with his body and she could only wait, biting back the questions that she knew would be useless and annoying. Several times, her phone vibrated, but the callers were work colleagues or clients, never Felix, so she ignored them.

It took twelve minutes before the door swung open. The man packed away his tools and got to his feet. He held the door, she stepped through, and it was closed behind them.

'She mustn't know we've been here,' she said.

In response, he pulled from his pocket two pairs of disposable gloves and held one out to her.

'We're looking for a piece of paper, A-four size, with handwriting on it,' she said. 'Also a film from a camera or possibly developed photographs. They could be in an envelope, or a plastic bag, something for safekeeping.'

'I'll start this end.' He got to work.

The room was small, with sloping ceilings, barely the size of

Talitha's youngest stepchild's bedroom at home. The plasterwork was a dirty cream, the wood of the window frame was rotting beneath the peeling paintwork and the carpet old and sticky, but the room was neat and the kitchen area clean. There were no dishes in the sink or on the draining board, no discarded clothes on the floor and the single bed was neatly made. Remembering what slobs they'd been as eighteen-year-olds, Talitha thought that prison, if nothing else, had given Megan clean habits.

She could hear the soft chinks of crockery and tinned goods as her companion sorted through kitchen cupboards, but she had yet to join the search. Her attention had been caught by a corkboard pinned above the bed. It was full of photographs and other mementos of the life Megan left behind when she was sentenced. Talitha's own younger face, and those of all five of her former best friends, stared back at her, with glazed eyes, wild hair and pursed lips: by the river in Port Meadow, dripping wet and shivering; lying drunk in the sunshine in University Parks; dancing like dervishes at Reading Festival; the punt race on the Cherwell, Xav powering one boat with Amber and Megan as passengers, Felix on the other with her and Dan, and suddenly it seemed the most important thing in the world to remember who'd won.

In the centre of the board was a picture of Xav. Taken outdoors, because there was a background of trees, and in summer, because the trees were in full leaf. She knew instinctively that Megan was the photographer. There was a smile on Xav's face that she hadn't seen in years. Maybe twenty years.

'Look on the back of that,' her companion told her and Talitha realised there were tears in her eyes. She did what she was told though, but there was no manila envelope pinned to the back of the corkboard.

'Bed,' she was told next. 'Strip it.'

There was nothing in or around the bed. The two of them

tipped it on its side so that they could see underneath the frame, but nothing. She went through the scant contents of the wardrobe and looked both on top and underneath it. She checked the drawers of the dressing table, lifting each cheap pair of pants, refolding both supermarket bras.

By this time, her partner in crime had finished searching the cooking area and was checking for loose nails in the carpet. When they had been in the room for nearly forty minutes, he shook his head.

'If it was here, we'd have found it,' he said.

Talitha couldn't disagree.

'Something important, people usually keep it with them,' he added.

They left the house together. On the first-floor landing, they came across a young woman who was unlocking one of the doors, but after a glance their way, she hurried inside.

'Still want to set a watch?' he asked, when they were back on the street. This was something they'd already discussed.

'She leaves work at five,' Talitha told him, although he already knew. 'Watch her till midnight, or until she comes home, whichever is the sooner. I need to know where she goes, and who she meets.'

'Till when?'

Talitha named a date four days hence, and they parted ways. As he drove away, she phoned Felix again.

'Nothing,' she said. 'She may have it with her. You need to search her bag.'

'How the fuck do I do that?'

'Use your imagination. Wait till she's in the loo, fake a fire alarm, lock her in a frigging cupboard. I don't care how you do it, just make sure it isn't with her.'

Annoyed, he hung up. It made no difference. He'd do it, of course. They were all criminals. Just a bit out of practice.

# 24

Several days passed before Felix had a chance to search Megan's handbag; she simply never let it leave her side. But on the Wednesday morning of the following week, needing to speak to her about a client invoice, he peered round the open door of the general office. She wasn't at her desk; her handbag was, though.

It sat beside her chair, a cheap-looking canvas bag, the sort the girls had taken to festivals when they were younger. Lumpy, a bit grubby, it slumped over on itself, straps trailing across the carpet.

*Come on then, it taunted him; I dare you.*

The main office wasn't empty. Three of the sales reps were at their desks and could see his reflection in the window if they looked up. The IT staff had their heads down, but they rarely let him leave his room without a question of some sort.

There was never going to be a perfect opportunity.

He approached Megan's desk, pulled out her chair and sat.

'Help you with anything, Felix?' Cath, his large-account rep – who hated her job title, probably because she was overweight and under no illusions about the jokes cracked behind her back – was watching him from several desks away.

He didn't look up. 'Nah, I'm good. Megan gone far, do you know?'

'Stockroom, I think.'

Nodding, he pulled Megan's in-tray towards him, pretending

to rifle through the papers. Without looking down, he hooked his foot around the bag and pushed it further under the desk, before knocking a felt-tip pen to the floor. Cursing, he pushed his chair back, bent double, and disappeared from sight under Megan's desk.

Close up, the bag smelled like second-hand shops and had a press-stud fastener. It looked full. He upended it, spilling the contents over the floor, before replacing them one by one: purse, mobile telephone, hairbrush, cosmetic bag, tissues, tampons, several pens and pencils, an A5-size brown envelope, sealed, something small but heavy inside. He pressed it between fore finger and thumb. Something cylindrical, about two and a half inches long.

Felix experienced a burning sensation in his chest that felt a lot like triumph; this had to be it.

In the room above, the outer door closed. He slipped the envelope into the waste bin, pushing it to the bottom, out of sight. As he emerged, Megan was walking towards him and, in his own room, the desk phone started to ring.

'Came to talk to you,' he said, in response to her raised eyebrows. 'Knocked everything off your desk. Sorry. I think it's sorted.'

She'd look for the envelope now, for sure. He'd blown it.

His desk phone stopped ringing and his mobile took up the summons in its place. His personal device, not the burner Tal had given him.

'What about?' Megan couldn't take her seat while he was in the way. Somehow, though, he couldn't move. Moving would feel like running.

'Sorry?'

'What did you want to talk to me about?'

'Oh, right.' He couldn't remember. He'd totally forgotten the excuse he'd had planned. Another phone sounded, in the main room this time.

'This?' she lifted the invoice off her desk.

'Ah, that's it. Not sure what's—'

'Felix, reception have been trying to get hold of you,' Graham in IT called over. 'Sarah's on her way up.'

The door opened and Felix's wife walked in.

'Morning.' She gave tight-lipped smiles to the staff as she crossed the carpet; some were returned, not all. Sarah had never gone out of her way to make friends with her husband's employees. She ignored Megan completely. 'Need a word,' she said to Felix.

Grateful for the reprieve, knowing it could only be temporary, he followed his wife into his office. Before the door was closed, she leaned over his desk, picked up his coffee mug and sniffed. He waited. She put the mug down without comment and gestured to the door.

'What's she doing here?' she demanded.

Felix walked around his desk and sat down. He wondered, for a second, whether pouring himself a drink in Sarah's presence was a good idea and did it anyway. She was smart enough to pick her battles and, right now, he'd rather be accused of being an alcoholic.

'We discussed this,' she added.

'No. You gave me your opinion. I said very little. Not my idea of a discussion.'

Sarah managed to make pulling out a chair and sitting down seem like an act of violence. She leaned towards him across the desk and, fair play, tried to lower her voice. 'She's an ex-con,' she hissed. 'You cannot allow her anywhere near the company accounts.'

The Scotch tasted like shit with the dregs of coffee contaminating it, but Felix drank all the same and was rewarded with the momentary surge of bravado. He said, 'She was convicted of murder, not corporate theft.'

'And that makes it OK? God knows what she learned in a high-security prison the last twenty years, and you've given her access to all our money? She could wipe us out, Felix.'

Actually, his wife was giving him an idea.

'What about the payroll?' his wife went on. 'There's the better part of half a million pounds waiting to come out at the end of the month. How will we pay the staff if she transfers the lot to an offshore account in Bermuda?'

Was he up to it though, this new plan that had crept into his brain the way a sewer rat steals through pipework? Finance really wasn't his thing or Megan wouldn't have been here in the first place. Xav, on the other hand – yeah, Xav could do it.

'Are you even listening to me?'

'Please keep your voice down, Sarah. I'm keeping an eye on her, checking everything she does. There are safeguards in place for that sort of thing – we had them even before she came. The bank will spot anything unusual. And you know what, she's been pretty efficient so far. She's well on her way to getting the books under control.'

Sarah got up, so quickly he thought she was going to come for him, but it was his desk cupboard she was interested in. She pulled it open and grabbed the bottle.

'You're a drunk, Felix. You're not capable of keeping an eye on anything. And she can't work here – I've checked.'

He took the bottle from her and put it away. 'What are you talking about?'

A knock sounded on the door, startling them both. It opened before he had a chance to speak and revealed Megan in the doorway.

'We're busy,' Sarah snapped.

'Talking about me – I heard.' Megan stepped inside and let the door close.

Faced with Megan herself, Sarah lost some of her bluster, but wasn't about to back down completely. She positioned herself to one side of Felix's chair and looked the other woman in the eyes.

'I don't wish to be unhelpful, I appreciate you're in a difficult position, but I don't think it's a good idea for you to work on the company's accounts,' she said. 'The shareholders wouldn't like it.'

'There are no shareholders,' Megan replied. 'It's a privately owned company.'

Felix heard the whistling of his wife's breath. 'Part-funded by my father,' she said.

It was a while since Felix had heard that one; a good couple of months, at least.

Megan said, 'Felix is managing director, it's up to him. With respect, you aren't even on the board.'

'It's against the law for you to practise accountancy,' Sarah said. 'You're a convicted criminal.' She gave Felix's shoulders a nudge to get his attention. 'I asked Claire, her sister's an accountant in one of the big London firms.'

'Claire's misinformed,' Megan said, before Felix could reply. 'I won't be allowed to join any of the professional bodies with my conviction, but there was nothing to stop me taking and passing all the relevant exams. It's entirely up to Felix whether he employs me or not.' As though losing interest in Sarah, Megan then addressed Felix. 'You didn't see a brown envelope in my bag just now, did you?'

Unable to speak, but grateful at last for his wife's presence, Felix shook his head.

'Shame.' Her stare became a little too fixed. 'I thought you

THE PACT

might have seen it when you were cavorting around under my desk just now.'

Felix forced himself to meet her gaze. 'Sorry.'

Megan seemed to lose interest. 'Must have left it at home. God, I'm losing everything these days. I've had to buy new sunglasses, two new umbrellas and a pair of gloves this week alone.'

'Dan has your red sunglasses,' Felix said. 'You left them at Tal's at the weekend.'

'He can keep them. Nasty second-hand pair.' She smiled at Sarah as she left the room. 'Good to see you again.'

Sarah didn't even wait for the door to close before she rounded on him. 'Are you going to let her talk to me like that?'

Felix sighed, although he had to admit Sarah's objections were entirely reasonable. 'Can we discuss this at home?' he asked.

'We're discussing it now.'

'No, we're not, because you haven't the first fucking clue what you're talking about. Now, I've a lot to do, so if you want the bills to be paid, you'd better leave me to it.'

Without another word, Sarah left his office. She attempted a door slam, but the soft-closing mechanism prevented even that. Megan had got the better of her for now, but by the time he got home that night, she'd have recharged her batteries and he'd face a fresh barrage of complaints.

Exhaustion swept over Felix; already the Scotch high was fading, and he could feel the familiar trembling creeping into his fingers. He wanted nothing more than to drop his head onto the desk and sink into oblivion. He wasn't sure he could get through the day, never mind face hours of petulance and recrimination once he got home.

The phone rang and he picked it up; there were motions to go through.

*

At five o'clock, the admin staff went home and Megan stayed at her desk. By six, the technical staff and the sales reps had all drifted out. Megan hadn't moved. By six thirty, the cleaners had reclaimed the building and it was empty but for them, Felix, and Megan.

From his desk, he couldn't see Megan, even with the adjoining door open, but was acutely conscious of her presence, not yards away. She was messing with him, she had to be; she'd found the envelope in the bin and was waiting for him to try to retrieve it.

Felix hadn't had a drink since lunchtime and that felt like a victory of sorts, but sometime in the last hour he'd opened his desk cupboard and let his right hand drift down to touch the bottle. For some reason, one that made no sense whatsoever, physical contact with the bottle was helping.

Within an hour of his wife's storming out, it had occurred to Felix that he could tell her the real reason for employing Megan. His wife was a practical sort. She had a lifestyle she valued, a son to take care of; she wouldn't willingly see him in prison.

Sarah would be unmoved by the fate of Sophie Robinson and her children, he knew that instinctively. His wife was almost totally lacking in empathy. She'd fight to the death for her own son, but the illness of other children left her unmoved.

Her charitable work was local and visible: riding for the disabled, Helen & Douglas House, Friends of Oxford Hospitals, all causes that got her noticed by the people who mattered. He had never known her send so much as a pound to charities overseas, or do a single good deed that wasn't visible.

Sarah's element was radon, an almost-impossible-to-detect noble gas that decayed in your lungs and slowly poisoned you from the inside out.

Sarah wouldn't give him away. On the other hand, there would be one more in the circle, one more potential liability.

No, somehow, he would avoid telling Sarah the truth for as long as he could.

The door opened and a thin, black man in his late twenties, wearing the uniform of the cleaning company, pushed a trolley into the room. The cleaners had reached the upper floor; they'd be emptying the bins and he was running out of time. A woman followed, small and dark-skinned, pulling an industrial vacuum cleaner, and he remembered how his wife invariably left the house when the cleaners arrived. Always polite to them, she didn't want to get embroiled in their stories. 'The minimum-wage brigade can be so needy,' she'd said to him once.

Felix felt he'd learned more about his wife in one afternoon than in seven years of marriage. He hadn't realised before, quite how alike, how well suited, the two of them were. He didn't love her, of course; love was something he'd watched slip away a long time ago.

He started. Megan was standing in the doorway, as though she'd been there for some time. 'Miles away?' she said.

Felix opened his mouth to ask if she'd found her envelope and realised it would be better to act as though he'd forgotten all about it. 'Lot on my mind,' he said.

'Tough at the top?'

He shrugged. 'You off?'

'I'm sorry about Sarah,' she said. 'Do you want me to talk to her?'

Megan's smile seemed a hair's width from sincere, her eyes holding a gloss of slyness. 'There's an awful lot I could tell Sarah,' she seemed to be implying, 'if I chose to.' On the other hand, he might be becoming as paranoid as Dan.

The sound of a vacuum cleaner filled the main office.

'It'll be fine. I'll sort it,' Felix lied, then, 'You're doing a good job, Meg. You've got this.'

A change in her stance, then, and in her expression. Felix couldn't have put it into words but thought about the glow around a newly lit candle, a second before the flame builds to its full strength.

'I'll see you.' She moved to leave the room.

'Meg!'

She looked back over her shoulder.

'I was thinking,' he said, 'if you need an advance on your salary, I can arrange it. We've got another ten days to go.'

'I'm good, thanks.' She seemed to think of something. 'Oh, that reminds me. I came across something that puzzled me.'

'What's that?'

'A monthly payment, quite sizeable, into a numbered account.'

Stomach churning, Felix kept his face blank.

'The amount fluctuates each month, which seemed odd, until I realised it was always exactly ten per cent of the company's profits.'

Ten per cent of their income, the agreement made long ago in an Oxford college library. He'd set it up that way, thinking an annual payment would be much more noticeable to anyone who went through the accounts.

'Trust fund,' he said, using the story he'd repeated to several accountants over the years. 'For Luke.'

'Ah. Very prudent. Do you want me to take a look at it? Financial advice isn't my strong point but there are certain boxes long-term investments should tick, you know, pension provision, balance of risk, that sort of thing.'

Megan could not be given access to her own trust fund – she would see that contributions came in regularly from Tal, Dan, Amber and Xav. 'You've got more than enough to be getting on with for the time being,' he said.

She half-smiled and this time, really did seem about to leave. 'I wouldn't have guessed it was for Luke,' she said. 'Because he's what – two years old? And the trust dates back as far as I could trace records. You must have always been sure you were going to be a dad.'

Once more they held eye contact for a second longer than seemed normal and he thought, *Dan's not paranoid, he's right. She does remember.*

'Don't miss your bus, Megan,' he said.

Determined to do nothing until she left the building, Felix watched Megan cross the car park and vanish behind a line of trees that hid the bus stop from view. Only then did he run into the main office. Her bin was empty. Tearing across the office, he found the cleaners in the corridor.

'Sorry, sorry,' he called.

They looked back at him as though he were breaking some unwritten rule, maybe, that there should be no interaction between company staff and contract cleaners. He certainly couldn't remember speaking to either of them, even seeing them before. It was possible the company sent different people every night – he'd never even thought about it.

'I need something from one of the bins,' he explained. 'I threw it away by mistake.'

They were staring, as though not quite following him. Giving up on explanations, he spotted the large bag suspended from the trolley.

'Excuse me.'

He pulled the bag from its fastening and tipped it upside down. The detritus of the day spilled out: papers, screwed up carrier bags, empty envelopes, lottery tickets, supermarket coupons, sandwich wrappers, banana skins, apple cores. A coffee cup that hadn't been emptied tipped a pale brown liquid over the blue carpet.

There. The brown envelope. He grabbed it and looked up, as though caught in the act of something shameful. The man and the woman were watching him, silently. Pushing the envelope to one side, he gathered up the rubbish and replaced it in the bag. Getting to his feet, he handed the bag to the man who took it without a word.

'Sorry,' he said, gesturing to the coffee stain on the floor. 'That was clumsy of me.'

'It isn't a problem, sir,' the man replied in a rich, accent-free voice. 'We will deal with it.'

# 25

Felix tipped the film out onto the pub table. He'd suggested the Turf Tavern in central Oxford because its dark rooms, low ceilings and access via a narrow, medieval passage, made it seem the right sort of place for clandestine meetings. As he'd arrived, he'd wondered if he was taking the piss out of Talitha and her insistence on meeting only rarely and always in different locations. It didn't matter; Tal wasn't remotely self-aware enough to realise.

At short notice, only four of them had made it. Amber was stuck in London and would be till late, but Xav had been on the train home when Felix called and had swung round to collect Dan from their old school.

'Shit,' Xav said, his eyes on the film.

'You were right, Dan, she is lying to us,' Talitha said.

Dan didn't seem to be enjoying his triumph; he'd lost weight since Megan's return, and his skin looked unhealthy, eczema breaking out on his wrists and temples.

'Looks like it,' he muttered, as he clutched his drink.

'What I don't get is why,' Talitha went on. 'Why not tell us what she wants and get it over with? Megan was never mean.'

'Nothing we can give her will make up for what she lost,' Dan replied. 'It's not only about claiming what she's due, it's about hurting us as much as she can.'

All four of them were keeping their voices low. The pub might be noisy, but fellow drinkers were very close.

'Was it a Kodak?' Xav picked up the round black tube and held it to the light. 'What about the letter?'

Felix shook his head. 'Just this. Nothing else.'

'The letter's irrelevant without this,' Talitha said. 'The letter could be fake, it could be a joke, it proves nothing if we all stand firm. It's the photograph that will bring us down.' She reached out and gently punched Felix's shoulder. 'Well done, Felix.'

Someone, a drunken student, stared in at them through the open doorway and Felix instinctively put his hand on top of the film to hide it.

'What do we do now?' Xav asked.

'We get it developed,' Daniel said. 'We have to be sure.'

'Yeah, well we can't exactly drop it off at Boots,' Felix told them. 'I've put in an overnight order for sodium thiosulfate, acetic acid and phenidone. Delivered to the house in case Megan gets suspicious.'

'Handy line of work you're in.' Xav, like Felix and Megan, had excelled at A level chemistry.

'Sorry, are those . . .' Daniel began.

'Agents I need for developing film,' Felix said. 'I've got the rest in stock. I can set up a darkroom in the shed at home.'

Talitha leaned back against the bare stone wall. 'I can't believe it could be over this time tomorrow.'

Felix said, 'We shouldn't count our chickens, not till we've seen it. Oh, and she found the trust fund.'

A moment of silence.

'How?' Talitha asked.

'She's doing my accounts. She has access to all my company's finances. And she's frigging good at what she does. In different circumstances, I'd employ her happily.'

'Are we going to release it?' Xav said. 'Amber wants to. She was on the phone last night.'

'It may soften the blow,' Felix said. 'Once we tell her the game's up. I can't keep her on at work – Sarah's doing her nut.'

'Mark isn't thrilled either,' Talitha said. 'I'm not sure what I'll do if she wants to come to the house again.'

'She phoned me today,' Dan said. 'Your office number came up, Felix, so I thought it was you and I answered. She wants to meet up.'

'Me too.' Talitha's face was grim. 'I'm having lunch with her on Friday. Five Arrows at Waddesdon. I can't wait.'

'I think she's been phoning my house,' Xav said.

Instantly, the others were interested; Megan contacting Xav seemed more serious, somehow.

'You think?' Felix said.

'Only when I'm out at work. I got home the other night and Ella came dancing up to me, wanting to know if I was having an affair, because she'd been answering the phone all day to find no one on the other end.'

'That's all you need,' Felix voiced his sympathy.

'She was joking,' Xav went on. 'I've never met a woman less possessive than Ella. She called the phone company the next day to complain about a fault on the line. But it could have been Megan.'

For a moment, no one spoke.

'Are you going to meet her?' Felix asked Dan.

Daniel picked up the film. 'I guess it depends what we find on this,' he said.

# 26

'We could have gone somewhere closer to the factory,' Talitha said, as she and Megan settled themselves in the alcove table at the Five Arrows. Talitha, who had her choice of tables at the Arrows so long as she gave them a few hours' notice, had thought long and hard about where she wanted to sit. In the main restaurant, Megan might be less likely to raise difficult subjects; on the other hand, were she to do so, the fallout could be a whole lot worse. In the end, she'd opted for the alcove; its stone walls on three sides offered the closest to privacy they were likely to get.

Megan was looking out at the garden and didn't respond.

'How did you even get here?' Talitha went on. 'I'd have picked you up.'

'I bought a car,' Megan told her. 'Mum left me some money. It's an old banger, but it will do for a few months.'

And now Talitha was wondering what was likely to happen in a few months that would enable Megan to replace the banger with something better.

'I love this place,' Megan said. 'Your parents brought us for your eighteenth, do you remember?'

Of course. Her eighteenth birthday had been before that summer, before everything was stained. Talitha spent a great deal of time thinking back to when life had been pure and full of promise.

'Dad's a mate of Lord R,' she said. 'It was practically the family dining room when we were growing up.'

'Nice table.' Megan turned back to the huge picture window that filled the outside wall. 'I thought they were taking us into the garden.'

'How long is your lunch break?' Talitha asked.

'I've got the afternoon off. I'm flat hunting.'

A new car, the promise of a better car soon, and now she was flat hunting.

'Oh?' Talitha said, as the menus arrived.

'I can't stay in the bedsit forever,' Megan said when the waitress had left. 'It's grim. And I'm sure someone broke in the other day.'

Talitha had had years of practice keeping her expression under control in public. Even so, eye contact at that moment was beyond her. She frowned into her menu. 'Really?' They'd left no sign behind, she was sure of it. 'The smoked salmon is good here,' she said. 'My treat.'

'Things seemed in different places. Hard to be sure, though.'

'Anything missing?' Talitha asked, keeping her eyes on the menu.

'What do I have to steal?'

If there was an answer to that, it didn't spring to mind. 'Are you looking in Oxford?' she asked instead.

'I think so. Want to come?'

Talitha closed the menu; she knew it off by heart, anyway. 'Full diary this afternoon. Invite me to the housewarming.'

She would be busy, out of town, maybe even out of the country, by the time Megan got round to throwing a housewarming party.

'Of course,' Megan said. 'I'll invite all of you. Spouses too. Although Sarah doesn't seem to like me.'

'Sarah doesn't like anyone. I'm not sure she likes Felix that much.'

Megan's eyes momentarily lost their cold glitter as she laughed and, for the first time since she'd returned, Talitha saw something of her old friend.

The waitress was back already. There were disadvantages to being so well known, and at times the service verged on the intrusive. There were only so many times you wanted your wine glass to be filled, or your conversation to be interrupted to tell the waiting staff that everything was fine, thank you.

'Dan said you'd been ill,' Talitha said, when they'd ordered and were alone again.

'Are you surprised?' Megan replied. 'Did you think prisons are healthy places?'

'I know they're not, of course.'

'The food is appalling, processed stodge. Everyone gains weight apart from the drug addicts. A stone a year, we worked out.'

Megan had not gained weight. If anything, she looked thinner than Talitha remembered her. Did that make her a drug addict?

'There's no fresh air, no exercise, healthcare is sub-standard and hygiene doesn't exist. The mental health problems are every bit as bad as you'd imagine. Average life expectancy for a woman in the UK is eighty-one years. Guess what it is in prison?'

'I can't. Less, I guess. Ten years less?'

'It's forty-seven, Tal. Had I stayed in, I'd have less than ten years to live right now. As it is, who knows how long I've got. So not only did I lose the twenty years I served, I've lost up to thirty more on the outside.'

'Meg, I don't know what to say,' Talitha began. 'We can help with that, at least. I mean, I can. I'll make an appointment for you at my private health clinic. I'll pay for it. And for any treatment you need.'

What the hell was she saying? Treatment for liver and kidney disease could run into hundreds of thousands of pounds. Mark would go apeshit.

Megan picked up her water glass and drank. 'That's kind, but not what I need from you right now.'

The trust fund would have to cover it. The others would agree, she'd make them. Hang on, what had Megan just said?

'What do you need from me?'

Megan settled back in her chair. 'I need you to be my solicitor, Tal.'

Talitha took her time. She refilled her glass, then Megan's and wondered where the urgent client calls were when you needed them.

'Why do you need a solicitor?' she said at last. 'You're out. And criminal law isn't really my thing.'

Criminal law had been Talitha's speciality, back in the day before she became managing partner. Megan didn't need to know that though.

'I'm not free, though, am I?' Megan said. 'A life sentence is exactly that. Life. I could be sent back if I so much as get a parking ticket.'

That was a good point, one Talitha should have thought of herself. Megan's sentence, technically, would never fully be served. 'I doubt that,' she said. 'You'd have to do a lot worse than a parking violation.'

An act of violence would do it. Being caught in the act of dangerous driving, almost certainly.

'My point is, I'm vulnerable,' Megan said. 'Anyone can accuse me of anything, set me up for anything, and I'm guilty till proved innocent. The law is turned on its head for people like me.'

Their starters arrived. Talitha had never felt less hungry in her life, but she was grateful for the few seconds reprieve.

'Who would do that?' she said, once the waitress had left them.

'Who would accuse you of something you didn't do?'

Megan held her cutlery in two gripped fists, like a savage, like she might need to use them as weapons at any moment. 'It's been happening for years,' she said.

'What has?'

Without replying, Megan began eating. Her starter, a smoked-salmon dish, was light, beautifully presented, but Megan shovelled it into her mouth in a few bites. 'The judge gave me a twenty-year tariff, do you remember?'

Of course she remembered. Talitha could write a transcript of that day in court and not get a word wrong.

Megan had finished already. She'd eaten like this at the house at the weekend, Talitha had noticed, the only one of them apart from the children who'd shown any real appetite. She reminded Talitha of a dog that had known starvation, and who would grab at anything put in front of her. And yet she was still so thin. She must really be ill.

Talitha put her knife and fork down and pushed her plate towards the other woman. 'Try this,' she said. 'I think it's the best thing on the menu here.'

The plates were swapped.

'After ten years, there was talk of appealing and applying for early release,' Megan said. 'On the grounds that I'd been very young when the offence occurred and been a model prisoner. And then a fight broke out in the canteen. Nothing to do with me at all, but I was charged with inciting violence and assault.'

'How could that happen?'

All too easily was the answer. Any number of people on the inside were prepared to kick off a fight for a small consideration; hell, most of them were so bored they'd do it for the laughs. Prison officers were even easier to bribe – after all, they could spend money on the outside.

'The prisoner I'd supposedly assaulted had a broken nose,' Megan went on. 'A fairly minor injury, you'd think, but five different witnesses, including two officers, testified against me. Funnily enough, the CCTV cameras were malfunctioning that day. I was advised to drop my appeal.'

'I had no idea.'

Another lie. Talitha had been told by her father when it happened. He'd admitted no involvement, he wouldn't incriminate himself, even to his own daughter, but she'd looked into his eyes. Barnaby Slater knew what his daughter had done and was protecting her, even if he despised her for it.

'And then I was accused of theft,' Megan said, as she wiped her plate clean with her fingertip. 'The cash was found in my cell, and no one believed me when I said I'd no idea how it got there.'

'How was it for you?' Unseen by either of them, the waitress had arrived to clear their plates.

'Best food I've eaten in twenty years,' Megan said.

The waitress's smile grew a little fixed. The plates went.

'Next up, I was accused of drug smuggling,' Megan said. 'Found in my cell again. By this time, I was starting to get paranoid.'

'Couldn't your solicitor do something? Get you transferred maybe?'

'My solicitor couldn't care less. I barely saw him in twenty years.' Megan leaned across the table towards Talitha. 'Here's the thing,' she said. 'I wrote to you, and your father, asking you to represent me. I wrote four times. I got one reply, from a junior clerk.'

'I asked Dad,' Talitha said. 'He said it could be too damaging for the firm. There was very strong feeling locally when you were convicted, Meg. The school was vandalised several times, did anyone tell you that? Admissions dropped. Fundraising took a hit. The following year, a whole year later, Oxbridge admissions from the school fell by fifty per cent. No one wanted to be associated with you, and Dad knew his firm would suffer if he was seen to be on your side.'

Megan's face was like stone.

'We're an Oxford firm,' Talitha said. 'He said you needed to be represented by a firm out of the area.'

'And then there was another fight that I got blamed for,' Megan said. 'And that's how it went on until I thought I was never going to see the light of day again.'

Talitha gave an uncomfortable look around. 'Megan, please keep your voice down. I know how let down you must feel, but we were teenagers. There was nothing we could do at the time.'

'You could have come to see me. Not once, Tal. Twenty years and not once.'

The waitress was back. 'Hi guys, got your mains for you.'

'Oh, for heaven's sake,' Tal snapped. 'No, I'm sorry. Please—' She gestured that the plates be put down. 'I do apologise. Thank you.'

The waitress fled.

Megan cut into her steak and blood bubbled out. 'You know what it felt like, Tal? It felt like someone with a huge amount of influence in the legal world was doing his damnedest to keep me inside for as long as possible.'

She shoved a huge piece of steak into her mouth, enough to keep her quiet for a couple of minutes at least. No such luck.

'Or *her* damnedest,' she said, through a mouth of semi-masticated meat.

# 27

The chemicals arrived on Monday, but Felix waited until Sarah had gone to bed before developing the film. He stapled Luke's blackout curtains to the window of one of the brick outbuildings in the garden, ran several litres of water from the outdoor tap into a container and turned on the infra-red light he'd borrowed from work. The process of turning photographic film into negatives wasn't hard; well, not for him.

Using a camping stove, he heated the developing chemicals to the required temperature and, in darkness, unrolled the film and wrapped it around the drum in the bespoke tub. He used a timer, agitated when instructed to do so, before returning the liquids to the bottles they'd arrived in. He could dispose of them at work.

The next part of the process involved halting the development, and these chemicals were the most foul-smelling and toxic. Several minutes in, his head was aching, and he was starting to feel dizzy. When the process was done, he switched on the overhead light – the film was no longer light sensitive – and opened the door for a few seconds.

He couldn't resist holding the film up to the light – was that the river? A scene in a park? He scanned the reel for the shot taken twenty years ago in the pool house, the one with the written confession. It was no use – the images were too small, and still in negative. Felix poured out the third blend that would fix the image in place. More time spent waiting, agitating the tub, rinsing. Finally, he used water to wash all the magical substances away. When the rinses were running clearly, he was done.

Resisting temptation to hold it up to the light once more, he pegged the long, thin strip of brown film to a line of string. While he was waiting for it to dry, he stepped outside.

The night was clear and cool, full of the scents of early summer. When he'd got home that evening, Luke had been in his bath with the window open – Sarah was paranoid about steam damaging the paintwork – and blossom was drifting into the room, falling like confetti onto his pink-skinned angel.

The thought that he might lose Luke, either through Sarah's leaving him, or – a thought he could barely allow to fully form – because of his own imprisonment, was crippling. Felix loved Luke with a passion he hadn't known he'd possessed. The moment his son was born, he'd known that he would die for this tiny scrap of a human. Right now, on the brink of finding what he needed to make everything all right again, he was asking himself a different, altogether darker question. Would he . . . ?

It was time, the film would be dry and that particular question could be asked another day. Back in the shed, Felix gathered up everything he'd used that night and left it in the boot of his car to go back to the factory. The film he carried carefully indoors.

Creeping upstairs, he pushed open the door to Luke's bedroom. The toddler was face down, his chubby legs and feet drawn beneath him so that his bottom – huge in the night-time nappy – was pointed towards the ceiling.

Easing the door closed, Felix crept along the landing to his home office. His Mac was already switched on, so that the sound of it firing up wouldn't disturb Sarah, and the Lightroom software installed. He scanned in the negative film. A few movements of the mouse inverted the images so that they became positive; a few more sorted out tone, contrast and brightness. They were still, though, too small to properly make out. He didn't bother with cropping, simply pressed print and sat by the printer, grabbing each image as it fed out. There were fifteen images.

The first made his heartbeat speed up. The bridge at Port Meadow. Kids were gathered at its apex, and the photographer – Tal, he guessed, it had been her camera – had captured a boy in mid-air, his feet breaking the surface of the water. Other kids sat around on the bank. The jumper could be Xav, Felix wasn't sure, but this had to be the right film. He swallowed down a lump in his throat and told himself to stay calm. The next image was another taken in Port Meadow, as was the third. Still no one he recognised.

The fourth sheet of paper showed a park; University Parks, he thought, a group of five people in the distance sitting in a circle. Tal must have taken it as she'd approached; she'd always been late. More shots of University Parks, of trees, of a cute kid at the playground. A couple of Oxford city centre, one taken from directly outside the window of the steampunk shop on Magdalen Bridge.

The next image puzzled him. Taken at night, it showed a statue, a huge angel with great, soaring wings. He had no memory of hanging around in graveyards, even during their steampunk phase, but Tal would have taken some of these when she was alone.

An apple tree – was it? – yes, the apple tree in Talitha's garden. Another of the garden at the Five Arrows, Tal's dad's favourite restaurant because the pretentious git had loved bumping into Lord Rothschild and pretending the two of them knew each other.

Shots of the school and Felix could feel the start of a nervous tick. Still no images of the gang, and something didn't feel quite right. He started to flick back through the pictures. The last one was coming out. It drifted away from the paper tray and landed, face down, on the carpet.

He didn't want to pick it up, knew he had to. He turned it over, put it on the desk in front of him and looked long and hard. Then he did something he hadn't done in years, had forgotten he was capable of doing.

Felix started to cry.

# 28

Felix didn't go into work the next morning, but drove straight to Talitha's offices in the city centre and announced himself at the reception desk. After fifteen minutes, he was shown into his old friend's panelled office with its Queen Anne furniture. Talitha was not pleased to see him.

'This won't look good if the shit hits the fan,' she said, when her office door was closed. 'You've never been here before. Why would you come now?'

'Clear your desk,' he told her. 'You need to see something.'

Standing in front of the window, Talitha's face was largely hidden, but he knew of old she didn't react well to being told what to do. Outside, Felix could see the timber-framed building that, despite being across the lane, looked close enough to touch. Each storey had been built wider than the one below, so that the whole building mushroomed out as it rose into the air.

Tal needed a reality check. 'I've got all day,' he said. 'My life is unravelling and pretty soon yours will be too.'

Without another word, Talitha moved the desk diary and laptop to a side table, enabling Felix to lay out the photographs he'd printed in the early hours. Tal didn't touch them, but as she looked from one to the next, her face seemed to relax.

'I remember that shop,' she said at one point. 'We stalked

around the Sheldonian at one in the morning and that German couple nearly shat themselves.'

'It's still there,' Felix told her. She hadn't got it yet. Fair play, it had taken him most of the roll, but this was, supposedly, her film, taken with her camera.

'What's this?' she bent closer to look at the picture of the angel. 'I don't remember taking that. Maybe someone borrowed the camera.'

He carried on laying the images down for her.

'Dear apple tree,' she said. 'I think I miss the tree more than the house.'

Felix put the last one down. Talitha stared at it, looked up at him, then picked it up.

The last picture on the film was a shot of Megan in Christ Church Meadow. In it, she smiled at the camera and held one hand up in a small wave.

Talitha was no fool. She got it at last. 'This is recent,' she said. 'This is Megan now.'

Felix had spent a long time the previous night looking at Megan, smiling – in triumph, he thought – at the camera.

'They're all recent,' Felix said. 'I got a bad feeling when I saw this one, I just couldn't place it.' He put a finger on one of the shots of the city centre. 'That car is not from twenty years ago,' he said. 'It's a modern model. And the bus doesn't look right either.'

'What the hell?'

'You didn't take any of these, Tal, she did. Remember in the pub the other night, when Xav asked whether the film had been Kodak? Probably wasn't. She's got hold of a new film and taken a load of photographs of the city.'

Tal looked bewildered and, suddenly, years younger. 'Why would she do that?'

'Well, two reasons I can think of. The first is that she's trying to recreate memories, going back to places where she spent her youth.'

'She has a smartphone now – she'd take pictures on her phone.'

'Yeah, I'm not sold on the first reason either. The second is that she deliberately found an old camera, bought a film and went around recreating shots that could have been on the original. And then she brought it into work, knowing I'd try to get a hold of it. She wanted us to find this.'

Talitha sank back against the window ledge. 'She really is fucking with us, isn't she?'

'Yep. Question is, what do we do about it?'

# 29

It was the end of the week before they were all able to get together, and once more Talitha had cautioned against panicking. *'We have to hold our nerve,'* she'd said to Felix before he left her office. *'She might be trying to provoke a reaction. We can't give her one. We have to act as though nothing's wrong.'*

*'Easy for you to say,'* Felix had snapped back. *'You don't have to spend eight hours a day with her.'*

Somehow though, he'd made it through the week, being politely friendly to Megan and palming his wife off with promises that her employment wouldn't be for long.

Now, at last, in the company of people he didn't have to lie to, he felt nothing so much as relief.

The private room at the Rose and Crown in Summertown was tiny, cramped, like the rest of the pub. Amber and Xav were sitting some distance apart, the way they always positioned themselves in public; if Xav weren't so clearly besotted with his young wife, Felix might long ago have suspected he and Amber of rekindling an old flame. Dan was on his feet, examining the contents of a bookcase – God alone knew why because the most recent thing in it was a ten-year-old *Good Pub Guide*.

Felix was by the window, looking out over the courtyard, on the watch for Tal's arrival.

'It's still not proof,' Amber was saying. 'I know you're upset,

Felix, but it's not. She may simply be trying to recreate some memories.'

For a politician, Amber was naive, verging on idiotic. Maybe it explained why she was so successful; her naivety made people believe her. Amber, he'd decided while they were still at school, was vanadium, strong and useful on the surface, especially when she had others to bounce off, but basically nothing under the hood.

Felix leaned across the pub table and gathered together the photographs. He felt like Megan was taunting him, even from a distance, and he didn't need to look at them any more.

'I mean, she's been out for nearly a month,' Amber was droning on. 'If she was going to ask anything of us, she'd have done it by now, wouldn't she?'

'She's made no contact with me,' Xav said. 'And if she really does remember what happened that summer, it's me she should be most pissed off with.'

*Small mercies,* thought Felix. Megan's wrath, once it was unleashed, would be aimed primarily at Xav.

'Maybe she's saving the best till last,' he said, spitefully. 'Still getting anonymous phone calls?'

'They stopped after Ella phoned the company,' Xav admitted. 'Might have been nothing after all.'

'Exactly, we shouldn't be panicked into doing something stupid,' Amber said. 'Dan, tell us about the lunch you had with her. How was she?'

Daniel tore his eyes away from a Latin dictionary and looked round at the group as though not entirely sure what they were all doing together. 'Shouldn't we wait for Tal?' he asked.

'I'm not sure how long I can stay,' Amber said. 'I've got a constituency meeting at eight.'

Felix glanced back out at the courtyard. No tall, dark-haired women striding in their direction. 'We'll fill her in when she gets here,' he said. 'Go on, Dan.'

'So, I took her out to lunch.' Dan topped up his glass from the bottle of red that he, Felix and Xav were sharing. 'Turkish place on Iffley Road. I tell you what, there's nothing wrong with her appetite.'

Daniel wasn't looking his best. There were patches of eczema on his hands and blotches on his neck and lower jaw that could be an allergic reaction but equally might be stress related. Xav too looked thinner and paler.

'How is she?' Amber asked as Felix sat down next to her. 'In herself, I mean. Before you get onto the other stuff, how do you think she's coping?'

'Looking a lot better than when she first came out,' Daniel said. 'Her skin's lost some of that unhealthy, yellow sheen, and she's not constantly looking over her shoulder, you know, as though worried someone might be creeping up on her.'

'I noticed that,' Xav said. 'When we were at Tal's. Jumpy all the time.'

Xav had become much the same, Felix thought, starting every time he got a text message or there was a loud noise outside.

'She mainly wanted to talk about us.' Daniel glanced Felix's way. 'How well you've done with the company.'

They were all reacting to the blow of Megan's return into their lives. Dan was breaking out into weird skin conditions, Xav had become jumpier than a maiden aunt, Amber was driving them mental with her endless virtue signalling and Felix himself was getting to the point where even he thought he'd lost control of his drinking. He pushed his glass further away from him. The trouble was, his hand went to it automatically; he almost didn't realise he was doing it half the time.

'And she's blown away by Amber's success.' Dan attempted

a smile, but it looked odd and forced. 'She'd asked me to bring photographs with me, of big occasions, you know. I showed her Amber's wedding pictures – not yours, Xav, I'm not that stupid. I said I didn't go to yours, so don't drop me in it.'

'She wanted to see my wedding?' Amber glanced nervously at Xav.

'Yeah, she made a big thing about how she'd have been one of your bridesmaids, or godmother to one of the girls. She wanted to know their birthdays. I couldn't remember exactly – sorry, Amber, but they're not my godchildren. I told her I'd find out. And she wants to know their favourite toys, books, films, and so on. For presents, she said.'

'This feels a bit obsessive,' Felix said.

'Yes, that's it exactly.' Dan picked up his glass. 'She asked a lot about Tal, too, whether her family still have that place in Sicily, why she never had kids of her own, were she and Mark happy? Every time I asked her about herself, she changed the subject as soon as she could.'

'Trying not to be caught out?' Xav asked.

'Who knows. In the end, I asked her straight up what had gone wrong with her exams that summer. I told her it had been almost as much a shock to us as the accident, given how clever we all knew her to be. To be honest, I think I laid it on a bit thick.'

There was a pinkness around Daniel's eyes, and even Felix, not known in the group for his sensitivity, could see the other man struggling. Amber covered Daniel's hand with her own. 'What did she say?' she asked in a tone you might use to a child about to kick off. 'About her exams?'

Daniel sighed. 'She said maybe she wasn't half as clever as she'd pretended to be. Well, she could see I wasn't falling for that, so then she spun me this story about suddenly developing exam phobia.'

'Is that even a thing?' Xav asked.

'Very much so.' Daniel looked happier on a subject other than Megan. 'There are very bright pupils who can't perform in exams. We've got a couple in school now, and we're working with psychologists to get to the bottom of it. It's unusual for it to come on suddenly, though, which is what Megan claimed happened to her.'

'How did she explain it exactly?' Amber said.

'She said that a few hours before each paper, she started to feel the onset of a panic attack. Her heartbeat would pick up, her stomach contents turned to mush, her breathing threatening to spiral out of control. In fairness, these are classic panic-attack symptoms.'

'How come we didn't notice this?' Felix asked. 'Megan was in every exam I took. Xav, you and she did the same papers. Did you spot anything?'

Xav shook his head. 'Nothing out of the ordinary. I mean, we were all on edge; all feeling the pressure.'

'Exactly,' Daniel said. 'We were all completely focused on ourselves, on what we could remember, what was likely to come up. We wouldn't necessarily have spotted a problem with someone else.'

'Where the hell's Tal?' Felix muttered.

'When she got into the exam room, things got worse,' Dan continued. 'She needed the loo every few minutes, thought she was going to be sick. Even the papers went blurry, as though her eyesight had gone. If all this is true, then to be honest, it's a wonder she did as well as she did.'

'What brought it on, though?' Felix asked. 'You don't go from being the most gifted student in the school to someone incapable of sitting a paper.'

'Yeah, thanks, Felix, I do know something about exam psychology,' Dan said. 'If she's telling the truth about her symptoms, something will have happened to cause them. But if she remembers what it was, she isn't admitting to it.'

'She aced her mocks,' Xav said from the window. 'I remember the master giving us both a lecture on the danger of complacency, about how kids who do well in January can mess up completely in June. She made us promise we'd keep our noses to the grindstone.'

'So whatever happened, it must have been between January and June,' Daniel said. 'Anyone remember anything?'

'Tal's here,' Xav said.

Talitha had inherited her father's habit of striding into a room like a hotshot lawyer on a TV show, bursting his way into court. They heard her heels on the flags outside and then she flung open the door as though expecting to catch them in the act of something disreputable.

Felix got to his feet. He couldn't cope with another orgy of air-kissing and pretend hugs. 'I'm going to the bar. I'll let Dan catch you up. Another bottle, chaps?'

Neither man took him up on it, which meant he probably shouldn't have another drink either, and he felt a moment of envy of both Dan and Xav for being happy with a third of a bottle of red wine each. Amber, of course, got tipsy on Perrier water if you stuck a slice of lime in it.

'Scotch please, single measure,' he told the barman.

The Scotch and a jug of water appeared in front of him. 'And a glass of white wine,' he went on. 'Chablis if you have it.'

He added a few drops of water before lifting the whisky glass and drinking down half of it. Wine and beer made no difference to him any more; he might as well drink sparkling water like Amber for all the effect either had. The Scotch, though, might take him through the next half hour.

'So what have you got for us?' he said, when he was back in the private room.

'For the most part, very little,' Talitha said, before holding her hand up to quash the moans of impatience. 'Hold on, I'm getting there.'

She swallowed back a mouthful of Chablis that she hadn't thanked Felix for and pulled a document from her bag. The report, probably the final one, from her private detective. In between sips, she began reading.

'She goes to work, stays there all day, apart from the time she met me at the Five Arrows, gets home about six and mainly stays home. When she does go out, she walks around the open spaces, along the river, in the parks, that sort of thing.'

Talitha glanced up, probably to see if she had everyone's attention.

'She eats takeaway food and bought a second-hand car a few days ago from that place on the Abingdon Road,' she went on. 'She paid nearly fourteen hundred pounds for it. Legacy from her mum, before you ask.'

'We didn't,' Felix muttered.

'A couple of days ago, she had a hair appointment and went down to Westgate where she made clothes purchases in John Lewis and Hobbs. She's also been to Finders Keepers three times. Flat hunting.'

Talitha put the report down on the table.

'One reason for flat hunting may be that the media seem to have found out where she lives,' she said. 'There've been people hanging around outside her house for three nights, stopping everyone who comes and goes, and there was paint daubed on the front door two nights ago.'

'I think people at work have found out who she is as well,' Felix said. 'No one's said anything to me yet, but there's been a definite atmosphere shift.'

'It won't make a difference though, will it?' Amber said. 'You're not going to sack her?'

Felix almost laughed. 'If I can cope with my wife treating me like I've just killed her puppy, I can deal with a few disgruntled lab technicians.'

'I'm not done,' Talitha objected. 'Last night, she went out at a few minutes after nine. Possibly waiting until everything was quietening down and getting dark. She got into her car and drove out of town towards the ring road.'

'Did your bloke go with her?' Felix asked.

Talitha's dark eyes flashed. 'Of course, he went with her, I'm not paying him to let her drive off alone. She picked up the A40 London Road. He thought she was going to go straight on to the motorway, but she turned off towards Thame and stayed on the A40 back towards Milton Common.'

Felix sensed a subtle shift in mood around the table.

'Your old house?' Amber said.

Talitha's dark curls bounced as she shook her head. 'No, she went here. Small place just off junction seven of the M40.'

Talitha pulled a photograph out of the envelope and the rest of them leaned in to see a night-time shot of a large, white-painted building with red roofs. Two storeys, close to the main road; it had a narrow, paved area at the front.

'Echo Yard?' Daniel read the sign fixed high on the wall to the right of the door.

'It's an architectural salvage yard,' Talitha said. 'It rescues material from old buildings – stone, wood, marble, brick work, et cetera – and sells it on, usually for a massive mark-up. There's a huge yard at the back, full of all sorts of weird and wonderful stuff.'

Amber said, 'Mum loves it. Most of the doors and door frames for their extension came from there.'

'Did any of you ever hear of Megan having a connection to the place?' Talitha asked.

The others shook their heads.

'So, you'll be as surprised as I was to learn that Megan let herself in through the gates by punching in a security code,' Talitha said. 'Which rather gave our intrepid detective a problem, because he didn't have the code and couldn't follow. He carried on snooping around, though, and thought he saw a light in a caravan towards the back of the yard. He made his way around the perimeter fence and happened upon a part of the railing that had the stump of an old tree alongside it. He managed to clamber over and got close to the caravan.'

Talitha broke off to show them more photographs: the salvage yard at night, a weird sort of cross between a junk shop and a gothic graveyard; a caravan with steam coming from a vent and several lights behind curtained windows.

'One of her prison mates?' Felix suggested.

'Hold on to that thought,' Talitha said. 'In the meantime, you might all like to think back to one of the pictures on that film Felix stole.'

'The stone angel,' Felix said. 'Was that taken at this place?'

Talitha drew out another picture and pointed to something in the background. Felix didn't need to look for long. It was the same angel.

'Last picture taken by our private eye,' Talitha said, 'because at that point what sounded like a large dog started barking inside the caravan and my man ran for it.'

'So what does that mean?' Felix said. 'We never went to Echo Yard, did we? I mean, not as a group. It wasn't one of our places.'

'It means the pictures you stole could have been entirely innocent,' Amber said. 'Nothing to do with us at all.'

'The PI did some digging the next day,' Talitha said. 'Seems the caravan is the official home of Echo Yard's resident stonemason. He's a part-owner in the business and the guy who goes out to rescue the various features from condemned buildings. He lives on-site, a sort of human guard dog, although there's a canine one as well, and his name is Gary Macdonald.'

She waited for the news to sink in.

'He's Megan's dad,' she added, in case they hadn't got it. 'And he's spent time in prison.'

# 30

'Gary Macdonald has been a part-owner of Echo Yard for nearly twenty-five years,' Talitha told them after a moment of shocked silence. 'He owned it back when we were in the sixth form.'

'I can't believe she never said anything,' Xav said.

'She never mentioned her dad,' Amber added. 'When I asked her, she said they'd lost touch years ago.'

'Probably because he's been in and out of prison for much of his adult life,' Talitha went on. 'Not exactly a parent to be proud of.'

'Could he be the reason her exams went pear-shaped?' Amber asked.

'Possibly, but what interests me more is that Echo Yard is very close to my parents' house in Little Milton,' Talitha said. 'Less than a ten-minute drive. You know how we've been asking ourselves what she could have done with that film and the signed confession between leaving us and getting home?' She looked back down at the photographs. 'I'd say we've got our answer.'

Felix could see his own excitement reflected in the faces around him. Daniel leaned back in his chair and exhaled noisily.

'You think it's still there?' Xav asked.

'We know it's not in her bedsit. And she doesn't carry it around with her.'

'But that stuff is for sale,' Daniel objected. 'She couldn't risk her hiding place being shipped off to some barn conversation in the Cotswolds.'

'That makes it easier,' Felix said. 'We can ignore anything with a price tag on it.'

'There must be some things they're hanging onto for sentimental value,' Talitha said. 'Or maybe that they can't sell. Maybe this angel. It's worth checking out.'

'Can your detective friend do it for us?' Daniel asked.

Talitha's face tightened. 'We can't risk him getting his hands on anything that will incriminate the rest of us,' she said. 'And frankly, I can't justify the cost any more. If we want to search the place, we have to do it ourselves.'

'At night?'

She shuddered. 'God no. Megan's dad has a frigging German shepherd. I'm not tangling with that. I'll go during opening hours and have a look round. Someone should give me a hand, though, it's a big place to search alone.'

'We can't all go,' Felix said. 'It will look too suspicious if she shows up.'

'I'll come,' Xav offered. 'We need to do some work on the house this year anyway.'

Felix said, 'We can't rely on finding it. We need a plan B.'

Talitha gave him a cold smile. 'So, why don't you share yours?'

Felix looked around the group. Amber, he knew, he was about to have trouble with; the others, not so much. Tal, in any case, was already on board.

'Tal explained to me that while Megan might be out of prison, a life sentence is never officially over,' he said. 'So, if she commits another crime, one that's sufficiently serious, chances are she'll be locked up again, probably for a considerable time, and our problem goes away.'

Silence. Even Amber didn't object as quickly as he'd expected her to.

'What've you got in mind?' Xav asked.

'Sarah gave me the idea,' Felix said, and wondered if he was, in some small way, passing the blame onto his wife. 'She was ranting about how Megan could clean out the entire company, just make a few cash transfers to an offshore account, and that's it. Company folds.'

'Megan's not a thief,' Amber said.

'I'm not suggesting we wait for her to do it herself,' Felix said.

It didn't take the others long to catch up.

'Is that even possible?' Daniel asked.

'Of course, it's possible,' Felix said. 'I can access any computer in the building. I know every password there is. Setting up a destination account will be harder, but luckily we know someone with investment and IT skills.'

They all looked at Xav.

'Possible?' Talitha asked him.

'Easy in theory,' Xav replied. 'I could probably do it remotely. It would be better if I come in, though, sometime when we're sure she doesn't have an alibi and could have been the one doing the deed.'

'We're not doing it,' Amber said.

'Let's hope we don't have to,' Talitha said. 'I had the same thought, although it would be trickier for me to organise something. I'd need the PI again, and it wouldn't come cheap.'

'What?' Daniel asked.

Talitha shrugged. 'Kiddy porn on her computer, stealing her car one night, driving it dangerously and abandoning it somewhere. She'd have to prove she wasn't driving and given that she lives alone, that would be quite tricky.'

'I can't believe I'm hearing this,' Amber said.

Tal turned on the other woman. 'So, what's your brilliant idea? Come on, Am, you can't keep shooting down our plans and not giving anything yourself.'

Amber wasn't backing down. 'We could take care of her. Give her the money, allow her back into our lives.' She looked around the group. 'It might not be so bad. She's good at her job – Felix, even you admit that. Tal, you can easily be her solicitor – you can do that with your eyes shut. I don't mind if she wants to become some sort of honorary aunt to the girls.'

Silence.

'We can deal with this,' Amber was pleading now. 'We don't have to throw her to the wolves. Again.'

'How's Dex going to feel about a convicted child killer getting involved in his daughters' lives?' Talitha asked. 'How will your constituents? The national press? I'm not sure about anyone else, but I reckon this could throw the Profumo scandal into shade.'

'OK, take it easy.' Xav reached across and put a hand on Talitha's arm. Felix expected her to throw it off, but to his surprise she took a deep breath and picked up her glass again.

'Sorry, Am,' she muttered.

'There's another way,' Xav said. 'If we're thinking outside the box.'

'What?' Amber asked.

'If we really do think the shit's going to hit the fan and that Megan won't keep quiet, we do what we did last time,' Xav began.

'I'm not following,' Daniel said.

'Twenty years ago, one of us took the blame for the group,' Xav went on. 'Megan took one for the team. So, if we have to face it again, someone else steps up.'

Felix saw his own puzzlement reflected on the others' faces.

'How can that even begin to work?' Talitha asked. 'If Megan drops one of us in it, she drops all of us in.'

'Not if we stick together, if it's our word against hers,' Xav said. 'One of us agrees to confess to being in the car with Megan that night, even though she took the blame. The rest of us support the story. That person will serve time, almost certainly, maybe even more than Megan did, but my point is, it's only one of us, not all of us.'

'And how do we decide which one?' Daniel's face had lost all colour.

'Xav, you're talking bollocks,' Talitha said. 'Megan has a signed confession.'

'She has a *false* confession,' Xav countered with a cold smile. 'That was her price for agreeing to take the blame and let Daniel – just plucking names out of the air – get away with it. We signed that confession for Dan's sake, but it wasn't true. The rest of us never left Tal's house.'

'I can't see that working,' Amber said.

'It will be Megan's word against the rest of us,' Xav said. 'Has to be worth a shot, doesn't it?'

'How do we decide who takes the blame this time?' Daniel asked again.

'Any volunteers?' Xav smiled around the group and Felix noticed he had one hand tucked inside the pocket of his jacket.

'Xav, we can't do this,' Amber protested. 'I have two children.'

'Oh, I think we all have a reason or two for wanting to stay on the outside,' Xav said. 'My point is, we might not be able to. Maybe we let Megan decide.'

'Well, she won't choose you, will she, not if she still has the hots for you,' Amber snapped. 'And she probably won't pick Felix either, or she loses her job.'

Xav pulled his hand out of his pocket. Sticking out from his clenched fist were five coloured plastic straws. 'Pick one,' he said.

Nobody moved.

'One is two inches shorter than the rest,' Xav said.

'This is bogus,' Daniel said. 'You know which one.'

'So I pick last. That's fair.'

Talitha slid her chair a couple of inches away from the table. 'I prefer my plan,' she said. 'We find the signed confession and the photograph, then no one needs to confess to anything.'

'Oh, I prefer your plan too,' Xav said. 'Don't get me wrong. This is plan B.'

'It's a shit plan,' Amber said.

Xav turned on her. 'So, are you reconsidering the transfer of money from Felix's company into a Channel Islands bank account?' he asked. 'And if that doesn't work, Tal's idea of crashing her car one night.'

Amber dropped her forehead onto her hands.

'Are you?' Xav insisted.

Amber let her head nod up and down. Xav pressed home his advantage. He pushed his clenched fist across the table towards her. 'Pick one,' he insisted.

She looked up at him, tears in her eyes. 'I agree. You win. Let it go.'

'You still need to pick one, we all do. We need a plan C.'

Without moving his hand, he looked around the group. 'If nothing else, it will focus the minds.'

Muttering something, Amber pulled an orange-coloured straw from Xav's hand. 'Well, is this it? Is this the short one?'

Felix leaned across the table and pulled the red straw from those remaining. Acting as one, he and Amber held their straws up to compare lengths. Both were the same. He was ashamed of how relieved he felt because this was absurd.

Then Talitha's hand shot out, like a snake after a mouse, and the blue straw was loosened. The same length as his and Amber's.

Only two straws left now in Xav's clutched fist: one green, one pink.

'Feel lucky?' Xav grinned at Daniel.

As though he was about to stick his hand in the fire, Daniel grasped hold of the green straw and pulled it out. Same length as the others.

Xav opened his hand and let the pink straw fall onto the table. Same length as all the others.

'Just kidding,' he said.

Amber suppressed a sob, Daniel ran his hands over his face and Talitha turned white.

'Fuck's sake, Xav,' Felix snapped. 'What the hell was the point of that?'

Xav got to his feet. 'Establishing a principle,' he said. 'Next time, we do it for real.'

# 31

Xav and Talitha went to Echo Yard late on Monday afternoon. A spring storm had broken over Oxfordshire when he pulled up alongside Talitha's white Range Rover. She waited until Xav had got out of his car before lowering the window.

'Think this is going to stop?'

'I've got a spare umbrella.' He opened the boot, took out his umbrella and the one Ella used and opened both. 'Come on, it closes at six.'

The yard didn't really feel like a yard once they were through the gates. Much of the salvage on show was intended for outdoors, so efforts had been made to fake the sort of gardens it might sit in. Scrubby patches of lawn held moss-covered birdbaths, the central feature was a pond, surrounded by reeds and flowering yellow marigolds, a fountain playing in its midst. Garden benches sat everywhere, most laden down with neglected pot plants. Wrought-iron gazebos on stone pillars, tall columns and huge statues formed a skyline, and rusting iron railings created paths and enclosures. Gates, all of them for sale, blocked the path at irregular intervals. Dozens of terracotta plant pots, every shape and size imaginable, sat on wheeled trolleys and in one corner Tiffany lamps hung from lamp posts. A hazel tree, its branches so gnarled and twisted it belonged in the darkest sort of fairy tale, was festooned with lanterns.

The rain, and the late hour, had deterred all other customers, and he and Talitha were alone in the yard as they made their way along the first gravel path. Even in the poor light, Xav's eyes were drawn to a huge golden globe towards the back of the yard. Nearly ten feet in diameter, it sat on top of an enormous stone box. Beyond it towered a massive concrete structure, not part of the yard, but strangely in keeping with it. A water tower from the mid-twentieth century.

'Christ,' came Talitha's voice from under her umbrella. 'Where do we start?'

'Let's go around the perimeter,' Xav suggested. 'I'll meet you at the far end. Ignore anything that could be for sale. And try to think like a kid. Megan could have been coming here for decades.'

Without waiting for a reply, he set off, following a line of fire-places. He passed a collection of urns on columns like an outcrop of fungi and moved on through a menagerie of stone animals – lions on pedestals, crouched griffins, recumbent hounds – feeling himself watched by dozens of lifeless eyes. Relieved to leave them behind, he reached an outbuilding of dirty brick.

The roof was hidden beneath the lowest branches of an ash tree and layers of trailing ivy. The part of the wall that he could see was covered, practically every inch, in stone gargoyles. Some had teeth, some fangs, even tusks, many stuck out thick, sponge-like tongues in his direction; all of them were screaming at him. Some covered their eyes, some their ears, others clutched weapons in claw-like fists. Many, dripping with rain, seemed to be weeping. The theme was continued at Xav's feet, where imp-like creatures gazed malevolently up at him. Gargoyles were hollow, he remembered, basically elaborate drainpipes; they all had an empty cavity inside.

'Help you, mate?'

A man of about sixty-five in a green oilskin coat and flat

country-style cap on his grey curls had approached. He looked like a farmer.

'Sorry,' Xav gave the bloke – who had to be Megan's dad; they had the same dark eyes – the smile he saved for clients with upwards of ten million to invest. 'I've got a bit of a thing about gargoyles. The wife'll kill me if I come back with one, though. She's sent me for wood.'

'Over that side.' Gary Macdonald gestured to the opposite side of the yard, beyond the golden globe, past a statue of dancing wrought-iron skeletons, to where wooden doors lay stacked up like packs of cards beneath a makeshift awning. 'What you looking for exactly?'

Macdonald gestured that they should cross the yard and Xav followed. As they walked behind the huge golden globe, he spotted a Victorian roll-top bath that might work in his bathroom at home. Maybe he'd bring Ella here if things ever went back to normal. On the other hand, maybe not; there had to be other salvage yards.

'We've bought a house in central Oxford,' he explained, as they circumnavigated the pond. 'We've got a lot of internal wood from the 1970s and my wife wants to replace it with something more appropriate.'

'Well, if you want to give me some details.'

Talitha found him thirty minutes later, ten minutes before the yard was due to close for the night. She shook her head at his raised eyebrows.

'I think we're wasting our time.' Xav kept his voice low. Megan's dad had vanished, and he wasn't entirely sure where he'd got to.

'You don't think it's here?'

'Oh, I think it's here, all right. Just not accessible.'

Xav had had plenty of time to think while he'd been listening to Macdonald senior drone on about reclaimed oak, South American walnut and Polish pine.

'She wouldn't risk putting it anywhere that could be sold or moved,' Xav said. 'Even things like this monstrosity,' he gestured at the golden globe, 'could tickle someone's fancy. She'd have left it somewhere permanent, somewhere not for sale, under any circumstances.'

'Where then?'

Xav nodded towards a structure at the very rear of the yard, one that loomed over everything in it.

Talitha said, 'The water tower?'

'Who visits a water tower?' Xav asked. 'The water authority, once in a blue moon. And I wouldn't be surprised if that one's no longer in use.'

'You think Megan climbed that?' Talitha shuddered and Xav remembered that a fear of heights was one of the very few weaknesses his old friend had ever admitted to.

'She was pretty fit at eighteen. She ran cross-country, and she was in the climbing team.'

Talitha gave the slow, slight nod of the head that indicated agreement. 'Can we get up there?' she said.

Xav had been asking himself that same question. 'I think we have to,' he said. 'I think we have to come back after dark.'

When Xav arrived home, his wife met him in the hallway; she was wearing her wedding dress.

He said, 'Did I miss something?'

Ella had a goofy, even weird sense of humour, but this was a new one. She marched up to him, heels tapping on the floor tiles; she was in full make-up, only the coronet of flowers was missing. Reaching him, she spun on the spot.

'Unzip me.' She told him.

Wondering how he'd explain to a wife, ten years younger and married less than two years, that he really didn't fancy sex right now, Xav did what he was told. His wife's skin, the gold of newly opened sunflowers, seemed to burst from the white silk.

'Easier, or harder?' she asked when the zip was fully down.

'Sorry?'

'Easier or harder than on our wedding night? This dress is my litmus test. If it's easier to pull the zip, I've lost weight; harder and I've gained. Tondy says I'm looking chubby.'

Tondy was his wife's agent. As Ella turned again to face him, he said, 'You couldn't step on the bathroom scales?'

'Pounds and ounces are deceptive, inches are what count.' She stretched up to kiss him, catching hold of his tie and tugging him closer. 'So, harder or easier?'

He hadn't a clue. ''Bout the same.'

She mock-glared at him, unconvinced, and then suddenly, her face was serious again.

'You'll laugh at this,' she said.

'Good. I could use a laugh.'

'I think I'm being papped.'

'Leave the house in your wedding dress and I can guarantee it.'

'Earlier, when I was still in leggings and an old T-shirt of yours, someone was right outside taking photographs through the window.'

Xav and Ella's house had no front garden; passers-by could rap on the windows, even look through them. As a rule, they didn't; the people of Oxford were, for the most part, civilised.

'Did you see who it was?' he asked as Ella turned and flounced back into the kitchen. She'd be reluctant to take her wedding finery off now; she loved dressing up. He followed more slowly, checking out the window that overlooked the street. They'd never bothered with net curtains; *'What am I, a maiden aunt?'* his wife had said.

Someone earlier that day had stood outside and taken a photograph of the inside of his house. Of his wife.

Ella could be right, it could have been paparazzi; it could also have been Megan.

'I made dinner,' Ella called back at him. She was a dreadful cook. 'Second time this week,' she added. 'Are you proud of me?'

'I'm a lucky man,' he said, as he went to join her.

# 32

Westminster might be in Whitsun recess but Amber had late meetings in town on Monday and didn't get home until after nine o'clock. Entering the house by the back door, she closed it quietly; the girls were always alert to Mummy sneaking in. Given half a chance, they'd both leap from their beds to say hi, whatever the hour.

The steam in the kitchen was heavy with cumin, lime and coriander; on the worktop a bowl of couscous was soaking in saffron water. Thank God she'd married a man who liked cooking. Dex appeared from the hallway, barefoot, ink on his hands, remnants of the girls' dinner on his T-shirt.

'Hey,' they both said. She let her head fall onto his shoulder; he helped her remove her coat.

'How've you been?' she asked, as she took the wine bottle from the fridge. They had a rule about not drinking mid-week, but maybe half term and recess didn't count as the working week.

'The girls are fine,' he told her, because she never asked about them first, and he knew she always wanted to. 'Swimming, lunch at Chloe and Amelia's house, afternoon at that hideous place in Thame. Ruby fell out with her best friend but made up an hour later, and Pearl, according to Ruby, has a boyfriend, but they haven't kissed yet.'

'That hideous place in Thame' was Wizz Kidz, the indoor adventure playground; the girls loved it, their dad was less keen.

He held out a glass. 'In less exciting news, we got the Canary Wharf job, and I'm lead architect.'

Amber kissed her husband, and felt less guilty about the wine, because now they could call it a celebration. She climbed onto a stool as Dex pulled a casserole dish from the oven.

'Emily did mention something.' Dex ladled out spiced chicken with apricots and pineapple. 'She wasn't too worried but wanted to be sure we knew and were OK with it.'

Emily was the girls' nanny. Amber made an 'I'm listening' face.

'She was approached by someone in Wizz Kidz, while the girls were on the big slide.'

'What do you mean "approached"?'

Dex spoke in between mouthfuls, very little got in the way of Dex and his food. 'The kids were all playing, and the nannies and mums were in the coffee area, keeping half an eye on them, you know how it works in that place.' He paused and chewed for a few moments. 'Anyway, a woman sat down at Emily's table.'

Something was bothering Dex; he was pretending to be fine, but the lines of his face were tighter, like his skin had been stretched.

'A woman?' she said.

'Megan.'

Amber put her fork down. 'Megan was in Wizz Kidz?'

'Yep. She said she was there with another family, although Emily didn't see anything of them, had recognised Pearl and Ruby, so wanted to say hello. She sat with them for a bit, Emily said, asking all sorts of questions about them, where they go to school, what after-school activities they do, that sort of thing.'

'Why the hell didn't Emily phone us? Why didn't you call me when you found out?'

Dex held up one hand, and God help her, if he said, 'Chill, babe' – she'd put a fork in his eye.

'Emily said she was in two minds, but she kept a very close eye on the girls after that, and she hopes it goes without saying that she didn't tell her anything about their habits or their movements. I believe her, Am. Emily knows she has to be extra careful with the girls.'

Amber got to her feet. 'I'm going to see them.'

'Babe, what's up with you? I know she's not exactly a role model, but she may have been telling the truth. She could have been with another family.'

He didn't believe that; she could see it in his eyes. Dex was trying to pretend that everything was cool, because that was his instinct, but his face told a different story.

Upstairs the girls, who still slept in the same room, were fast asleep, the unusual activity of half term having exhausted them. Pearl, who saw pixies in the undergrowth and monsters in every cupboard, was tucked away beneath the duvet, with nothing to reveal her presence but a few coils of dark hair. Ruby, though, with her super-fast metabolism producing heat like a mini furnace, had pushed the duvet down to her feet and lay curled on the mattress, a soft toy clutched between her chubby hands. Amber bent to kiss her daughter's forehead, to breathe her in for a few seconds, and felt her heart stop.

The toy Ruby clutched was not one Amber had seen before: an elephant, with silver-grey fur, softer than velvet, from a range that Amber knew, from years of buying baby gifts for friends, to be ridiculously expensive.

'Hello, Mummy.' Ruby's huge eyes looked black in the dim light.

'Hey, baby.' Amber kissed her daughter again. 'Who's the new friend?'

'It's Elly.'

Elly the Elephant – of course it was. Ruby had no imagination, her mother had used it all up, giving birth to Pearl.

'Where d'you get her?'

Ruby's eyes were closing again. 'Auntie Megan.' She murmured something else, something so low that Amber barely caught it. Getting to her feet, she crossed quickly to Pearl's bed, lifting the duvet cover to reveal her older daughter's sleeping face.

Pearl, too, had a gift from 'Auntie Megan'. Another Jellycat toy. Curled up on the top of her head, a little like a soft pink crown, was an octopus, its many legs entwined around Pearl's hair as though it would never let her go.

Amber left the room with Ruby's sleepy mumble ringing in her ears.

'Auntie Megan said she's an ellyfant. Cos ellyfants never forget.'

## 33

Xav went back to the salvage yard after midnight, grateful that the bad weather was making the night extra dark. As he'd suspected, the water tower wasn't in Echo Yard itself, but in a separate area of adjacent land, entirely contained within high steel fencing. Xav tucked his car against the hedge – it was black and unlikely to be seen from the road – and then retrieved his loft hook, borrowed from home, out of the boot.

He'd had plenty of time to plan. Ella had gone out after dinner to the official opening of one of the new shops in the Westgate centre, and had arrived home late, too tired to chat. He'd hoped it would have stopped raining by now, but it had at least slackened off, and the cloud cover was a definite bonus. Feeling the damp steal across his face, Xav was surprised at how calm he felt, but as he approached the eight-foot-high steel railing and stepped into the shadow of the tower, he felt a stab of nerves. Maybe it hadn't been such a good idea to come alone. But Felix was rarely sober these days, Dan was afraid of his own shadow and he could hardly ask either of the girls.

Xav was dressed in black, like a cat burglar, and while he had a head torch, he didn't want to switch it on just yet. He pushed the loft hook through the railing before using a Thames Water sign, firmly screwed into the metal uprights, to give him a leg-up and allow him to leap over.

Close up, the tower soared above him. Built of concrete some-time in the 1950s, it was a great circular tank of water held high on six concrete columns. It looked alien, even predatory, like early film adaptations of *The War of the Worlds*, and climbing it was the last thing he wanted to do.

Even so, he used the loft hook to bring down the ladder and began. Before he was ten feet in the air, the wind picked up and at fifteen feet an unreasonable fear gripped him. Telling himself the ladder was sound, that water engineers must still use it from time to time, he forced himself to keep going. At twenty feet the tower seemed to be moving, as though conspiring with the wind to shake him off.

The first platform, when he reached it, gave him chance to rest but from this point on, the climb became harder. Once he set off again, he'd be climbing a ladder that sloped backwards to snake itself around the giant cylindrical tank. Only a narrow safety rail, that could have rusted years ago, would stop him tumbling if he lost his grip. For a short while, he'd have to climb practically upside down, and Xav was a long way from being as fit as he used to be.

The moment his feet left the platform, panic hit him. As his body began to tremble, Xav fixed his eyes on the concrete and told himself it wasn't far. He could support his own body weight for a minute or two. Chilled by rain all day, the cold metal stung his hands, but he could ignore that. His feet were sliding on rungs no longer parallel to the ground, but the ladder was sound.

He'd reached the trickiest part of all, pulling himself around the curved lower edge so that he could once again climb verti-cally. If he slipped now, he'd break his back. A last pull and he was upright again. Gritting his teeth, he climbed the last few rungs.

Pulling himself onto the upper platform, Xav collapsed and, only when he'd caught his breath, took stock of his surroundings.

He was on a narrow ledge that ran around the circumference of the tower. The water tank, a large, contained mass of dark water, was directly below him.

As a stronger gust of wind hit the tower, Xav looked up. Above the centre of the tank was a smaller, circular structure that appeared to be some sort of control room. He struggled to his feet and, holding tight to the railing, made his way around the perimeter. The countryside surrounding the tower was flat and empty; the closest villages, and they were all tiny, at least a mile away.

Back at the door to the control room, he tried the handle. It was locked, of course, and no window to allow him to see inside. Xav took a step back, kicked out, and the door sprang open to reveal a circular space, like the uppermost room in a lighthouse, but without windows. Free at last from the risk of being spotted, Xav switched on his head torch.

The room was a teenager's den. A square of threadbare rug covered the concrete floor and an oversized teddy leered at him from the far wall. A beanbag close to his feet smelled rotten. A pile of magazines had melted into each other and he thought he recognised one of the A level chemistry textbooks. Hanging from a hook on the wall was a battery-operated lamp. Megan had brought all this stuff up here herself, climbing that treacherous ladder.

Xav didn't know whether he was more sad or annoyed that Megan had never told him and the others about this place. So much they hadn't known about her.

There was no sign that anyone had been here in decades and yet his heart was thudding again, this time with excitement. Megan could surely not have two such hiding places; the film and signed confession had to be here.

The torch beam landed on a satchel, stuffed away behind the

bean bag. Inside, Xav found a scrapbook and put it to one side while he emptied the bag. A crumpled tissue fell out, blood-stained, as though someone had used it to stem a nosebleed.

There was nothing else in the satchel, even in the zipped pocket at the back, so he settled himself on the bean bag and opened the scrapbook. On the first page, he saw his own face looking back at him.

It was all about him. The whole bloody album. Often the pictures were of the whole group, but he was centre stage in all of them. Lying full length along a row of seats in the common room at school; striding out of the river at Port Meadow, water streaming off his body; throwing wood onto a fire pit, as sparks flew into the night around him. He came across his old school library card, ticket stubs from bands they'd seen, a programme from Reading Festival.

On the back page, he found his old school tie stuck to the paper. He lifted the flap, just to check, and saw his nametag, *Xavier Attwood*, on the reverse side.

The blood-stained tissue had been his too, he remembered now, or rather one Megan had given him when Felix had kicked a football directly into his nose. She'd kept it. All that time, Megan had been in love with him, and he never knew.

But there was something, worm-like, wriggling away inside him. *You did know, though, didn't you? You just pushed it to the back of your mind because it was too much to deal with.*

'And no sign at all of the confession? Of the film?'

When Xav had got back to his car, he'd been surprised, and grateful, to see several text messages from Talitha. She was the only one he'd told about his plans. When he'd texted back, she'd replied immediately, letting him know she was awake. Needing to talk to someone, he'd phoned her.

'None,' he said. 'I turned that place upside down before I left. It isn't there.'

'It's probably where she hid it though, twenty years ago, when she knew she was going to prison. It would have been there all the time she was inside.'

A car flashed by on the road, too fast to have noticed Xav's car, still tucked away close to the hedge.

'Yeah, well that doesn't help us now, does it?' he said.

'Did you leave the place as you found it? Will she know someone's been in?'

'I kicked the bloody door in – of course she'll know. We have to confront her. We can't keep on like this.'

Silence. Then, 'Christ.'

He'd never heard Talitha sound so defeated. 'Yeah,' he replied.

'Where are you going now?'

'Home. Where else would I go?'

He hung up on Tal as the thought occurred to him that before too much longer, going home might no longer be an option.


Xav parked a little way down the street and sat in the car for a while. He'd never in his life felt more tired or less able to sleep. There were no lights on in his house, thank God.

Oxford city centre at one in the morning was rarely still – the clubs kept going until the early hours – but St John Street was far enough away from Jericho not to attract the drunks and the stragglers. The stone-faced terraced street, shining gold in the lamplight, was empty, and its occupants asleep.

For years, Xav had envied those who slept well and easily. He lay awake, for hours sometimes, haunted by waking dreams of what his life could have been like; what all their lives could have been if that night hadn't happened.

Sophie Robinson would have been fifty-eight by now, her

daughters grown women. She might even have been a grand-mother. Years ago, Xav had found out their birthdates – by chance, he hadn't been looking – but now every year on 10 January, 17 June and 25 August, he found himself thinking about the three women he'd helped to wipe off the face of the earth. When he saw young women in their twenties, pale-skinned and with dark hair, he thought of the two Robinson girls whom he'd never pass in the street or bump into in a bar. As the years had gone by, he'd started to ask himself if this crippling guilt would have been less if he'd taken his share of the blame twenty years ago. There'd even come a time when he'd started to envy Megan.

Conscious that tomorrow he had to be on the first train, that he had a full day ahead of him, and that the world's bond markets wouldn't close while he lost his mind, Xav at last got out of the car. The sound of the door slamming bounced off the buildings with a half-hearted echo, and he crossed the street.

'Xav!'

It was half a call, half a whisper, and on any other city-centre street, he might not have heard it, but in the dark silence, it came floating across the tarmacked road. He turned and saw a woman on the opposite pavement, half-hidden behind a blue car. Megan.

# 34

Xav felt a sweat break out. He was afraid, and it was worse than the fear he'd felt climbing the water tower. The risk then had been definable. This new one was not.

Megan stood still as stone, letting him stare. A thought crept into his mind, one so disturbing he didn't give it air to breathe, but dismissed it, never to be considered again. He held up both hands in a questioning gesture and she took his movement as a signal to approach.

'I thought you were never coming home,' she said when she was close enough to touch him.

'Meg, what are you doing here?'

He could smell her perfume, could name it, God help him, even after twenty years. Coco by Chanel, her eighteenth birthday present from the gang. They'd all chipped in, but he and Amber had bought it in Debenhams one Saturday and the final choice had been his. Years later, she was still wearing his perfume.

'I've had to leave my flat,' she said. 'I've nowhere to go.'

'What do you mean you had to leave?'

What did she mean, she had nowhere to go?

'The media have found me. They've been camped outside for three days now and the other people in the house know who I am.'

Xav glanced around; the street was still empty. 'So? I mean, what's their problem? You've served your time. And you're not exactly dangerous.'

The words faltered on his tongue, Megan could very easily be dangerous.

She took a step closer. 'Try telling them that. I'm a child killer, Xav – no one wants to live in the same house as me. The front door has been vandalised – someone wrote *murderer* on it in red paint. And my own door has been kicked in, my room wrecked. They smeared shit all over the walls and peed on my bed. They've been messing with my food too – I've had to throw it all away. I can't lock the door. I'm not safe.'

And with that, he knew why she was here.

'What about the others?' he managed.

A flicker of annoyance crossed her face. 'I can't go to Dan's – he lives in a monastery. And Amber has more security around her house than the Beckhams.'

To know that, she must have been snooping around Amber's house. He wondered how many times she'd stood in this street, maybe watching him and Ella through the windows, and his stomach twisted at the thought of Megan coming anywhere near his wife.

'Tal?' he tried. 'What about Felix? I mean, you work with him.'

'Sarah and Mark can't stand me. Sarah's trying to get me sacked – there's no way she'd let me stay with them. And I went to Talitha's house. Mark wouldn't let me in.'

That probably wasn't even true. He'd spoken to Tal not half an hour ago. She would have told him.

'Ella's never met me.' Megan pushed out her bottom lip and widened her eyes at him. 'She can't throw me out before she's even met me.'

Ella knew nothing about Megan, nothing about her former friendship with Xav, her long incarceration, or her reappearance.

228

Even so, few wives would admit a strange woman into their house without question. Actually, Ella might be one of the few; nothing ever seemed to ruffle Ella's zen-like calm.

Xav glanced at the windows of his house, two doors away; still black and empty. Unless his wife had an early job, in which case her packed suitcase would be in the hallway, she rarely got out of bed before eight. It was possible he could sneak Megan in and out without Ella even knowing.

'Did you drive here?' He looked up and down the road for a car he didn't recognise. 'You'll need to move by seven or you'll get clamped.'

She held up a hand, car keys looped around an index finger. 'No problem. I still have a job, in spite of Sarah's best efforts.'

Megan waited quietly while he unlocked the door. No suitcase in the hall, thank God, and he hurried her through to the kitchen.

'Coffee?' he said, before wondering if Ella would hear the kettle. Probably not, she slept like a child.

Megan ignored the offer. 'So, where have you been?' she said. 'I was beginning to think I'd have to sleep in the car.'

'Work.' He turned to the kettle, picked it up and put it down again – she hadn't said she wanted coffee. 'Lot on at the minute. Had a conference call with the team in New York.'

He had to stop talking. He'd never been a good liar, and he wasn't even dressed for work. 'I parked at Uxbridge.' He pulled a Tube station out of the air. 'Got a cab there. The firm have an Uber account for when we're pulling all-nighters.' Christ, he had to stop. 'Do you need anything? Towel? Toothbrush?'

She raised a shoulder so that her bag bounced against her hip. 'Emergency supplies,' she said. 'I've been expecting this for a while.'

'Tal said you were flat hunting. Any luck?'

'Tal's house is lovely, isn't it? I always wanted to live in Summertown.'

'I guess.'

Megan turned on the spot, taking in the high-ceilinged kitchen, the conservatory that led out into the walled garden.

'This is great too, though, and handy for the centre of town.' She looked up at the ceiling. 'Four floors, including the basement, four bedrooms, two bathrooms, and a study. Some work needed, but potentially the perfect family home.'

She sounded like the estate agent who'd sold him the place.

'I Googled it, in case you're wondering,' she went on. 'Properties for sale stay online for months after the sale goes through. I think I prefer Tal's on balance. No offence. But the parking will be easier, and the garden's a lovely size.'

She was talking as though Tal's house, his house, were hers for the asking. Maybe they were.

Megan turned away without waiting for a response and froze, her eyes fixed on something. For a moment, Xav had no idea what she could be looking at. Then on the dresser, he saw the wedding photograph of him and Ella.

It had been a snapshot, taken by one of the guests, of the two of them walking along a country path from the church to her parents' garden.

*'Marry me, Xav. That's your favour. Get rid of Amber, she doesn't deserve to have her hopes built up and dashed. You'll have a few years to sow your wild oats – I won't ask any questions – but you have to stay single. Stay single and when I get out, you have to marry me.'*

They'd stood, he and Megan by Felix's mum's car, the last time that summer the six of them had been together, and he'd thought how beautiful she was, and that he'd never really appreciated that before, and that she looked desperately sad and, at the same time, cold as polished steel. It had been all he could do not to throw himself on the ground at her feet and sob how sorry he was, how grateful that she was doing this for them and that he would do anything to make it up to her. Marry her? Of course, it was the least he could do.

Now, as he stood behind her, almost in touching distance, he wondered if she hadn't been acting in her own interests after all. With crap A level results, she'd have had to wave goodbye to the glittering career the rest of them could look forward to. With no university place, she'd have been dropped from their circle eventually. Maybe Megan had seen the accident as her last chance to bind the group to her forever; her last chance to keep Xav in her life.

She hadn't known that night about the police evidence of all their other attempts. She couldn't possibly have known she'd be charged with murder, not dangerous driving, that the sentence would be longer than the worst she could prepare for. By the time she'd realised the full force of the case against her, it would have been too late to back out. In fairness, though, she hadn't even tried. She'd done everything in her power to protect them. To protect him.

'She looks like me,' Megan said.

She turned to face him, even seemed a little surprised at how close he'd moved, and then nodded down at the photograph, and the traitorous thought that had crept into his head in the street was back. At twenty-nine, Ella didn't look much older than Megan had at eighteen. Her hair, cut short, dyed platinum blonde, was exactly how Megan had worn hers at school. Her tiny face was the same, her pointed chin the same, her big, dark eyes the same. He'd married a woman who could be Megan's younger sister.

Xav had had no idea, until that moment, how totally fucked up he was.

'Do you think so?' he managed.

Megan put her hands behind her back and stared up at him. 'Nothing like Amber,' she said.

'Amber and I were a long time ago.'

'So were you and I, almost.'

Of all the things she could remember, why did it have to be that? The party on the hill, high above Oxford, when pavilions and fires and lanterns had transformed an already wild garden into something akin to fairyland. As most people had either gone home or passed out, he and Megan had been sitting by the fire pit, talking, and it had almost happened between them. She'd been so brave, dropping huge hints about how she felt about him, and he'd bottled it. He'd let her go, and in doing so, may have changed the entire course of both their lives.

His wife was upstairs. His wife was feet away, possibly awake, although he and Megan were making no sound at all now. He might almost have been grateful for a squeaking floorboard, for a sudden coughing fit, but the night stayed treacherously silent as he took the last step that brought them to within inches of each other.

'Every night,' she whispered.

He knew exactly what she was going to say next. *Every night I thought about you.* He didn't give her a chance. He took hold of her face and kissed her.

# 35

Every time Xav's phone rang that week, he expected it to be Megan. By the Thursday, he was seriously considering throwing it into the Thames; the sound of it was shredding his nerves. Halfway through the morning, it rang and he knew, this time, it had to be her. He fumbled for his jacket, somehow managing to knock it off the back of his chair. *Number withheld*. He pressed accept.

'Xav, it's me.'

Not Megan, but Amber and, Christ, that was a stab of disappointment in his gut.

It had been Megan who'd brought the kiss to an end on Monday night, not him.

'*Not with your wife upstairs,*' she'd whispered, and he'd managed to pull himself together. The two of them had crept upstairs, he'd shown her to the spare room on the second floor and then lain awake beside his sleeping wife.

'Hi.' He could do without Amber right now.

'I need to see you,' she said. 'Are you free for lunch?'

'I don't do lunch, Am.' He'd lost count of the number of times he'd explained this.

'Later then. I've got meetings, but I can rearrange.'

'Is this really—'

'It's about Megan. Xav, you need to hear this.'

He met Amber at the entrance to Portcullis House; she signed him in through security and walked ahead to her office on the third floor. She was wearing a mauve close-fitting suit with high-heeled navy shoes.

'Thanks for coming here,' she said, after she'd told her assistant to hold all calls. 'It's difficult for me, you know, restaurants and things.'

Amber's office window looked out over the river. Xav could see St Thomas's Hospital on one side of the bridge, the old County Hall on the other, a constant stream of people pushing their way along the embankment. Further downstream, the London Eye moved slowly.

'I haven't got long,' he told her.

Amber took a seat in one of the easy chairs. She'd taken off her jacket. Her shirt was silk, tailored, and he could see damp patches beneath her armpits. 'She's been stalking the girls.'

For a second he was confused. 'Who? Megan?'

'Yes, Megan.' Amber's face twisted. 'She's going after my daughters, Xav.'

He'd seen that look on Amber's face before, just not for many years; it meant she was about to cry. He reached out and took hold of both her hands. 'OK, take it easy. Are they both OK?'

Megan wouldn't hurt Amber's children. Amber had got it wrong somehow, but the look on her face was scaring him. She'd reddened, was breathing too quickly, and her eyes were filled with tears. She seemed to be struggling to speak.

'Come on,' he urged. 'Take it easy. Start at the beginning.'

She gulped in air like a drowning woman. 'She followed them and their nanny to an indoor play area on Monday,' Amber managed at last. 'And then yesterday, she was waiting for them outside their ballet class. I've no idea how she knew where it was – I certainly didn't tell her.'

He let go of her hands. 'I think we should assume Megan knows as much about all of us as it's possible to find out. So, what happened?'

'She was there when I went to collect them. You know how I like to be around for them when I can – and it's not so that people will see me being a good mother, it's so I *can* be a good mother. They like me to pick them up, not Emily.'

Xav tried to remember who Emily was; of course, Amber's nanny.

'So, we were waiting in the car park outside, and one of the other mum's was bending my ear about how she didn't agree with the increases to child benefit and then Megan appeared.'

The way she had to him in the street. Xav had to admit, it was disconcerting. 'Did you ask her what she was doing there?'

'She said she was in the area – don't ask me why, I didn't think to ask – and wanted to see the girls again. She said she'd been thinking about them such a lot, about how beautiful they are, and how much she wants to be a part of their lives now she's back in Oxford. That's her new euphemism for being released from prison, Xav, she's "back in Oxford again", as though she's been on some sort of fancy sabbatical.'

'Yeah, focus, Am. I can understand why you don't want her turning up unannounced, but this doesn't sound too bad.'

'Oh really, well keep listening because it didn't take her long to get on the subject of you.'

Xav pushed away the image of Megan's face, inches from his own.

'What did she say about me?'

Amber sniffed. 'Oh, now you're interested? Well, I'm getting to that. She'd brought presents for them both – she did the same thing on Monday too – and you know what kids are like with gifts. They were all over their new Auntie Megan, wanting to bring her home for tea, and I tried to make excuses, but she focused all her attention on them, not me, and practically invited herself round.'

'You took her home with you?'

'She gave me no choice. Other people were watching by this time. You don't know what she's like, Xav—'

Oh, he did. He knew exactly what Megan was like. He knew what she smelled like, what she tasted like.

'I couldn't say no without making a scene, I'm sure some of the other mums were getting suspicious, so she followed us home and now she knows where we live.'

She'd have known anyway. 'Am, I think you're over-reacting.'

'Oh, am I?' Amber's voice rose. If she weren't careful, they'd be heard in the next room – Amber never tired of saying the Commons was leakier than a sieve. 'Well, tell me something,' she went on. 'How did Ella take the news the two of you are getting a divorce?'

'What?'

'That was her bombshell while the girls were getting changed. She said she had something important to tell me. She wanted me to know first, because of the history you and I had, that you and she are getting together.'

Xav half got to his feet. It had been one kiss. One fucking kiss.

'What the fuck?' he managed.

'News to you, is it? Because it surprised me a bit, but apparently the two of you had a thing, even back when we were going out. She said something about Will Markham's party, when I wasn't feeling very well. She said you were going to break up with me once we went to uni and start seeing her instead. She said that's why the two of you both applied to Cambridge so that you could be together.'

Will Markham, that fabulous house on Boars Hill, a garden that seemed to go on for miles; and the best party he could remember.

'Well, first, that's bullshit, and second, it was twenty years ago. What the hell does it matter – to you, I mean – now?'

Looking affronted, Amber said, 'Oh, it doesn't, but I thought you'd want to know.'

'I do, thanks, Am. But why does she think the two of us are getting back together? Not that we were ever together in the first place.'

'Well, it could be something to do with the fact you actually promised to save yourself and marry her when she got out of prison, but she didn't mention that. She's keeping up the can't-remember-anything nonsense. She said it's been obvious since she got back that the attraction is still there. You can't keep your eyes off each other, apparently. She said that's why Ella didn't come to Tal's that first Saturday – you didn't want the two of them meeting up. She said you don't love Ella, you never did, she was just second best because you got too lonely but that it's over now. Xav, she sounded mad.'

He couldn't look at Amber. 'She came to the house on Monday night.'

For a moment, the admission seemed to hang in the air.

'Shit. Was Ella there?'

'Asleep, upstairs. I was late back.' He hadn't yet told anyone else in the group about his visit to the water tower, and it looked like Tal hadn't either. Events were going too fast to keep up with.

'You didn't let her in, did you?'

Oh, like it was that easy. 'She spent the night,' he admitted as he got to his feet. Sitting still didn't feel possible any more.

Back at the window, watching a man buy flowers from a stand near Westminster Bridge, he told her about Megan's sob story, installing her in the spare room and about her leaving, calm and grateful, shortly after he'd dragged himself downstairs the next morning. He didn't tell Amber about the kiss, or that he'd lain awake most of the night. By the time he was finished, Amber was pale-faced and scared. He didn't blame her.

'Xav, I know I've been the first to argue we should cut Megan some slack, but I'm not sure any more.' Amber seemed calmer, having got the worst off her chest. 'I haven't told you everything.'

Xav felt something harden in his stomach. 'Go on,' he said.

'Once the girls came back, she started making a big fuss of them again. And she's good with them – she's got a sort of natural gift for talking to children. She was telling them about Antigua, where Dex's family come from. She must have read it all in a book because there's no way she's been to the Caribbean, but she was talking about folk legends and magic, people who could turn into animals and spirits who lived in the mountains and the rivers. It was fascinating, even I could see that. They thought she was fabulous, but you know what occurred to me after a few minutes?'

'What?'

'She was luring them away. She was trying to charm them, casting some sort of spell over them.'

Xav took a step back towards her. 'Am, I thin—'

She held up a hand to ward him off. 'No, listen. I put the TV on in the end. Me. I never encourage them to watch TV, but I couldn't stand it and then she started saying that the worst thing about being inside for a young woman was the lost opportunity to have children. She said even with you in her life, she was never going to have a child of her own. She told me she had a bad accident in prison – I guess it must have been the one Tal and Dan told us about, when she supposedly lost her memory. There was massive internal damage and she had to have a hysterectomy. She can't ever have kids.'

'Not a problem as far as I'm concerned. Am, let me be clear, I'm not leaving Ella for Megan.'

He wasn't, he realised. It didn't matter what strange, twisted attraction she had for him, and maybe Amber was right to call it a charm or a spell. It made no difference. Xav loved his wife.

'You don't get it yet, do you?' Amber hurried on. 'She started looking at Pearl and Ruby as though she was going to eat one of them, and she said, "I'll never have anything as precious as these two, will I?" and when I tried to think of something to say, she looked at me, all mean and cold, and she said, "So you're going to have to give me one of yours."'

For a moment, Xav wasn't sure he'd heard her correctly.

'What?' he said, after seconds had gone by. 'I mean, you're not serious?'

'Oh, she laughed about it, and made out she was joking, but she was perfectly serious. That's my favour, Xav. I have to give her one of my children.'

# 36

At a little before eight on Friday morning, as his train was pulling into Paddington, Xav got a text from Felix on his burner phone.

*Good news. Found it! Meet tonight at Tal's old house. By the pool. 8.30 p.m. Don't call, I can't talk. See you later.*

*Found it.* He had to mean the film and signed confession, the proof. Xav found Felix in his contacts and was on the point of pressing call when he remembered he'd been told not to. Amber then, she'd still be at home, getting the girls ready for whatever half-term activity was planned. He typed quickly.

*Did you get the text?*

A minute later, she replied.

*A little while ago. Tal too. Sounds great. Best not to talk, though. See you later.*

Xav put the phone away. Was that it then? Was it over?

The day passed maddeningly slowly and Xav's train home was delayed. On top of that, traffic out of Oxford was worse than usual. The heavens had opened that afternoon and vast glistening puddles lay across the tarmac, slowing everyone down.

The rain was slackening by the time he reached Talitha's old village. The huge electronic gates of her parents' house were open and Xav pulled into the drive with a sense of foreboding. He hadn't been back here in twenty years, not since that summer. Even Talitha rarely came here any more; she and her parents hadn't got on for years.

It was nearly quarter to nine in the evening.

So, Megan had left the proof here after all. He'd been wracking his brains all day to work out how she'd done it because that last night he'd walked her to her car and watched her drive away. Somehow, though, she had, and Felix had worked it out. As he parked and switched off the engine, Xav was conscious of a sense, not of disappointment, exactly, more of missed opportunity. If anyone had been meant to get the better of Megan, it should have been him. Megan aside, he was the smartest.

He'd look after her though, even if the others weren't prepared to play nice. She could have his share of the trust fund, he might even be able to find some more funds he could direct her way. He'd see her taken care of, as long as she dropped the psychological torture.

By the pool, Felix's text had said, but the pool was in darkness, bouncing with a life of its own as the rain fell into it. There was a light on in the pool house though, and Xav thought he could see silhouettes beyond the window. He tapped on the door before pushing it open. Talitha appeared.

'We were getting worried,' she said. 'Everyone's here, even Amber.'

Shaking the rain off his hair, Xav followed Talitha inside. The pool house was smaller than Xav remembered and smelled of mildew and pool chemicals; the bamboo chairs had splintered with age and the cushions were stained. It felt wrong to be in here, like coming back to a place he'd spent his adult life trying to escape.

Felix was at the bar, no surprise there, and Daniel stood by the pool table, gripping one of the cues like a weapon. Amber sat on the edge of an easy chair, her hands clenched. She gave him a smile, though, one that made her seem, for a moment, like the old Amber.

Xav had no sense of having interrupted a discussion; Felix had waited for him before breaking the good news. No wonder the others were looking edgy.

'Parents?' Xav asked Talitha. The last thing they needed was an elderly Barnaby Slater QC barging in.

'Palermo,' she told him. 'They like to go before it gets too hot. It's only us here.'

'Drink?' Felix offered.

Xav shook his head. 'I'm good.' He crossed to Amber and sat down, but when he looked up, the others were all watching him. They all looked tense, even annoyed.

'Sorry, guys,' he said. 'Trains, then traffic.'

The sound of the rain outside seemed to grow louder.

'So?' Talitha said. She was by the door, as though guarding the entrance, in spite of what she'd said about them being alone on the property.

Talitha was talking to him, not Felix. Four pairs of eyes were still fixed on him.

'End the suspense, please,' Talitha went on. 'I mean, we all appreciate the discretion, but I've been beside myself all day.'

'Where was it?' Amber asked.

Felix pushed himself away from the bar. 'Never mind where was it, are you sure you've got it,' he said. 'I mean a film could be anything, we know that already. We need to get it developed.'

Xav looked from one face to the next; still the same expression on all of them. 'Guys,' he said, 'I don't know what you're talking about.'

No one spoke.

'Xav, this isn't funny.' Amber's voice was unsteady. 'Why would you do that?'

He'd missed something, something massive.

Daniel said, 'Did she put you up to it?'

Xav pulled his phone from his pocket. Getting to his feet, he found Felix's text and held it out as he strode to the bar.

'This arrived early this morning,' he said. 'When I was on the train. What good news? What did you find? And what the fuck are you all talking about?'

With a trembling hand, Felix took the phone. A few seconds later, he handed it back. 'I didn't send this,' he said.

They were messing with him. 'What do you mean, you didn't send it? It came from your phone, from your number.'

Talitha grabbed the phone from Xav and read the message. 'Shit,' she said.

'What?' Amber was on her feet now, even Dan had put the cue down.

Talitha held her own phone out towards Xav. He read the message on screen, a message from him:

*Good news. Found it. Meet tonight at Tal's old house. By the pool. 8.30 p.m. Don't call, I can't talk. See you later.*

The same message he'd got from Felix, except this one he'd sent himself, apparently, to all four of the others.

'We got it at six forty-five this morning,' Talitha said. 'You asked us to meet here.'

'No,' Xav shook his head. 'No, I didn't. I thought Felix did.'

'How is that possible?' Amber asked.

'Megan,' Dan said.

Amber turned on him. 'Well, obviously Megan, but how did she do it?'

Felix had pulled himself upright. The tallest, he could see over their heads and his eyes were fixed on the window. Xav was conscious of the others turning around as he did. Outside, the pool lights had activated and, at the far end, a solitary figure stood on the tiles, looking down at the water.

Felix said, 'I think we're about to find out.'

## 37

Felix led the way outside. It may only have been Dutch courage, but of all of them, he seemed to have the most. Talitha and Daniel walked together, sharing nervous glances. Amber hung back and even took hold of Xav's hand as they followed the other three.

'She scares me,' she whispered.

Megan scared Xav too. She hadn't dressed for the weather, and already her light summer dress was soaking wet. Her long hair clung to her skull and streamed down her back. She had a satchel-style bag, its strap crossed over her chest, as though it held something precious.

Felix led the group to the opposite edge of the rectangular pool.

'Hi, guys.' Megan looked up at the sky and water poured down her face. 'Can you believe it? Raining on my parade.'

'What do you want, Megan?' Felix had taken his stance directly across the water. The others gathered behind him.

'I thought we should end it here.' Megan had to raise her voice to be heard above the rain. 'Where it all began, by Tal's pool.'

Amber squeezed Xav's hand. 'She does remember. I knew she did.'

Amber's whisper shouldn't have been heard over the rain, across the distance, but somehow it was.

'Well, of course I remember,' Megan yelled back. 'You think I'd forget what you lot did to me? For a second? You could batter half my skull away and I'd remember that.'

Xav dropped Amber's hand. 'Meg, let's go inside. We can't talk out here.'

For a moment, he thought she'd refuse, that she'd carry on screaming until, storm or not, the neighbours called the police, but then she looked over their heads.

'The pool house,' she said. 'OK. That's where we hatched our vile little plan.'

Megan entered last and stood with her back to the door. Water fell off her body and pooled on the linoleum. Nobody switched on the lights.

Megan spoke first. 'Just to get it out of the way, I let myself into your house first thing this morning, Xav, and used your phone to text the others. I kept a key from the night before. I'll hang on to it, if you don't mind. When I got to work, I used Felix's phone when he was out of the office and, yes, you both need to change your passcodes now.'

Felix was leaning against the rear wall. He didn't look frightened, like the rest of them. He looked furious. 'I'll ask again,' he said. 'What do you want?'

'Felix don't.' Amber was huddled on the edge of the old sofa. 'Don't make things worse.'

Talitha, too, had taken a seat, directly opposite Megan. Daniel was standing behind her, his hands on the chair back. It was possible he meant to look protective; equally possible that he was hiding behind Tal.

'Oh, I think things are about as bad as they can get.' Felix hadn't taken his eyes off the woman by the door. 'What do you want, Megan?'

'What do I want?' she said. 'I want to look you all in the face and say, you bunch of cowardly, miserable, treacherous shits!'

Xav had expected it, had said the same thing to himself over the years; even so, the force of Megan's rage felt blistering.

Felix, who seemed to have become their spokesman, said, 'OK, so now you've done it, what—'

Megan didn't let Felix get any further. 'Oh no, I'm not nearly done. I gave you my entire life. I gave up everything for you lot, and all I asked of you, in fact, the last thing I said to you, was don't forget me.'

There was a tremor in Megan's voice; to his shame, Xav found it giving him hope. Emotion was the opposite of strength.

'We didn't forget you, Meg, not for a second,' Amber said.

Megan turned on her, making Amber cringe into her seat. 'Oh really? Because not one of you phoned or wrote or came to visit me in twenty bloody years.' She sneered at Dan, who had his eyes fixed on the back of Talitha's head. 'You, you snivelling piece of shit – you were less than a mile away for four years and you didn't come. And now, finally, when I'm out, you treat me like a pariah, some sort of wannabe mate from the old days trying to hang out with the rich, cool kids.'

'Nobody asked you to do what you did,' Felix too had raised his voice. 'You volunteered.'

Megan gasped, and Felix seemed to think he had her on the run. He even took an aggressive step towards her. 'You failed your A levels, or as good as. You crashed and burned, Megan, so don't whine at us about missing out on your fabulous future. You didn't have one.'

'I could have re-sat, you miserable git,' Megan yelled back. 'I would have lost a year, at most. Instead, I lost twenty.' She pointed her finger at Talitha. 'You, you were supposed to represent me, you promised you'd get your sleazebag of a dad to act for me and what did he do instead? He's been representing Michael Robinson for twenty years. And you didn't even leave it at that, did you? Did you think I wouldn't wonder why everything went so badly for me inside? Why I was constantly being picked on and abused and set up? I knew someone big was on my case and it could only have been you and that bunch of criminals you call your family.'

Talitha opened her mouth; nothing came out.

'Why did you tell us you couldn't remember anything?' Daniel asked, in a voice that managed to sound aggrieved.

'Because I wanted to see what you'd all do,' Megan told him. 'I wanted to give you a chance to behave well, to do the right thing, even if you didn't have to.'

Xav gave a deep sigh. He should have known; it had been a test. They'd all failed.

'Meg, it's not as bad as you think, I promise you,' Amber was in tears now. 'We set up a trust fund, years ago. We've all been paying into it. It's a lot of money.'

'Yeah, yeah, I know all about the trust fund.' Megan gave a dismissive glance at Felix. 'Your IT security wouldn't keep a nursery safe. I found it my first week and I used your passwords to get into it.'

'You can have it, all of it,' Felix said. 'We can transfer it to you tomorrow.'

Megan lowered her head to lift the bag strap over it. 'I've already got it, you moron. I helped myself to Xav's laptop first thing this morning, and I put it all into my account. So, thanks, guys – it's a start.'

Xav wondered if he was going to be sick. What else had she done? And what did she have in that bag she was unbuckling?

'So, what do you want?' Felix repeated.

The effort of loosening the bag seemed to tire Megan. She leaned back against the door, her eyes half closed, and took several quick breaths. Xav was reminded that she was, supposedly, very ill.

'First of all, forget looking for the proof,' she said, when she appeared recovered. 'You'll never find it. Oh, that reminds me, who broke into the water tower the other night?' She looked from one face to the next. 'Amber and Dan wouldn't have the nerve. Felix wouldn't be sober enough to tackle that ladder. Tal, maybe. No, my money's on you, Xav. You'd have been closest on my tail.'

She held eye contact with him, and he knew she was thinking about what else he'd done that night.

'Enough.' Felix held both hands into the air, the way a schoolteacher calls for silence. 'Tell us what you want, Megan, or don't. Either way, I'm not listening to any more crap.'

'Shut the fuck up, Felix, and open this.' From the satchel, Megan pulled a large brown envelope and held it out to him. For a moment, Xav thought it might be the proof they'd been looking for, that Megan was simply going to hand it over, but Felix's face as he pulled out a typed document, several pages long, told him that was impossible.

'What is this bollocks?' Felix held it back towards Megan. She didn't take it.

'A legal document making me a full partner in your company. You'll need to get your lawyers to look over it. Maybe Tal will do the honours. I've changed my mind about having her act for me – you're welcome to her.'

Xav had never, before, seen a look of such fury on his old friend's face. For a second, and another, he thought Felix would rush at Megan. Getting a hold of himself, Felix said, 'You think I'm giving you half my company?'

'Fifty-one per cent.' Megan gave him a tight smile. 'I'll be managing partner because that way, we've a chance of saving it. I give it less than two years with you at the helm, Felix. Your drinking is out of control and your cash flow is at crisis point. I'll let you give Sarah the good news – she really doesn't seem to like me.

Although to be honest, I'm not sure she's going to be married to you for much longer.'

Megan was done with Felix. Leaving him pale with shock, she turned from him as though he'd ceased to exist and pulled another envelope from her bag. Xav's stomach clenched as she turned to him.

'On the subject of marital discord,' she said, 'here are your divorce papers. You need to sign and serve them. Don't take too long.'

Xav took a deep breath. At least his favour wasn't a surprise. 'I'm not divorcing my wife. Megan,' he said, 'I'm sorry about what you've been through and you're right to be angry, but I'm not doing it.'

He was conscious of nervous looks shooting between the others as Megan came towards him. He could smell the rain on her hair and a faint note of Coco Chanel. She came close enough that she had to tilt her head to make eye contact. 'Then, sometime in the next few days, you will wake up in the middle of the night to find me sitting on the end of your bed,' she almost whispered to him. 'I will tell your wife everything you did. Then she'll be the one serving divorce papers.'

The relief, as she turned from him to focus her attention elsewhere, made Xav want to sit down. He forced himself to stay upright. Daniel was next, and he too received a brown envelope.

'Medical forms,' Megan said to the white-faced man in front of her. 'I need them completed by the end of the week and sent to the address in the top right-hand corner. You'll have to go through a psychological assessment and I expect you to pass it. The favour is only considered redeemed when I have a fully functioning kidney in my body.'

As though to demonstrate the point, although she gave the impression of doing it unconsciously, Megan put a hand to the small of her back and leaned into it.

'You're insane,' Daniel muttered, but he couldn't look her in the eyes.

Megan threw back her head and laughed.

'Oh, cheer up, you wimp,' she mocked Daniel. 'As long as you live through surgery and don't get a post-operative infection, you'll be fine. You'll barely notice your loss. I'd say you're getting off lightly compared to the others.'

Amber startled them all with her sudden movement. She jumped to her feet and half ran towards the door. 'I'm not staying,' she announced. 'I'm not listening to this.'

Reptile-quick, Megan caught hold of her old friend by the sleeve of her jacket. 'Not so fast,' she said. 'No one walks away from this.'

Tears were rolling down Amber's face. 'Please don't,' she begged.

'Ruby, I think.' Megan had a small, tight smile on her face, as though she'd just chosen a puppy from a litter. 'She'll find it easiest to adjust, being younger. Tell her she's going to stay with her Auntie Megan for a while. She'll be thrilled – she really liked me. She'll probably ask to go home a lot in the beginning, but children are very adaptable. She'll get used to it. Eventually. And I promise to look after her.'

Xav swallowed hard. He was feeling sick, and it wasn't even his kid this deranged woman was threatening. Amber, unsurprisingly, looked ready to faint.

'Megan, you're going too far,' he said. 'You can have the trust fund, no one's arguing with that. Felix will give you some shares in his company – shut the fuck up, Felix – and if you really want me to leave Ella and give it a try with you, then OK.' He stepped closer and tried to soften his face, even to smile. He couldn't do it, if he'd had a gun with him, he'd have shot her, but he made himself keep talking. 'There was always a bond between us,' he said.

'I admit it, and who knows, maybe it will work. But Daniel's not giving you his kidney, and Amber's certainly not letting you have one of her children. You can't ask that.'

It was working. Megan was smiling back at him. She even reached out and touched his arm. Then her smile slipped from her face like melting ice.

'You don't get it, do you?' she said. 'I can ask whatever I like, because all of you face losing everything.' She started pacing the small room, pointing her finger at people as she spoke to them. 'Dan, you won't survive five years in prison – they will eat you alive. Losing a kidney is nothing compared to that. Felix, your company will collapse when you're convicted, and your wife and kid will be penniless. Of course that mercenary bitch will divorce you and you'll never see Luke again. Xav, your wife will leave you like a flash when she finds out what you've done, and Amber, what would you really prefer? Keep one of your girls and know the other is being taken care of, or see them both for an hour, every month, for the rest of your life.'

She stopped moving and turned to address the group. 'You have until July the first, the night of Amber's party. By then, I want all arrangements to be in place. And yes, I do expect an invitation. I'll be coming with Xav.'

'What about me?' Talitha said. 'What's my favour?'

Megan turned to smile at Talitha, almost as though remembering her presence was a wonderful surprise. 'I'm glad you asked,' she said. 'Amber, sit down, you're going nowhere yet. Xav, back off, you can't win this.'

Xav led Amber back to her seat. She collapsed into it and started sobbing quietly.

Megan's mood seemed to change. She sat down on the coffee table, making herself smaller than most of them, almost in a position of vulnerability. Xav wasn't fooled; she'd been planning this for a long time. He watched her lean forward, as though about to confide something important.

'Let me ask you something, guys,' she said. 'Did any of you wonder why I failed my A levels twenty years ago? Did you wonder for a second what had gone wrong?'

'Of course, we did,' Xav said. 'But given everything else going on at the time, it wasn't top of our list of things to talk about.'

Megan's eyes hardened. 'And true to form, you were only concerned with how things affected you. You hadn't the slightest interest in what was going on in my life.'

'Oh, for heaven's sake, Megan, we were kids,' Talitha snapped. 'What eighteen-year-old isn't self-obsessed? So, you had some personal stuff that threw you off track? Big deal.'

Megan's eyes flashed. 'Personal stuff? I'll tell you what happened to me in May of that year, just a couple of weeks before the first exam. I was gang-raped by my dad and four of his mates. How's that for personal stuff?'

The revelation seemed to reverberate around the room. Even Talitha seemed to have paled. 'You're kidding,' she said.

Megan shook her head. 'I'm going to give you the short version,' she said. 'The time for crying on shoulders has long gone. I never really knew my dad. When he wasn't in prison, he wasn't interested in his daughter. But naive idiot that I was, I wanted a dad in my life. I kept hanging around him, hoping he'd show an interest. I turned up at the caravan one night when he and his mates were out of their heads on cocaine and things got out of hand.'

'When?' Talitha asked. 'When was this?'

'You want a date? The seventh of May. Friday night. I was supposed to be meeting you at The Old Firestation and didn't turn up. I told you the next day I'd been throwing up all night. That bit was true.'

'I remember,' Amber said.

Xav remembered it too. By May of that year, Amber had been starting to get on his nerves, and he'd found himself dwelling on the events – the unfinished business – of Will Markham's party. Almost without realising it, he'd fallen into the habit of waiting for Megan to show up, actively looking for her when she didn't.

'Why didn't you go to the police?' Talitha said.

'Because I'd been drinking too. I'd been with them for about an hour before it all kicked off. I'd taken some coke too, and I thought I'd be blamed, that people would say I'd led them on, that I'd been a willing participant. Because I was ashamed that my dad, my own dad, would let that happen to me, would even take part himself, and because I was eighteen and when we're eighteen, we fuck up.'

'You should have told us,' Talitha said. 'We'd have helped.'

'Would you? Would you really? Because I don't remember any of you being interested in me.'

'That's not true,' Amber said, but she did so without any conviction.

'Meg, I'm sorry,' Felix said. 'That's really fucked up. I wish we'd known.'

For a second, Megan almost seemed touched by Felix's words; even to Xav they'd sounded genuine. Then she pulled herself together and turned away from him.

'So, here's what you have to do, Tal. You have to use your unsavoury family connections to deal with my unsavoury family connections. Get in touch with that bloke who helped you break into my room the other week, or someone else if he doesn't do the wet work, and get my father out of my life once and for all.'

Talitha gave a scared look around. 'What the hell are you talking about?' she asked.

Megan got to her feet. 'That's your favour, Tal. You have to murder my father.'

# 38

They watched their old friend walk away through the rain. As the church clock chimed ten, Felix got up and vanished behind the bar. He reappeared a few minutes later with a bottle of Scotch and glasses. Nobody complained when he poured five large measures.

'Any suggestions?' he asked.

'I'm not giving her Ruby.' Amber jumped in before anyone could speak. 'Even if I was prepared to, which I'm not, Dex won't allow it. I could tell him everything and he'd still never give up one of his daughters.'

All five had taken separate seats, Xav noticed, some distance from each other, neither offering nor seeking comfort; it was as though they'd all decided that, ultimately, they were facing this alone.

'Would he see you go to prison?' Daniel asked Amber.

'Yes, I think he would.' Amber looked from one face to the next, as though pleading with them. 'It can't be done. I'm sorry, guys. Even if you all agree, I can't go along with it.'

Xav waited for Felix, possibly Tal, to argue. Neither did.

'Well, the bitch isn't getting half my company.' Felix spoke up loud and clear, almost making Xav jump, and he gave Amber a grim smile. 'Don't worry, Am. It's not going to happen.' He looked round at the group. 'None of it is.'

'We're all dying to hear your plan,' Daniel said, after a second.

'She gave it to us herself.' Felix had finished his drink and was glancing, almost guiltily, at the bottle. 'You just had to be listening.'

'I'm not following,' Xav said.

Talitha was watching Felix. 'I am,' she said. 'And I agree.'

The two of them held eye contact for a second, an unspoken message flashing between them, and Xav felt something small and revolting, insect like, creeping down his spine.

Felix said, 'Megan wants Tal to take a hit out on her dad. In different circumstances, I'd be OK with that – the guy's an absolute sleazebag. In the current one, it feels like a waste.'

No one spoke. Tal's eyes were on the floor, Amber's shooting around the room. Daniel was staring at Felix as though he couldn't tear his gaze away.

'Is it possible?' Felix asked Talitha, after a moment or two.

'In theory,' she said. 'It could be done. It's risky. And expensive.'

'We've got the trust fund,' Felix said. 'Xav, do you think you could get it back?'

Xav gave a non-committal grunt. He didn't know; it would depend how carefully Megan had hidden her tracks. And frankly, he wasn't sure where this was going.

'What would be expensive?' Amber wasn't either.

Although Xav felt maybe he was, on some level. He was suddenly restless, wanting nothing so much as to run out into the rain.

'Hiring a hitman,' Talitha said, as though discussing any employment contract. 'I'd need to go home, talk to some people.'

By home, Talitha meant Palermo, where her mother's family lived. It was happening then, Talitha and Felix were contemplating hiring a professional killer. Xav waited for someone – Amber, Dan – anyone, to object.

'You're actually going to do it?' Xav asked when no one else spoke. 'Hire someone to kill Megan's dad?'

'Half right,' Felix said.

'I'm not following,' Xav said again, although by this time he knew that he was. Even Amber had lost her puzzled expression.

'We hire the hit man,' Felix said. 'And we kill Megan.'

## 39

Xav was on his feet. 'You're out of your mind. You're not turning me into a murderer.'

'We're all murderers, Xav.' Unable to resist any longer, Felix reached for the Scotch. 'For twenty years we've had the blood of three people on our hands. This is just one more, to save all of our lives.' He unscrewed the bottle top but paused on the act of pouring.

Xav turned to Amber. 'You're not going along with this? Am, this isn't you.'

Unhappy as she looked, Amber's voice didn't waiver. 'She's not taking one of my babies, Xav. She crossed a line.'

'Dan, are you in?' Felix asked.

Daniel put his fingers to the centre of his forehead, and Xav thought for a moment he was about to cross himself. But then his eyes closed, his hand fell back to his side and he let his head nod up and down.

The bottle clanged as Felix put it down; his glass remained empty. 'OK, so we buy time,' he said. 'The first of July's a month away, and we can probably get some more time if we need to. Dan, send those forms off. It will take weeks to get everything sorted. You can invent a cold if need be. All you have to do is avoid going under the knife till Tal can get her side organised. Amber, tell her you agree but it has to be towards the end of the summer.

You and she can start looking at schools together in Oxford. The key thing is to make her think you're going along with it.'

Amber, pale-faced and trembling, nodded her agreement.

'I'll do the same,' Felix went on. 'Pretend to be making plans for the share transfer but slowing the pace. How soon can you fly out, Tal?'

'I don't believe I'm hearing this.' Xav heard his voice, unnaturally loud, even over the hammering of the rain. 'What the hell is wrong with you all?'

'She hasn't given us a choice,' Amber said.

None of them, not even Amber, could look at him.

'And what she's asking of you isn't that bad.' Daniel half glanced up, and his face looked sly and mean.

'Oh, you think?' Xav made for the door. 'No. I'm not doing it. I'm not having a hand in killing anyone else. I'll give myself up before I do that.'

'You can't make that decision for the rest of us,' Daniel said.

'Watch me.'

'OK, wait.' Felix could move fast for a big bloke; he caught Xav on the doorstep, blocking his way out. 'You're right. We're rushing into this.' He caught the look in Xav's eye and stepped back a pace. 'Let's sleep on it – no, sod it, let's take the weekend to clear our heads – and talk again in a few days. OK, mate?'

Felix stepped back further, hands up in a placatory gesture. 'We'll talk on Monday, for the rest of the weekend, we just chill. Maybe we can persuade Megan to be reasonable. The red lines are Amber's kid and Dan's operation, am I right?' He glanced round at the group.

'And the contract killing,' Xav added.

Felix was suddenly Mr Reasonable, as though Xav were the one with the outrageous demands. 'Right, so maybe we can talk her into dropping those,' he said. 'I can make her a shareholder in the company. I draw the line at fifty-one per cent but I can offer her something. Maybe she can go abroad for the transplant. And we can persuade her to go to the police about her dad. Tal, you could act for her in that, couldn't you? Really, I mean, this time, not screwing her over.'

Tal nodded, her eyes shooting from Felix to Xav.

'Could that work?' Felix asked Xav. 'Maybe she's bargaining with us, and what we heard just now was her opening gambit. We can make a counteroffer. That could work, couldn't it?'

'Maybe.'

Felix patted him on the shoulder. 'OK, go get some rest. We'll talk in a couple of days.'

Desperate to be out of the room, away from them, Xav strode out into the night and ran through the rain back to his car. It was only when he was pulling out of the driveway that he realised none of the others had left the pool house. They were all still inside, talking.

About Megan? Or about him?

# 40

Over the weekend, Xav felt as though he was losing the ability to think rationally. Each time he tried to maintain a train of thought, the ideas slipped from him, the way they typically did in those last moments between being awake and sleeping. He tried using pen and paper, plotting different courses of action: he could quash his conscience and go along with Felix's plan, telling himself that Megan's life had effectively ended twenty years ago, that they were simply putting a wounded animal out of its misery; he could persuade Megan to run away with him, live off the trust-fund money, never seeing or contacting the others again; he could support the rest of them in a counteroffer, hoping Megan would see reason. As the weekend went on, different possibilities occurred, some reasonable, others downright outlandish, but they all had one massive flaw: the Robinson family. Whatever he did now, there was no escaping the knowledge that he had taken three lives, and never really paid the price.

Still no way out that he could see. He couldn't confess without taking the others down with him. Luke, Ruby and Pearl would grow up without one of their parents; Mark, Dex, Sarah and Ella would all see their lives shattered; the children he'd thought might appear in his own future would fade like a forgotten dream. As the minutes stretched into hours, Xav found himself looking at his wife's lovely face. He'd never seen her cry, wasn't sure she'd known real unhappiness in her life. And now he was going to break her.

The others had been as good as their word; not one of them had been in touch. But he was getting paranoid. Maybe they were meeting without him. Maybe his refusal to go along with the plan had turned him into the outcast. Was it completely out of the question that Felix and Talitha had decided the contract killer from Palermo could solve two problems for the price of one and that next time he got into his car, he might find the brakes no longer worked?

Xav started checking that the doors to his house were locked. When Ella was offered a ten-day job in Iceland for the following month, he agreed so enthusiastically that she looked hurt, but in Iceland, he knew, she'd be safe.

A little after noon on Saturday, a plain white envelope was pushed through the door, marked, *Xav.* Inside he found a business card for the Travelodge on the Abingdon Road with the single word *Megan* written on the rear. What the hell did that mean? Was she expecting him to join her there?

By Sunday evening, he was losing it. He'd barely slept the night before, hadn't eaten all day, and couldn't keep still. Enough. He had no idea what he would say to Megan, but he was bringing this to an end.

The traffic was light and it didn't take long to reach the Travelodge. Megan's car was parked close to the exit. The young man on reception rang Megan's room, told Xav he needed room twenty-four on the second floor and buzzed him through the secure door. Xav climbed the stairs, walked the corridor, found room twenty-four and knocked. She opened the door and, without speaking, stepped back to let him enter.

Megan's hair was wet, sleek as a seal's fur. She wore no make-up. Her eyes and lips were less startling than he'd grown used to, but her skin was paler and had the sort of radiance his wife talked about endlessly. Her dressing gown was made from a thin cotton and it clung to her damp skin. She didn't look surprised to see him.

'I'm sorry,' he said.

Megan raised her eyebrows, perfectly shaped and dark as her hair.

'We shouldn't have let you do it, twenty years ago,' Xav went on. 'We should have taken the blame together.'

Apart from the blinking of her eyes, Megan gave no sign of even hearing what he was saying.

'We should have known something was wrong, that something terrible had happened to you, and that you needed us. We were shit friends. You were supposed to ace your A levels, Meg, and it was our fault you didn't.'

Something softened in Megan's face; it wasn't a smile as such, maybe the memory of one. 'No,' she said. 'That, at least, was nothing to do with you.'

'Real friends would have stuck by you, even when you went to prison. We should have written and visited and let you know that we were there for you, that we always would be.'

'Yes,' she said. 'That would have been good.'

'And we should have welcomed you back; told you about the trust fund straight away; taken you back into our lives and helped you in any way we could. Waiting until we were forced into it, going along with the fantasy that you were guilty all along, is possibly the worst thing we've done in twenty years.'

Her mouth turned down, her head swayed from one side to the other; she was miming thinking about it.

'But that's it, Megan.'

Her eyebrows rose again.

'This is where it ends,' Xav went on. 'I'm not giving into any of your cruel demands, and I don't think the others will either. I'm not divorcing my wife. I love her. It took me a long time to find someone I loved, and possibly that was because of the promises I'd made to you and how I felt about you, but I found her and I'm not going to leave her. You and me are never going to happen.'

He saw her jaw clench as she swallowed; her eyes became a fraction shinier.

'I'll confess before I let you blackmail me,' he went on. 'I've been on the point of it all weekend anyway. Twice I put my shoes on to walk to the station.'

'What stopped you?' Her voice was cold as ice now; she'd show him no mercy.

'I think I should give the others fair warning before I do,' he told her. 'But I will, make no mistake.'

'So, you finally got your balls back,' she said.

He deserved that.

'Goodbye, Megan,' he said. 'I'm sorry.'

As he opened the door and stepped out into the corridor, Megan uttered a sound that he couldn't identify, halfway between a gasp and a cry. He didn't look back.

## 41

Felix was already awake when the alarm on his phone sounded at three thirty on Monday morning. In the darkness he caught a glimpse of what seemed to be a younger face in the bathroom mirror. The coarsening of his skin, slacker jaw and the lines around his mouth had gone, leaving the face in front of him the one he remembered from his teen years – only with one big difference. The light had gone from his eyes.

His face, now, was that of an evil man. The mindless behaviour that ended three lives and ruined six others had been at his instigation. His idea, born on a late-night journey home in the passenger seat of his dad's car, when, from nowhere, he'd pictured himself driving at speed into oncoming traffic. He'd been unable to get it out of his head, had introduced it into the group conversations, subtly at first so they were barely aware of what he was doing, but by the time he'd said, '*Come on, let's do it,*' they were primed and ready.

All his fault.

Sarah hadn't moved as he crossed the bedroom. She slept on her back and a beam of light had fallen onto the side of her face. How easy it would be for him, an evil man, to drop a pillow onto her face and hold it down until she stopped fighting. He probably wouldn't even feel remorse. He'd been struggling to feel anything since Megan had returned; it was like the evil inside him, kept in

265

check for so long, had been unleashed by her sudden reappearance. Sarah's face twitched, as though she'd sensed the danger hovering close.

Felix slipped soundlessly from the room. He wasn't going to smother his wife, of course. Luke needed her, and besides, he had nothing against Sarah. Before Megan's return, he'd felt something close to affection for her. Not love, of course; Felix had only ever loved one woman in his life, and she'd left it a long time ago.

Quietly, he climbed into Sarah's car; his wife's black, mostly silent, electric BMW was far more suited to his purpose than his own vehicle. Before turning on the engine, he checked his mobile phone, opening a recently installed app that he'd told no one about.

After discovering Megan's trick with the photographs, he'd ordered a simple tracking device on the internet, the sort typically attached to lively dogs, and when he'd known Megan was in a meeting, he'd borrowed her car keys and slipped it under the spare wheel. It meant he knew exactly where she was twenty-four-seven, and right now she was tucked up at home in . . . actually, she wasn't – her car was on Abingdon Road, about a mile from the city centre.

It didn't matter, as long as she was nowhere near where he was heading.

He set off towards the motorway. Halfway there, his headlights caught the eyes of a fox at the roadside and the animal seemed to shrink into the undergrowth, as though instinctively avoiding him. When he was close to Echo Yard, the architectural salvage place where Megan's father lived, he pulled over and parked beside a gated entrance to a field. It was two minutes to four in the morning; still time to change his mind.

Out of the car he stood listening for a moment, to the sound of a lorry heading up the M40 and the cry of an animal he couldn't identify, and told himself he was stopping to think. If they'd done that twenty years ago, things could have been so very different. They might have changed their minds, driven back to Tal's, got drunk and crashed out, and life would have gone on as planned. Except for Megan.

Felix had done enough thinking; he wasn't going to change his mind.

From the boot, he took a small rucksack and an old university baseball bat. Pulling on gloves and a ski mask, he jogged a quarter of a mile down the road until he was directly outside the caravan where Megan's father lived. From something Tal had told them previously, he knew there was a tree stump nearby that would get him over the fence.

The verge between fence and road had been neglected. The coarse grass was over a foot high and he had to stamp on a tangle of brambles. He was glad of the vegetation, though; it would keep him hidden.

Felix pulled the rucksack off his shoulders and rummaged around inside. The whistle he'd found on Amazon had a frequency of forty kilohertz, practically inaudible to humans but easily within the hearing range of dogs. Blowing it produced, to his ears, a quiet hissing sound, and he was rewarded by a yelp from the inside of the caravan.

He blew again.

The dog barked. Felix blew the whistle a third time and the barking turned into a frenzy as the animal began scrabbling against the caravan door. As his stomach twisted with nerves, Felix saw the door opening and the dog leap out. A male figure stood in the doorway.

Felix dropped to his knees and opened the rucksack again. He found the plastic bag, cold and squishy beneath his fingers, upended its contents and tossed the piece of meat through the fence. It landed directly in the path of the bounding German shepherd.

'Duke, what's up?' Megan's father called.

The dog, close enough to make Felix nervous in spite of the fence, emitted a low growl; but it had seen the meat.

'Duke!' called Megan's father.

Torn between greed and duty, the dog remained where it was, eyeing up Felix, keeping his nose directly above the six-ounce piece of rib-eye steak. He growled; he licked the meat. Felix turned and crawled away. Knowing nothing about animal psychology, he figured removing himself from the scene might give the dog the victory it needed to give into temptation. A few feet from the road, he waited, knees and hands on damp ground. A nettle stung his wrist.

Megan's dad called for the dog again. Felix heard the dog running and then the door of the caravan closing. Getting to his feet, he checked his watch.

The drugged meat would take fifteen to twenty minutes to work, taking him to around a quarter past four; Felix knew from reading every Lee Child book published that four o'clock in the morning is the time when the human body is at its lowest point, when sleep has its tightest grip. Attacks, invasions, ambushes are planned at zero four hundred hours for a reason.

At sixteen minutes after four, Felix climbed the fence and dropped down into the yard. He left his rucksack behind but kept a tight hold on the baseball bat. There was no trace of meat on the ground.

Not a sound could be heard from the caravan as he rapped quietly on the door. No response – from dog or human. Felix turned the handle and was unsurprised to find it unlocked; Megan's dad thought himself safe, surrounded by a seven-foot-high metal fence and sleeping alongside a large dog.

The dog lay on the floor, out cold; the man was on a bunk at the far end of the caravan. Felix stepped over the dog.

'Hey,' he said, when he'd checked that he had plenty of room to swing. Then, 'Hey!' a little louder.

Megan's dad sat bolt upright. 'What the fuck—'

Felix didn't let him finish. He swung fast and hard, and the bat made contact with the side of the other man's head. Macdonald fell back and Felix struck again. A sound, something between a grunt and a moan came out of the other man's mouth and he half fell off the bunk. His arms wrapped around his head, but he made no other move to defend himself.

Felix brought the bat down again, on the man's shoulders this time, on his clenched hands, and thought he heard a bone snapping. On the caravan floor now, Macdonald curled himself into a foetal position. Short of breath, Felix grabbed hold of the collar of his victim's T-shirt and dragged him across the floor to where he'd have more space. He kicked him, once, twice and then a third time where he judged his kidneys would be and then, when Macdonald uncurled, struck him once more across the face. A sickening crunch told him the man's nose was broken.

On his way out of the caravan, Felix bent to check the dog. Assuming its weight to be around thirty-five kilos, he'd calculated the amount of ketamine needed to keep it unconscious for about an hour. Its chest was rising and falling more or less normally. He propped the door open, so that the dog could escape if Macdonald didn't regain consciousness. He might be evil; he wasn't a monster.

'You're welcome, Meg,' he whispered to the wind, as he walked back to his car.

# 42

Felix got home, climbed back into bed without disturbing Sarah and, to his surprise, slept for several hours. His wife had to wake him, long after his alarm would normally have gone off, and he was running late when he arrived at the factory.

Climbing the stairs to his office, Felix braced himself to come face to face with Megan for the first time since Friday night. What he'd done to her dad made no difference. Beating up Macdonald had been an aberration, something entirely removed from the current situation. Hurting, maybe even killing, Megan's dad had been something his eighteen-year-old self should have done. He owed it to her.

Didn't mean she was getting half his company. And while he didn't have any strong feelings about Amber's kid, or Dan's kidney, he wasn't letting her go that far either. She might come for Luke next. No, the Megan problem hadn't gone away and he hadn't changed his mind about how he and the others should tackle it. He pulled open the door to the main office and got ready to face her.

She wasn't at her desk.

He walked the length of the room, nodding to anyone who made eye contact, responding to those who wished him a good morning. Most of his employees, as usual, did not.

'Megan not in yet?' He'd reached her desk and could see no

sign of anyone having worked at it that morning.

'She's on a week's leave.' His head of HR gave him the briefest of glances.

'Since when?'

In a flash, the woman's face became defensive. Jeez, could he not ask a simple question any more?

'Since she filled in the form and put it on my desk,' she told Felix. 'I signed it off. She said she'd cleared it with you. Is there a problem?'

'No, course not.' He made himself walk on. 'She probably did tell me and I forgot.'

Of course, it was a bloody problem – Felix pulled open his own door – and she sure as hell hadn't told him. He pulled out his phone and opened the tracker app. She, or her car, was still on the Abingdon Road.

He was about to text the others but stopped himself after the first name came up. Talitha had warned them more than once against texting anything to do with Megan, even on the burner phones. Tal was an opinionated cow at times, but she was right on this.

Felix sank into his chair as another thought occurred to him. The police. Megan could have had a change of heart. She could be with the police even now. Except she wouldn't have booked leave for that – what would be the point? No, she probably wasn't with the police. Even so . . .

Feeling panic growing in his chest, he picked up the green-cased phone. Talitha wasn't available, of course, because Talitha was never bloody available, and he wasn't going to waste his time trying Amber. He left a message for Tal and tried Dan at school.

'I haven't got long,' his friend said, when he answered. 'I'm teaching in ten minutes.'

Did the bloke think he'd phoned to arrange a squash match?

'Megan's gone,' he said. 'She's booked a week's leave. Did you know anything about it?'

A slight pause. Then, 'No. Has she told anyone where she's going?'

'No one in the office knows anything.'

Felix was on the point of telling Dan about the tracking device but held back. Frankly, he wasn't sure which members of the group he trusted any more. He'd known about Megan's visit to Xav's the previous week, about her overnight stay, from the tracking app, but had Xav owned up about that? No, he bloody well hadn't. Another reason he wasn't sure he trusted Xav.

Dan said, 'What's she up to?'

'Exactly what I asked myself. Do you know where she's living now? Someone should pop round to her old bedsit, see if she's still there.'

By someone, he meant Dan, of course; he was the closest.

Dan said. 'I can go at lunchtime.'

Sooner would be good, but even Felix had to accept that the head of a school couldn't simply walk away from the premises.

'Soon as you can,' he said. 'This is something new. And she's been planning it for a while.'

# 43

There was no sign of Megan at the bedsit. By pressing bell after bell on the communal intercom, Daniel eventually found what sounded like an elderly man willing to talk to him. The bloke didn't know Megan by name but did refer to the murderess in room seven.

'She's gone,' Dan made out over the crackling of the intercom. 'No one wants her here.'

Booked leave without telling anyone and left her bedsit? Jesus, if Megan was going the extra mile to make them sweat, he really had to tell her it wasn't necessary.

'You all right, sir?'

Somehow, Daniel was back at school, by the bike racks, and two third-year boys were watching him, their faces a mix of concern and glee. He'd pulled off his jacket, a thing forbidden on school premises until the usher declared that summer had arrived, even loosened his tie, and had been staring down at the tarmac. He had to pull himself together.

Attempting a joke about needing to work on his fitness, Daniel hurried upstairs and phoned Talitha. He caught her on her way out to a client lunch. 'I was about to call you,' she said, sounding out of breath. 'Have you heard?'

He could hear the clipping of her high heels echoing along a tiled corridor. 'Heard what?' he asked.

'Hang on a minute.'

In the background, a door closed.

'It was on BBC Oxford an hour ago,' Talitha went on. 'Police are attending a salvage yard by junction seven of the M40. A man in his sixties has been badly beaten and left unconscious. The dog sounded the alarm first thing this morning. It has to be Megan's dad.'

Unable to stay on his feet any longer, Daniel dropped into the chair behind his desk. Megan gone, now this.

'That could explain why she's not at work.' He spoke slowly, trying to make sense of it in his own head. 'She could be at the hospital.'

Talitha said, 'What do you mean she's not at work? Have you spoken to Felix?'

Even without his jacket, Daniel was too hot. He closed his eyes and took a deep breath. 'Megan booked a week's leave without telling him. And she's left her old bedsit.'

Talitha didn't reply immediately and Daniel felt as though, if he opened his eyes, he would see the edges of the world melting away.

'She's more likely to be with the police than the hospital,' Talitha said.

His eyes were open again; the world still as it was. 'You think Megan beat up her dad?' he said, as lurid pictures of Megan wielding a blood-stained cosh sprang into his head.

Talitha took her time. 'Not really. Why ask me to get rid of him if she was planning to do it herself? Besides, Megan's dad looked as though he could handle himself when I saw him.'

Whereas a strong wind would blow Megan over. 'Who then?' he asked. 'Seems a bit of a coincidence.'

'Oh, I'm not saying it's coincidence. I'm saying I don't think it was Megan.'

'Who then?' Dan repeated.

For a moment, the line was silent, then, 'This is between us, right?'

'Of course.'

Another pause, then Talitha said, 'I think it was Xav.'

# 44

Work was impossible. He didn't think he'd ever be able to chair a meeting again, never mind stand in front of twenty sixth-formers, some of whom spoke Greek and Latin better than he did. Daniel cleared his diary for the afternoon and jumped on his bike again to ride to Xav's. He was damp with sweat by the time he arrived, and his heart was doing something weird. Not racing exactly, although the short ride had exhausted him, but almost dancing in his chest. It would beat hard and fast, then appear to stop, before flopping about lazily like a fish on a beach. He'd have to get it checked out if this crisis was ever over.

As he waited for someone to answer the bell – he'd already spotted Xav's BMW up the road – he wondered if having a heart condition would make him ineligible to be an organ donor. Christ, that he'd got to the stage where having a weak heart would be good news. He pulled out a handkerchief to wipe the sweat off his face; it sprang back almost immediately.

The door was opened by Ella, Xav's wife. Daniel could never see anything particularly attractive in Ella when he met her in the flesh: her angular cheekbones, eyes so large they were almost cartoonish and her androgynous hairstyle lacked all appeal for him. As for her body, if she wore revealing clothes, he almost felt as though he were back in anatomy lessons. The photographs though, in magazines and online, were stunning.

That day, her hair showed a centimetre of dark roots and he could see two pimples on her chin. She wore a loose, long-sleeved shirt and black leggings, showing off legs and a bottom that could belong to a nine-year-old girl.

'Sorry to arrive unannounced. Is Xav in?'

Ella liked him, he knew. Most women did. Talitha had told him once it was because they thought he was gay.

'He's not himself,' Ella said, as she led the way into the house. 'He insists he's not ill, but he's never missed work before. Can I get you a coffee?'

Coffee was the last thing Daniel needed, but he sensed Ella wanted to talk.

'Has he had bad news?' He kept his voice low; Xav was in the house somewhere.

'Not that he's told me. But he's spending ages on the phone. He's getting calls from all sorts of people, his solicitor, his financial adviser, but he won't tell me what's going on. I think he's moving money around. And look . . .'

Agile as a monkey, she climbed onto the worktop. Reaching up to the top shelf, she pulled down a jar and held it out to reveal rolls of cash.

'There's nearly a thousand quid in here.' As she spoke, she kept darting nervous glances towards the stairs. 'I think he's in financial trouble and he's afraid to tell me. Dan, what if he's been sacked?'

Dan was sweating again. 'OK, where is he? I'll see what I can find out.'

'He won't tell me a thing; I've given up asking him because I'm just stressing him out more. And there's another thing. He's cleared out the freezer.'

He turned back in the doorway. 'He's done what?'

'All the meat, chicken, fish; all the stuff he eats and I don't. I found it all in the outside bin. It's like he's planning to leave me.'

Tears were running down Ella's face by this stage. Daniel reached out and put a hand on her shoulder. It was the closest to a hug he felt comfortable with.

'Xav adores you,' he said truthfully. 'I'm sure you're wrong,' he lied. 'Let me go and have a word.'

Ella watched, anxiously, as Daniel climbed the stairs. Xav met him on the landing. 'What's up?' he said.

Xav looked like shit, as though he hadn't shaved in days, and his T-shirt had stains on the front and beneath the armpits. He wore jogging bottoms that were baggy at the knee and his feet were bare.

'A question more properly directed at you, I'd say.' Daniel followed the other man into a small sitting room. The snug, Ella called it, where she curled up to drink mint tea and watch soap operas.

'Felt lousy all weekend. Couldn't be arsed going in.' Xav dropped into an armchair. Daniel caught a whiff of unwashed male body that reminded him of the sixth-form boys' changing rooms.

'Ella's in a real state about you,' he said. 'What's going on, mate?'

'Never hurts to put your affairs in order.' Xav's eyes were flat and cold, but at least he didn't pretend he didn't know what Dan was talking about. 'So, what do you want, Dan? Tal send you on another errand?'

With a growing sense of unease, Daniel too sat down. 'It's about our mutual friend,' he said.

'What else? Well, we can't talk about it here. My wife listens at doors.'

Dan had never heard Xav criticise Ella before. He got up again and walked to the top of the stairs. A moment later, he returned. 'She's on the phone in the kitchen,' he told Xav, who'd let his head fall back and his eyes close. 'Megan has gone. Do you know where she is?'

Those deep blue eyes flicked open. 'Gone where?'

It was possible, thought Daniel, that Xav was drunk. He couldn't smell alcohol, stale or otherwise, but this slob wasn't the Xav he knew.

Daniel said, 'I don't know, that's why I asked. She booked a week's leave without telling Felix, and she's gone. I thought she might have said something to you, seeing how the two of you are to be married.'

For a second Dan thought he'd gone too far, then Xav got up and left the room, brushing clumsily against the doorframe on his way out. He came back a few seconds later, his wallet in one hand, a business card in the other.

Dan took the card. 'Travelodge,' he read. 'The one on the Abingdon Road. When did she move in there?'

'Haven't a clue,' Xav replied. 'She put that through the door on Saturday. I was bloody lucky Ella didn't open it.'

'So, she's still there?'

Xav's eyes fell. 'How should I know?'

'I think we should go round. Can you drive?'

Xav looked up. 'And what? What would we say to her? She has a right to take time off work.'

He had to tell him. There was no way around it. 'Mate, there's something else,' he said. 'If you don't know already.'

Xav's eyes narrowed. 'What?' he said.

'Something happened to Megan's dad,' Dan told him, thinking, *Watch him closely now, watch for the flicker of the eyes.*

'What?' Xav said again.

'He was attacked in the early hours. Beaten up quite badly.'

Eye contact remained steady. 'Where? In Oxford?'

'In his caravan. Someone broke in.'

Xav's face registered puzzlement, then shock. 'Shit.'

'Exactly.' Daniel could see nothing, nothing at all, to suggest that Xav wasn't as surprised as he'd been. 'It's been on the local news all morning,' he said. 'I'm surprised you haven't heard.'

Xav had become very still; he hardly seemed to be blinking any more.

'I don't listen to it much myself,' Daniel admitted. 'Talitha told me.'

Xav dropped his head into his hands. When he spoke, his voice was muffled. 'That reckless, irresponsible cow. How the fuck did she get it organised so fast?'

OK, this wasn't following the script.

'You think Tal did it?' Dan tried. 'Had someone do it, I mean?'

Xav's head snapped up to face him; his hands had clenched into fists. 'Of course, she fucking well did. She's ruthless.'

'I don't know—' Daniel began.

'She had Megan attacked in prison, for God's sake, she conspired to keep her in there for twice her sentence. She's an evil cunt, Dan, and she'll throw us all under the bus if she needs to.'

'She thinks you did it.'

Xav's face screwed up in disbelief.

Daniel braced himself. 'That's what she said, she thinks you did it. She thinks it was your knight-in-shining-armour party piece.'

Xav sneered at him. 'She's talking bollocks.'

Fair play, he was convincing.

Xav breaking into the salvage yard and beating Megan's dad to a pulp? Dan had never suspected Xav of having a violent streak. Felix, well, that was different, you watched yourself when Felix had had a few drinks, even when they'd been teenagers, but not Xav.

'Why?' Daniel said. 'Why would Tal do it? We'd agreed to slow everything down, to stall Megan, make a counteroffer.'

'Yeah, while I was in the room. Who knows what you agreed after I left. Maybe you decided Megan's dad should be roughed up a bit so you could tell Megan it was a down payment on what was to come later.'

Daniel blew out a heavy sigh. Xav was a good liar; on the other hand, so was Tal. He honestly had no clue. Worse than that, the solidarity of the group, that he'd have bet everything he owned on a matter of days ago, was falling apart.

And without the group, what did he have? Nothing.

'It'd be good to know for certain where Megan is,' he said at last. 'Even if we don't talk to her. And if we do, we can tell her about her dad.'

'I'll get some shoes on.' Xav got to his feet, as though making a huge effort, and made for the door.

'Mate,' Daniel called. 'Have a shower.'


It took a little over thirty minutes to drive to the Travelodge on Abingdon Road, and Daniel spent most of the time trying to decide who he believed was behind the attack on Megan's dad, and what Xav was really up to.

He'd felt no surprise when, after both Megan and Xav had left the pool house on Friday night, the others had confided a suspected attachment between the two of them.

'*He always liked Megan,*' Amber had said. '*I could tell. And she obviously feels the same about him.*'

Xav had known where Megan was staying – were the two of them colluding now? Was Xav planning to leave Ella and run away with Megan?

The car park outside the Travelodge was about a quarter full.

'Megan's car.' Daniel pointed over to a small blue hatchback. 'She's here. What are we going to say?' he asked, as he and Xav walked towards reception.

'Good question,' Xav replied. 'Can't say anything springs to mind.'

Watching Xav pull open the door to the Travelodge, Daniel realised he'd made a big mistake. Xav wasn't thinking rationally any more. The two of them had no plan and things, already bad enough, might be about to get a whole lot worse.

The woman behind reception looked up and smiled.

'We've come to see a guest of yours,' Xav announced. 'Megan Macdonald. Would you mind calling her room?'

Cleaned up a bit, Xav was back to his normal handsome self and the receptionist's smile widened.

'Of course, sir. Bear with me.'

The receptionist picked up the phone. 'Who shall I say is calling?' she asked after several seconds.

'Xav.' Another exchange of smiles. Daniel took himself away to wait by the window. This was a big mistake. He picked up his phone; he had to call Tal, even Felix. This wasn't something he could deal with alone.

'I'm not getting any response,' the receptionist said. 'Do you have a mobile you can try?'

Xav turned to Daniel. 'Do we have a mobile we can try?'

Of course, they had Megan's mobile number. Xav wasn't asking him that, he was asking whether they should dial it. No, they bloody well shouldn't; as far as Dan was concerned, coming here had been stupid, maybe even dangerous.

Without waiting for him to reply, Xav made up his mind, pulled out his own phone and dialled a number, presumably Megan's. He held it up so Daniel could hear the ringing tone. It went to voicemail.

The receptionist had put the phone down. 'Would you like to leave a message?' she said.

'Her car's in the car park,' Xav said. 'The blue Nissan. I'm a bit worried she's not answering. Can you send someone to her room?'

'I don't have anyone to send, but I can ask the cleaners when they finish. They'll have noticed any problem.'

It was the best they could do. Xav thanked the girl and the two of them left the building. As Xav walked back to his own car, Daniel strode ahead to where Megan's was parked. He wasn't entirely sure what he was looking for or planning. Maybe leave a note tucked behind the windscreen wiper?

The small blue Nissan was entirely unremarkable: clean, completely tidy on the inside, no hint of the woman who drove it. Daniel peered in, shielding his eyes from the sun to see into the dark interior, then looked back up at the Travelodge. He had no idea which was Megan's room, but he felt her eyes watching him. She was here, not at the hospital, not helping police with their enquiries, but here, yards away. He scanned the windows, looking for a pair of eyes.

Xav called over, 'Do you want a lift back to school?'

Xav looked ready to leave and it was a long walk back. Daniel joined him and they pulled out of the car park and onto the Abingdon Road. Xav drove as though on autopilot, his jaw clenched, saying nothing.

'What now?' Dan asked after the silence was making him uncomfortable. 'Do we contact the hospital, find out how he is?'

Xav kept his eyes on the road. 'Do you give a shit?'

Daniel thought about it. 'Not really.' Gary Macdonald's state of health felt like the least of his worries.

They pulled up at the school gates. Xav sat silently, without even looking his way, waiting for him to leave the car.

'Xav,' Daniel said. 'What are you going to do?'

His friend didn't look at him. 'What I have to. I suggest you do the same.'

# 45

'Amber? Amber, is it you? I have to say . . . I mean . . . some very disappointing news in my inbox this evening.'

The distinctive voice boomed out from the car's speaker as Amber sped down the A34.

'I'm sad about it too,' she said, 'but I think it's for the best.'

'But, but, I mean, you were managing so well. You're the – what's the word – the pin-up girl for working mums on the green benches.'

'You know that's disgustingly sexist, don't you?'

It was nice to hear, all the same. She'd taken pride in being exactly that.

'Oh, blast it, I'm upset. I don't mind telling you, I mean to say, I'd never have normally made this public – and it's not to become public, not in a million years – but we had our eye on you for a top job at the next reshuffle.'

She'd known that, of course; half of Westminster had known that. She'd wanted education, would have settled for environment.

'I'm grateful. But the truth is, I may be experiencing some problems in the next few weeks. Personal ones. And I really don't want to embarrass the government. Better if I stand down now.'

The pause lasted three seconds. 'I see. Well, in that case . . . Umm, maybe you're right. I trust your judgement, Amber. Good luck. And thank you for all you've done.'

'It's been an honour, Prime Minister.'

The call ended, and so did her career. Even if she kept her seat, she'd never have the nerve to clamber over the green benches towards ministerial positions again. Amber felt a sob forming at the back of her throat. Two things she'd wanted, since she'd been sixteen years old: to become prime minister, and to marry Xav. And Megan had stolen both from her.

Turning off the A34, she drove the short distance along the Godstow Road to reach the Trout Inn as Talitha was climbing out of her own car. The car park was already filling up and the gardens of the pub on the river were full of people enjoying the evening sunshine.

Talitha joined Amber without offering a greeting, not even breaking a smile. Sometime in the last few weeks, they'd ceased to be friends.

'I said we'd meet at the abbey.' Talitha walked ahead towards the bridge and Port Meadow.

No; she'd stopped being friends with Talitha a long time ago.

Amber followed, keeping her head turned away from the crowds on the pub deck; this hadn't been the wisest place to meet on a warm evening. She crossed the weir, its churning waters sparkling silver in the sunshine, and then the navigable part of the river. Boats were moored on the banks and the smell of barbecues filled the air. She could hear the squeals of children in the distance. Port Meadow sucked in the families of Oxford like a magnet.

On the opposite bank, the two women – Talitha had let Amber catch up – dropped down onto the towpath. From there, a short walk across ancient grazing land took them to the ruins of Godstow Abbey.

Dating back to the twelfth century, once the home of Henry II's mistress, Rosamond Clifford, the abbey had crumbled to little more than a surrounding stone wall and the shell of a chapel. The women walked to where once the entrance gates would have stood. Felix's height and fair hair made him easy to spot by the old chapel, but there was no sign of either Xav or Daniel.

'Shit,' Talitha muttered, but when Amber looked a question at her, she shook her head.

'There's Xav.' Felix was looking over their shoulders as they reached him.

A hundred yards behind them Xav was a mess: unshaven, wearing clothes that needed washing.

'I thought you might bring Dan,' Felix said when Xav was close enough.

Xav shook his head. 'Can't get hold of him.'

Talitha pursed her lips and breathed out a heavy sigh.

'Any news on Megan's dad?' Felix looked from one to the other.

'He'll live,' Talitha replied.

'Anyone here want to say anything about that?' Xav, Amber noticed, was keeping his eyes on Talitha as he spoke.

'Good question.' Tal held Xav's stare.

'What's going on?' Amber asked.

'Tal thinks I beat up Megan's dad,' Xav replied. 'I think she did.'

'What am I missing?' Amber turned to Felix, who shrugged.

'Guys, I don't give a shit who beat up Megan's dad,' Felix said. 'The bloke was scum, probably into all sorts of stuff we know nothing about, and anyone could have done it. If he takes a turn for the worst, that's one problem out of the way as far as I'm concerned. So, Tal, what did you want to see us about?'

They were standing, conspicuously, in the middle of the square of grass, surrounded on four sides by medieval stone walls. Amber wanted to suggest they move to a bench or walk along the towpath, anything to draw less attention, except they weren't all here yet. 'Shouldn't we wait for Dan?' she asked. 'Is he actually coming?'

'OK, I'm going to start.' Talitha ignored Amber. 'First, Megan is still in the area. She's been seen at the JR, in the ward where her dad is.'

'Are you sure?' Xav asked.

'Unless Macdonald has another daughter. The ward sister I spoke to said his daughter had been in once to check on him. She didn't stay long.'

Amber said, 'So, she's just avoiding us. Well, we can't exactly blame her.'

'I think she might be stalking Ella,' Xav said. 'She came home the other day with a daft story about the market. She'd been waiting at a wholefoods stall and when it was her turn to be served, the stallholder, who she knows a bit, asked if her sister was staying with us for long. He said there'd been a woman standing right next to Ella while she was waiting who was the absolute image of her, only a bit older. They looked around, but whoever it was had gone.'

'So?' Felix looked mystified.

'Ella is the image of Megan when she was younger,' Xav said. 'I didn't realise it until – well, until recently, but she is.'

'Mate, the pressure's getting to you,' Felix began.

'No, he's right,' Amber interrupted. 'I spotted it when the two of you met. It gave me the chills, to be honest.'

Xav turned to Amber in surprise. 'You never said anything.'

'What purpose would it have served? You were so happy – why would I risk spoiling that? But if Megan's hanging around Ella, that is a worry.'

'Was that it, Tal?' Felix asked. 'Because I have other places to be.'

'Oh, there's more,' Talitha said. 'I can't find Daniel.'

She waited for the news to sink in.

'Sorry, what?' Xav said.

Talitha seemed ruffled for once. 'I've been phoning him for three days,' she said. 'He doesn't answer my texts and the school are being very circumspect. I finally got them to admit that he's had to take some unexpected time off to deal with a family emergency, but they wouldn't tell me anything else over the phone.'

Amber felt as though she was struggling to absorb the fresh news. First Megan, now Daniel?

'Well, I felt sure he would have told me about a family emergency,' Talitha went on. 'So I called his parents.'

'You're still in touch with them?' Felix asked.

'We've acted for them a few times,' Talitha said. 'They still have the farm at Waterperry. Anyway, they haven't heard from him. Don't you think they would know about this so-called family emergency?'

'He doesn't have any other family,' Amber said. 'No brothers or sisters.'

'I went to school,' Talitha continued. 'It's a lot harder to fob people off when they're right in front of you. I told them I was his solicitor and worried that he'd missed some appointments. They brought the usher down and he did his best to get rid of me, but in the end, they let me see an email message they got from Dan early Tuesday morning.'

'And,' Felix prompted, when Talitha stopped for breath.

'First of all, it was sent from his phone.'

She looked around for a reaction, letting a flicker of annoyance show when she didn't get one. 'It said he'd been called away to a family emergency and would be gone a couple of weeks. Could they please reschedule any urgent meetings and arrange cover for the classes he took? They were obviously embarrassed. It's not the sort of behaviour you expect from the master of All Souls.'

'You think he's hiding out somewhere?' Xav asked. 'What would he gain?'

'No, I don't think he's hiding out,' Talitha snapped. 'That message was all wrong. It wasn't the way Dan speaks.'

Still, Amber felt the rest of them were playing catch up.

'School wouldn't have noticed,' Talitha went on. 'They don't know him like we do. And it was sent from his phone. How do we even know Dan sent it?'

No one spoke.

'So, first things first, has anyone heard from him since Monday morning?' Talitha said. 'That's when I last spoke to him.'

'Me too,' Felix added.

Xav said, 'I saw him Monday afternoon. He came to my house.'

Talitha turned on Xav, almost angrily. 'Why? What did he want?'

'To ask if I knew where Megan was, to tell me that she'd done a disappearing act too. Christ, what is this, the Harry Houdini show?'

'Focus,' Talitha snapped.

'I told him she was staying at the Travelodge.'

Talitha's face twisted with strain. 'Why the hell didn't you tell us?'

'You didn't ask.' Xav's voice, too, was rising. 'I didn't know she'd gone AWOL till Dan showed up. The two of us drove round there. Her car was outside, but there was no sign of her. And for what it's worth, that was the first I heard about Megan's dad. I haven't been near the bloke, so wind it in, Talitha.'

Amber took a nervous look around. No one was close enough to hear them, but their body language would be giving a lot away. She said, 'Is it possible they're together?'

Felix said, 'Dan and Megan? What the hell for?'

'No, I'm her co-conspirator according to you lot,' Xav said. 'What is it you think the two of us have planned, exactly?'

'Mate,' said Felix, 'this isn't helpful.'

Energy seemed to seep out of Xav. 'Don't you think we're beyond help?'

'Stop it,' Talitha said. 'We need to—'

'Hold on,' Felix held a hand up to silence Talitha. 'There's something I need to tell you guys.'

'What?' Talitha didn't like being interrupted.

'Just over a week ago, I put a tracking device in Megan's car.' Felix looked around the group, as though daring any of them to object. 'I had a feeling we should know what she was up to.'

'Why didn't you tell us?' Talitha again.

'Because he doesn't trust us, either,' Xav answered her.

'No, you're right, Xav. I don't. You didn't tell us she spent the night at your house a matter of hours after I installed the device. What else haven't you told us?'

Talitha's mouth fell open. 'Are you kidding me?'

'He told me,' Amber said. 'Back off, Felix. You too, Tal.'

Felix held up both hands in mock surrender.

'So, where is she now?' Talitha asked.

In response, Felix took out his phone and stared at the screen for a few seconds. 'Blackbird Leys,' he said, naming a housing estate on the Oxford ring road. 'Her car's been there, more or less permanently, for the last twenty-four hours. She must have left the Travelodge.'

'New bedsit?' Talitha said. 'She said she was flat hunting.'

Felix shrugged.

'OK, thanks for telling us,' Talitha said. 'It will help. Keep an eye on her, won't you? For now though, we need to find Dan. I'm going to his order, see if I can bullshit my way in. Amber, you'd better come too. If they don't find a government minister intimidating, I won't have much luck by myself.'

'I've resigned,' Amber said.

Felix and Xav allowed their surprise to register on their faces. Talitha didn't so much as blink.

'Is it public knowledge?' she asked.

'Not yet.'

'Then we're good to go.'

# 46

The Holy Innocents order of lay brothers lived in a sixteenth-century house set some way back off the Cowley Road but within walking distance of the school. The two women sought admittance via the intercom at the front gate, a huge, wrought-iron affair that swung open silently before slipping back into place behind them.

'Have you been here before?' Amber found herself whispering.

The courtyard felt austere, more like the yard of a prison than the garden of a medieval house, in spite of the lines of lavender and the neatly trimmed box hedging. The stone wall that surrounded them on three sides looked close to twenty feet tall and along its length, Amber could see the outline of inner walls and arches long since demolished. Ahead lay a mill-like building, three storeys high, through which ran a central archway.

'Never.' Talitha too seemed unnerved by the place. 'He told me visitors aren't encouraged.'

Maybe it was the silence. The huge stone walls were holding back the sounds of the city, giving the illusion of a time when motor vehicles hadn't even been dreamed of.

'It's not exactly homely,' Amber said. 'Where is everyone?'

Bees danced around them as they crunched their way over the gravel and, gradually, the smell of traffic fumes became the scent of lavender, but as they stepped into the shadow of the archway, the insects fell back. 'This far we'll go,' they seemed to say, 'but no further.'

All heat fled from the day, as though the sun had been turned off, and Amber glanced nervously at two wooden doors tucked away into the sides of the archway. Hoping Talitha wouldn't notice, she stepped a little closer to her.

The second courtyard, smaller and without planting of any kind to soften the endless stone, had even more resemblance to a place of confinement, only this time the walls were replaced by wings of the building. Dozens of black, mullioned windows glared down at them.

From a door directly opposite, a man emerged, dressed as a monk in a long robe of a colour somewhere between brown and grey. He looked about fifty, close-shaven, with short cropped hair. His eyes were grey and his skin pale; his hands, peeking out from very wide, long sleeves, reminded Amber of hands she'd seen on waxworks and his fingernails were unusually long. When they were close, he looked from one to the other without speaking.

'Thank you for letting us in,' Amber said.

The monk made no sign of having heard her.

'As I explained at the gate, we're looking for Daniel Redman,' Talitha said, after a moment. 'We're old friends of his. I'm also his solicitor. I expect you know Amber Pike, the junior minister?'

The monk's eyes flickered to Amber's face. 'I'm afraid I can't help you,' he said, in a voice that carried the faintest hint of a stutter. 'Perhaps you would be good enough to ensure the gates close firmly on your way out?'

Talitha took a sharp breath. 'He does live here?' she asked.

The monk inclined his head.

'We've been to school. They told us he hasn't been in for some days. Is he ill?'

'I'm afraid I can't say.'

Talitha took a step closer to the monk. In her heels, she was almost his height. 'Well, *I'm afraid* that isn't good enough. We're concerned for Daniel's wellbeing. If you can't tell me anything, I'm going to insist on being shown to his room so that we can speak to him directly.'

The monk stood his ground. 'Impossible.'

'Why?'

'This is a holy order. Women are not allowed within our confines. Daniel has a telephone, although it is against our rules for it to be switched on when he is here. I suggest you call his number and leave a message.'

'We've tried, many times,' Amber jumped in. 'We're very worried about him. We've been seeing him regularly for weeks now, and suddenly he disappears. It's unheard of for him to leave school before the end of term and, if he was ill, I'm sure he would have told us.'

For the first time, the man seemed hesitant. His eyes fell, and when they rose again, they'd lost some of their conviction.

'I understand that we can't go to his room,' Amber pressed on, 'but is it possible that someone else could go? To put our minds at rest?'

'I'm afraid it would be pointless,' the monk said. 'Brother Daniel isn't here.'

Sensing Talitha was about to start speaking again, Amber put a hand on her arm. 'So can you tell us where he is?' she said. 'Or how long he's been gone?'

'Neither, I'm afraid, because I don't know. He was seen at dinner on Monday evening, but I can't say further than that.'

Monday evening – directly after he and Xav had gone to the Travelodge to look for Megan.

'Have you spoken to the police?' Talitha asked.

A frown line had broken the monk's complacency. 'No. At this stage, we've no reason to be alarmed. Our brothers are free to come and go as they please. It's possible that Daniel felt the need for some solitude and reflection and consequently has gone to one of several retreats that we use.'

Amber shared a look with Talitha and knew exactly what the other woman was thinking. Wouldn't it be typical of Daniel to run away when it all got too much?

'Can you give us any details?' Amber asked, 'So that we can try to get in touch?'

'I'm afraid not. When our brothers go on retreat, they have deliberately chosen to eschew the modern world.'

'What if he's come to harm?' Talitha asked.

'Then he's in God's hands,' the monk replied.

This was too much for Talitha. 'Are you kidding me?' She looked around, as though planning her next move. Short of pushing her way past this monk, though, there wasn't one. 'Come on, Amber, we're done here.'

Amber felt herself pulled, faster than felt comfortable, back along the path.

'I can tell you one thing,' the monk called after them.

The two women turned on the path.

'Daniel has left most of his personal effects behind,' the monk said. 'His wallet and telephone are both in his room.'

# 47

In the days that followed, Talitha was taken by surprise to learn how much she missed Daniel. It was a bit like having an annoying little brother who'd been sent away to school – thank God, at last – but after the initial hour of euphoria, you remembered how he always came to find you when meals were ready, and that he was OK with you having first scoop out of the chocolate ice cream and that he hadn't told your parents about that time you'd accidentally, OK, on purpose, broken his DS.

On their first day at pre-school, Daniel had sat beside her in the lunchroom and said that he'd liked her hair. He'd shared his chocolate buttons with her and had been a constant presence in her life since. They'd spent a while – university years and immediately after – some distance apart but had never lost contact, and the arrival of social media had meant they could be in touch daily, even several times a day. She was closer to Daniel, she realised, than to her husband.

She simply couldn't get her head around the fact that he'd gone, without telling her.

After leaving his order on Thursday evening, Talitha had instructed her private investigator to look into religious retreats, but few were publicly listed, even fewer answered the telephone and none, none at all, would divulge details of who might be staying with them. By close of play Friday, she'd reluctantly agreed that she wasn't going to find Daniel's retreat. If indeed he'd gone to one. Somehow, she didn't think he had, because that was something he would have told her.

Sometime on Saturday, she concluded that it was her fault; she should have noticed how badly Dan was taking Megan's return. He'd never been emotionally strong, and the stress of the last few weeks had been too much for him. She should have realised, taken more care of him. But he'd always been the one to demand the least attention, the member of the gang they never really worried about because he was so self-contained, and he had his school, and his God. She should have seen beyond that. Daniel had been driving the car. However much they might say they shared the blame, his hands had been on the steering wheel.

By late Sunday, the thought that had been lurking in the deepest part of her subconscious could be ignored no longer. Daniel did tell her everything, and there was only one reason she could think of why he might not. One by one, she called the others and told them to meet her the following evening.

This wasn't something she could do alone.

# 48

Daniel's parents lived in a medieval millhouse, on a tiny island in the River Thame, not far from the village of Waterstock, and Amber had been to it many times before. Not, though, since the girls were born, because even thinking about its steep garden walls plunging into deep water gave her the horrors now that she had young children to worry about.

Remembering Talitha's instructions to park away from the house, she pulled up in the lane. She was five minutes early, but Felix was ahead of her. As she was getting out of the car Xav pulled up.

'I'm not sure I can face Dan's parents,' she said, when the three of them had gathered in the lane. 'And why worry them before we know anything?'

'I don't think visiting them is the plan.' Xav had made an effort since Amber had last seen him. He'd shaved and looked cleaner; he still looked tired though. 'Why would we be parking down the road?' he finished.

'Tal's here,' Felix said, as a white Range Rover appeared from around the corner.

'What?' Tension seemed to be radiating from Talitha as she approached them; as usual, her aggression came Amber's way.

'I didn't know you owned such clothes,' Amber replied. Talitha was wearing cotton cargo pants and a faded T-shirt, on her feet were scuffed hiking boots. It was a bit like seeing the Queen in an apron and Marigolds.

Felix glanced down at Talitha's footwear and gave a nervous laugh. 'What's up?' he asked her. 'What's going on?'

Talitha couldn't seem to look directly at any of them. Saying, 'You need to come with me,' she set off towards the mill.

Puzzled, Amber and the two men followed along a short stretch of road and onto the public footpath that took them across the River Thame. They went so close to Daniel's parents' house that, had his mother been at the kitchen window, she would have seen them, and then on past the property and onto another bridge on the opposite side of the small island.

On the apex of the second bridge, the noise of the weir still loud in their ears, Talitha stopped.

'I spent half my childhood here,' she said, looking around at the ring of trees, the disappearing footpath, the fields and meadows beyond. 'I used to wish Dan's parents were mine because they seemed to love me more than my own did.'

Amber had never once heard Talitha admit that her life had been less than perfect.

'Dan's mum told the most amazing stories,' Talitha leaned out over the water as she spoke. 'She used to tell us that fairies lived in the trees here and that they'd come out at night and make sailboats out of laurel leaves, with cobwebs for sails, and hold races on this stream. She told us to look for laurel leaves on the bank and that they'd be boats left behind for the fairies to use once night fell. I must have been ten before I realised she'd made it up.'

Amber saw her own puzzlement reflected on both men's faces; this wasn't the Talitha they knew.

'In summer, when I wasn't in Sicily, I was here,' Talitha went on. 'We weren't allowed to play near the water on our own, but we sneaked out when Dan's mum was busy. I know every inch of this island.'

Amber saw Felix glance at his watch. He didn't say anything, though. Even Felix, not known for his sensitivity, could tell this was important.

'Tal.' Xav seemed to have lost weight, even in the few days since Amber had seen him. 'Whatever it is, just tell us.'

Talitha hadn't looked up. She said, 'This bridge is taller than it looks from up here. And directly beneath us there's an old iron hook.'

Amber saw Felix's eyes flash wide.

'We played under this bridge,' Talitha said. 'We tied a rope to the hook and used it as a swing. Our parents would have had a fit, even mine, but they never knew.'

Felix stumbled away, out of Amber's eyeline, to lean over the other side of the bridge. She glanced at Xav, in time to see him swallow hard.

What did they know that she—

'He said to me once –' Tal went on, 'I pretended he was joking, but I knew deep down he wasn't – that if he ever wanted to kill himself, he'd do it here, under the bridge, because no one ever looks under this bridge.'

Amber was aware of Xav moving closer. 'No,' she managed, looking from him to Felix, to Talitha, seeing identical looks of horror on each face.

'So now I have to find him,' Talitha said. 'I'm sorry to drag you all out here, I just didn't think I'd be able to do it by myself.'

As though sleepwalking, she made for the bank. 'Wait here,' she said. 'Phone the police when I call up.'

'Oh, no you don't.' Felix caught up with her. 'You're not going under that bridge on your own. Xav, look after Amber.'

Talitha shook her head. 'I'm dressed for it, you're not. What's the point in ruining a decent suit?'

'Daniel's worth a decent suit.' Amber pulled away from Xav and joined the other two on the bank. 'We'll all go.'

The water was colder than Amber expected, and the mud deeper. She'd taken off her shoes, as had the men, and she held onto Xav as she made her way over the uneven, pebble-strewn riverbed. Felix and Talitha were a pace ahead.

Felix reached the stone abutment of the bridge. A few more steps and he'd be able to see directly underneath. Steadying himself against the stone with one hand, holding onto Talitha with the other, he moved on, the water over his knees. Xav and Amber followed. She saw the swinging shadow and gasped, pulling away from Xav, on the point of fleeing the water. Then the shadow moved, it was Felix's shadow, not Dan's. She took Xav's hand again.

Amber was the last to see the dark, slime-ridden cavern beneath the old bridge. It was a grim place, and would have been dreadful had it been the last thing that Daniel saw in this life.

It wasn't. The iron hook was exactly where Talitha had said it would be, and their childhood swing remained. Daniel was nowhere to be seen.

# 49

It took fifteen minutes of angry sobs, and most of the contents of Felix's hip flask, but eventually Talitha was calm enough to talk again.

'I'm glad we haven't found him,' she said, wiping mascara streaks across her face. 'But I'm not wrong. Daniel wouldn't leave us. Not now, not with everything going on. And he couldn't go anywhere without his wallet.'

'And there's the passport thing,' Amber reminded her. 'The mad monk at his residence told us none of the brothers have passports,' she explained to the men. 'He found an old one in Dan's room, the same one he had when we were students. It hasn't had a corner cut away, which means he's never applied for a new one. He has to be in the country somewhere.'

'I can't believe those idiots haven't called the police,' Felix said. 'Not that it's in our interests for the police to get involved right now.'

'Talitha made exactly that point,' Amber said. 'It didn't go down too well.'

Talitha sighed. 'I simply pointed out that the wallet and phone suggested he hadn't planned a trip of any length and that their presence in his room was cause for concern. Father Ted replied that when the brothers go on retreat, they take just enough money to cover a return journey. He did not see any reason to invade Daniel's privacy.'

'Can we track down these retreats?' Felix asked.

'Not a chance – we've already tried,' Talitha told him. 'And its pointless – he hasn't gone on a retreat.'

Running footsteps sounded a few seconds before a Lycra-clad runner appeared on the path. They stepped aside to let him pass.

'We played Poohsticks here,' Talitha said, when the runner had gone. 'Dan would spend ages collecting twigs and as soon as we got within sight of the bridge I'd nick most of them off him. He burst into tears every time, but he never told his mum. So I kept on doing it.'

'You were born to be a blood-sucking lawyer.' Felix bent to the ground and picked up two twigs. He gave Talitha the longer, thicker one. After a moment, Xav found two sticks, one a little bent, and offered one to Amber. The four friends stood on the apex of the bridge and looked down at the water.

'It's not exactly fast-flowing,' Felix said.

'It never is,' Talitha told him. 'It's a backwater.'

'One, two, three, go,' Felix announced, and four sticks fell into the water. As one, the four of them turned and took the steps that would bring them to the opposite side of the bridge.

'That's Amber's,' Xav said, when a broken twig appeared, followed by three others. 'Well done, Am, always the dark horse.'

'I wish we'd done this before,' Talitha said in a small voice. 'When there were six of us.'

Out of the corner of her eye, Amber saw Felix take a step closer to Talitha and wrap an arm around her waist. A second later, she felt Xav's arm steal its way around her own shoulders. She leaned into him and let her head fall against his chest. Closing her eyes, smelling the scent of Xav that had never properly left her memory, she allowed herself to dream, only for a second, that life had been so very different.

If she'd been less drunk that night, she could have pleaded with Xav not to do it; she could have made him change his mind, she knew it, and without him, it wouldn't have happened. They could be six old friends now, catching up on old times. Tears gathered behind her eyes.

'So where is he then, Tal?' she heard Felix ask.

Talitha said, 'Something's happened. I was wrong about him being here, but I'm not wrong about that.'

Amber opened her eyes again. 'You mean, like an accident?' she said.

'He'd have been found if it had been an accident.' Talitha's voice was tight with emotion and she didn't look up from the water.

Felix said, 'It's not like you to be coy, Tal.'

Talitha's shoulders heaved as she took a deep breath. 'In the last few days, Megan's dad has been badly beaten up and Daniel has vanished,' she said. 'What, or rather who, do those two men have in common?'

'Megan's disappeared too,' Xav pointed out.

Talitha turned at last, and now she wore what Amber called her court face. 'We know Megan's alive and kicking because she was seen at the hospital. We don't know Dan is.'

'Her car's still at Blackbird Leys,' Felix said, 'but it has been moved from one street to another. She's alive.'

'Megan wouldn't hurt Dan,' Xav said.

'Excuse me, Megan was prepared to have Dan cut open and one of his kidney's ripped out,' Talitha replied, 'so I beg to disagree. She's also prepared to abduct one of Amber's children and have me take out a contract kill on her father. I think we can safely say there's little she isn't capable of.'

'She's been in prison a long time,' Felix said. 'Nobody comes out of prison unchanged.'

'She still wouldn't hurt Dan,' Xav argued. 'She needs him.'

Talitha took a deep breath. 'Well, maybe she's realised that plan of hers isn't going to work, that we won't go along with her favours. Maybe this is plan B.' She looked around the group. 'Guys, you saw her last Friday night. She was furious. One way or another, she's going to get her own back.'

'Then she shops us to the police,' Felix said. 'If she wants to screw us all over, that's the way to do it, surely?'

Talitha nodded her agreement. 'It is, if she still has the proof, but what if she doesn't? What if it got lost or destroyed during those twenty years? Xav, what was that water tower like?'

'Not exactly waterproof,' Xav admitted. 'Cold and damp.'

'So, how about this scenario – Megan comes out of prison, determined to get payback for our neglect of her over the years. She hasn't got the proof any more, but we don't know that, so she blags it. She demands the favours and keeps her fingers crossed we go along with her. When she realises, or even suspects, we're not going to, she hatches a different plan.'

'The flaw in that,' Felix said, 'is that for all Megan knows, we will go along with it. We haven't told her otherwise.'

In a voice that sounded exhausted, Xav said, 'That may not be strictly true.'

'What do you mean?' Talitha asked.

'I went to see her last Sunday night,' Xav admitted. 'At the Travelodge. This was two days after she confronted us. I told her I wasn't going to divorce Ella.'

'You did what?' Felix had gone white.

'I told her I was sorry, but that I wasn't going to be blackmailed and I didn't think any of you would either. I told her I'd confess before I let that happen.'

Felix and Talitha exchanged looks of horror, and Amber saw Felix's fist clench.

'Xav—' Amber began. He stepped away from her.

'You got Dan killed.' Talitha's eyes were wide with horror. For a second she seemed about to rush at Xav. 'Dan is dead because of you.'

'Take it easy, Tal.' Felix stepped in between them.

'You think she'll stop at Dan?' Talitha yelled at Xav. 'She went for him first because he's the easiest to get to, and he's mild as a lamb.' Her head shot round to Amber. 'You're next, Ex-Junior Minister. You'll be a sitting duck now you don't have security. Then, I don't know, probably me. She's picking us off one by one.'

'OK, stop. Stop.' Felix took hold of Talitha by her upper arms and gave her a gentle squeeze. 'Do you mean it?' he said, when he'd turned back to Xav. 'About confessing?'

'I do.' Xav's voice was shaking. 'I'm sorry, guys, I really am, but all this – looking for Dan's body under a bridge – I can't do it any more. I won't drop any of you in it. I'll say it was just me in the car with Megan, that she agreed to keep quiet because she was in love with me.'

He took a step backwards, then another, until he'd left the bridge. He was leaving them. The group was breaking apart. First Dan, now Xav.

'She won't go along with that.' Talitha sounded desperate.

Xav kept walking. 'Probably not,' he said. 'But it will be her word against mine. And yours, if you decide you can still live with this.' He'd reached the path that would take him back to the mill. 'In fact, that's what we do: those of us who can't live with ourselves any more, go to the police and admit to being in the car. Those who can, well, I won't give you away.'

'Mate, don't do this,' Felix said.

'I'll give you a week,' Xav called. 'I'll do nothing till this time next week. That gives you time to make your minds up and sort out anything that needs sorting. Then I'm going in.'

'Xav, you're throwing us to the wolves.' Amber felt tears springing to the back of her eyes as she took a step after Xav. 'If you reopen the case, the police won't stop till they've got all of us. Felix and I have children.'

'And Talitha and I have lives, even without kids,' Xav said. 'Only I can't live mine any more.'

He raised one hand in a farewell, a motionless wave that became something akin to a salute, and then he turned and walked away. A second later, he'd gone.

# 50

Xav had spent the previous week cancelling his life: moving assets, updating his will, paying off his mortgage. Ella was hopeless with money, but he'd done the best he could to protect her. On the Friday, he'd resigned from his job, citing personal difficulties that were impossible to surmount.

Physically clearing out the house, taking clothes and sports equipment to Oxfam, had been harder and he wasn't entirely surprised when he got home from Waterstock to find Ella, cross-legged on the floor of their living room, red-faced and sobbing as she turned the pages of a photograph album she'd pulled from the outside bin.

He joined her on the rug, enfolding her with his arms and legs, the way he might have done, one day, to a child of his own, had it not been for that summer.

'I love you so much,' he whispered into her ear.

'You never even showed me this,' she mumbled. 'Why would you throw it away before I had a chance to see it?'

Pictures of his teenage years that made his heart burn to look at now: a party, high on a hill, a house in one of the most exclusive areas in Oxford, a garden strewn with lanterns and candles; children, almost grown, wild and beautiful with brightly coloured clothes and glitter on their skin. A fire pit, the faces of his friends glowing in the flickering light, Amber's strawberry-blonde hair falling almost to the ground as she dozed on Xav's shoulder; Felix, tall and golden like a young Nordic god; and Daniel, pale and pretty, almost feminine at seventeen; Talitha, too, a coronet of buttercups on her messy, dark hair; and, slightly apart, silver-haired and slender, Megan.

'I wish I'd met you sooner,' Xav said, as he got to his feet, the album in his hands now. 'I wish I'd known you longer.'

Talitha and Felix called round that evening to try to persuade him to change his mind. The big sacrifice, they argued, would achieve nothing; he'd still live with the guilt, but in a place where he'd be powerless to atone. There was more than one way to find redemption, they urged: he could work for a charity, donate most of his money to the less fortunate. He was an immensely capable man, with so much to offer, and shutting himself away to a life of toilet cleaning and vegetable peeling was the real crime. He told them of the preparations he'd made and advised they do the same.

An hour after they left, Amber called him. In between sobs, she repeated everything the others had said. He told her he was sorry and put the phone down.

When darkness had fallen over St John Street, he phoned his parents at their home on the outskirts of Banbury and had the longest chat with them he could remember having in years. He told them he loved them; both asked him what was wrong.

He woke early on Tuesday morning, some time before the sun came up. As he lay in the half light of his bedroom, his wife breathing softly beside him, he knew, as though someone had whispered it to him in a dream, where Megan had hidden the proof.

# 51

Xav said nothing to the others, because he was a long way from knowing whether or not it would make any difference to him now. All day long he could think of little else but made no move to leave the house. When light was fading, he drove the few miles out of town to a stretch of woodland on the south side of the city. He parked and began the long trek that would take him to his destination.

Will Markham's family might not live on Boars Hill any more, but the house would probably be there still and the garden unchanged. If it weren't, if the land had been sold off, the trees felled and a housing estate sprung up, then he was wrong. But it hadn't, and he wasn't.

He was out of breath by the time the rooftop came into view above the tree canopy, but he'd remembered every detail of that night twenty-one years ago.

It had been mid-June when Will celebrated his seventeenth birthday, and a marquee extension to the family home had meant he could invite the entire sixth form and a good chunk of those from neighbouring schools. Nearly three hundred sixteen- and seventeen-year-olds had been on the property that night. Many had gone home at midnight, but Xav and a small group had gathered around the fire pit at the foot of the garden, nearly a quarter of a mile downhill from the house. One by one, the others had wandered away, until only he and Megan were left. He'd been teasing her about boys she was keen on. She'd dismissed each of his suggestions, but not the idea that there was someone, and for some reason, it became very important to learn the identity of the boy Megan liked.

She'd left the fire as it began to die down, heading towards the woods; Xav had grabbed a blanket and lantern and followed her. By the perimeter fence, a few yards from a gate that led to open countryside, they'd stopped by a huge beech tree. The two of them had sat, and he'd had a feeling that something, something special, was about to happen.

'Look,' she said. 'It's a trysting tree.'

Around the tree's huge girth, couples had scraped away patches of bark before scratching out hearts, enclosing two sets of initials. Xav pointed to one shaky heart. 'Felix and Ari Hughes,' he said. 'Remember the gathering we had here at Christmas?'

'They lasted, what, six weeks?'

Xav found his keys, and the bark came away easily. 'Go on,' he said, handing the keys to Megan. 'Give me a clue.'

Megan scratched out the outline of a heart, much neater than the one Felix had carved months earlier, and then her own initials: *MM*. Xav waited, feeling his heartbeat pick up a fraction, and then she'd stopped.

'He can carve his own initials.' She handed the keys back.

Maybe if he hadn't drunk so much he'd have known what she meant, and in a way he had known. But he wasn't even seventeen and girls were a foreign country, one he'd feel comfortable in one day, but back then, he'd been treading carefully down the strange high street, a tourist map in one hand, his phrase book in the other. He'd stared at her, waiting for the words to come, but they'd let him down. Feeling stupid, Xav put the keys away in his pocket, and a second later, Megan got to her feet and set off back towards the house.

The next day, he went abroad with his family and didn't see Megan again until the start of the upper-sixth year at school when she'd become uncharacteristically cool and distant. By half term, he'd been desperate to have sex for the first time and when he'd heard that Amber was keen on him, well, she was one of the prettiest girls in the sixth form, of course he wasn't going to say no. So, he and Amber had become an item and Megan – well, she'd become unfinished business.

She still was.

The gate at the bottom of the Markham garden was unlocked, and Xav slipped quietly through. The fire pit was still there, and the pale stone of the seats around it glowed in the moonlight. The huge beech tree stood out against the midnight-blue sky. Dropping to his knees in the long grass at its foot, he shone his torch on the carvings. There were more than he remembered, but Will had had younger siblings; there would have been other teenage parties, other couples to carve their initials. Xav moved the torch beam around until he found the patch of bark he'd cleared himself two decades earlier.

The heart shape he remembered had carried only one set of initials, two capital letter Ms, but it now had a second. Twenty-one years later, Megan had finally carved into the tree the initials of the boy she liked. *XA*. Him. And a tiny arrow, pointing downwards.

The part of the trunk closest to the ground wasn't visible beneath a tangle of grasses and ferns, but Xav pulled enough away to expose the root structure and saw a small hollow. Dropping flat, he shone in the torch beam, but it revealed nothing other than a dark hole. He pulled up his sleeve and pushed in his hand. Soft ground, decomposing leaves, something sharp that scratched against his fingers, a mesh of twigs that he thought perhaps was an old nest and then cool, smooth plastic.

The Ziploc bag he pulled from beneath the tree was entirely unremarkable, as was the brown, A4-size envelope. Inside that were a reel of photographic film and the admission of guilt they'd all signed in Talitha's pool house twenty years earlier. And a second, smaller envelope, hand addressed to him. Xav tucked the plastic bag into his pocket and took a seat by the fire pit to read the letter.

Eight hours later, the gardener, who'd been instructed by Mrs Markham to clean out the ashes in the firepit, had his day completely ruined by the discovery of Xav's body.

# 52

Amber pulled up in St John Street with no recollection of the journey over. It wasn't entirely impossible that she'd died on the way and was stuck in some weird purgatory because the world around her was not the one she knew. The graceful Regency terrace had lost its sharp outlines, edges had blurred, and the tarmac of the road was shimmering, as though in a heat haze, although the morning was quite cool.

Xav could not be dead; it was a cruel joke on Ella's part.

Amber left her car without thinking to lock it and crossed the street, telling herself it was all a prank, that Xav himself would answer the door, apologies tripping over his tongue, and she wouldn't care, she wouldn't give a flying fuck, because the nightmare was over, Xav was standing right in front of her, and he wasn't bloody well dead.

She pressed the bell. *Open the door, Xav, open the goddamned door.* The door opened and Ella towered above Amber on the steps, her lovely face a mass of blotches.

It was real then; Xav was dead.

'Tell me what you can,' Amber said, a few minutes later, when the two of them were sitting in the front room of the house that was no longer Xav's, and her hands were being gripped so tightly by the other woman that her rings were digging into her fingers.

Ella continued to sob and Amber glanced around for tissues, kitchen roll, a towel, anything, and wondered when she too could break down and scream.

'None of it makes any sense,' Ella managed at last. 'What was he doing up there? We don't know anyone up there.'

'Up where? Ella, start at the beginning. What did the police say?' Amber continued to look around, this time in the hope that a uniformed constable might be lurking in the kitchen. 'They usually leave someone with a bereaved relative.'

Ella made a visible attempt to pull herself together. 'I sent her away. She was making it so real, Amber. I thought if I couldn't see her any more, it wouldn't be.' More sobbing, then, 'It could be a mistake, couldn't it? Mistaken identity. Do you think that's possible?'

Amber would have given anything to think that possible.

'It's unlikely, Ella. The police are usually pretty sure about these things. What did they say?'

'They asked me to confirm that I was Mrs Attwood, and then they said they were very sorry, but they had reason to believe my husband was killed in the early hours of this morning.' She stopped, sniffed noisily. 'But it can't be him. We didn't know anyone on Boars Hill. Why would he go to a house on Boars Hill so late?'

Ella was right, they knew no one on Boars Hill. Amber hadn't set foot on one of the most expensive residential roads in Oxford for over twenty years. Not since Will Markham's seventeenth birthday party.

'They want me to identify the body – they say I have to as next of kin, but I can't, Amber. I've never seen a dead body. How can the first one I see be Xav's?'

'Ella, did they say what happened to him?'

Was it possible this was a road traffic accident? She hadn't seen

Xav's car outside. An RTA would be dreadful, but not totally out of kilter with the normal order of things.

'Head injury, they said.' Ella was having trouble both breathing and speaking; it was possible she was asthmatic. 'They found him in the garden of a big house. By some stone seats. They think he may have fallen and banged his head badly and died waiting for help. I can't bear it, Amber, him lying there all night, bleeding to death.'

Later, Amber, too, would struggle to think of it. For now she was thinking, stone seating area, sitting around a firepit, smoking weed, because they thought they were too far away for Will's parents to smell it.

'Ella, have you told anyone else?' she asked. 'Talitha or Felix? What about his parents?'

Ella shook her head. 'No, I called you. You were always his best friend.'

A fresh stab to a heart that Amber didn't think could hurt any more. His best friend. He'd actually said that. To his wife.

'Will you come with me?' Ella said. 'To see him, I mean. I can't go by myself. I'll make his dad do it if you won't.'

She meant to identify the body. Amber had never realised, before, quite how young Ella was, how completely unprepared for the harsh side of life. She would make that sweet elderly man look at his son's corpse.

'I'll come,' she said. 'Is he at the John Radcliffe? Go and get dressed. We'll drive up there now.' Amber pulled the other woman to her feet. 'Upstairs,' she said. 'Get dressed and I'll drive you up.'

The second Ella left the room, Amber dialled Talitha's number. 'I don't care who she's with,' she told Talitha's secretary. 'You need to interrupt her right now and tell her that Amber Pike, the junior minister, is on the phone, and that it's a matter of the utmost urgency.'

She waited. She counted to ten. She wouldn't put it past Talitha to refuse to take even the most urgent of calls. She counted some more.

'Amber, what the fuck?' Talitha said, after twenty-three seconds. *Don't think about it, don't choose your words, just out with it.*

'Xav's dead.'

'What?'

'I'm not repeating it. Don't make me repeat it.'

Silence. A weird gasp. Then, 'Give me the facts.'

'Early hours of the morning, up at Will Markham's old house on Boars Hill. He was found with a head injury by that stone seating area. The police think he could have fallen.'

Another strange sound, that, if it were anyone but Talitha, would sound as though she were holding back sobs. 'He didn't fall. Amber, you know he didn't fall, don't you?'

Talitha had to shut up right now. Xav's death was bad enough; the thought it could have been anything more than a terrible accident was too much for Amber to get her head around.

'No, Tal, we don't know anything.' She had to be calm for a little while longer. 'I'm taking Ella to identify the body. I have to go and see him, I have to look at him – the man I've known since we were kids and thought at one time I was going to marry – and I have to see his corpse. His parents don't know yet, that sweet, old couple. I'll probably have to tell them. It will kill them. They don't even have grandchildren.'

'Amber, for heaven's sake, get a hold of yourself.' Talitha sounded more like herself. 'First Dan, now Xav. It was not an accident. Jeez, have you spoken to Felix this morning? What if he . . .'

Whatever the thought was, Talitha couldn't finish it. 'I'll call him now,' she said after a moment. 'You take Ella to the mortuary. The police are likely to be there, so be very careful what you say.'

'They'll want to talk to me this morning?' That was blind panic, rearing its head again. 'What will they ask? Tal, I'm not sure I can do this.'

'Yes, you can. The last time you saw Xav was at Waterstock on Monday. The four of us met up because we were worried about Daniel. That's on record, and we've done all the right things, so no reason not to mention that. We met there because it's a convenient place for you and Felix, who don't live in Oxford, but we didn't go into the house because we didn't want to worry Dan's parents. Before that, you don't remember when you saw him, you'll have to check your diary, and you don't remember him being particularly worried about anything. Can you do that?'

No, she couldn't; she wasn't sure she could leave the room. 'I think so,' she said, 'but Tal, I can't bear it. It's Xav.'

'I know, I know. But listen to me, Amber, you have to be careful.'

'I will, I won't say anything stupid.'

'I don't mean that. Do you still have close protection?'

For a second, Amber was puzzled by the sudden change of subject. 'No, I resigned, remember.'

Talitha sighed down the line. 'Well, you're going to have to take care of yourself,' she said. 'If Megan contacts you, do not meet her alone.'

'Megan? You think Megan had something to do with this?'

'Amber, grow up! If Xav didn't have an accident – and I would put money on him not having – then of course it was Megan. Don't let her into your house and don't let her anywhere near the kids. Call their school, make sure the staff know there's a risk.'

Amber would not have thought it possible to feel any more afraid.

'She wouldn't hurt Xav, she loved him.'

'Hell hath no fury, Amber. He turned her down. She saw her plans falling apart. Promise me you'll be sensible.'

The girls, oh God – she had to phone school. 'I promise.'

'I'm calling Felix. He should have been keeping track of her car. I'll let you know. Now, I mean it, Amber, be very careful.'

# 53

'Felix? Felix, are you still there?'

The line had gone silent. Talitha turned away from the window and wondered if she was about to scream.

'I'm here.' The man on the line sounded nothing like Felix.

She asked, 'Are you OK?'

'Yeah, I'm good. I'm— Shit, Tal.'

'I know.'

Silence, but she could hear his breathing, fast and loud.

'Felix, we need to know if it was Megan. Were you tracking her car last night?'

Another pause. 'I checked a few times early evening,' he said after a few seconds. 'The car hadn't moved. At least it didn't look as though it moved, but the signal's been weak. The battery may be on its way out.'

'When was the last time you checked?'

'Not sure. About ten. Hang on, I can find the last journey.'

Talitha waited. She heard sounds in the background, a clunk that might have been the phone being dropped, a drawer being opened, a mumbled curse, then—

'Oh, Christ, Tal.'

'What?' When you think you can't possibly be more afraid, you learn that you can be, that there is no limit to fear.

'It was Megan,' Felix said. 'She was in St John's Street a few minutes after eleven and then she drove up to Boars Hill. She followed him up there.'

Tal had to sit down. She opened her mouth to yell down the phone, to demand to know why he hadn't checked the app last night, because if he had, he'd have seen the danger, would have been able to warn Xav.

There was no point. What was done, was done.

'We have to tell the police,' she said. So this was it, then. The end of the road.

Felix said, 'We can't. Not unless you can come up with a good reason why I put a tracker in her car.'

'We have to stop her. She's coming for us next.'

No sooner had the thought entered her head than Talitha was on her feet again, at the window, looking out to see if Megan was on the street below.

'I know,' Felix said. 'And we will, but we can't panic. We'll take some time, we'll speak later. And don't tell Amber. It might just push her over the edge.'

There was no sign of Megan outside. 'I'd say she's teetering already.'

'All the more reason. Come on, Tal. You and me, we're the tough guys. We can do this.'

# 54

In death, Xav looked more beautiful than he had in years. His hair, left to grow long since Megan's return, fell around his head in dark curls. His face was untouched by whatever injury had killed him, and his shoulders could have been carved from marble. As the curtain slid back, Amber held Ella's hand and thought there was a bitter-sweet serendipity in that the two people by Xav's side at the end were the first woman he'd loved, and the last.

'Mrs Attwood, is this your husband?' The detective who'd accompanied them into the mortuary was standing a respectful distance behind them.

Ella gasped, nodded and resumed crying.

'This is Xav Attwood,' Amber said.

The detective was playing with some sugar grains on the cafeteria table and Amber wanted to slap his hands, to yell at him to be more respectful.

'Ms Pike, can you think of anyone who might want to harm Mr Attwood?'

And so it begins.

'Harm him?' Amber made herself look mildly shocked. 'I thought it was an accident.' Over the detective's shoulder, she could see Ella talking to a second detective and told herself it was a good thing that neither of them had been asked to go to the station or to submit to a formal interview. Yet.

'That was our first thought,' the detective acknowledged. 'Mr Attwood, possibly having had too much to drink, stumbled in the garden and banged his head on one of those stones.'

Amber waited. The detective examined the pad of his right index finger where sugar grains had stuck.

'Two problems with that theory though,' he said. 'The first, there was no alcohol in Mr Attwood's blood and, secondly, the post-mortem shows three distinct contusions to the back of his head. No one falls three times in a row.'

'I guess not.' Amber felt the last trace of hope slip away. Talitha had been right, of course; she always was. Xav had been murdered.

'So, can you? Think of anyone who'd want to harm him?'

Amber shook her head. 'Not a soul,' she lied. 'I've never met anyone who didn't like Xav.'

The detective glanced down at his notebook. 'You say you saw him on Monday at Waterstock. How did he seem to you?'

Tortured. At breaking point. On the verge of throwing his entire life away. 'He seemed fine,' Amber said. 'Normal. Busy at work, making tons of money, normal Xav.'

A fresh pain around her jawline, tears threatening again.

'Interesting,' the detective said, 'because his wife says the opposite. She claims he hasn't been himself for weeks.'

Amber told herself to take it slow, give the appearance of thinking.

'Well, she'd know him best, I guess. Maybe he let her see things he didn't show the rest of us.'

'And he'd resigned from his job, only four days ago.'

She hadn't known that. 'I didn't know that.'

He'd meant it then; Xav had been putting his affairs in order. No, he'd been closing his life down, getting ready to leave it.

'His wife says he spent the weekend clearing out his things. She thought he was planning to leave her.'

Well, he had been, in a way. Amber shook her head. 'News to me.'

'You're an old girlfriend of Mr Attwood's, aren't you?'

'Xav and I went out at school. That was twenty years ago.'

'So, the two of you haven't been seeing each other recently?'

Amber felt a stab of relief at being able to answer a question honestly. 'If you mean having an affair, no we definitely weren't.'

'And yet you resigned only the other week, for personal reasons. Within days of Mr Attwood doing the same thing. Were you worried something might embarrass the government?'

'Xav and I were not having an affair. As far as I know, he wasn't having an affair with anyone.'

Funny, but until it was taken away, one never appreciated the simple satisfaction of being able to tell the truth.

'So why did you resign?'

'I was missing too much of my daughters' childhood – I can return to the front benches when they're older.'

'Can you think why Mr Attwood might be in the garden of the house on Boars Hill at midnight?'

Another question she could answer honestly. 'I can't, I'm afraid. We knew one of the boys who grew up there, Will, the oldest, but I haven't seen him for twenty years. I don't know if Xav was still in touch with him.'

'Will Markham is in the United States.' The detective consulted his notebook again. 'Mr Attwood is the second friend of yours to cause you some concern in the last two weeks, isn't that right? A Dr Daniel Redman, head teacher of All Souls' School, has been reported missing by the staff there.'

'We've been worried about Dan,' Amber said, 'but his residence told us he'd gone on a retreat.'

'We?'

'A group of old friends.' She named Tal and Felix, the only two left now.

'I wonder why you didn't report his disappearance to the police.'

'We thought about it. I wanted to. But Tal argued that if Dan simply needed some time to himself, we could be causing him huge embarrassment by making a fuss. We decided to give it some time.'

'You see, I ran Mr Attwood's name through the police computer, and it came up in connection with yours and Daniel Redman's. You were all friends with Megan Macdonald, weren't you?'

'A long time ago.'

The detective put down his notebook and fixed Amber with a long stare. 'Did you know that she's missing too?'

## 55

Talitha realised, as she pulled into the driveway and saw the huge black windows of her home, that she hated coming back to an empty house, and she had no idea why it had taken her so long to acknowledge it.

When she'd met Mark, she'd told herself his three sons from a former marriage were a point in his favour. Loud, smelly, frequently obnoxious, occasionally hilarious, the boys had been all the children she'd ever need and would present her with grandkids one day that, again, she wouldn't have to get too close to because they wouldn't be her – you know – *real* grandchildren.

Fortnightly visits and mid-week sleepovers had been all the family life she'd needed, but now, when Mark was away, as happened so often, she wandered the endless stone floors of the house with a heaviness inside.

She sat in the drive a while longer. Gus, the youngest at seven, had stuck Marvel stickers on his bedroom window, and she'd been annoyed; the garish pictures cheapened the minimalist frontage of their home, but Mark had taken his son's side. Now, she found herself longing for Gus's warm, stocky body next to her own on the sofa. Gus was a cuddle machine, prepared to snuggle up to anything warm that stayed still long enough, and she'd never been especially patient with him.

Was it too late, she wondered, to have a child of her own?

The rain, that had been pouring down since she left the office, was blurring the windscreen. Talitha left the car, ran the last few paces, and let herself in. Remembering her own advice to Amber and Felix, she checked the deadlock and was putting the chain on the door when she realised that something was wrong. She should be hurrying to the burglar alarm, punching in the code that would prevent it going off, and yet the low-pitched alert hadn't sounded. The alarm was disabled.

Only she, Mark and their housekeeper knew the alarm code, but she'd spoken to Mark earlier from his hotel room in Berlin and the housekeeper never came outside her normal hours. On the other hand, it was entirely possible that she'd forgotten to activate the alarm that morning; she had a lot on her mind at the moment.

Raindrops fell from Talitha's coat as she hung it in the small cloakroom. As usual, it was almost impossible to find a hook and numerous coats and jackets formed a great shapeless mass that the door could hardly push back. She would have to speak to the boys about leaving so much junk here.

Her heels echoed down the hallway and the buckle of her handbag strap clattered against the granite of the kitchen work-top. She'd never realised before how noisy a house it was. The windows, taking up the entire back wall, had become a huge mirror against the darkness outside and the mezzanine gallery behind her was perfectly reflected. She could see five bedroom doors, one ajar.

Something – a twig, litter – rapped against the kitchen window, making her jump.

'Alexa,' she said. 'Close the blinds.'

A second of silence and then the vertically hung blinds hummed into place. Cutting off the night should have helped, but no sooner was she enclosed in the kitchen, unable to use the windows as a mirror any longer, than Talitha had an undeniable feeling that someone was watching her. She pivoted. Still no one on the gallery, of course, but the open door was a problem. The bedroom doors were kept closed when the boys weren't here. Someone had been up there.

On the way out of the kitchen, she stopped by the knife block. All seven knives were exactly where they should be, which was good in itself, she supposed, and she certainly wasn't going to carry one around the house because the idea was too ridiculous.

But this was not her life as she'd known it, this was a world in which Dan had vanished and Xav had been killed. She chose a medium-sized knife, one she'd seen Mark use for chopping vegetables, because the bigger meat knives really would be absurd, and this one could be almost concealed in her hand.

The ground floor was empty. Mostly open-plan, devoid of hiding places, it was easy to inspect. No crouching assassin behind any of the leather sofas in the sitting room; in the cloakroom by the front door, the mass of coats was exactly that, a mass of coats; Mark's study was a mess, but it was Mark's mess, as he always left it. The upper floor would be trickier.

The knife handle had become slick with sweat as she climbed the stairs.

Starting with the room she and Mark shared, Talitha checked the bedrooms in turn, not forgetting the en-suites, stepping back as she pulled open wardrobe doors, all the while conscious that on the upper floor, there was no easy way of escape from the house. On the upper floor, she was trapped.

The door that wasn't quite closed belonged to Rupert, the eldest. She stopped on the threshold and slid the knife properly into her hand. The beating of her heart became almost painful.

*OK, go!*

The door slammed back against the wall; out of sight, a high-pitched voice yelled. Talitha screamed, even as she leapt forward to see a sixteen-year-old boy on the bed. A smartphone had dropped to the floor, and he wore headphones that had blocked out the sound of her arrival.

'Rupert, what the fuck?' The sudden release of tension made Talitha yell. 'What are you doing here?'

The thin, dark-haired boy stared back with wide-open eyes and a pitiful expression. 'Sorry, sorry, I let myself in.'

Heart still thumping, Talitha slid the knife, unnoticed, into her pocket.

'We're not expecting you till the weekend. Does your mum know you're here?'

Rupert's face flicked from apologetic to sullen. The idiot thought he was in trouble; she'd never been more pleased to see him.

'She thinks I'm staying with Stan,' he said. 'I had an argument with him.'

Stan was one of Rupert's less pleasant friends. 'So why not go home?'

'Mum's best mates with Stan's mum. She'd make me go round and apologise so it wouldn't be awkward.'

Stan's mum was head of the school PTA and the sun around which the other mothers circled like lesser planets.

'What if she phones to check on you and finds out you're not there?' Tal asked. 'She'll panic.'

'She's texted me three times with instructions on how to be-have.' Rupert held up his phone. 'I replied. She knows I'm alive, just not where I am.'

Talitha sank onto the bed beside him. 'So how did you get in?' she asked.

'I found a spare key last time I was here.' Rupert's eyes dropped.

'You've got others, I knew you wouldn't miss it.'

'Charming. And the burglar alarm?'

He shrugged. 'Known it for months. We all do.'

Talitha raised her voice. 'Alexa, remind me to change the burglar alarm code.'

As Alexa scheduled a reminder, Talitha let herself smile. 'Hungry?' she said.

Rupert's eyes lit up. 'I had some crisps,' he offered.

'Your dad put some lasagnes in the freezer. Fancy one?'

Rupert jumped up and pulled her to her feet. He'd be taller than she was soon; he was already much stronger. Talitha touched his shoulder. 'It's good to see you,' she said.

As Rupert left the room, Talitha stepped to the window to draw the blinds. On the upper floor they weren't automated. They'd reached the halfway point when she spotted movement in the street outside. She switched off the bedroom light and gave her eyes a few seconds to adjust before going back to the window.

There was someone on the pavement outside, standing beneath a streetlight, mainly shielded by an umbrella, but her face was revealed a split second before she walked away. Megan.

'We said we wouldn't do this,' Felix's voice sounded muffled, as though he were talking through a scarf.

'I think Megan's outside my house,' Talitha replied.

'Hang on.'

The phone clattered onto a hard surface. Talitha waited.

'If she is, she's on foot,' Felix said, when he'd picked up the phone again. 'Her car's back on the Blackbird Leys estate. Different street but same area.'

'She was on foot.'

'Doesn't make a lot of sense, though. It's a long way from Blackbird Leys to Summertown. Why walk in this weather?'

Why indeed? And now she came to think of it, the hair had been wrong. It has been short, blonde, like the Megan of old.

'It may not have been her, I suppose?' She'd only seen the woman for a moment.

'Want me to come round?' Felix offered.

Talitha could feel the tension slipping from her body, leaving it exhausted. 'No, it's OK. Rupert's with me.'

'Well, keep the doors locked.'

Late supper over, Talitha and Rupert were huddled together on the sofa – turned out Rupert was a great cuddler too – watching one of the old Marvel films, when the doorbell could be heard above the sound of the Hulk taking out an attack helicopter. Rupert groaned. 'Mum,' he said, opening an app on his phone.

Talitha paused the film.

'Not Mum.' Rupert sounded puzzled. 'Find My Friends says she's still at home.'

'Wait here,' Talitha told him.

The hallway was dark, apart from the dimmest of beams from the security lighting, meant to ensure no one need walk around at night in the dark. Talitha made no move to switch on lights, because then she'd be less able to see through the glass of the front door and make out who was standing on its threshold.

From the sitting room, came the sound of the film resuming, and that was a good thing, because it meant Rupert wouldn't hear anything she called through the door.

Whatever happened, whatever excuse she offered, Megan was not coming in.

The dark outline of the figure on the doorstep took shape slowly as Talitha moved down the hall. Two steps away, she saw hair, shoulders, the curve of a face that she knew.

*

The credits were rolling before it occurred to Rupert that his stepmother hadn't returned to the sitting room. Nor had he learned who'd been at the door. He got up, expecting to find Talitha at the kitchen counter, hunched over the laptop, as she usually was, but the great open-plan room was empty. He was about to try upstairs when a door slammed somewhere in the house; he felt a cold draught, and realised the front door was open.

'Tal?' He stepped cautiously along the hallway.

It was still raining outside. Rupert had his phone in his hand – of course he did, he was sixteen years old – and keeping his eyes on the doorway, he found his dad's number. His finger hovered over the call button, but he made himself wait.

On the threshold, he could see Talitha's car parked in the driveway; she hadn't gone anywhere.

'Tal? What's going on?' The gravel of the drive bit into his feet. He hadn't thought to put shoes on, and the rain would soak him if he stayed out here for much longer. Already it was running into his eyes, dripping down his neck.

He didn't need to stay out long.

The body of his stepmother lay on the gravel by the side of her car.

# 56

'Do you believe in coincidence, Mr O'Neill?'

'Of course,' Felix said.

'So, you'd put the deaths of two of your oldest friends, and the disappearance of a third, all within a few days, down to coincidence?'

'No, that would be absurd,' he said. 'Megan Macdonald killed Tal and Xav, probably Dan too.'

The more senior of the two detectives interviewing Felix slid a photograph of Megan across the desk towards him. 'This Megan Macdonald?' he said.

The picture had been taken in prison, against a stark white background. Megan's hair clung to her scalp, damp, possibly unwashed; in a face devoid of make-up, her skin seemed a mass of tiny blemishes and eczema patches.

'That's her.' He pushed the photograph back. 'Have you found her?'

'We're following some leads. Tell me why Miss Macdonald would want to kill two of her oldest friends.'

'Three. The fact you haven't found Dan's body doesn't mean he's alive. Dan wouldn't disappear like that.'

Dan would totally cut and run, but these bozos didn't need to know that.

'Why would Megan want to kill anyone?'

'There's something not right about her. She was never right. Look what she did twenty years ago. It was brutal. And she's spent twenty years in prison – that's enough to send anyone nuts.'

Hardly convincing, it was all he had.

A heavy sigh answered him. Then, 'And yet most people come out of prison as sane as they went in. Megan Macdonald has never been considered as having anything other than normal mental capacity.'

'She's clever, I'll give her that.'

'OK, let's go with your theory for a moment. Why would she choose her oldest friends? Why not some random stranger in the street?'

'She was angry at us. She thought we betrayed her.'

'How so?'

Felix had spent much of the previous night awake, planning his response to exactly that question. 'When Megan was arrested, it was a massive shock,' he began. 'We couldn't believe what she'd done. I guess we turned our backs on her. We were under a lot of pressure from our parents to cut her out of our lives, and I suppose we did. The last time we saw her, not so long ago, she had a real go at us for abandoning her.'

'And had you?'

Deliberately, Felix dropped his eyes to the desk. 'I guess so. We didn't visit or write. I think Talitha made some childish promise that as soon as she was a qualified lawyer, she'd represent Megan, try to get her sentence reduced, but she didn't. Daniel was at university in Durham, where Megan was in prison, and even he hadn't been to see her.'

'What about Xav Attwood? Why would she want to kill him?'

Felix risked a glance up; the detective's eyes were bloodshot. 'That's the easiest to explain,' he said. 'She had a major crush on him back in school. I think he may even have promised he'd wait for her. So, when she came out and found he was married, with no intention of leaving his wife, she flipped.'

'You said earlier you've seen a lot of her since she was released?' the detective said. 'Every weekday in your case. Why is that?'

Felix leaned back in his chair, although it was the last thing he felt like doing. 'None of us wanted to particularly. But she wormed her way back into our lives. She wasn't taking no for an answer. It was getting embarrassing, to be honest, causing problems with our families.'

'And yet you gave her a job?'

'I felt sorry for her.'

'She's been working for your company for, what? Five weeks?'

Felix mimed thinking about it. 'Sounds about right.'

'Getting on all right, is she?'

'Yeah, she's not bad, in fairness. She got to grips with the finances quickly. Turned up on time every day. She was OK.'

'So, she probably wouldn't wish you any harm? Seeing as how you were her employer.'

'I'm sure she hates me as much as the others. Maybe I'm next.'

'When did you last see her?'

This was where he had to be careful, where any information he gave could be checked against what the others said. Except, there weren't any others now. Only him and Amber. And Megan.

'I'm not sure,' he said. 'She didn't come into work last week. She'd booked leave, but only for a week, so she should have come back on Monday.' He dropped his head into his hands, to give himself thinking time. 'Sorry,' he said. 'I'm struggling to take all this in. Xav was my best man, I've known him since we were kids. Tal was a good mate too.'

Silence, then, 'Take your time, Mr O'Neill.' A glass of water was placed in front of him. 'In fact, why don't we take a short break?'

The interview was suspended and Felix left alone. He wiped his eyes with the back of his hands – they came away damp, who'd have thought it? – and swallowed some of the water. It was lukewarm and contained too much fluoride. By the time the detectives came back, he'd made a decision.

'There's something I need to tell you,' he said.

The two men settled themselves down, switched on the recording equipment, and waited.

'Twenty years ago, we set up a trust fund for Megan.'

The lead detective's face betrayed no surprise. 'A trust fund?'

'I can't remember whose idea it was, but we thought about it the day she was sentenced.'

'Sorry, who is "we"?'

'The gang, the five of us. Me, Xav, Tal, Amber and Dan. We were in court that day, although I don't think Megan ever knew. We agreed that once we'd finished university and were earning money, we'd set aside ten per cent of our income every year and put it in a trust for Megan when she was released.'

A glance between the two detectives. 'That's exceptionally generous.'

'We were kids. And we were gutted about what happened. We did it, too. Even Dan, who only had a teacher's salary for most of the time. Xav managed it for us, and it was pretty sizeable by the time she was released.'

'She must have been grateful.'

Felix dropped his gaze again. 'We didn't tell her.'

'Why not?'

He looked up and hardened his stare. 'We weren't kids any more. Something we'd done when we were teenagers felt childish, unnecessary. It was a lot of money. We were all reluctant to give it to her, to be honest. We were heels, I'm not denying that. Anyway, the thing is, she found it.'

'Found it how?'

'She noticed I was making regular contributions to a trust fund and managed to access it. She really is very clever. But instead of being grateful, she was furious, because she knew we'd been holding it back.'

'I suppose I can see her point.'

'Yeah, me too. I'm not defending what we did. But she didn't just find it, she stole it. I mean, she accessed it. The money's gone. She has it. So, wherever she is, and whatever she's got planned, she's very well resourced.'

'We'll need to access your company's computer system,' the detective said.

Felix nodded the permission that he knew wasn't necessary. He'd realised in the night that, sooner or later, the police would go into his company accounts. It didn't matter. Short of the trust fund – and he'd owned up to that – there was nothing that could incriminate him.

'There's something else,' he said. 'Something she told us last time we saw her.'

'I thought you couldn't remember the last time you saw her?'

'The occasion I can remember,' he told them firmly. 'It's the date I'm struggling with. Maybe it was the second to last time, I don't know, OK, but I think this is important. She told us she'd been gang-raped by her father and several of his friends the summer we did our A levels. We were knocked for six. She'd given no hint of it twenty years ago, but it obviously explained why she'd gone off the rails. You know, failing her A levels so spectacularly, doing that stupid driving thing? She was trauma-tised. Probably suffering PTSD, not thinking properly. I wish now we had known – we would have made sure the police knew and it would have been taken into account in her sentencing, but we didn't.'

Both detectives were making notes.

'Her dad was attacked not so long ago,' Felix went on. 'Beaten up in his caravan. It was on the news. I think she arranged it, using our money. She's using the trust-fund money to get her own back on everyone she thinks let her down.'

'Do you have any idea where she might be?'

Felix shook his head. 'She might have contacts, people she knew inside. I don't think she has any family in the area other than her dad and he's still in hospital.'

'We're nearly done, Mr O'Neill. Just a couple more things to run past you. What car did Ms Macdonald drive?'

Felix let his eyes drift and pictured himself standing at his office window, looking out at the car park. 'A Nissan Micra. Quite an old model. Metallic blue.'

Another photograph slid across the desk towards Felix. Taken at night, a car, that might have been blue, but it was hard to say, was heading out of town towards Boars Hill.

'This one?' the detective asked.

The registration number wasn't visible. 'Looks similar,' Felix said.

'Ms Macdonald hadn't registered the car in her name so was in effect driving illegally,' the detective said. 'It would help if you knew the registration number.'

Felix closed his eyes and thought for a second. 'PD54 RZM,' he said.

'You sound very certain.'

'I'm good with numbers too,' he said. 'Is that the same car?'

'It is. It was caught on camera going up Boars Hill and then coming back down again around about the time of Mr Attwood's murder.'

Felix felt a rising excitement. 'Is that proof?'

'Not quite, we can't see who's driving the car. But it is strong circumstantial evidence.'

'One more thing, sir.' The other detective produced a clear plastic evidence bag. 'Do you recognise these?'

Megan's sunglasses, the same pair she'd been wearing at Talitha's lunch party.

'They're Megan's,' he said.

'Are you sure?'

'Absolutely. She wore them in her hair most of the time, but when she took them off, I could see the ends were chewed.' He pointed. 'Like that.'

The bag was removed.

'Thank you for your time, Mr O'Neill. We'll be in touch.'

The recording equipment was switched off and all three men got to their feet. At the door, Felix turned back.

'Are you able to tell me where the sunglasses came from?' he said.

A brief look was exchanged. 'Don't see why not. We found them on the driveway of Talitha Slater's house. Not far from her body.'

# 57

The sound of the security gates opening caused Amber to slice a sliver of skin from the top of her thumb. A bubble of blood appeared a second before the pain kicked in and, as always, she wondered how she might cope with real pain when even a tiny cut hurt so blinking much. Well, she might find out soon, exactly as Tal, Xav, and Dan had.

She had to calm down; blind panic would kill her for sure. The gates had opened to let Dex in; he was due home round about now.

She'd been cooking – she often did when she was stressed and needed a simple, productive way of filling her time. Each election night, and Amber had known four since becoming an MP, saw her peeling, chopping, flash-frying and casseroling. By the time the result was declared, her freezer would be full and her kitchen looking like the oven had exploded.

Dripping blood over the worktop, she found some paper towel and wrapped it around the wound. Only then did she realise that Dex hadn't entered the house. Nor had she heard the wheels of his car on the drive, and the security light outside the back door remained off. And just like that, the fear was back.

Amber left the kitchen, grabbing her bag on the way, because it contained both her phones and she never let them leave her side any more. In the dining room, she approached the big bay window that overlooked the drive. No sign of Dexter's car. She was reaching for her bag to call him, when the burner phone began to ring. Felix was calling. Well, of course it was Felix – he and she were the only ones left.

No, no, she couldn't think about that, not now.

'Hi.'

Without preamble, Felix said, 'I need to talk to you.'

Amber was still listening out for her husband's arrival. 'I may have to call you back.'

'No, not over the phone. Remember what we talked about? When a certain person first came back?'

No phone conversations because you never knew who might be listening. Amber, especially, had to be careful.

'Are you on your own?' Felix said. 'Is anyone with you?'

'No, but I think Dex is about to come in.'

Felix seemed to breathe out a heavy sigh. 'OK, good. Listen, I need to see you. Can you come over?'

Not tonight. Not now.

'I don't think I can.'

Another pause, another audible intake of breath. Felix, too, was upset, maybe afraid, and this made everything worse. Felix was supposed to be their tough guy. If he fell, they all did.

They all had, though. Only two left.

'Am, this is important.'

She could hear the tremble in his voice that he was trying so hard to hide. 'You and I have to talk,' he went on. 'We need to decide what we do next. Something's happened.'

Well, of course something had happened. Megan, released from prison, had become an avenging fury, taking down everyone in her path. She'd killed Dan, Tal and even Xav, whom she'd loved, so she'd have no mercy for the best friend who'd stolen the love of her life and left her to rot in prison.

'What's happened?' she managed.

'Am, I'm not going to tell you again. You're in trouble. Where are the girls?'

The sudden subject change threw her.

'What?'

'Pearl and Ruby, where are they? I've sent Sarah and Luke to her parents. I don't want them anywhere near here.'

A stab at her heart, sharper and colder than anything she'd felt so far. 'Me too,' she said. 'They're at Dex's mum's place in Finchley. I told her I'd be busy in the House for the next few days. Dex wasn't sure when he'd be back but he's here now.'

Maybe he wasn't though – she still hadn't heard her husband enter the house. Amber was suddenly aware of how big the house was, and how far from those nearby.

'That's good,' Felix told her. 'Right, can you get yourself over here? Come to the factory – we'll be safe there. No one has keys but me and the cleaners, and they'll have finished by now.'

Safe. She had no idea what that meant any more.

'Amber, are you listening?'

'Of course. OK. If you think it's important.'

'And Am, don't trust anyone. Don't talk to anyone and don't stop driving. Just get here, OK?'

Felix ended the call and the silence of the house seemed to surround Amber. In spite of what she'd just told Felix, she was alone. Dexter wasn't capable of being quiet for more than a few seconds; even when he slept. She'd never known a man snore and talk in his sleep the way her husband did. This oppressive, unnatural silence meant he wasn't in the house.

She grabbed a jacket and was on the point of unlocking the back door when she remembered why she'd thought Dex was home. She'd heard the gates opening and closing.

The huge, state-of-the-art gates, installed when she'd been

appointed prisons and probation minister, recognised the number plates of a handful of cars permitted automatic entry. To open them at any other time required a six-digit key code that, she'd been assured, was impossible to guess, as long as she didn't use anything obvious like her birthday, her husband's or either of her children's. She hadn't, so the gates couldn't have opened; she must have heard next door's gates.

Taking heart, Amber slipped outside. As she locked the door, her jacket was nearly pulled from her shoulders by the force of the wind. A scattering of twigs and branches on the ground told her the storm had been raging for some time. The gates were closed, exactly as they should be, and she wasn't going to worry about the garage door being open, because she usually left it that way for Dex. Her car was facing outwards, ready to drive away, something that had been impressed upon her by her security team. She was in the driver's seat in seconds.

Leaving the property, Amber turned onto the A-road outside her house. She'd driven about a hundred yards, was reaching fifty miles an hour, when she realised her terrible mistake. When she'd remote unlocked the car it had responded, not with its customary clunk of locks disengaging but simply with a turning on of the internal lights. Her car had not been locked. At the same time, she became aware of a smell that didn't belong: rain on clothing, the chemically created floral scent of a shampoo and a hint of body odour.

Her foot froze on the accelerator and she knew exactly what she was about to see in the rear-view mirror. It was almost a relief when the road behind vanished from view and a pair of dark eyes in a pale face appeared. When the worst happens, dread, at least, is over.

'Hello, Amber,' Megan said from the back seat. 'Keep driving.'

# 58

'Don't slow down. No, I'm serious, Amber, you have to keep driving. Don't even think about pulling over on this road.'

Megan's face left the mirror momentarily, replaced by the back of her head as she glanced behind. 'If you stop and another car comes along, we're both toast,' she snapped. 'Keep your eyes on the road, keep driving, and for God's sake, get a grip. You're hyperventilating.'

Amber could hear what Megan was saying, but her brain couldn't process it.

'What the hell do you want?' she managed.

Her voice, thin and unnaturally high-pitched, might have been squeezed out through a tube. It was a stupid question anyway. She knew what Megan wanted. She wanted to kill them all. Felix must have known she was on her way over and damn him for not just saying it. Sooner or later, when they reached a layby or a turn-off, she'd be told to pull over and that would be it.

'Only to talk.' Megan's voice was calm, low-pitched; the tone people use when soothing a panicking animal. 'Wait a sec, I'm coming through.'

She moved forward; Amber cringed and the car swerved.

'Oh, for God's sake,' Megan snapped. 'I'm only coming to join you in the front.'

Out of the corner of her eye, Amber watched Megan squeeze through the gap between the seats. Why, when she needed it most, could she remember nothing of what her close-protection officers had told her about self-defence?

Megan waved both hands in front of her face. 'Look,' Megan said. 'No gun, no knife, nothing. I'm not going to hurt you.'

'What do you want?' Tears sprang into Amber's eyes. 'I'm really sorry about what we did. I know we were wrong, and I don't blame you for hating us, but you're turning into a monster.'

She should be braver than this, she knew, but Pearl and Ruby – she might never see them again.

A hand landed on her arm and she shook it off, the way she'd shake off a spider or a wasp.

'Amber, listen to me—'

'My little girls, Megan. How can you do this to my girls?'

'Amber, get a fucking grip. I'm not the one you need to be afraid of.'

She risked a sharp glance sideways. Megan's face was unreadable, but somehow, she didn't look like a cold-blooded killer about to strike. If anything, she too looked scared and that made no sense, none at all.

'What do you mean?' Amber said.

'Where are we going?' Megan replied. 'Right now, where were you headed before you saw me? Come on, that's not hard.'

For a moment, Amber had to think. Of course, she was meeting Felix, that was it, at the factory.

Megan said, 'You took a phone call on that burner phone Tal gave you. I could see you from the drive. Was it Felix?'

Amber let her head fall and rise.

'And he wants you to meet him somewhere?'

Another nod – what else could she do? Megan flopped back

onto her seat as though struck by a sudden thought and a phone rang, startling them both. It was Amber's burner phone. Felix was calling.

'Don't answer him,' Megan snapped. She leaned across and killed the call. A few seconds later, Amber's own phone began ringing through the car's internal system. Felix again. He'd be at the factory by now. When she didn't show up, he'd do something, wouldn't he? He wouldn't abandon her.

Megan pressed the reject button.

Of course he would; this was Felix.

'Amber slow down, this is dangerous.'

The speedometer was at sixty-two miles an hour, too fast for this narrow, dark road. Amber eased up on the accelerator.

'OK,' Megan said. 'I need you to stay calm and listen to me. Can you do that?'

She could do that. She let her head tremble – it would do as acquiescence.

'I was leaving,' Megan said. 'I'd paid a dodgy lorry driver to smuggle me to France in the back of his lorry. No one gives a toss about lorries heading out of Britain – all they care about are the ones coming the other way. I was in Dover last Tuesday, ready to go, and you would never have heard from me again.'

This couldn't be true, it made no sense. 'So why didn't you go?' she risked.

'I heard on the news what someone did to my dad. Someone broke into his caravan in the middle of the night and beat him within an inch of his life. I had to turn back.'

Still not making sense. 'You hated your dad.'

'I don't give a shit about the bastard, but I knew something was up. Even Talitha couldn't have organised a hit that quickly. This was something else.'

Amber heard the words, but they might have come out in the wrong order for all she understood them.

'I'm not ill, Amber,' Megan sighed. 'I would never have made Dan give me one of his kidneys – I was messing with him. You too. As if I'd ask for one of your children.'

The woman was mad. She'd broken Amber with that demand; now she was saying it had been a joke? Suddenly, it was all too much. Amber took her hands away from the steering wheel and her foot off the accelerator.

'I can't do this.' She shook her head. 'I can't.'

Megan grabbed a hold of the wheel. 'OK, OK, pull over. There's a layby coming up. Look, four hundred yards, pull in there. But you have to promise me you won't run away.'

'I promise.' She'd promise anything. It didn't even matter if this had been Megan's plan all along, to get the car parked up before smashing Amber's skull to pieces. She was past caring.

As Megan glanced repeatedly behind, and at her watch, Amber drove the last few yards and steered the car into a layby. She let the engine stall and her eyes close.

'Listen to me.' Megan's voice sounded loud and too close. 'I was messing with you, with all of you. I was bloody furious at the way you left me to rot in that place, not giving me a second thought all those years.'

Hearing movement, Amber opened her eyes in fright. Megan was staring directly at her.

'And, if I'm completely honest,' Megan went on as Amber closed her eyes again in shame, 'there have been times when I could cheerfully have killed Talitha for keeping me in there.'

'I didn't know about that, I promise,' Amber sobbed.

A hand landed gently on her arm and this time she didn't shake it off. 'I know,' Megan said. 'But this is important, I wasn't going to do anything. Amber, please look at me.'

Amber opened her eyes, but tears had filled them again and Megan was a blur.

Megan said, 'I know what you've all been going through these last twenty years, I know that what we did has been eating away at you. You've all been punished too.'

Yes, that was true, they had. 'Not like you, though.' Amber wiped her eyes in time to see Megan smile.

'No, not the same,' she said. 'Arguably worse. At least I paid for what we did. There's some solace in that.'

Tears were threatening again as Amber felt Megan take hold of both her hands. 'I'm so sorry,' she said again.

'Listen to me.' Megan squeezed Amber's hands. 'I put the film and the letter in a place where I knew Xav would find them. I knew he'd remember that tree in the Markham garden. I don't even know if the film could be developed after all these years, but I was never going to try. I left a letter for Xav too, explaining exactly what I'm telling you now. It was over, Am. I'd taken the money, and I'm not going to feel guilty about that, but I was never going to bother any of you again. For one thing, Talitha was capable of a lot. I was never going to trust her.'

Amber was trying to process what she was being told. If Xav had found the proof in the Markham garden – in a tree? – then the police must have it now. Except that didn't work either, because if the police had it, they would know everything. Megan had to be lying.

'Talitha is dead,' she said to Megan. 'You killed her.'

Dark eyes stared directly into Amber's. 'No, not me. I'm not saying I didn't hate her, but you think I could kill Xav? Even Daniel?'

She didn't know. 'I don't know you any more. I don't know what you're capable of.'

Amber's hands were released. 'So why haven't I done it already?

Why wasn't I waiting outside your back door, ready to cosh you over the head with something heavy?'

It would have been so easy. 'Your car was seen heading up Boars Hill the night Xav was killed,' she said. 'The police know you did it.'

Megan flinched, as though Amber had struck her, and for a moment, she seemed lost in thought.

'I left my car at the Travelodge last Sunday,' she said at last. 'I left the keys under the carpet on the driver's side. I knew I couldn't take it away with me, and I didn't want it used to track me down. It was collateral damage.'

So much to process, and no way to tell truth from lies.

Megan dropped her head into her hands, maybe giving herself thinking time, a chance to invent more lies, and Amber heard a car approaching. She looked around in time to see the vehicle – a small blue hatchback – draw closer and seem to lose speed, before accelerating away again.

'We should get moving.' Megan had raised her head. 'Are you OK to drive?'

Amber started the engine and pulled out of the layby. 'Where are we going?' she asked.

'Not sure.'

The wind was still furious. Every few seconds, flotsam blown from the trees hurtled across the road like tiny weapons. Her car phone sounded, Felix again; this time Amber made no attempt to answer.

They passed a turning to the left and Amber caught sight of a small blue car waiting to pull out. It took its time, even though the road was empty but for the two vehicles, and then its headlights were lost around a bend.

'Why are you even here?' Amber asked, after she'd driven a half-mile. 'If you don't want to hurt me, why would you climb

349

the fence to get onto my property and sneak inside my car?'

Megan gave a short, mirthless laugh. 'Well, first up, I didn't climb a twelve-foot fence with trellis on top. I used your mother's birthday on the keypad and it worked. I figured of all of us, you'd be the least likely to change your passcodes, even after twenty years. Your car was open. And I'm here because someone does want to kill you and is planning to this very night. I would prefer that not to happen. I couldn't go to the police for obvious reasons, so I had to come myself.'

Amber felt the fog in her head gathering again. Who on earth wanted to kill her if Megan didn't?

'Who?' she asked.

Megan said, 'Felix, of course.'

'Are you mad?'

'Felix has had access to my car keys for weeks. He could easily have had a copy made.'

Felix had put a tracker in Megan's car too, he'd known where it was all the time.

Megan said, 'What did he say to you on the phone?'

Something about wanting to see her, not being able to talk on the phone. He'd bullied her into meeting him, and it was so in character for Felix to expect the rest of them to jump when he told them that she hadn't questioned it anything like as much as – maybe – she should have done.

'He said I was in danger,' she told Megan. 'He said we needed to talk.'

'Think about it, Am. Talitha, one of the smartest people we know, left the security of her house after someone rang the door-bell late at night. At a time when she knew she was at risk. Do you seriously think she'd have opened it to me?'

She wouldn't. Of course, she wouldn't.

'You tricked her.' Amber knew she was clutching at straws. 'You rang the bell and hid.'

'And she'd have fallen for that? Come on. Whoever rang Talitha's doorbell was someone she trusted. She did not trust me.'

Talitha had been so convinced of the danger they were all in, had impressed upon Amber the importance of being cautious.

'The attack on my dad was something to do with you lot,' Megan said. 'I knew the chances of Talitha arranging something so quickly were slim, so I figured it was one of the guys. Dan didn't have the guts for it, never mind the muscle, so it had to be one of the other two. Who, out of Xav and Felix, would you say was the most capable of violence?'

Felix, of course. Amber had never seen Xav so much as lose his temper.

Megan assumed from Amber's silence that she'd come to the right conclusion. She said, 'Where are you supposed to meet him?'

'The factory.'

'Well, we're not going.'

No, they weren't, Amber realised. She was not going anywhere near Felix. Somehow, in the last few minutes, she'd transferred her trust from one old friend to the other.

'Where are we going?' she asked again.

'Somewhere he won't find us. We need a plan, Amber.'

## 59

Before leaving home for the factory, Felix checked the tracking app on his phone, expecting to see Megan's car on the Blackbird Leys estate where it had been immobile for over twenty-four hours. When he saw it on the A329, only a couple of miles outside Drayton St Leonards, where Amber lived with her family, he thought his heart might stop beating.

He called Amber's home phone, her personal mobile and then the burner phone that Tal had given her. No answer.

He was too late.

# 60

*Echo Yard.* Amber read the sign and wondered why on earth they were at Echo Yard. If Felix had nearly killed Megan's dad here, he knew how to get in. Too late to ask questions, though. Megan was already approaching the huge steel gates.

Aware that, at last, she had a chance of escape, Amber knew she wasn't even going to try. Sometime, over the last few miles, she'd made a decision that she hadn't even needed to formulate in her head. She trusted Megan more than she did Felix; it was as simple as that.

It still didn't make being here a good idea. Amber watched Megan tap in the lock code and then the gates slide open. Following her old friend's signal, she drove forward and into the yard. The heavy gates clanged shut behind her. Megan walked ahead of the car, leading the way.

So unnerving, this place at night. Surrounding trees, all of them huge, were being tossed around like straw, and their shadows raced everywhere. As the car crawled forward, statues loomed pale in the moonlight and from the walls of the lock-up shed gargoyles sprang like stone pimples, dozens of hideous faces peering out at her. Others hung from trees, like devils leering from above. Hair blowing like a flag in the wind, entirely at home in this unearthly place, Megan ignored them all and directed Amber to tuck the car behind the shed.

'It won't be seen from the road,' she called through the glass of the driver window.

The car parked, engine switched off, Amber climbed down. 'Is anyone else here?' she asked. The yard was full of sound and movement; impossible to believe it was just she and Megan.

'The other owners don't sleep on site.' Megan set off towards the caravan. 'Dad's the nightwatchman as well as everything else.'

After a glance at both her phones, Amber followed; there'd been several calls to each of them from Felix.

The caravan wasn't locked. Once inside, Megan checked each window to make sure the flimsy curtains were pulled tight before switching on a low piece of strip lighting over the sink.

The caravan was tiny; a two-man, Amber guessed from her memories of her grandparents' caravan. She was standing in a kitchen area. To her right, a desk and chair sat under one window and an internal door led to what was probably the bathroom. To her left was a small dining table and, beyond that, a double bunk.

'Have a seat,' Megan stepped around two holdalls that filled the floor space. Another bag, smaller, with a sports logo, sat on the narrow table.

'Have you been living here?' Amber asked. There was a faint smell of Megan in the cramped space, floating somewhere on top of stale clothes and wet dog.

'For the last few nights.' Megan squeezed herself onto the narrow bench seat. 'I was only going to stay a day or so, till I found out what happened to Dad. Then I heard about Daniel vanishing. Those aren't mine, by the way.' She nodded to a half-full bottle of Bell's whisky and two dirty glasses on the Formica table. 'They're Dad's. I've been trying to touch as little as possible. You shouldn't either – you don't want your prints found here.'

That really wouldn't be a problem. You could write your name in the grime around the sink, and the floor was worse.

Clusters of dog hair and grit had caught in each corner, and the small square of rug was littered with debris. Empty beer cans lay in a disordered heap on the draining board and the remains of a takeaway dinner tumbled out of an over-filled waste bin. She could hear the buzzing of flies above the wind and as she sat opposite Megan, Amber felt something small and light hit her hair. She brushed the insect away and shuddered.

Megan's mouth pursed. 'To answer your unspoken question, prison is a lot worse,' she said.

Amber looked down. 'Sorry.'

'And that needs to be your last apology.' Megan pulled the sports bag towards her and unzipped it. 'You have to see this.'

The contents of the bag spilled out onto the Formica. Clothes, all of them black, a large pair of trainers, jeans, a hoody, gloves and, weirdly, a ski mask. Also . . .

'That's a baseball bat,' Amber said, looking at the long smooth piece of wood.

'Look at the logo immediately below the handle. Don't touch it.'

Amber did what she was told. 'Beit Hall,' she read. 'Felix's hall of residence at Imperial. Is this Felix's stuff?'

'Given that I found it at the back of the store cupboard in the factory, I'd say yes,' Megan replied. 'I let myself in there last night. I think this is the weapon used to beat my dad half to death. And quite possibly Dan, Xav and Tal as well.'

Amber pulled back. If there were bloodstains on the thing in front of her, she didn't want to see them.

'And you took it?' she asked. 'He'll know. He'll be coming after us.' She thought of the huge steel fence surrounding the yard. It might keep them safe; equally it could hold them trapped.

'Amber, he was coming for you anyway. You were a sitting duck.'

She still was. Felix's brain was unfailingly logical. If he was looking for Megan, then sooner or later, probably sooner, he would think of this place. He would come here looking for Megan, and he would find Amber too.

Megan said, 'Come on, Am, pull yourself together. I need you at your best.'

Easy to say, but Amber had lost her best a long time ago. They all had.

'Why is he doing this?' she said. 'He's our friend, why is he hurting us?'

Felix was doing so much more than hurting them, but it was hard, somehow, to use the word *kill*. So much easier to pretend it was all a series of terrible accidents, born out of a misunderstanding, because that way, there was still a possibility it could all come right.

'Because he thinks you're going to crack under the pressure and confess,' Megan said. 'Pressure that I'm largely responsible for. So, I do accept my share of the blame for what happened to Xav and Dan.'

Even in the dim light Amber could see that Megan's eyes, too, were shining.

'Not Talitha though,' she went on. 'That bitch deserved it.'

'You're not to blame,' Amber said. 'We set events in motion that summer. Sooner or later, they were going to catch up with us all.' Her eyes went to the bottle of Bell's. She'd never needed a drink more.

'In Felix's psychopathic brain, it only needed one of you to go to the police and that would bring you all down.' Megan said. 'He's been struggling for years, Am. His drinking's out of control, and his company is on the verge of going under. He's made some stupid decisions. I wasn't entirely kidding when I said it needed someone like me to turn it around.'

'We've all been struggling,' Amber said. 'None of us are normal people.'

'No. I could tell as soon as I met Dan again that he wasn't robust. I'd say he's had mental health problems for years.'

'It wasn't him, though,' Amber said. 'It wasn't Dan who cracked first. Xav was the one who was going to the police. He even gave us notice.'

Megan let her head shake sorrowfully. 'Well, there you are. Felix couldn't let that happen. But we don't know what might have happened between Felix and Daniel. I wouldn't be surprised if Daniel was the first to die.'

'But why Talitha? There's no way she would have gone to the police. Not ever.'

'I think Felix realised the only way he can be safe is if he's the only one left.'

Impossible to sit still any longer. Amber got up, stepped over Megan's holdalls and crossed to the far wall of the caravan. She pulled the curtain back a couple of inches. The road beyond the fence was empty.

'He won't be the only one left though.' She turned around to face Megan again. 'Even if he gets me, there's still you.'

'Oh, I'm easy to deal with,' Megan said. 'I'm going to get the blame. He'll have DNA that he's picked up from the factory: stray hairs, fingerprints on pens, the odd tissue from the bin. He's going to spin the line that I'm out for revenge on the friends who abandoned me, so I'll go back inside, probably for another couple of decades. I'll die in prison.'

'That's why you need me alive.' Amber said. 'You need me on your side.'

Megan didn't argue but began replacing Felix's clothes and bat in the sports bag. She did it carefully, using the ski mask as a makeshift glove. 'This will prove his guilt,' she said. 'His prints should be on the bat. There'll be DNA that ties him to Dad, Xav and Talitha. Maybe Dan as well. But you're a loose end we need to tie up.'

What the hell did that mean?

'I've got a plan, Amber, want to hear it?'

With no other option, Amber nodded her head.

'We leave here, and we drive straight to the police station in Oxford,' Megan said. 'We tell them the truth about what happened twenty years ago.'

So that was her choice: confess and serve time or be bludgeoned to death by the man who was once her friend. At that moment, Amber wasn't entirely sure which she'd choose. The latter would be quick, and she'd die leaving her reputation intact.

'And when I say the truth,' Megan went on, 'I mean a version of it.'

Amber walked back towards the table. 'I'm listening.'

'I tell them that the others – Dan, Xav, Felix and Tal – were in the car with me that night,' Megan said. 'But not you. You'd had too much to drink and you'd passed out hours before we even decided to go.'

It wasn't so very far from the truth. She'd been almost totally out of it that night.

'I'll tell them I offered to take the blame because I knew I'd screwed up my A levels,' Megan went on. 'The deal was they'd all support me. Tal would get her dad's firm to represent me, make sure I didn't get too harsh a sentence, and then, when I came out, they'd all take care of me.'

'Take care of you how?'

'Give me a job, help me find somewhere to live, set me up with some money. I can be vague about the details – it was a long time ago. The important thing is, you knew nothing about this until very recently, maybe the last week or so. We need to agree a date, say the time I made you all meet me at Talitha's old house.'

It wasn't possible. This would never work. And yet, that was a tiny glimmer of hope she could feel, wasn't it?

'You were horrified,' Megan went on. 'You couldn't believe it. We knew you wouldn't keep it to yourself – the others went into a full-on panic and Felix decided to take matters into his own hands.'

'I resigned,' Amber said. 'That would fit. I would have had to resign from government once I found out what my old friends did.'

Megan gave a cold smile. 'Yep, that actually works quite well. So, what do you think? Can you do it?'

She wasn't sure. 'Why would you let me get away with it?' Amber asked.

Megan got to her feet. 'Because enough lives have been ruined, Am. You really were out of your head that night. You barely knew what you were doing. Of all of us, you were the least to blame.'

Amber shook her head. Much as she'd like to believe that was true, she could remember every moment of that drive along the A40.

'And you have two little girls.'

'What will happen to you? You'll be confessing that you lied to the police, committed perjury.'

Megan shrugged. 'I may have to go back inside for a while. Not long, I shouldn't think, not now Tal's no longer around. When I'm out again, I'll take my money and go.'

Could it really be that simple?

'Felix won't let us get away with it,' Amber said. 'If we take him down, he'll drag me with him.'

'He'll try,' Megan agreed. 'And he may succeed. But it will be our word against his, and why would I lie now?'

It would be the end of her career. Her entire life would change. But she'd still have a life.

'You're right,' Amber said. 'I'll do it. Let's go.'

Megan picked up the sports bag and Amber opened the door as a massive gust of wind almost blew it into her face. The night had grown even wilder. Waiting only until Megan had jumped down, she set off at a half-run along the path towards the car. She'd started the engine before Megan had climbed inside. Throwing the car into reverse, she backed away from the shed and turned the vehicle around before driving at the gates. A few yards away she stopped, waiting for Megan to jump out and open them. The other woman didn't move.

Amber said, 'What's up?'

Megan was staring at something in the dark beyond the windscreen.

'Put your lights on full beam,' she told Amber. 'And make sure these doors are locked.'

Heart thudding, Amber followed Megan's instructions. In the bright glare of the car's headlights, she could see clearly what Megan had only suspected. A heavy-duty chain had been wrapped and padlocked around the inner-most rungs of the gates. Megan's knowledge of the key code wouldn't help them in the slightest. They were trapped.

## 61

'He's here.' Megan was looking beyond the gates to a car parked on the other side. 'That's my car. I told you he had it.'

It had never occurred to Amber before to ask what car Megan had been driving. Now, she saw a small blue hatchback, a little – no, a lot – like the one that had passed them on the road over. Had they been followed this whole time?

Megan's pale face had blanched; she couldn't seem to tear her eyes from the locked gates, and the small blue car facing them. There was no one in the driver's seat.

'What do we do?' Amber's heart began to thump against her chest wall. 'Back to the caravan?'

'He'll break that lock in seconds,' Megan replied. 'We're safer here. Give me your phone. No, not that one. Your real one.'

Megan had dialled one digit of the 999-emergency number when they heard a cry from the other side of the yard. Both women turned to face the rear window. A dark figure was running towards them. They lost sight of him for a split second as he vanished behind the globe.

'It's Felix,' Amber whispered.

The tall man, his fair hair plastered to his face by the rain, reappeared. He was shouting something.

'All he can do is break in.' Megan's voice was shaking. 'When he tries, drive forward and back, as fast as you can. I'll call the police. Our story stays the same, Amber. Hold it together.'

'Amber! Wait up! Amber, wait!' Felix was yards away. Amber revved the engine and gripped the handbrake.

He reached them. His hand slapped down hard on the driver's window as Amber released the brake and the car shot forward.

'Amber, for God's sake.' Felix ran alongside, banging on the window. Amber kept her eyes straight ahead.

'Reverse!' Megan yelled. 'Hello, hello, police?'

Amber could see nothing behind but did as she was told. A second later, the car hit something and crashed to a noisy halt. Megan's phone clattered onto the dashboard and then the floor as she braced herself against the windscreen. Felix caught them up. His eyes went briefly to Megan before he banged on the window again.

'Let me in, you need to hear this, both of you.'

He tugged on the door handle.

'Move, Amber,' Megan yelled from the footwell. She was trying to locate the dropped phone. 'Drive forward.'

The car shot forward and Felix vanished. Amber heard what sounded like a cry of pain. She stopped inches from the gate and looked back. Felix had gone.

'He's on the ground.' Megan, too, was looking back, peering over the seat. 'I can't find that phone, give me your other one.'

'It's in my bag. Did I hit him?'

'No.' Megan was rummaging in Amber's bag. 'He's tricking us.'

A rapping on Megan's window made them both leap in fright. They turned, as one, to see Daniel, soaking wet, pale and thin, staring in at them.

## 62

Through the open window, as though afraid he might dissolve before her eyes, Megan reached out to Daniel.

'You're OK? What the hell happened? Where have you been?'

'I knocked him out.' Daniel looked dreadful, his face gaunt and covered in scaly patches of eczema. He seemed out of breath, close to exhaustion. 'I saw his car parked off the road a few hundred yards away.'

A coughing fit grabbed hold of him and he bent double for several seconds.

'I've been watching him for days,' he said, when he'd recovered his breath. 'I wasn't sure I'd be on time.'

He glanced over at the gates. 'We need the key to that padlock,' he said. 'We have to get you both out of here. Can you watch him while I look for it?'

'I'll do it,' Megan said as she wound up the window. 'Amber, stay in the car.'

Something was wrong. How could Dan have seen Felix's car parked a few hundred yards away when, according to Megan, Felix had been driving her car?

'Hang on, Megan, I'm not sure—'

Too late. Megan had unlocked the car and jumped out. She and Daniel were staring at each other, exchanging words that Amber didn't catch. There was a brief hug. Amber pressed the button that would open the window again.

'Come on,' Daniel was saying to Megan as he led her away from the car. 'Watch yourself. I didn't hit him that hard.'

'Meg!'

Amber wasn't heard. Knowing something was going horribly wrong, she put the car into reverse again and followed them. Megan glanced back but didn't stop. Within seconds, she and Daniel had reached the point where Felix lay slumped on the ground.

Amber twisted in her seat so that she could see the tableau being played out in the red gleam of the car's reverse lights. As her two old friends neared Felix's prone body, Daniel dropped back and Amber saw what she hadn't noticed before. Daniel was carrying something in his right hand, slightly behind his body, as though trying to conceal it from Megan. In the darkness, it looked like a hammer, presumably what he'd hit Felix with. He was still carrying it like a weapon, and why would he need to do that unless—

Amber's hand hovered over the car horn. This wasn't right. The car, for one thing – Megan's car, parked directly outside the gates – and yet Dan said he'd seen Felix's car up the road. Felix could not have driven two cars here. How had Daniel got here when Daniel couldn't drive? He could though, he'd learned years ago. Was driving something you forgot?

She had to get Megan back in the car.

Megan was peering down at Felix. As she crouched to – Amber wasn't sure, check he was still alive, look for the padlock keys? – Daniel swung his right arm up and back, before bringing it down. Megan collapsed beneath the blow, and then Daniel turned and ran straight at Amber's car.

# 63

Amber put the car into drive and slammed her foot down. She drove straight at the steel gates, losing her nerve at the last moment, taking her foot off the accelerator a heartbeat before she hit them.

Several airbags exploded on impact and for a second, Amber thought the thundering noise against the side of the vehicle was a weird echo of the crash. Then the passenger-side window splintered as Daniel swung his hammer at it a second time. On the third strike, she saw the metal tip break through.

Amber ran. Flinging open the driver door, she sprinted away along the gravel track, past the prone bodies of her two friends. If she could get to the caravan, the locks might hold long enough for her to call the police. As she darted behind the huge golden globe, she glanced back to see Daniel reach Megan's unconscious body. He raised the hammer to strike, then seemed to change his mind; the hammer dropped to his side again.

'Amber!' he yelled.

The caravan was twenty yards away, but if she ran for it, he'd see her.

'Amber, where are you? I only want to talk.'

She needed a weapon. Not two yards away was the statue of a cherub, less than two feet high. If she could get to it, if she could lift it . . .

Daniel didn't know where she was. He was moving, but slowly, checking every possible hiding place. For the moment, he'd lost track of her.

'I had to do it, Amber,' he called. 'They're in it together.'

He was getting closer.

'I've got a plan. I need to talk to you.'

Felix could not have driven two cars here, so Daniel must have been at the wheel of Megan's blue hatchback. It had been Daniel who'd been hanging around outside her house earlier, who'd followed them here.

Talitha would never have opened her door to Megan at night. To Felix, possibly, but to her old friend Dan, back from the dead, she wouldn't have hesitated. Talitha had loved Dan, and it had got her killed.

Amber bent to the ground and picked up a small stone. She waited until Daniel was looking the other way, then threw. It landed, noisily, by the gargoyle shed and Daniel turned on his heels.

Amber backed out of her hiding place until she reached the stone cherub. Heavy though it was, she managed to lift and hold it against her chest. Daniel, meanwhile, thought she was behind the shed. Using a torch to light his way, he was peering into the bushes, pulling at the ivy.

The caravan was ten feet away. Amber quickened her pace as Daniel straightened up, turned, and saw her. She ran, made it to the caravan door and up the steps. Once inside, she drew the bolts that might hold Daniel back for a minute or two. Only then did she reach for her phone.

She didn't have it. She didn't have either of them. They were still in the car.

The door buckled inwards with the force of a hammer strike. Daniel's second blow broke the upper bolt; the lower one went on his fourth strike. A gust of wind blew in and Daniel followed. He and Amber made eye contact, and he took a moment to get his breath. Then he swung the hammer, as though firming up his grip.

Amber felt the table edge digging into the back of her legs. Nowhere left to run.

'You don't have to do this,' she begged, as she crawled backwards along the padded bench seat. 'I won't tell anyone, I promise.'

Daniel closed the door, as though it would make any difference. There was no one to hear her screams.

'Dan, I have two little girls. I won't do anything that risks losing them, you know that. I won't tell.'

'I wish I could believe you.' He was moving slowly now, trying to get his breath back. He really did look very ill.

'Megan phoned the police,' Amber tried. 'They're on their way.'

'Megan's still alive,' Daniel said. 'She'll come round in a while, with a hammer in her hand.' He waved the weapon in the air. 'A hammer with Felix's blood on it. And Xav's, and Tal's. Yours too. By that time, I'll be back at my retreat in Cumbria.'

He smiled at her then, showing his perfect white teeth. She'd never seen anything more terrifying.

'I've been having a nervous breakdown, Amber,' he said. 'That's why I had to go away. I'll be devastated when they break the news to me that all my old friends are dead.'

The bench ran out and Amber could stand upright again. She glanced left then right, hoping for the miracle, a door to the yard she'd missed, but to one side were Gary Macdonald's clothes and to another a shelving unit. His bed was behind her.

There was a window over the bed. And Daniel had not yet manoeuvred his way around the table.

Amber turned and leapt onto the evil-smelling bed, pushing

aside the curtains, fumbling with the window lock. The night air rushed into her face as the window opened and she pushed herself through it. Gravity took over and she was falling to the ground.

Her ankles were grabbed.

Pain tore into her thighs as she was pulled back up. She reached out for leverage of some sort, something to grab hold of. She kicked out and squirmed against the side of the caravan, but the edge of the window felt like a knife blade as she was pulled against it. Then she felt a hand on the waistband of her jeans and she was moving upwards.

She splayed her elbows, but he had her around the waist now, and she was almost back in the caravan. She grabbed hold of the window frame. For a second, the hands pulling her released, but then the hammer slammed into her right hand and she felt the bones crumble beneath it.

As she fell onto the bed, a hand grabbed hold of her hair and she was dragged along the tabletop. She caught a glimpse of the whisky bottle flying across the caravan. Her scalp was burning and then the floor was rushing up to meet her and she was re-leased for what she knew would be the last time.

The air whistled above her head as the weapon that would kill her hurtled through space. Solid matter met solid matter, and the weaker of the two gave way. Bones crumpled and broke; blood burst free like a firework. A cry sounded, that might have been human, and then a final breath was released like the last wave before the tide turns.

Someone was touching her head. 'Amber? Are you OK? Amber, talk to me. It's over.'

Megan's voice. Megan, pale and blood-stained, was coaxing her upwards. Amber risked looking up. Not inches away, Felix was kneeling over Daniel's supine body, fingers at his throat.

The cupid statue, with blood on one of its wings, lay a short distance away from Daniel's head.

'He's dead,' Felix said.

'Good,' Amber replied.

# 64

After he ended the call, Felix felt as though he could breathe again. He'd had serious doubts about Megan's ability to drive with a head injury, not to mention Amber's with a broken hand, but the two women had made it back to Amber's house. They'd spend the following day there and then, the next night, Megan would drive her car to one of the long-stay car parks at Heathrow Airport. From there, she'd take public transport to Kent and contact her lorry-driver friends who would get her to the continent.

She'd be wanted for the rest of her life in connection with the deaths of Xav Attwood and Talitha Slater, but she hadn't seemed fazed.

'I know people,' she'd told Felix, seconds before the two women had driven away. 'I know how to vanish. And I have money, thanks to you guys.' She'd smiled and touched the curve of his jaw in a gesture that might almost have been affectionate.

Felix let his hand stray to where she'd touched him. He could feel her fingers still.

Oh, Megan, of all the lives he could have lived, the one with you most haunts his dreams. You would have got over that childish crush on Xav, he would have made sure of it.

Felix took hold of Daniel's body under the shoulders and dragged him out of the caravan. It was still a few minutes short of midnight.

Amber would resume her life as normal. In time, it was possible she'd rise to the cabinet once more. Felix wouldn't bet on it though. He had a feeling Amber's future would see more meetings of the PTA than Parliamentary Select Committees. Amber, he believed, would be spending a lot more time with her family.

His head was aching, and he could feel blood sticky in his hair. He still had a lot to do.

After the girls had driven away, he'd returned, briefly, to the factory and filled the boot of his car with sodium hydroxide powder and a loading trolley. He'd used the trolley to transfer the tubs to the roll-top bath tucked away behind the golden globe. Using a hose attached to the gargoyle shed, he'd half-filled the bath with water. He had a cast-iron sheet at the ready to keep the rain off.

All things considered, there were worse places to dispose of a body than an architectural salvage yard.

Daniel hadn't been a heavy man, but his body was awkward to manoeuvre out of the caravan and across the yard all the same. Felix put his old friend face up in the bath, as though in a coffin, and crossed his hands over his chest. It seemed the least he could do.

When Felix had seen the red sunglasses in the evidence bag at the police station, everything had fallen into place. The sunglasses were Megan's, but they'd never been returned to her after the lunch party at Talitha's house. Daniel had kept them; Daniel had used them to frame Megan for Talitha's murder.

Bubbles floated to the surface of the water as though Daniel were still breathing, but Felix was neither fooled nor spooked. He was a man of science. He knew Daniel was dead, and what he was doing now was entirely practical and necessary. Megan, though, had closed Daniel's eyes and, foolish or not, Felix was glad of it.

His sports bag with the baseball bat went in the bath too, along with Dan's various possessions. Then, one tub at a time, he poured in the sodium hydroxide powder. Daniel's flesh began to sizzle as the compound ate away at his body's proteins, and a flicker of steam drifted upwards as the water temperature rose. Putting the iron sheet over the tub to keep the worst of the rain off, Felix went back to the caravan. He'd already registered that the bottle of Scotch was intact.

Five hours later, when heavy cloud was holding back the dawn, Felix returned to the bathtub. Using industrial-strength gloves, he released the plug and let the thick crimson liquid drain away. The rain would clear all traces of it and if the grass around the tub's base refused to grow for a season or two, well, who would give it much thought?

All that was left of Daniel was a shrunken and brittle skeleton; sodium hydroxide will not destroy bone. Felix scooped his old friend up, the bones crumbling and breaking as he moved them, and carried them in buckets to the back of the gargoyle shed where he'd dug a shallow trench. Once the bones were in the ground, it was easy to use Daniel's own hammer to smash them to pieces. By the time he'd finished, the bones were unrecognisable as human. Felix turned over the earth a few times. Another couple of hours of rain and even someone venturing behind the shed wouldn't spot anything unusual.

In the pocket of his jacket, Felix had the half-empty bottle of Scotch that had belonged to Gary Macdonald. It was untouched. The stopper fell to the ground and he smelled the familiar warm, peaty scent.

Upturning the bottle, Felix emptied its contents onto his old friend's grave.

'You can sleep now, mate,' he said, and walked away.

# Acknowledgements

Readers who know Oxford will quickly spot some physical resemblances between the fictional All Souls' School and the real-life Magdalen College School, which my son, Hal, was privileged to attend for seven years, latterly as a senior prefect. The similarities, though, are entirely superficial.

MCS is a wonderful school, high-achieving, but with a strong moral code, staffed by exceptional teachers and attended by bright, talented, hard-working, funny and kind students. Being part of its community over the years has been a great pleasure.

*The Pact* is a work of fiction, derived entirely from my own imagination, inspired by no real-life events. To the best of my knowledge, every student and alumnus of MCS is a considerate and careful driver!

I'm grateful to Hal for making Felix's knowledge of chemistry credible and to Dani Loughran of Aston Chemicals for giving him the work experience that made all the difference. Thanks also to my friend Lucy Stopford for helping me plan the Oxford locations, and my husband Andrew for being my first reader.

The talented triumvirate that is Sam Eades, Alex Layt and Lucy Cameron have been brilliant, as have all their colleagues at Trapeze and Orion. As always, my love and thanks to my agents: Anne Marie Doulton, Peter Buckman, Rosie Buckman and Jessica Buckman O'Connor.

# Credits

Trapeze would like to thank everyone at Orion who worked on the publication of *The Pact* in the UK.

**Agent**
Anne-Marie Doulton

**Editor**
Sam Eades

**Editorial Management**
Georgia Goodall
Charlie Panayiotou
Jane Hughes

**Copy-editor**
Rebecca Millar

**Proofreader**
Melissa Smith

**Audio**
Paul Stark
Amber Bates

**Contracts**
Anne Goddard
Paul Bulos

**Design**
Lucie Stericker
Debbie Holmes

**Production**
Claire Keep
Fiona McIntosh

**Finance**
Jennifer Muchan
Jasdip Nandra
Rabale Mustafa
Elizabeth Beaumont
Ibukun Ademefun
Afeera Ahmed

## Sales

Laura Fletcher
Victoria Laws
Esther Waters
Lucy Brem
Frances Doyle
Ben Goddard
Georgina Cutler
Jack Hallam
Ellie Kyrke-Smith
Inês Figuiera
Barbara Ronan
Andrew Hally
Dominic Smith
Deborah Deyong
Lauren Buck
Maggy Park
Linda McGregor
Jemimah James
Rachel Jones
Jack Dennison
Nigel Andrews
Ian Williamson
Julia Benson
Declan Kyle
Robert Mackenzie
Imogen Clarke
Megan Smith
Charlotte Clay
Rebecca Cobbold

## Marketing

Lucy Cameron

## Publicity

Alex Layt

## Operations

Jo Jacobs
Sharon Willis
Lisa Pryde

## Rights

Susan Howe
Richard King
Krystyna Kujawinska
Jessica Purdue
Louise Henderson